Advance Praise for Ascer

D1073479

"*Ascending Spiral* is a metaphysical novel wit̲   ̲ ̲ ̲
violence marking each episode is a deliberate evocation of the darkness that
is inherent in mankind, and the theme, therefore, shines like a silver thread
of promise—the idea that we are capable of loving forgiveness of ourselves
and, more particularly of others. The way of karma rings true for many
people, and this book is a very well written and thoughtful explanation of
its message. It is also an exciting, historically accurate series of linked stories
that will hold the reader in his chair for a single sitting. Highly recommended."

Frances Burke, author of Endless Time

"Dr. Pip Lipkin has lived for 12,000 years, in many lives, different sexes,
and even different species and he's here for a reason. Dr. Bob Rich's
Ascending Spiral is a true genre-buster, incorporating elements of historical
fiction, literary fiction, science fiction, and even a hint of nonfiction to
create an entertaining novel with an important message. *Ascending Spiral* is
a book that will take the reader to many different places and times,
showing, ultimately, that our differences and divisions, even at their most
devastating, are less important than our similarities. This is an important
and timely novel full of wisdom and insight."

Magdalena Ball, CompulsiveReader.com

"Bob Rich evokes the powerful wounded healer archetype in his latest
novel *Ascending Spiral*. He takes readers along on Pip's painful and
insightful journey through several lifetimes. His tale serves as a shining
example of how to turn misery into virtue. Highly recommended."

Diane Wing, author of
Coven: The Scrolls of the Four Winds

"I believe the author's goal for *Ascending Spiral* is for his reader to enjoy
these pages filled with controversy and adventure, and to join his efforts in
thwarting greed, promoting love, and to secure the preservation of the
Earth, as well as the human race. I give this book five stars plus, for content
that grips, stories of true emotion that entertain, and intent that serves
others. Great book!"

Susan Hornbach

"*Ascending Spiral* is unlike any I've read before. I made the mistake of skimming the beginning one night, even though I was in the middle of reading another book and was committed to reading several others before it. By the time I got to the end of the first chapter, I was hopelessly and happily hooked. I couldn't seem to get my eyes to read fast enough. I don't usually like any type of historical fiction or metaphysical books, but maybe I'd be a fan of the genres if they were all as well written and engaging as this book. My heart was completely invested in the main character's story from the beginning, even though I had to find out about him first when he was several other people."

Joyce Sterling Scarbrough, author of *Different Roads*

"*Ascending Spiral* by Bob Rich is not your typical read. A novel told in stories joined together by a common thread or two, the novel defies genre distinction, provokes thought, causes the reader to recall the past, and hope for the future. The cycle of life is woven through history, the psyche, and spirituality. Rich invites you to follow his character, Pip Lipkin, on his spiritual journey through space and time. This atypical tale is thought-provoking."

Cathy Thomas Brownfield

Ascending Spiral
Humanity's Last Chance

Bob Rich, PhD

Marvelous Spirit Press

3rd Printing -- April 2013

ISBN 978-1-61599-194-5 (hardcover)

Library of Congress Cataloging-in-Publication Data

Rich, Robert, 1943-
  Ascending spiral : humanity's last chance / Bob Rich, PhD.
    pages cm
  ISBN 978-1-61599-186-0 (trade paper : alk. paper) -- ISBN 978-1-61599-187-7 (ebook)
  1. Metaphysics--Fiction. 2. Humanity--Fiction. 3. Theological anthropology--Fiction. 4. Science fiction. I. Title.
  PR9619.4.R53A93 2013
  823'.92--dc23
                                           2012051420

Distributed by Ingram (USA/CAN), New Leaf Distributing (USA), Bertram's Books (UK/EU).

From Marvelous Spirit Press, An imprint of
Loving Healing Press
5145 Pontiac Trail
Ann Arbor, MI 48105
www.MarvelousSpirit.com

Tollfree 888-761-6268
Fax 734-663-6861
Email info@LHPress.com

Contents

Prologue

Pip 2011 AD

In 2008, a young woman came to me as a victim of crime. I'd been warned that she was suicidal. She started to cry when I asked her to tell me her story. For five minutes, every time she tried to speak, tears ran down her face, sobs shook her body and she needed to wipe her nose. Hunched forward, hugging herself, all she could do was to feel her despair.

"Come on, Alison," I said, "we're going for a walk." I led her outside. Speaking gently, calmly, and just loud enough to be heard over the noise of the traffic, I said, "Alison, look at the sky. See the color. Don't put a name on it, just see it. The clouds. They're just shapes."

A truck went by. "Hear that sound. It's just a sound. And now the smell. Don't judge it, don't name it, just experience it. And look at this wall, that pattern on it." We walked a few steps. "Feel the pressure of the ground on your feet. Just feel it. And how your legs work. And your breath: chest rising and falling. That tree. Look, every leaf is different."

Slowly we walked around the block. Waving blades of grass... the pressure of her T-shirt on her back... the look of a rose... the crunch of gravel under our feet... the pattern a butterfly wove in the air... I focused her on Now. This moment. This instant. This.

In ten minutes, we were back in our chairs. She could now tell me of her tragedy. She'd been pregnant. While tidying, she found the tools for shooting up heroin. When her guy came home, she confronted him: drugs or me. He bashed her up, so severely that she lost the baby.

We needed two more sessions. Then she left my area, back to her family.

Last week, I met her again. Health and contentment shone out of her. She carried a two-year-old girlie. "Hi Pip, remember me?"

"Alison. Of course I do."

"Claire, sweetheart, say hello to Dr Lipkin."

Kids are my joy. I made friends with little Claire.

"I'm so glad to see you! I now have a lovely husband, and this little darling, and life is terrific!" To my delight, she blamed me for her great improvement.

Then there are the emails, from all around the planet. Mostly they're from kids. So, I have hundreds of grandchildren, most of whom I'll never meet. Here is one I'll call Maria Rodriguez:

Dear Dr. Pip,

I don't really know how to do this because I never ask for help but I typed "I hate myself" in Google and you came up first so I clicked it. I saw what you've done for other people and I was hoping that maybe you could help me.

I just turned 16. Ever since I was 14 I've thought about suicide. My mom found out a few months ago and she yelled at me, said I was disappointing her, and to be honest I don't think she understands how serious I am about it.

I hate myself because I'm ugly, stupid, fat, can't be loved, and I'm a liar. Kids made fun of me, so I made up stories about myself so that someone would talk to me and have even the slightest interest in me. However, I've been thinking that if something happened to these people, they'd die not knowing that I lied. So, I told my two best friends. One was completely understanding and is helping me. The other hates me and won't talk to me which is a constant reminder of what a terrible person I am. I can't tell some people because I have no idea how to find them and I feel terrible because I can never take back what I did. And there's one person I want to tell but I'm afraid of her hating me too. My friend said to tell her when we get older but I can't guarantee how long I'll live. Then she said just to tell her. I can't because she has been my role model since I was 5 and now she talks to me and I don't want to lose that.

I hate what I've become, and I want to change. I've tried really hard but I couldn't do it. No matter what I did something always kept me back whether it was the kids at school calling me fat, whore, lesbian, and retarded or my parents just making me feel inadequate to my other siblings, something always messed me up. I feel like suicide is my only way out. I don't have money to pay you but I was hoping that you could help me despite that. Please help...I don't want to live another day where I wish I was dead.

With love, Maria

We have now exchanged eight emails. The second-last was:

> Dear Pip,
> I'm sorry this has taken me so long but I've been meaning to thank you. You really changed the way I look at life. I just have one last question:
> How can I forgive myself for all the mistakes I've made?
> Love, Maria

And my answer:

> Maria my darling, thank you for cheering me up. I've been very tired after work all day, and dropped my bundle a bit. Then you picked me up.
> There is no such thing as a mistake, a fault, or a defect. This is my view of everyone:
> You are perfect.
> Some of the things you do are excellent.
> Most of the things you do are OK.
> The rest are the growing opportunities.
> If you find that a past act was a mistake, that's proof that you've gained in wisdom. If you could do it again, you'd do it better. So, congratulate yourself.
> If a past mistake has caused harm to yourself or someone else, then apologize within your heart. If it's possible and appropriate, apologize to the other people affected. If possible and appropriate, make restitution. But there is no need for guilt or shame. Celebrate the fact that now you know better. Work out how to do the same kind of thing if the situation arises.
> Maria, only two things matter in this life: what you take with you when you die, and what you leave behind in the hearts of others. Everything else is Monopoly money.
> What can you take with you: Lessons learnt, gained wisdom—or the opposite: hate, bitterness, blame and the like. So, you either advance in spiritual development, or go backward, or of course a bit of each.
> Look after the heart, the Love, and you can let go of everything else.
> Thank you for sharing the planet with me.
> Love,
> Pip

And finally, for now:

> That helped so much. Thank you so much.
> Love, Maria

I have this ability to heal hurt, to lead people from despair and helplessness to strength and Love. This gives me joy, so, whatever may go wrong in my life, I am content. I am content despite seeing all the terrible things on our world. I see the craziness, the suffering, the way people hurt themselves, each other, and the wonderful natural environment we're a part of. But it's all right. I hate it but accept it, both at the same time.

What craziness am I talking about? When people ask me to introduce myself, I often say I'm a visitor from a faraway galaxy. At home, I'm an Historian of Horror, so Earth is my favorite place in all the Universe. Where else do you find an organized game (called war) in which intelligent beings kill each other? Where else are child-raising practices designed to damage children? And best of all, where else do you see the entire economy of a species designed to destroy the life support system of their planet? For an Historian of Horror, that's delicious.

Well, one day I learned that this joke is based on truth. Indeed, I am a visitor to your planet. Don't believe me? I'm just an old guy with a gray beard, right? A professional grandfather children love, a fellow whose sense of humor keeps getting away from him... not so. I really am a visitor from off planet, and I'm here to do a job.

I was not always content with life. For much of my existence (which, as you'll read, has lasted over 12,000 years), I was hurting. But, you see, a person is like a diamond. Put some coal into a place of great pressure and heat, and it becomes the hardest jewel known. A person is like steel. Put iron in red-hot coke and blast it with oxygen for nine hours, then drop it, red hot, into cold liquid, then heat it again, and you have hardened and tempered steel. I needed all that suffering to turn me into a tool designed for my job. That job is to help you save your life, and the lives of those you love. Like everyone on this planet, you're in great danger, and my reason for being here, being a human for now, is to be part of the effort to save us.

When it was time, I was shown what I had to know for my task. This book is the account of what I learnt. Let me tell you my story, and you can judge for yourself. I'll start with the earliest recall of living on your planet I've been given, on an island off Ireland.

Padraig

805-806 AD: Vikings

The first time I saw my love, she had long dark hair with a red band holding it in place, pansy-blue eyes, and a long elfin face that was quick to flash into a shy smile.

We were watering our sheep at a sizable creek, before descending to the next village. We followed this route every year of course.

She came striding up the path, a little bit of a girl, a yoke over her shoulders holding two wooden buckets that bounced around at every step.

I ran over. "Will I take those buckets off ye?" I asked. "The sheep done made the creek stirred up. I'll happily fill it for a lovely colleen up above where the water is clear."

"Oh, I can do that meself," she replied with that smile that grabbed my heart. But she did nothing to stop me when I unhooked the buckets off her yoke and sprinted up the path.

I filled one, then the other. As I turned, she stood just behind me. "Thank ye," she said. "You got a name, boyo?"

"Sheilagh," I said for a joke.

Her eyes grew wide and her mouth opened. "That's my name! Go away!"

"Well then, if I've guessed yours, you guess mine."

Then Da spoiled it, "Hey Padraig, there's work to be done!"

I picked up her buckets and started down the track. "Thank ye, Padraig," she said behind me, a laugh in the voice. "But y'know, I carry those buckets full every day."

I handed them over, and as our hands touched for the merest instant, I felt a jolt of lightning go through me. She hung them on the yoke and fair danced her way down the path.

Of course my big sister Meaghan had to spoil it for me. "Smitten, are we, Paddy?" she asked.

But Da chased me back to work before I could reply.

That evening, we sat around a blazing fire in the center of the village, hosted by the fifty or so people. They were hungry for news, we were hungry for contact beyond ourselves. The adults passed the whiskey along, and I managed to snare the pot, but not for long.

Then Sheilagh sat next to me. "I envy your life of moving around. Y'know, all me life I've never been away from this place?"

I don't know what made me say it, but say it I did, "Come with us, and be me wife."

Again her face got that look of surprise, like when I'd guessed her name. Then she grew serious. "I'm too young, boyo. Mebbe in a couple of years, if you still be interested..."

I grasped her hand, to again feel that jolt of lightning. I knew, two years, two lifetimes, I'd still be interested.

She squeezed my hand. "Only, Padraig, don't you dare take up with another girl instead, or I'll find you and cut your head off!" Still holding on to me she stood, and pulled me up. Strong little thing she was. She led me to a couple, talking with my parents. "Da, Ma," she said, "This is the boy I'll marry when I'm of the age."

Well, this was a joke to everyone else, but no joke to us. And the next day, when we moved on, it was a hard parting for me. My heart dragged in my feet for many a day.

As the year turned, and the seasons changed, and we moved from place to place, often my dreams cherished her voice, the way she moved, the glint of firelight in her eyes.

Midwinter it was when we reached the village of Fearann, only the village was no more. Smoky walls stood without thatch roofs above them. Bits of rotted meat and skin stuck to scattered skeletons. I felt as sick as everyone else looked.

"Vikings," Da said heavily. "Heathen savages from the north."

"Why?" Meaghan asked, looking ready to vomit.

"They abduct young women and children, and sell them into slavery. May the Devil take them."

We moved on the next day, and for many a night the horror visited my dreams. But as things will, it receded as spring replaced winter, and summer replaced spring.

Then one morning, Meaghan said to me, "Hey Paddy-boy, y'know where we'll be by eventide? Or forgotten, have ye?"

No, I did not forget. I knew every twist of the path, every hill and tree and view of the sea. My heart near stopped for worry, because things can go wrong and people can get sick and die, and fair colleens can be swayed by others than a wandering shepherd-boy.

But she waited for us at the same place, by the creek where it is fresh and clear. She had no buckets this time, and a fine blue dress she wore, specially for me, that was obvious.

Taller she stood, and her figure fuller, but the smile was the same.

Then she ran forward and I must have too, for there we were, ahead of the others. She was in my arms, and her arms around me, and I felt the pressure of her bosom against my chest, the scent of her clean hair in my nose.

"I knew you was coming." She pulled away but took my hand. "Last night you came in me dream, and I always know when I dream true."

"I have to do me work," I said, "but tonight we can talk."

Indeed, that evening she snuggled against me by the fire. Oh, I wanted to take her off into the darkness, but you can be sure that many eyes were on us to prevent such a thing.

"And," I asked, "are ye ready yet?"

White teeth glinted in the firelight. "Nay, I'm but fifteen, six weeks gone."

"They say the Virgin Mary was but sixteen when she had Jesus."

"Oh Padraig, we have a lifetime together!"

"Oh Sheilagh, do I need to trudge around the Island another year without ye?"

She whispered in my ear, "Come out an hour before dawn and I'll meet ye."

Of course, I could hardly sit still after that, and hardly managed to get to sleep when it was time to do so.

All the same, before morn I was up, washed and dressed, and, careful to make no sound, walked from our camp down toward the village. Here she came, a shape lighter than the path. Our hands found each other, and for the first time her mouth met mine. I was on fire, we fit perfectly together, and I lost myself in her embrace. As my hands rested on her shoulders she wriggled, like a cat relishing a stroke does.

At last we separated.

"Sheilagh, you I love. Only you."

"And I you, Padraig. But I will not lie with you till we're wed."

Did I not know that? All the same...

Holding my hand, she led me along a path till we came to a cliff over the sea. There we stood, my arm around her shoulder, hers around my waist, looking out at endless peace, until the dawn light started behind us.

"I must go back," she said, but I'd seen something below.

"Look!"

Two long, lean shapes swooped along the water, seeming from here like beetles with many legs. Those legs were oars, pulling hard.

She whirled for the village.

"No!" I shouted. "Go wake me folk!" That'd put her further from the danger.

But she paid no heed, and I had to chase her. I shouted as loud as I could, "Awake! Vikings!"

It was too late. Big armored men were sprinting into the village, swords and axes waving. Some carried torches, which they threw onto thatched roofs.

I grabbed Sheilagh's arm and spun her around. "Run! To my folk!"

I found a spade leaning against a wall, and used the handle to trip a raider. He sprawled in the dirt with a yell. I thrust the blade into the throat of the next man. Blood spurted.

Dawn light shone on the bared teeth of the third raider. His axe was coming for my face.

Then terrible pain.

Then darkness.

Then, somehow, I was up high. I saw a man catch my Sheilagh and knock her down, and I saw the unequal battle as men and women were slaughtered, and girls and children dragged onto the longboats, aye, my sister Meaghan and my brother's wife Caitlyn with her little child, and all our dogs killed as they valiantly fought to save us. The sheep scattered mostly, but gloating big men caught a few.

And I could do nothing but witness.

Book 1: Dermot

1. 1784-1798

Over the cliff

The second time I saw my love, she had golden hair, a square face and a terrible temper. She was two years of age, and me four, and when her parents and mine worked in the potato fields, it was my task to keep her from mischief. But as she lay in the dirt and screamed with her face going blue and her heels hammering the ground, that was when I knew I loved her, and always had and always would.

Granny came over. "Good boy, Dermot," she said to me, "You was right to stop her going into the creek." Then she scooped Maeve up and carried her to their cottage.

After this, I sometimes saw deep blue eyes looking through the sky-blue, and dark hair shadow the gold.

One winter's day, our fathers were both out to sea, fishing, and her Ma came over. She walked carefully in the mud, because her tummy was great, like my Ma's. I knew there was a baby in each. Maeve held her Ma's hand and carried a small basket of her own.

I rushed to open the door. Being a big boy, I could now reach the latch on tippy-toes.

In they came, and we shared some fine baking and a hot drink of milk, then were sent off to play in a corner. I had some bits of firewood I'd polished up into dolls. Some I called people, some horses or sheep or dogs. I got these out. "Hey," I said, "this is you and this is me."

"Nah. No it isn't."

"Jus' pretend."

"Nah."

"C'mon Sheilagh..." Huh? Where had that name come from? I knew no one called Sheilagh.

"Me name's Maeve. MaevEEEE!"

Her Ma shouted, "And Maeve, keep it down you hear, or I'll paddle your bottom!"

She did grow out of being Tantrum Monster Mistress No. Then my fun was to play with the other boys, but all Maeve wanted was to tag along behind me, and I couldn't get rid of her.

The first time Da took me out fishing, she stood on the beach, great tears wetting her face for being left behind. So, on my return, I triumphantly made her a gift of the first fish I'd ever caught. "Oh Dermot," she said with a great grin, "doesn't it even look like you!" With that she whirled, fish clutched to her chest, and ran to her Ma, cooking at the fireplace. As I followed, she said, all sweetness, "Ma, look at the wonderful fish Dermot caught, just for me!" That was her, during all our childhood: the needle and the honey.

Sometimes, I needed to get away from her. Twelve I was when I made a fishing rod, and learned to tease the trout in the creeks above the fields. I cut a long willow branch and carefully seasoned it to stay supple, and saved the long strings that came on the occasional parcel from the city of Dublin, over on the other side. This string was the thickness of my finger and rough, but it made do. I fashioned a hook from a knot on a twig, and a sinker from a stone, and on the first day came back with three trout.

It was good I caught them, because Ma could not say I was wasting time, but for myself I cared not. It was a blessing to be away from all people, all noise, the smell of the pigs, the chatter and worry. I could be alone under God's sky, at peace, dreaming of nothing much.

I was now old enough to listen in on adult conversations. This was most interesting when traveling traders passed through. One had a name I thought funny: Mr. Connor O'Connor, but he was a wise man with gray in his beard, so I kept the laughing inside. On one of his visits he talked about a new kind of gun the English had, and used against the French. It had rifling in the barrel and so could shoot accurately for surprising distances. Only, and I found this funny too, Mr. O'Connor told us he had no idea what rifling in the barrel may be.

Trouble was brewing in the land. The accursed English took everything, and gave nothing but grief to anyone who complained. If you were a Catholic, or even a Presbyterian, whatever they were, you could not vote in Parliament, though I didn't know why that mattered. "There will be bloody rebellion, mark my words," Uncle Dan, the oldest in the village, said whenever anyone would listen, or even if nobody did. The words gave me a thrill. I dreamt of heroic deeds, of being part of a mighty army smashing the overlords, sending them back home.

On Sundays Father Liam arrived on his horse about mid-morning, and held mass. We all ate together after this, then he left for the next village. Uncle Dan got out his tin whistle, my Da his drum, and all the young men and girls lined up to dance. One Sunday, Maeve grabbed my hand and dragged me into the line. We'd watched the dancers many a time, so were quick to pick up the steps of every dance, and I will admit it was fun, even when little cat Maeve dug her fingernails into my hand, with the sweetest of grins. And after this day, I could not get out of it if I'd wanted to: when the young men and maidens danced, so did the two of us.

But life was mostly work now: hilling the potatoes, braving storms in our boats to bring in the fish, slaughtering a pig in the snow, carrying stones to terrace a new field, helping father to make whiskey, repairing a leaking thatch roof, whatever was needed.

I had a special bond with my father's best horse, Harry, a large young gelding who was as happy pulling a cart or a plough as being ridden. He was the first horse I'd ever trained, under Da's supervision. One summer day I was up on his back, returning from a message for my father from the next village, when somehow I felt uneasy. I looked up at the scrub on the hillside above, and out to the right over the sea, then turned to look behind. A yellow dust cloud rose above the hill I'd just descended, and that was when I noticed a vibration in the ground. Before I could do anything a group of galloping riders burst over the rise, two abreast along the narrow road. The lead man's arm moved in a circle, then a terrible sting along my side, and Harry jumped, crashed into something, and I was falling off the edge, falling, down toward the sea.

Over the drumming of hooves, I heard laughter.

* * *

Agony beyond bearing. I opened my eyes, but made no sense of what I saw. Through a blur, I was looking at something brown. Salt water washed over my head, into my mouth, nose and eyes. I coughed, and must again have fainted for a moment from the pain.

Very, very carefully, I managed to raise myself on an elbow. Under me, wedged between two sharp rocks, was poor Harry, very clearly dead. I'd landed on top of him, missing those rocks.

My left arm was bent halfway between elbow and shoulder. Every breath was a sawtoothed knife there, but I had to move, or die. Bit by bit, I managed to kneel, holding my left arm with the right hand, but when I tried to stand, an even worse jolt of agony speared into my left leg. I looked down to see bloody bone poking through the skin. I knew I was as good as dead.

After an unknown time of despair, I heard, "Hey, down there!"

I looked up to see Mr. O'Shea, the man I'd visited.

"Oh Dermot. Don't move, lad. We'll get you out by boat."

I don't know how long it took them, but the tide was well out by then. They beached the boat, gently put me on a scrap of fishing net and the four of them lifted me in. Then they rowed out, hauled up the sail and headed north, away from my home.

When the first wave pitched the boat, I screamed, to my shame. A man gave me a flask and I took a mouthful. The whiskey burned its way down, dulling the pain. They gave me a rope to bite on, and I closed my eyes and endured. Twice more I got a slug of whiskey, and at last we pulled in to a big wharf. It was the dark of night by then. Again they carried me on some netting, into a building. I heard Mr. O'Shea say through the fog in my head, "The blessing of God on you, Doctor. The accursed English threw this lad over a cliff." Someone held a cup to my lips. I swallowed, more burning liquid but tasting different, then darkness came.

When I awoke, my arm and leg hurt no more than from a bad cut, but my head pounded with a terrible pulsing rhythm. I'd often seen men with the hangover of course, and knew it was the price for the relief of the whiskey. I must have made a noise, for a door squeaked and a woman said, "Awake, are ye, lad?" She came into my view: an old woman with a haggard face but kind eyes. She helped me to sit, and I saw that my broken arm was nestled between two shaped bits of timber, with padding under. She'd brought a big cup with steam rising from it, and I drank, a tasty broth that filled my stomach and settled my headache. Then I slept.

Father arrived the next day. "Sorry you're laid up, son," he said, "and sorry to have lost Harry. Good horse he was."

"The best, Da." I sat up, and he put an extra pillow behind me.

"Bernie O'Shea came and told me about it. Bloody English. This can't go on."

"What were they doing here?"

"Surveying the land, they said."

"What's that mean?"

"Lookin' over to see which bits they'll steal next."

"Da, buy me a gun. By the time I'm grown, I want to be the best English-killer in the land."

"Dermot, we've got a gun."

"That little old thing? It's fine for shooting birds. I want a modern gun with rifling in the barrel, like Mr. O'Connor told us about. I'll make it pay, hunting."

He thought. "We can afford it, just sell more whiskey. Finding one to buy, and the ammunition for it, that's something else. Oh... I nearly forgot." He reached into his bag and pulled out a parcel, wrapped in a clean white cloth. "For you from your sweetheart."

"My she-cat you mean?" We laughed together while I unwrapped it. And as I chewed the first sweet mouthful, I heard Maeve's giggling laugh.

Hunter

I healed. We did buy a rifled gun, all the sweeter for having been stolen from the English. The man selling it said that you needed the same size bullet as for a redcoat's musket, but wrapped in a bit of paper, and that you had to keep the barrel clean. Ammunition proved easy: we bought powder and shot for our fowling gun, and re-melted the balls into bullets of the right size. Soon the rifle started paying for itself. I provided enough meat for several families, and also we made money from the skin and fur. Father and I built a tanning shed well away from the village, and several women sewed the skins I supplied into ladies' handbags, fur coats and wallets, I know not what else for that was not my concern.

Hunting gave me many days of blessed solitude, and although tanning was a smelly business, I didn't mind. Fishing is smelly too.

Of course, as I grew, so did Maeve. Every man's eye shone with lust upon seeing her. I noticed even old Uncle Dan looking at her with more than appreciation. And the two best memories of my life are from this time.

One was the pleasure of dancing. She was joy in motion: curly golden hair a flag behind her, white grin, that lissome figure a moving poem. Our favorite dance was the stomp. There were six beats of double notes, followed by a rapid triple. The dance was steps forward and back with my arms folded across my chest, then three rapid stomps of the foot when the drum did its triple beat, then grabbing Maeve's hands and swinging her around so we ended up in the place the other started from, then repeating over and over. It was a simple dance to simple music, but we both loved it. The memory of this dance has kept me alive, many a time.

Then there was the spring day she proposed to me—as always, she led and I followed.

I had to get a load of furs from the tanning shed, and harnessed our mare Blackie to the cart. As I headed up into the hills, Maeve came running after me. "I'm coming with you," she said, blue eyes glinting with mischief.

"What will your mother say?"

She laughed. "It's easier to say sorry after than to ask permission."

We soon arrived, and piled the cart full. I gave Blackie a drink while Maeve gazed up at the breathtaking beauty of the flower-covered hillside.

"Dermot, come here," she ordered, and I came. We meandered all over with my arm around her shoulder, hers around my waist, till she stopped, near the edge of a sudden drop, with the sea below. I had the feeling that I'd been like this before, with her, in just such a place, but of course I knew this couldn't be true.

She turned to face me, eyes luminous, mouth slightly open.

I raised my hands, and stroked her face from temples to chin.

She stepped even closer. I felt both love and lust for her. I gently pulled her head toward me. She came willingly, and as we kissed, her arms went around me and she hugged me so I felt her breasts against my chest. My erection almost hurt, although this was anything but lewd: more like religious worship in feeling.

As my hands held her shoulders, she wriggled, like a cat relishing a stroke does. "Dermot," she murmured, "it's time you and me got married."

It was arranged with Father Liam, for three weeks ahead.

Word came the next week: rebellion had broken out. The village was abuzz. Maeve came to me. "You're going, aren't you?"

"I have to go."

"Yes, and you may not come back. I want your child, in case..."

We didn't need to talk, just walked up above the tanning shed, into the field of flowers, and there gently undressed each other. Naked, she looked even more lovely. Often have I wished I were a sculptor, so I could make a statue of her.

With the soft green grass caressing our skin, our bodies and spirits became as one. Then it was my time to go to war.

2. 1798-1801

War

War was disaster. Oh, I heard that we'd had great victories in Wicklow, but I never saw one battle where we got the better of them. Our leaders knew not what they were doing. Our men were brave enough, but without discipline, without skill. I've seen a hundred English soldiers devastate Irishmen five times their number. They acted as one man, and after each of their victories, their confidence grew, ours shattered.

I was usually safe enough, because of my rifle and my skill with it. Typically, I was sent to some high place alone, and from there picked off one Englishman after another. I started with the officers, and worked my way down. Indeed, my wish as a boy came true—I may have killed more English than any other man.

Still, it was all for naught. Battle after battle they won, and captured men by the hundreds. Hidden safely up some hill, often I saw the slaughter of the prisoners. These English were less than human. They tortured wounded men, killing them as slowly as they could.

Guilt ate me as I escaped, time and again. But what good could I do by dying or being captured also? My duty was to stay free, and kill as many of the monsters as I could.

I did so, even when alone, living off the land. I slit the throat of many a sentry. They were easy to find by their smell alone, for these English didn't seem to wash themselves. Several times I set fire to buildings they slept in, then picked them off with my rifle as they rushed out, clear to see with the flames behind them. Then I ran, dissolving into the dark countryside long before they could shoot back at me.

When I needed to, I stripped my victims of powder, shot, and also food and good Irish whiskey, which they liked as much as we did. Then I spent an hour or so, wrapping each bullet in paper, which I also borrowed when I could.

Often I thought, I may have been the last Irishman to carry on the fight.

Slowly I made my way over to the west coast, toward home.

Slaves

Ever cautious, at last I reached country I knew, the steep, rugged hills where I'd hunted for three years. Something was wrong: I sighted the tracks of a pig, then of a couple of sheep. I knew what this meant: devastated villages. Domestic animals are too valuable to the living to be let loose.

I looked west from a tall peak. The forest, my forest, had a big bare patch in it, like the mange on an old dog. I already was a killer. If not, this would have turned me into one. That forest had been my church, my connection to God, but for the English it was merely timber with land under it.

For the first time since childhood, I cried. I knew they were dead. They had to be dead: my parents, sisters and brothers, all the people of the village I loved... and above all Maeve. Horrid visions tortured my inner eye, of what the savage, barbaric English must have done to her, to my love, to my all. I'd seen them at it elsewhere, and many a time had I avenged poor girls and women, raped before being killed.

But here, no doubt I was too late. The soldiers were sure to have moved on years ago, leaving ruins and corpses behind.

I waited till dark, and made my way to the tanning shed. It still stood, but the lack of a stink showed that it had been unused for a long time. A few old, brittle skins remained, and with amusement I noticed my ancient fishing rod leaning against the back wall.

I ghosted down the well-known path though it was overgrown, the starlight enough for my experienced eyes. There was the ocean, a luminous darkness, and the dark shapes of the cottages.

All was silent. I detected no scent of smoke, no smell of pigs or horses or last evening's dinner. My heart was a black stone within me.

The door of our house hung askew on one hinge. Inside, I could see stars above, through what had once been the roof. I searched around, but found no bodies, and my hands noted things missing that should have been there. Maybe... maybe they'd fled rather than been ravished and massacred?

I returned to the door and watched a while. All was still, so I crossed the space to Maeve's house. There also, some things were missing, and there was no roof. In front of the fireplace I did find a body. I couldn't make out who it was in the dark, so, using the patience of the hunter, I sat on the floor in a corner, and did my insufficient best to sleep.

At last I saw what was within the house: broken and charred furniture, ash everywhere, and the absence of various tools of living. I stood to have a look at the body by the fireplace.

I could see it was Granny from the remnants of her clothing. Her body was a skeleton with black skin on. She'd been dead for so long that there was no stink. I found no sign of wounds, so guessed she may have died from a natural cause, and they were hurrying too much to be able to bury her. I hung my head and said a prayer for her soul.

I checked my rifle, and stood a full five minutes in the doorway. Only the seagulls moved. I took some cooked meat and a couple of apples from my backpack, ate them, then followed with a drink of water.

This place, the center of my world till the war, was dead, but its people, my people, had to be somewhere. Could they find safety anywhere in Ireland?

I decided to wait till night, then walk to the next village north. Maybe I could find someone there, or more indications of what had happened. To spend the time, I returned to our cottage and looked around more carefully. Nothing of use remained after the senseless violence of the conquerors: things I'd cherished lay there, smashed. There was my father's drum, flat and broken as if stepped upon. It probably was. There was the cradle he'd made before my birth. It had held all my sisters and brothers after me, and now was part-burned kindling. My parents' bed was destroyed, straw everywhere, and with a sob I noted the dark stain of long-dried blood.

I had to get out of there.

Again I paused to watch and listen, and heard a dull distant thump. I'd heard such sounds before: the falling of a large tree. It came from somewhere way above the village.

The wise thing was to wait for my friend the night, but I had to know. Every sense alert, careful to take every cover, I moved uphill.

Nothing was amiss for awhile, then I heard a distant creaking. I hid behind a boulder.

A hundred yards away, four oxen dragged a large log on wheels. I didn't know the two men who tended them, but was shocked at their appearance. Their clothes were rags. They were nearly as gaunt as Granny's long-dead body, walking skeletons. They moved like old men, though their hair and shaggy beards were dark with no gray visible, from this distance anyway.

I waited for their passing, but no English came after. Still using every cover, I approached them, hid behind a bush until they were beside me, then softly said, "God be with you." I smelt the sour stench of their unwashed bodies, as bad as the English soldiers, though no doubt on them it was imposed.

Their eyes jumped to me. Without stopping, the older one said, equally softly, "God be blessed, a free man."

I shrugged my backpack off, pulled out a large piece of cooked meat, cut it in two and passed it to them. Still moving forward at the same painfully slow pace, they devoured the food like they hadn't eaten in weeks. Perhaps they hadn't. "Why don't you run?" I asked.

"Because they'll kill a few children. Take some unfortunate and torture him, or God curse them, her, for our sin."

"How many English?"

"A hundred of them, guarding maybe four or five hundred people including the women and children. We're locked up in a fenced enclosure at night, near-starved, worked from dawn to dusk on destroying our own land."

"The O'Hallorans and O'Donnells. Are there O'Hallorans and O'Donnells among you?"

"Surely. They stripped all the local villages. Killed the old folk too weak to work, just to show us who is top dog."

We were steadily descending toward the coastal road. The younger man spoke for the first time. "Lad, you better hide. They're waiting for us below. Catch us on our return."

"One more question: did they ravish the young women?"

I couldn't bear the pain in their eyes. The older man answered, "And when someone objected the first few times, they made an EXAMPLE of him."

My hands hurt from grasping my rifle so hard I thought it might break.

I stopped while they kept going, but shadowed them to see where they were taking the trees. It was two villages to the south of ours, at Bride's Bay. It's a sheltered cove, and as I looked down from the hill above the road, I saw that men were constructing a jetty sticking out into the bay. The buildings were undamaged, with complete thatch roofs. Redcoats were walking in and out of them. Stacks of seasoning timber were in a flat area near the village, and I saw men laboring at various jobs. Each group had a guard near it. Women worked in the fields, also under guard.

I couldn't attack, since I didn't want their prisoners punished for my actions. I retreated up into the scrub and waited for the returning ox drivers. With time on my hands, I thought about how to do something without inviting retribution on my people. Of course, I'd have to see the situation for firm plans, but I did have an idea.

I heard them, then they came into view. One pair of wheels was loaded onto the other, and bags and parcels were tied all over. As they approached, I noticed red wax seals on the ties holding the bags closed.

They were right beside me without either man noticing company, so once more I spoke.

They both jumped, startled. "You surely are good at this, lad," the older one said.

"I used to be a hunter of animals. Now I'm a hunter of English sub-animals. All I want to do is to kill the monsters."

"And may God strengthen your arm."

I fell in beside them. "Tell me, how do they talk with us?"

"Three traitors are with them. Well fed, wearing expensive clothes, lording it over us. Also, some of them, including two officers, are English living in Ireland. One of the lieutenants can speak the Gaelic like you and me, but a cruel little bastard he is."

"All right, here is what I want you to do. Spread a story that on the way back you were stopped by some Little People, who told you they'll use their magic on the English."

"They'll laugh at it."

"No doubt they will... until it comes true. I'll do the magic. Hopefully, this way they won't punish us for it."

The younger man spoke. "We-ell... anything is worth a try. From what I've seen, if any man can pull it off it's you."

Another team was coming downhill with a log, two bedraggled men driving the oxen. I faded back into the scrub, and heard the older of my friends give an excited account of meeting with the Little Folk.

Grinning to myself, I went off to the south, circling around to a secluded place I well knew. I reached it in an hour or so, but it was considerably closer to where I took the English camp to be, perhaps directly above it. This was a clearing in the forest where the bedrock was too close to the surface for trees to thrive. There was an overhang, not quite a cave, maybe thirty yards long and ten yards deep, although the deepest part narrowed down to nothing. Many loose stones and boulders lay around. A spring bubbled out of the ground about twenty yards below it. I had something to eat then rested till late afternoon. I hid my pack and rifle in the overhang, piling stones around them, and set off to see the lie of the land.

I was right: the camp was on the southern shore of the same creek, swollen to a decent size at this lower height, in a channel maybe three feet below ground level on each side. The fenced area drew my attention first. Solid posts were set in the ground at regular intervals, with something shiny between. From the distance, I couldn't make out what this might have been. The area looked way too small for five hundred people, or even four hundred. There was no shelter, just bare muddy ground. I wouldn't have kept livestock in such conditions. Something to the south of the fenced area puzzled me at first: a long zigzag of canvas. Occasionally I saw a man or woman go in there, then I realized that was latrines.

The English camp was uphill from the enclosure: ten big tents no doubt for the common soldiers, a number of obvious storage tents that were too low to walk into, and smaller square tents for the officers. I counted eight small tents, and one more set aside, even smaller. Again, to the south, I saw another zigzag canvas line, this one with a canvas roof. The Irish didn't even have a roof for sleeping under, while the soldiers could shit out of the rain.

There were also several other fenced enclosures. One held farm animals, another horses, while a third was empty. I also noted a row of small square tents to the south of the English camp, with sentries standing near them.

I watched the activity. Women tilled fields beyond the fenced area. I noticed a guard's arm suddenly move in a circle, and even this far away, a faint scream reached my ears as a woman pulled away. I well remembered the feeling of the whip, way back at my first meeting with the English. The vegetables were planted among hundreds of tree stumps. A small group of men were butchering some animal near the enclosure holding pigs, sheep and cattle, and I wondered how much of that meat would find its way to the Irish.

On the southern side, at the edge of the already large clearing, men worked at felling trees, chopping branches off them, digging up the bushes and scrub.

Alert-looking soldiers were on guard everywhere, but there was lots of activity among the tents too, and that was my main interest. I identified the commanding officer, three more junior ones—a scrawny fellow I thought must have been the "cruel little bastard," one about my build and a fat fellow who seemed to be the second-in-command. I also saw two men dressed like gentlemen, but didn't spot the third traitor.

Patiently I watched. At last, the fat lieutenant gave an order and a bugle sounded. Work stopped, and the Irish were herded toward their enclosure in the systematic way I was used to seeing from the English. They left little to chance. A small group came from somewhere with a horse-drawn cart and stopped by the gate. Each entering person was given something, no doubt a scrap of food.

Finally the gate was locked. People were squashed in so that I wondered if there'd be space for them all to lie down.

The English then ate, and sentries were posted at dusk. I counted ten pairs of soldiers around the perimeter, walking back and forth along their area. They timed it so that each pair met its neighbor, then returned to meet the pair on the other side. I knew I'd have no trouble penetrating past them. Two more sentries stood at the gate of the open-air prison.

I moved closer with dark, and climbed a large oak by the creek. It must have been left standing because it had several twisted stems instead of a single trunk. I took particular note of which officer went into which tent, and was happy to see that the commander was close to the creek, with only one big tent in between. I spotted the fourth lieutenant and the third traitor too. He was a huge man with a shock of blond hair, like a Viking of old.

Occasionally sipping from my water bottle, I waited out the night. They changed guard at midnight, and again two hours before dawn. While the new lot were getting their eyes used to the dark I climbed down and returned to my camp. The action would start the following night.

3.

Magic for the Captain

Having slept much of the morning, I got a couple of empty bags from my backpack and went down to the village. After checking it was deserted, I dug up enough potatoes to fill my bags. On the way back, I stopped at the tanning shed and cut a length of string off my fishing gear. It would make an excellent garrote. No blood, no noise. I spliced the ends, then went on.

Back at the camp I made a little fire, boiled the potatoes one potful at a time, then put them back in the bags, which I protected from any wildlife with stones. While watching the water boil, I set up a piece of rotten wood as a target, and spent the time throwing my knife at it. At ten paces, my average was nineteen hits out of twenty with the right hand, seventeen with the left. I wanted to improve to a perfect score.

At dusk, I darkened my face and hands with charcoal and set off along the creek, arriving after dark. My back against the twisted old oak, I watched the sentries trudging their endless walk, back and forth, until guard change at midnight. There was good cloud cover, but I knew I could get through even in moonlight.

As the new guards set off, I shadowed them along the three-foot deep channel, bent double. I made sure to step in shallow water so I wouldn't leave footprints. When they met the other pair then turned, I lay still, hard against the muddy drop, let them go a few steps, then was up and shielded from them by a big tent.

I found the commander's tent and lay on the ground outside its entrance so I wouldn't stand out for any soldier waking to urinate, and listened. Inside, I heard the soft breathing of one man. Garrote ready, I untied the entrance flap and slipped within.

This man didn't stink. Clearly, gentlemen washed, only the common soldiers didn't. Good to know an Irish peasant is as good as an English gentleman.

The dim light was enough for my dark-experienced eyes to see that he slept on a low pallet. There was a folding table and two chairs, his uniform neatly laid out on one. A couple of books lay on the table. Good. I was getting short of paper to wrap my bullets in.

His two arms were uncovered above the blankets. I took a deep breath then jumped, my knees landing on those arms. I whipped the string around his neck and dug my knuckles into his throat, pulling hard.

His eyes and mouth opened. He tried to buck under me, to no avail. His heels drummed on the bed under him, but this made little noise. I saw the terror in his eyes, then they glazed over. I held the pressure for several more minutes.

Under the blanket, he wore a singlet and short pants. I couldn't take his white skin through the sentries, besides I wanted all of him to disappear, not just his body. It was a struggle to dress the floppy corpse in the uniform, but I managed. His sword belt I buckled around my own waist. Then I tore out widely separated pages from the books and stashed them in the waterproof oilskin packet I always carried for that purpose.

I'd brought charcoal in a pocket and used it to blacken his hands and face too, and the white trimmings on his coat. Now came the dangerous part: getting him out. This had to be just after the next guard change, so I dumped him on the ground and rested on his bed—why not? I actually slept until woken by the noise of men emerging from the tents.

After giving the returning soldiers a chance to settle for sleep I neatly folded his blanket, ensured everything was tidy, and lifted him out through the entry. I put him down and lay on the ground. Nothing stirred. I heard the chattering of water over stones, the occasional loud snore from a tent, then an owl in the distance. The footsteps of the guard sounded loud as they tramped by, then silence returned. I tied up the flap and hoisted the body over my shoulders. It took but a moment to reach the creek, but the sword nearly tripped me as I descended the slope, careful to make minimal marks of my passage. I already knew the English were hopeless at tracking, but saw no reason to make it easier for them.

The body tucked neatly against the drop, I also lay still as the guard went by again. They were softly talking to each other.

I took the sword and sheath off, dug a shallow channel in the creek bed below the surface of the water, buried them and hid my work with a few stones.

Now came the fun part. As the guards walked uphill, I followed them, wading in the water and towing the corpse behind me, then again lined up two bodies—one dead, one alive against—the bank. Once at the perimeter, I waited for two turns of the guard to gather my strength, then just at the right time scurried for the twisted oak, the corpse over my back. The well-fed English officer was a great weight, so by the time I reached it, I was sure they'd hear my breathing on the other side of the camp. Having dumped my dead weight, I rested a while, then moved uphill in shorter bursts.

The eastern sky was alight when I reached my camp. I now saw that my victim was a captain. I hid the body under a pile of rocks in the overhang.

After a good dose of celebratory whiskey, I uncovered the top of a potato bag, had one for breakfast, replaced the stones, then, tired as I was, returned to see the show.

The English camp was an ant's nest, soldiers scurrying every which way. The fat lieutenant stood in the middle, bellowing. The Irish were still locked up. It took maybe half an hour for things to settle down. Again the cart was moved to the entrance and the prisoners were released, each being given something to eat. They wolfed down the food while moving.

The scrawny lieutenant and four soldiers set off downhill on horseback. I circled around the occupied area, then hurried west, catching them on the coast road. If I'd had my rifle, I could have got the officer and escaped without trouble, but what then? No, he had to be the target of the next episode of Little Folk magic. At least he'd be a lot lighter than the captain.

Predictably, they went to Bride's Bay, no doubt to report to a superior. I could imagine that man's incredulity at having a hundred soldiers misplace their commanding officer.

I returned to my camp for another swig of best Irish whiskey and a well-earned sleep.

In the evening I took a bag of potatoes to visit the Irish. This time I walked a fair way downhill, then approached the camp from the west, along the creek. I watched the two pairs of guards meet at the corner of the fence, gave them a few steps lead, then shadowed the pair walking along the creek-side. Stopping about three-quarters along their beat, I waited for them to pass me again, then approached the fence.

People lay on the ground, squashed like five children in a single bed. The fence consisted of a dozen horizontal wires, pulled very tight. I didn't know how they could tension wire so well. Vertical wires were tied to the horizontal ones, so that even a small child would find it impossible to get through. If I'd had a pair of pliers I could have cut a hole, but I didn't, and anyway, what could my poor people do then?

I hissed. A woman opened her eyes. They became large with surprise. I held a finger to my lips and she nodded. I returned to the lower level, waited for the sentries to pass one way, then back, and ascended again with eight potatoes, all I could carry. I gave them to her through the fence, signaling that she should pass them on. She nudged the man next to her. He stirred. She whispered in his ear, and gave him all the potatoes. I turned to return for my next load, delivered after the guard had gone by again.

My bag held maybe fifty spuds. I saw the woman bite into the last one after I made a hand gesture she correctly read as "finished." All right, I'd fed only a tenth of the crowd, but that was much better than nothing. I knew the word would spread, and feed the spirit of the captives.

After a quiet day, I came for the little lieutenant. This was much easier because thick clouds covered the sky and there was a steady drizzle, besides he was much lighter. Instead of wearing his sword, I tied it onto his back. I stacked him on top of the captain, who was well on the nose by then. I didn't think the cruel little bastard would mind. After breakfast I celebrated with another drink of whiskey, then settled for sleep once more.

The next night I took my remaining potatoes past the previous place, into the beat of the next pair of sentries, and repeated my approach. The nearest person was a lad. He slept soundly in the light rain even when I hissed. So while hiding along the creek waiting for the sentries to pass, I found a stick, and next time up, poked him with it.

He sat up, and despite the dark, I recognized my brother Dan. "Dermot!" he said.

I signaled silence, then rushed for the creek. I heard movements among the Irish, but no reaction from the sentries. All the same, I let them go by a couple of times before approaching again, with the first load of spuds. A dozen people sat in the mud, looking at me with wonder. As I passed my treasure over, I whispered, "The rest of us?"

"Ma's dead. They wounded her at home, and it went poisoned. She died two weeks later."

I had to go. When the guards were past, I came with the next load.

He continued, "And darling Sarah. Some men tried to escape. They shot them all down, then grabbed three little ones, she among them. They, they, oh... threw her up in the air, then three men stood under with bayonets and..."

I had to run to the creek, but cried as I went. Sarah was our youngest, a beautiful child of three when I'd left, so if she'd lived she'd have been what? Five now? Six? How could they?

When I passed over the next load, I had to ask, "Maeve?"

Dan looked at me, tragedy on his face, but I had to know. "She was swelling with your child, and did her best to seem dowdy. All the same, Lieutenant Harvey wanted her. She spat in his face, and, and, Dermot, I'm not going to tell you."

I had to go. All I wanted was to kill all the English, to die by going out in a rampage, but instead I hid until these two Redcoats tramped by, then returned with more potatoes.

"Her Da tried to protect her. They poured melted tar on him and ripped it off, and his skin came with it. Then they cut him to pieces."

"Which one is Harvey?"

"The fat bastard. He's the worst of them."

Each time I brought a load of spuds I pressured him, but he would not give any details about Maeve's suffering. Maybe he was right.

At last I returned to my camp, and spent a sleepless morning thinking about how to make fat Harvey disappear. By noon, I still had no workable plan. With a sigh, I took my empty bags and visited the potato fields of another devastated village. There I found a spade on the ground among the plants. It was a bit rusty, but perfectly serviceable. On the way up to my camp I wondered if I could dig in to the enclosure, allowing some at least to escape. It'd be good to have helpers.

I slept the rest of the day, and dozed during the night when torturing thoughts about Maeve allowed me to. In the morning, I went to intercept the log transporters. I heard the creaking not long after, but it was three teams fairly close together. I couldn't talk with six men on the move at the same time, so let them pass, then watched them ascend again. I ate my last cooked potato and had a drink of water. Then fat Harvey came to my mind, and Maeve, so I took a drink of whiskey as well to dull the anger.

At last another log made its way down. I allowed it to go past, watching and listening, but no one followed. Soundlessly I passed them, then waited. Like the previous pair, they were startled when I spoke, but one with red hair asked, "You the source of the spuds?"

"That I am."

"May the good God bless you. My wife was about dead, but that extra potato brought her enough strength to keep going a little longer."

"I'm also the magic the Little Folk use to make officers disappear in the night."

This got two appreciative grins.

"Only, the next one I want is Harvey, and he's a great load to carry."

The other man said, "You get rid of that one, my friend, and you'll be doing the world a service. A worse devil I've never seen."

"I can kill him, no problem. But then I'll need four strong men who are used to moving softly and silently, like me."

A sound came from above, so I dived onto the ground and rolled behind a bush. It was yet another team, well away still. The redhead looked back, then kept walking. "You're safe from them. All of us have a fair idea we have an angel around."

As I stood, he asked my name and I introduced myself. He did the same. He was Adam, the other man Sean.

Sean said, "My younger brother Jim used to spend all his time hunting with a bow and arrow."

"That's just the kind of man I want, and three more. I'll come with more potatoes tonight. If you can find a team for me, tell them to sleep right next to the creek, at the place I brought the spuds to the first time."

"Got you, Dermot," Adam said. "Could I be one?"

I grinned at him. "You failed the test: I managed to sneak up on you. Nobody could do that to me."

"How will you get your helpers out anyway?"

"I've got a spade, so we can dig a tunnel, but it has to be hidden by morning, like it was never there." I left them then, returning home to boil spuds.

4.

Uniforms

I woke with an idea. Since officers had disappeared from the middle of their camp, the English would not be too surprised to find the odd sentry missing too. If I could steal some uniforms for common English soldiers... And I'd need a night with fog or rain.

The corpses were stinking out my campsite, so now that I had a spade, I found a spot and dug a hole. After uncovering the two bodies, I dumped them into it, though handling the captain was disgusting. I had a good wash, dressed in clean clothes, and washed the dirty lot. In the evening, I headed out with a bag of wife-life-savers, hoping to meet my team.

A quarter moon shone, bright enough to cast shadows. But then, shadows are a killer's home, and I made my way to the agreed place. As I ascended the slope from the creek, a whisper came: "Dermot? We heard you coming."

These were just the men I needed. I whispered so while passing over the first lot of spuds.

There were six of them, not four. Talking in short bursts as the unaware English walked back and forth, they told me, all had been hunters, all had fought in the war, and they figured that in their weakened state they'd need the six of them to carry the fat bastard.

I explained that I'd be away for a few days, obtaining uniforms for them to wear. Cheered by the thought of future company, I returned home and got out my rifle and pack. I cleaned and oiled the rifle before starting my walk to get far away from the area. I decided to go north, back the way I'd come. I walked well into first light, breakfasted on a couple of spuds, and slept in a little hollow under the tangled roots of a great tree.

I traveled to the city of Sligeach before judging myself to be far enough, then hid my rifle and pack under the hay in a barn of an outlying farm, and entered the city by night. In the morning, there were plenty of Irish about, in relative freedom but looking dispirited. The English were everywhere like they owned the place, which of course they did, having stolen it by force. I simply fitted in, like any other fellow sent on an errand by a master.

I didn't want my actions to endanger the locals, and needed uniforms with no blood or damage. All day I moved around, getting more tired and hungry all the time, but had no money to buy food. In late afternoon, I headed out into the countryside again, and at night stole some vegetables from a field, with a silent apology to the farmer. I returned to the shed and made a cave in the hay, so a cursory inspection would find everything undisturbed.

I took what rest I could through the night, then listened to the farm waking up, but didn't count on one thing: farmers have dogs, and dogs have noses. There was growling with the occasional yelp, and the sound of the animal digging at the hay. A woman said, "Gobbles, what are you at?" I heard footsteps, and her muttering, "Some animal in the hay no doubt."

"Top of the morning to you," I said. "This animal is an Irishman hiding from the English."

She laughed after a short silence. "And I suppose you want a breakfast of a couple of fried eggs on fresh-baked bread as well."

The dog had stopped his noise, so I crawled out, dragging my pack but leaving the rifle.

She was a grandmotherly woman, with gray hair and twinkling blue eyes. She laughed again. "And a good sweep with a broom might go well too."

I swiped at myself to get the hay off.

She led me to the farmhouse, the dog now waving his tail and sniffing at me. "Hey James, a visitor we're having for breakfast!" she called.

Her husband was as thin as she was rounded, bald but with a white beard. "Welcome with the blessing of God," he said quietly.

I gave the customary reply: "And the blessing of God and Mary on you, Sir."

I did get the promised wonderful breakfast while I told them of my people's terrible fate. I wished I could have taken this food back to them instead of eating it.

As the woman stood to clear the table, the farmer asked what I hoped to do.

"Sir, I need to find a group of them, away from our people so nobody gets blamed for my actions. I'll kill some and take their uniforms. I need the disguise for my men."

He thought, stroking his beard. "They often have messengers going back and forth along the coast road, both ways. All the villages there are deserted now. You can waylay some maybe, but what can one man do against them?"

I grinned. "What I've done for the past year or three. If I may, I'd like to stay for the day. I'll do some of your hard work, then set off at dusk." So I chopped firewood, helped the woman shovel out the chicken shed, had a great lunch, shared a beautiful, mellow drink of whiskey, fixed up a leak in the thatched roof, then settled for sleep, in a proper bed. And as I set out, he pressed a flask of the whiskey on me, while she gave me a great parcel of food for the road.

* * *

I lay in the tall grass of a rounded hill, above the road a night's fast walk south of Sligeach. Indeed, I'd passed two destroyed villages. A light rain pattered on the oilskin on my back. I welcomed it, knowing that soldiers are less attentive when a bit miserable.

The first English I'd seen rode south just before noon. An officer led four soldiers, as if on a casual jaunt. It'd have been easy to shoot one, but, unlike every time before, I couldn't kill and run. So I let them go, and kept pace with them on the other side of the rise, up and down the hills. Just as well— a few minutes later, I heard a jingle from the north, and soon another patrol rode into sight. Instead of the red coats I was used to, these wore black coats with yellow facings. Their breeches were white, which I didn't think to be very practical. The two officers held a confab, then each went their way, allowing me to get ahead of them.

I saw smoke hours later, as the sea turned red when the setting sun fell below the clouds. I waded a creek, and stopped under the partial shelter of a tree up on the hillside, above yet another ruined village. Two of the houses were undamaged. Smoke came from the chimney of one, and five horses with feed bags on their heads were tethered outside. Wonderful. I could kill ten Englishmen.

I watched the two groups meet. Pleasingly, all ten were redcoats, like those torturing my people. Soon, smoke came from the second chimney. To my surprise, the two officers settled in one house, the soldiers in the other. Maybe the gentlemen objected to the stink too. I approached at nightfall, waiting for sentries to be posted. Eventually, one fellow sauntered out, looked up at the drizzle, and snuggled against the closed door in a most unsoldierlike fashion. I ghosted around the next ruin, left my pack and rifle under the oilskin, and sidled along the side of the house till I stood next to him, out of sight. I could smell him, hear his breathing. A fist in his guts, then the garrote went around his throat. I held him through his last struggles, then hoisted him over my shoulder and carried him back to my pack.

The door was sure to creak, but sooner or later his relief would open it for me. So, I pulled the oilskin over my head and waited. At last I heard the door—creaking—then a call, something in English, sounding both impatient and puzzled. I suppose the guard was to have woken his replacement, who called out again.

Angry with myself for not anticipating this, I moved fast, knife in hand, having no time for finesse. Before he knew it, I had a hand over his mouth and the blade in his heart. My own heart was trying to escape from my chest, and I sweated despite the cold and wet as I dumped him by his mate. Then I returned to just beside the door.

A man spoke over a snore, sounding more sleepy than worried. When no answer came, I heard his footsteps approach. I sheathed the knife and got the garrote out.

A big man, he stepped out into the rain. I had the string around his neck and my knee in his back. He stiffened, struggled for a while, then collapsed.

When I was sure he was dead, I left him in the doorway and tiptoed in. It was easy to locate the other six from the sounds of breathing, and their smell. Actually, one was trumpeting rather than breathing, and thankful I was to him for it.

Feeling with a careful hand, I found that they slept on loose straw. Good. One by one, I sent them to hell, leaving the snorer last.

One uniform spoiled, but that left just enough for my six mates and me. I now wanted to dispose of the officers, and here I didn't need to be either subtle or silent. My victims' muskets were neatly stacked against a wall. I loaded one, and stuck a bayonet onto it. Then I walked to the other house, opened the door and shot one of the prone figures. As the other sat up, I planted the bayonet in his throat. I felt nothing but satisfaction at a good job, well done.

Now came the heavy work. I stripped seven bodies, and carried them uphill. I found a blackberry thicket, although its thorns found me too, and hid the bodies in there. The two officers and the soldier with the bloodied uniform could stay were they were.

The next problem was that seven uniforms were quite a load even dry, and two were sodden. So, I set eight horses free and chased them off, keeping the best two. I saddled them, loaded one with the uniforms and weapons I'd liberated, and also all the food and ammunition I could find, and mounted the other. By the light of dawn, I picked my way up into the hills.

Helpers

Two days later, I waited for the first log of the day behind a boulder. To my delight it was escorted by Sean and red-headed Adam. "Hey, may the arrows of life hit your enemies," I said.

Startled, they stopped for a moment. Adam said, "Dermot! We thought you dead!"

I fell in beside them as they resumed their trudge, and gave them a boiled egg each, courtesy of the farmer's wife. "Not yet. The Little Folk are back. But what are the news?"

"We have a replacement captain, as bad as the last one, two new lieutenants, and fifty more soldiers. They now have fifteen pairs of guards out every night, not ten, and another pair standing at the officers' tents. They moved all those together."

"Oh well, we'll have to think about this then. Are my team ready to play?"

Sean said, "I guess. My brother Jim is, but like Adam said, we'd given up on you."

"Pass it on: I'll talk to them tonight, same place as last time if I can get to it with the new pattern. If not, the center of the nearest guard beat. Anyway, I wish you seven thousand blessings." I stopped and let them go on.

Back at my campsite, I looked after the two horses, had a good feed and a nice swallow of whiskey, and settled to sleep in the overhang. In the evening I grabbed the spade, loaded a bag with food and went visiting. A light breeze carried soft rain from heavy black clouds. Indeed the guards had shorter beats, turning every three-four minutes. All the same, I had no trouble making my way to the agreed spot. The men were waiting. In the couple of minutes I had, I dug out a few square bits of sod to make space under the bottom wire, and passed the spade through. When I returned with some cooked meat, they had enlarged the hole, so the next time I brought the whole bag and gave it to them.

Next time, I saw that the inside of the hole was large enough for a man to squeeze through. The nearest fellow passed me the spade, and I managed to match the size from the outside. As I scurried down the bank, I heard and smelt a man behind me. After this, one came during each safe couple of minutes. Grinning at each other, we lay hard against the slope. The last one took two passes of the sentries, and had both the spade and my empty bag with him.

I whispered, "One at a time, spaced well out. Follow me." I allowed the two Englishmen to be three steps ahead of me, then advanced bent double, head below the upper level. I stopped in darkness as the pair facing me approached, then waited motionless again while the men above me walked back. Then I was up and running, repeating the same game with the next pair.

Soon I was hiding behind the twisted oak. One by one, my team reached me, all grinning. "Stupid bloody English," one whispered, "they trip over their own shadow!"

"They did well enough in pitched battles," I reminded him. "All right men, let's go home."

Soon they were scrubbing themselves in the creek, preferring goosebumps to stink. I gave them the stolen uniforms to dress in, but looked at their shaggy beards. No doubt mine was similar, and soldiers shaved.

We sat around a little fire and introduced ourselves. There were three Js: James, John and Joshua, three Ds: David, Dylan and Dermot (me of course), and Gavin. "I'm always the odd one out," this one said.

Looking around at the haggard, gaunt faces in the firelight, I saw that every one was older than me. All the same, I felt I had to be boss. "Look you," I started. "The bloody English won their battles against us because they have discipline. They act as a team. They practice what they do till they can do it in their sleep. We lost because we were a bunch of individuals, each following his own path. Now we have advantages, because we dictate the terms. But this is important: I've been at it for years, living off the land. I'm strong and well-fed. And this is my country. I've hunted in these hills since I've been fifteen. So, I need your agreement. I'll ask your counsel before making decisions. But the decisions are mine, and in action I give the orders, you do them. Or get the hell away from here and enjoy your freedom."

Some agreed straight away, others thought about it, but none argued.

"All right, my friends," I continued, more relaxed now. "I've got a plan, and need your thoughts on it. I hope you can improve it. Our first job is to get you stronger with some good food inside you, and also we need to gather food for our poor friends like I've been doing when possible. Right?"

Dylan, an older man with gray at the temples, said, "Except every day we spend on that is more trees cut, and more poor prisoners worked to death."

"You're right. But you see, we need a night when it pours more than it rains."

"Well lad," Sean's brother Jim said, "Western Ireland is the best place for that!"

Gavin interrupted the laughter. "And I don't want to spend all me time dressed like a bloody Englishman!" They all nodded.

I told them, "I've seen plenty of clothing in the villages they've trashed. I'm sure the owners won't mind us borrowing some. Also, you know all the fishing boats have their bottoms staved in, but the rigging on them is still fine. We'll need some rope and pulleys."

David, with blond hair and even eyebrows, spoke very softly: "Dermot, you've been thinking about this. Tell us your idea then."

We started some serious planning. I insisted on dealing with Howard all alone, and this led to argument. "He may be fat," Dylan said, "But he's a big fellow and powerful. You'll have a fight on your hands." So, I had to tell them a little about Maeve.

Not only did we need to get the fat bastard out, but also make at least four guards disappear at the same time, in pouring rain. Josh suggested dumping them in the creek, because that'd be running in full spate. Dave disagreed: it needed only one guard to look that way at the wrong time, and we'd have disaster.

Gavin came up with the solution that had us laughing for days: "Look you, one of my jobs for the bastards a while ago was to dig these huge holes for them to shit into. Hard enough it was too with all the tree roots. We can drop the bodies down the shitholes!"

We all started shaving again, and it was a little like returning to peace. It took them a week to get used to sleeping in the daytime and being active at night, but this was a busy week. Every night, two of us fed the prisoners, and my team ate all they could too. Despite the lack of tending, we found plenty in the fields of the abandoned villages, and Jim was a marvel at catching rabbits and hares with a snare.

The third night had a thick fog and the kind of drizzle that gets into everything, so we returned to the Little Folk's magic. Dylan and David wore their soldier uniforms while Gavin, Jim, Josh and I dressed in black, with charcoal on faces and hands. Because we needed even numbers for this adventure, John fed the captives.

We approached the English camp from the south where they were devastating the forest, penetrated the guard line and waited for guard change at midnight. Our two false soldiers got behind a couple of real ones and knifed them in the heart. They took their place, and no one the wiser in the fog as long as they kept their mouths shut. Then it was easy for us four porters to carry the load away, in the segment guarded by our friends. The joke was of course when Dylan and David quietly deserted their posts. It took maybe three minutes for the first shout of alarm, then it was pandemonium. One even fired off his musket, I know not what at. Maybe he was shooting a Leprechaun. We laughed all the way home.

I cut a garrote for each man from my fishing line in the tanning shed, and we rescued the rope and pulleys from a wrecked boat. Jim and I went off with the bigger horse, whom I named Harry after my old four-legged friend, and found the escaped pig within a couple of days. This was far enough away from the English for a shot to be unheard. We gutted the carcass, built a triangular platform from a couple of saplings, and got Harry to drag Howard Pig back home. At my insistence, we then used him to rehearse our planned actions over and over, and waited for the mother of all rainy nights.

On a moonlit night, we borrowed guards from near the creek. On rainy nights we hit the other sides, avoiding any predictable pattern. In ten days, we killed eight.

We regularly talked with the ox drivers, and so knew there was a lot of panic among the English. But also, the cruelty increased, not because they blamed the Irish—how could people locked behind wire do anything—but because that's what terrified tyrants do.

The northern shore of the creek had not been despoiled yet, and the forest was quite thick there. About thirty yards from the creek we found a tree with a strong horizontal branch, and rigged up a pulley system. We also loaded fifty yards of rope onto a horse and took it there, laid out almost to the water's edge and covered over with leaf mulch and soil.

At last the weather was right for my revenge on Howard.

5.

Howard

The sun shone, but from our high vantage we saw a growing black line on the horizon. By late afternoon it swallowed most of the sky, lightning flashed almost all the time over the sea, and the distant thunder was a constant rumble.

We got ready.

The three Js and Gavin dressed as soldiers, the three Ds in black. In the pouring rain, we just sauntered through the line of miserable guards, then walked west among the tents. The drumming of the rain on canvas made so much noise that we could have sung and danced without anyone knowing. Even the frequent lightning was on our side, blinding more than illuminating.

Orders were not needed, after all the practice. Jim and Josh relieved the pair of sentries along the creek of their duties, and while the three of us watched, Gavin and John did the same for those guarding the officers.

Then I entered the tent.

Howard lay on his side, facing the entry, and snored so loud I heard it over the racket of the rain. I got behind him, and had the garrote around his neck with a foot against his back.

He struggled and threw himself around. One huge fist whipped back and hit my arm hard enough to numb it, so I let go of the string with that hand. I staggered back, but as he turned with the arm still extended, I jumped, both booted feet landing on the arm. I felt bone snap under me, at pretty well the same place where my arm had broken after my first meeting with the English.

His mouth opened in a scream that was probably soundless, thanks to the few seconds of string around his throat.

I continued over him, turned and kicked hard at his kidney. The big body jerked and started turning back again. "This is for Maeve," I shouted as I jumped again, one foot landing on his groin, the other on his gut.

He half sat up in automatic reflex, then fell back, the fight out of him. He may have fainted from the pain, though I hoped not.

I whipped the string around his neck again and finished the job.

A wave out the entry brought John over. He shouted above the drumming of rain on canvas, "They've got rid of the two guards from here, and about now the river ones are meeting their final resting place."

The two black-clad men pushed past him, and John returned to his guard post. "Go all right?" Dylan shouted, then saw the all too obvious signs of struggle.

It took maximum effort from the three of us to dress Howard Sub-Pig in his uniform. Then we rolled the corpse onto an oilskin and tied two short ropes on him for lifting handles. We tidied the place, then got Gavin and John to help us lift him out. I tied up the entrance flap.

Outside, it was easier on the wet ground. Dylan pulled on the oilskin while the four of us lifted him almost off the ground with the ropes. We went past the big tents without trouble, then reached the creek.

The water was only about six inches below ground level, and the creek swirled by with great force. We'd anticipated this, but had underestimated the difficulty. I now had to cross over. I backed well off, sprinted along slippery muddy grass and launched up high. I got over halfway before plummeting into the raging torrent. It swept me way downstream before my feet found bottom, then I was up to my chest in it. I dived forward and swam diagonally downstream till I managed to grasp a clump of grass. It came off in my hand but slowed me enough to eventually clamber ashore.

Well, I was no wetter than my mates. Panting, I trudged the long way back and found the rope. I gathered up a few circles and threw it hard across. An indistinct shape that had to be David lunged for it, held by someone else on a short rope. He missed, so I waited for him to get back, and threw again. This time I felt him grab the rope.

I followed the rope to Harry, patiently waiting. I gave him a carrot I specially had in a pocket, and kept a hand on the rope. When I felt a double tug I got Harry to walk. I could only imagine the struggle of the six men with the fat corpse across the raging stream.

At last, I felt another double tug, stopped the horse and walked back.

Howard was right under the tree with the pulleys. My mates lay on the sodden ground, doing their best to breathe. "Rest a while," I said, unnecessarily.

"Funny bastard," Gavin answered between gasps for air.

Having already had a bit of a rest, I got the lifting system ready. Then I returned to Harry, and tried to untie the rope from the harness we'd fitted to him all so long ago, in the afternoon when the sun still shone. I couldn't budge the knot, so cut it, saying a few choice oaths. Soon, we had Harry in place. It took only a few moments to lift the fat bastard's corpse and drape it across the saddle. Poor Harry.

Back home, we dumped Howard in the hole waiting for him though it was full of water, then thankfully joined Mary, the other horse, under the overhang.

We stripped, and dressed in dry clothes. I gave Harry a reward and a good rubdown while someone relit the fire. I found the farmer's whiskey, took a good swig and passed it along.

But, as the others celebrated, all I felt was a great empty sadness. Although I took my share of the whiskey, big tears wetted my face. I sank to the ground, bent my head and cried.

I felt a strong arm around my shoulder. Dylan said, "Tell me, son."

I looked up, to see all eyes on me. "I thought, well, I thought when the bastard was dead, I could be at peace. But, but, it doesn't bring my Maeve back."

* * *

Although it should have been dawn, the English encampment was still almost dark. No sentries patrolled this eastern boundary. Rain still fell, but more quietly. Dressed in black, we stood near the twisted oak and watched.

What we hoped would be an entertaining show turned into tragedy. Looking along the aisle between the neat rows of tents, I saw the new captain stand, facing the prison area, shouting something. We ran closer as the Viking-looking traitor started in Gaelic. It was safe enough, all the English being ahead of us, facing forward. His words were, "Someone has taken Lieutenant Howard away, and more soldiers. We don't care if it was Irish or Leprechauns or the King of Bombay. We'll now send him a message."

At a word from the captain, a group of soldiers rushed at the open gate of the enclosure, and grabbed six women and four men.

Their hands were wrestled behind their backs and manacled there. They dragged the first man to the captain. He whipped out his sword and struck the man's face. He must have used the flat of the blade, because the man sagged in his captors' hands, but there was no blood. The captain flipped his sword, and in the rapidly growing light I saw something fly off and this time blood spurted.

Softly, David said beside me, "Bastard's cut his ear off. I've seen them do this before."

"Let's go home, change into uniforms and get the guns," I said, turning.

We made it uphill in record time. The four wet uniforms were still steaming around the fire but my mates didn't complain. We reloaded our weapons with dry powder, then wrapped them in oilskins. We raced downhill even faster.

As I reached the twisted oak, I heard a scream of agony. I climbed up the tree, took aim and shot the captain an inch above the joining of his legs. I threw the rifle down to see John catch it, and descended in three big jumps.

"Mingle with them. I want to rescue whoever is left from those ten."

My mates all nodded, with grim looks on their faces.

The captain lay on the ground, a great pool of blood between his legs. Several men bent over him, but I knew he was as good as dead, dying slowly as he should.

A lieutenant was organizing the soldiers into a rapidly widening fan toward the east. We joined other soldiers who were herding the Irish back into the pen.

I led my men to turn. Only three captives were left alive: two women and a middle-aged man. The others were bloody torsos with bits and pieces of meat and bone around them. My eyes lit on one woman's head, bare of skin, with her hair sticking out of a lump of tar next to her on the ground. I felt sickened.

Each captive was held by two soldiers. I marched up to the one holding the right arm of the man. As I shoved my knife into his heart from behind, I said, "Too good for you, monster."

We couldn't remove the shackles from the captives' wrists, but formed a square around them, and urged them east. I didn't know how we'd get through, but was angry enough to take on the entire English army to do it.

Ahead, the soldiers formed an efficient skirmish line like I'd seen them do in battle. Had we been facing them, we'd have had no chance.

Behind the line nearest to us, a corporal went from group to group, issuing orders. He looked back and saw us. The three of us in the front made sure to shield our charges from him. I stopped and stood to attention.

The fellow rushed toward us, shouting something. For the first time in my life, I wished I could understand and speak English.

His face a mask of rage, he shook a fist at us, still rushing forward.

When he was ten steps away I whipped out my knife and threw it into his heart. I jumped forward and caught him before he fell, and Josh was on his other side at the same time. I retrieved the knife. "Hang onto his belt," I said. We turned him and lifted his feet just clear of the ground. Luckily, he was a short fellow, with no fat on him.

His upper body started to buckle forward, then an arm reached past me and someone grabbed the back of his jacket.

Three of us supporting him, we advanced toward the backs of the enemy, but I crabbed to the right. I hoped that from even a short distance, it'd look like he was leading us.

I diverged more to the right, toward the partly destroyed forest. We reached a small open-fronted tent with axes and saws neatly stacked inside, and rested behind it. This was the closest of several such tents, standing fifty yards south of the camp.

Jim said, "Change places. I'll help carry the bastard for a while."

One of the women said, with wonder in her voice, "You're Irish!"

I realized, till then none of us had spoken near her, so all she'd have noted would have been our uniforms.

"Surely, girl," Dylan told her. "This is Dermot's army of Little People."

I peeked around the tent, assessing the situation. The English were still advancing east. I decided that their tactics might have been developed by geniuses, but the men using them were anything but. "Keep going south, into the forest," I said. "We can leave the corporal here."

"Wait," David said. "We need a key for the shackles. I wonder..." He searched the corporal and found a key. We freed the captives but took the shackles with us. We set off, reaching the cover of the forest in a couple of minutes.

6.

Daytime magic

The young woman with dark hair was Katie, the motherly-looking woman Abby. The man was Kieran. Of course, all three were walking skeletons, wearing muddy, sodden rags.

I searched our borrowed clothes for the smallest. We'd have to get women's clothing when we could. We fed them, then gave the women privacy for a wash in the creek.

"We're in trouble now," I said while stoking up the fire.

"Why is that?" Gavin asked.

"The Little Folk use magic, not guns and knives. Now they'll take it out on our people."

"Didn't realize you were stupid, Dermot. Guess how we got three new recruits."

"Oh." Gavin was right.

"Will they find us here?" Kieran asked.

At a glance from me, Jim took his musket and went off into the rain again. By the time he returned, the women were huddled by the fire in overlarge men's clothes, with Kieran on the other side of the flames. "It's fine," Jim said. They've called off the hunt, and the Irish are back to ravaging the forest under guard. A messenger has gone to Bride's Bay."

I looked around at them. "Never before have we struck on successive nights. Let's do something to really upset them tonight."

Gavin got a big grin on his face. "We could borrow a whole tentful of them."

Everyone liked the idea, but David, always cautious, pointed out that we'd have up to twelve bodies to dispose of.

"Plenty of room in the shitholes," Gavin replied. We got to planning—but when we arrived at dusk, I saw with dismay that the English tent town had swelled in size. I counted twenty-five ten-man tents. Some men were still hammering pegs into the ground. Soldiers were everywhere.

I called the action off.

Back home, I looked around at the faces of my friends as we sat around the fire. "Look you, the old hands are scared. The new lot will be cocky. Let them talk to each other for a few days to pass the fear along, then we'll do it anyway."

Gavin disagreed. "Isn't it better to hit the new fellows before they're settled?"

We talked around it, and at last I gave in. Dylan and I returned to see the new disposition of sentries. The storm had passed, but ragged clouds flew overhead, with the moon playing hide and seek. We reached the twisted oak and climbed up.

Rather than pairs of guards walking a beat, now they stood singly, thirty yards apart. Given the enlarged area, this needed a lot of men for each shift. If nothing else, we were making the bastards uncomfortable.

It'd be easy to borrow several guards at the one time, whenever the weather favored us with fog or heavy rain. But to penetrate their camp, and maybe carry out bodies...

As we were returning to report to the others, I suddenly had to laugh.

"What?" Dylan asked.

"We still only need two false guards on a foggy night. Doesn't matter how many disappear in between."

But certainly there was nothing we could do then, nor could we bring food to the prisoners.

Our three visitors slept, but we were used to being active at night, and anyway too restless. To avoid disturbing them, we went for a walk, over the top of the hill.

"Look you," David said softly, "it annoys the hell out of me that we can only strike at them when we have fog."

Gavin waved his arms for attention. "Yes, because we're trying to hide."

We all looked at him.

"Best place to hide a tree is in a forest. We rescued our friends by doing just that, in daytime, right?"

* * *

Dressed as a soldier, I stood beside a tree and watched the camp awake. The first sign of life was smoke in a particular area, clearly their kitchen.

Idly I noted that one tree had the notch already chopped out of it, and even the back cut started. Another quarter of an hour would have seen it safely down. But clearly, stopping time was stopping time, and that was that.

A bugle sounded, and the perimeter guard departed in an orderly manner. It took nearly an hour before the slaves were escorted to their places of work. Tools were handed out at the line of tents, and after this the soldiers looked more alert. I ducked behind a thick tree as they approached, and glanced to each side to see all the team do the same. I got down low and peered through the foliage of a bush.

Widely spaced guards took up position, but they had more attention for the Irish than for the area beyond them. After all, there had never been any problem in the daytime. I thought Gavin to be a genius.

Things got busy. Two gaunt men used a large two-handed saw to continue on the tree I'd noted, with the fall area being kept clear.

I advanced with care, then my opportunity came. There was a loud shout and activity ceased. The tree swayed a moment, then fell with a mighty thump, all eyes on it.

I was beyond the guard, walking purposefully like I belonged there. Many other soldiers were doing the same.

The problem now was to find the other false soldiers. I noted a man sitting cross-legged, with four alert soldiers standing over him. I approached to see that he was sharpening axes with a honing stone. No doubt the guard was more for the axes than for the sharpener. I stood near them, copying their stance. They wouldn't see me unless they looked behind, and to anyone else I hoped to seem just part of the guard.

Three soldiers marched to a group of Irish who were digging up bushes and small trees with picks and long-handled spades. One pointed at two of the men, who obediently rested their tools on their shoulders and started walking away with the soldiers.

A fourth soldier joined them, and I recognized Dylan from his walk. He could never march quite right.

I took a couple of steps back, turned, and joined the group.

"Good," John murmured. "Jim and Gavin to come."

"There," David said, pointing with his eyes. A pair of soldiers seemed part of the guard over the men starting to cut the branches off the freshly fallen tree. Even from behind, I also recognized Gavin's distinctive shape: tall, broad shouldered but thin as a broom handle.

I left the group, who continued purposefully walking toward the camp, away from the tree felling activity, and marched to my friends. I saw Jim's eyes flick toward me, so just kept walking with apparent purpose. Soon the three of us joined the rest of them.

Other groups of escorted slaves, and soldiers on their own, crossed the space back and forth, so we didn't stand out in the slightest.

"To the latrines," I said.

Soldiers were going in there and coming out. Away from others was a sergeant, marching with urgency in his movements. We diagonally approached him, nobody paying us attention. As he flipped the canvas flap aside on one of the openings, John and David pushed in after him, shielded by the rest of us.

John came out almost immediately, then David after a short break. I approved: this'd look more natural, even if someone noticed. "He's head down in his final resting place," John said.

As unobtrusively as possible, we kept repeating this act, me and Josh handling the second one, a private. As he entered, we were behind him, my knife in my hand. I shoved it into his chest while looking him in the eye. Surprise and indignation turned into an instant of terror, then we tipped him upside down, and tucked him out of sight.

After the sixth victim in as many minutes, I felt we'd better change our pattern. "Let's put those digging tools to use," I said. I led the team to the end of the line of latrines, and the two slaves started digging the next hole. I left John and David to guard them, the five of us marching off to escort ten more men with spades and picks to perform our important task. I found two who, although they were as skeletal as the others, had a naturally solid build. I thought that if someone didn't come too close, they could pass as better-fed English. On the walk back to the latrines, I instructed these two in their task. All the men started grinning, till Gavin roused at them: "Look dispirited and hopeless!" We set up five pairs digging holes.

One at a time, I took each new man into a latrine enclosure and hacked his beard off, striking a compromise between a captive with a poorly growing beard and a soldier with a quick-growing one who'd forgotten to shave.

I left three men on guard, and the rest of us took the two solid Irishmen to the nearest group of tents to seek victims.

As we approached the first tent, I heard soldiers chatting. A glance as we passed the opening showed five or six men lounging inside. The next tent was the same, but no sound came from the third.

I stepped in. At first I thought the tent was empty, till I met the curious but unafraid eyes of a fellow sitting cross-legged next to the entrance. He'd been maintaining his musket, which was shining with oil, almost reassembled. I put a smile on my face, stepped toward him and bent. Before he knew it, I had the garrote around his throat.

The others were in. One of the new men was about to shut the entrance flap, but I shook my head. This tent had to look like every other.

With quick gestures, I stationed Gavin and John to guard the entrance, out of sight, and one of the strangers to take off his rags. Jim and Josh stripped the soldier while I quickly finished assembling his weapon. In probably less than a minute that felt longer than a lifetime, we had an additional false soldier and a dead false Irishman.

In a compact group we escorted—well, carried upright—our dead companion to the latrines, and dropped him into one.

We returned to the rows of tents to seek another victim, but everywhere, there were too many to attack. On one of our futile passes, we approached a small tent, which my nose identified as a latrine. A lieutenant was just coming out.

I took a step and blocked his path. As he opened his mouth in outrage I shoved hard and followed him in, my left hand clutching his throat while my right snatched for the knife. One thrust in the heart, then I lowered him into his own shit, ensuring he was out of sight.

The others were making a show of checking the pegs of this tent and a couple of nearby ones when I peeked out. No one was paying us attention, so I joined them.

"Bit risky that was," Gavin whispered. "A private soldier would never go into the officers' shithouse."

I thought we'd better get well away, so led my group back to our holes, unfortunately without having found another uniform.

A bugle sounded as I was inspecting the impressively deep holes. The diggers had done well. "They'll eat now," one of the new men muttered from the corner of his mouth, "then guard change."

I left David and the new man on guard, and had the rest of us line up for midday rations. It wasn't inspiring stuff: a lump of dry bread with a slab of stringy meat, and a refill of the water bottle with cold water. We managed to return to our station and passed the food to our recruits, who devoured it.

We had a problem: no guards could have been rostered to relieve us, and an officer might notice this. I hoped that they'd still be disorganized, since yesterday's great influx of men. Fortunately, no one paid us attention. As the relieved guard lined up for their feed, six of us again returned and got a second ration without anyone noticing.

This was the time to go back to hunting, I thought, but suddenly there were shouts, men running toward the officers' tents. The bugle sounded, with a very different note.

Like every other soldier, we made a show of looking warlike, ready to repel an army of Little People or the King of Bombay.

A corporal followed by three men came running toward us. He asked something, and once more I wished I had knowledge of the English language. I looked as stupid as I could and stood to attention.

Like the corporal during our previous escape, this one got angry at my reaction. He came closer. My men knew what to do. In less than a second, our four visitors each had a garrote around his neck.

There was too much activity for us to take bodies to the latrines, but our new holes each had a large heap of soil next to them. I tossed the corporal's body down the nearest hole and jumped after. It was a tight squeeze at the top, but considerably bigger below, widened into a bell shape. The depth was of course what a spade could reach, about four feet, but I managed. Even while stripping the body, I was impressed with the number of tree roots the diggers had had to cut through.

"Safe to come up?" I asked the man looking down at me.

He nodded, and gave me a hand out of the hole.

"Go down and become an English corporal," I told him. "Then dress the bastard in your clothes and hoist him up." In a few minutes, the bodies were hidden under loose soil.

"We need seven more uniforms to get my Da and his mates out," John said to me quietly as the others were similarly treated.

"Your Da?"

"Yeah, that's why I picked him out from among the crew at the trees."

One of the new false soldiers came up to me, an older man with a lot of gray in his hair and what I'd left of his beard. "You're the leader?" he asked.

"Guess so. I'm Dermot O'Halloran."

"I'm Ryan McCarthy. I was a traveling trader till they caught me. If it helps you, I can speak the English."

"Oh, it helps us all right!" I looked at the false corporal. "You two, down a hole and change jackets!" Then a bit louder, "All those dressed as soldiers, when you get a chance go down a hole, and use your bayonet to shave a bit better."

Our seven slaves were still digging away, piling soil on the four bodies. I was looking at them when David nudged me. "Company."

This was more than we could handle: a Lieutenant built like a bear followed by twenty soldiers. Our false corporal stepped forward and saluted. I was relieved to see that his face was now pretty well free of hair.

Looking down his nose, the officer snapped something, and my corporal answered. The officer barked a short answer, then walked on with his escort.

Phew.

Ryan said, "Let me translate. He told me, 'Corporal, Lieutenant Gordon is missing, and some men failed to report for guard duty. Have you seen anything untoward?' I answered, 'No Sir. We've been here extending the latrine line as ordered, Sir.' Then, 'Very well. Carry on.' So, I reckon I passed."

"Surely. We'd probably be dead by now otherwise."

7.

Escape

With the camp in turmoil, and groups of soldiers alertly inspecting everything, I felt it too risky to continue our hunt, but I still wanted uniforms for the remaining men. I raised my eyebrows at Gavin.

He came over to Ryan and me. "What's the problem, Dermot?"

"We need more uniforms, and survive till dark, and get these men out. No problem really."

"Look you, we came here to borrow a tentful of the bastards. When we do that, we have the uniforms."

Ryan looked like he couldn't believe what he heard. "There are more problems. There'll be hell to pay if the tools are not returned when work stops. And after that, the Irish are herded into the pen. And when the soldiers stop their duties, which tent will we go to sleep in? They have roll calls, that's how they noticed men missing just now. And I expect men in neighboring tents will know each other."

"How are our holes going?" I asked myself aloud, and we went to look. All were big enough to be considered done, and the men were digging as make-work. "Right. Let's return the tools now, and then the men can hide in the holes. It's uncomfortable, but better than back in the pen."

Gavin added, "That can include the new soldiers. Then us old boys can wait our chance, and hit the nearest tent. Get all ten of them."

Again Ryan looked incredulous, but said nothing.

So, we marched toward the tool tents, five of the seven still-slaves carrying both a pick and a spade. Ryan steered us to a tent with a couple of bored-looking soldiers on guard, and a few digging tools neatly stacked inside. He spoke in an angry voice to the guards, who snapped to attention in response. We handed the tools over, and one of the guards made chalk marks on a slate. Ryan then spoke sharply to us, and marched us over to a work detail where men were loading broken-up branches onto a cart with a patient pair of oxen harnessed to it. This man was worth his weight in gold, I thought.

With the extra help, the cart was soon full, and Ryan now marched us back to our holes with no one taking any notice. On the way, I said, loudly enough for everyone to hear, "All of you will hide in the holes till dark. We'll come and get you when it's safe. Then we have to walk through their camp to the creek. Simply walk like you belonged there. You'll all be soldiers by then, just returning to your tent after a pleasant shit. The seven of us will then kill fourteen guards. You'll need to be flat on the ground behind us, and stand up at the same time as the killer ducks down. That way, neighboring Englishmen will only see one guard. Got that?"

I could see some of the faces, all looking apprehensive. "Don't worry, we've done this kind of thing before."

Cautiously, our twelve new men dropped out of sight. The two holes with three occupants would be particularly uncomfortable, but I wasn't about to dig a new hole for them.

The seven of us simply hid in the latrines. Despite the stink, it was reasonably safe, and if an Englishman visited me, I could dump him in the hole. This didn't happen, though I heard a sudden noise I interpreted as one of my mates acquiring a new victim. I got heartily sick of just standing there, doing nothing, but at last the bugle for the evening meal sounded. As the occupants of the tent nearest our first hole went to line up for food, we snuck in and waited for their return. Four men entered, chattering. They didn't even look behind, so I waited an instant to see if there were more. Then I nodded. Jim and Josh on one side, me and Dylan on the other jumped forward and used our garrotes.

We dropped the bodies so that to a casual glance they were men lounging on the ground, and barely in time. Two more came in. Dave and John dealt with them just as another two entered. One fellow opened his mouth to shout, but Gavin punched him in the guts and dragged him in.

We waited for the remaining two. Voices came from the next tent, but we couldn't copy—there was too much risk that someone would identify Gaelic speech. Yet again, I wished for a knowledge of English. Maybe I'd ask Ryan to start teaching me.

"I'll have a look around," Dave whispered and walked out. He was soon back. "All the tents along here have eight in them," he reported. "I reckon two from each are on guard duty."

Still we couldn't do anything. Occasionally, one of us went for a stroll, and it was dark when at last John reported that the flaps were down on the other tents. We closed ours. "Time to take our companions for a trip to the latrines," I whispered. I left Dave to watch our backs, and two teams of three each took a body for a walk. There was no trouble about stripping them, tossing them into a shithole, then passing the uniforms down our holes. We kept repeating this till the tent was empty.

With the last body gone, we collected all their powder and bullets, gathered their muskets and went to the holes.

The line of sentries was clear to see just beyond the tool holding tents. Naturally, they faced away from the camp, and we had the five heaps of dirt to shelter us. I called the poor, cramped fellows up, then we rehearsed them in their coming duties.

Gavin whispered in my ear, "We have time to borrow another tentful."

In turn I whispered to Ryan for the new men to keep practicing how to crawl soundlessly, and the seven of us departed. I kept walking west along the row of tents closest to the latrines, to get a fair way from our previous act of magic. Eventually I chose one with two snorers inside. Dylan untied the flap, and we ghosted in. The nearest man was huge. After my wrestle with Howard, I knew the garrote would be a mistake, so I whipped the blanket off him and stuck my knife into his heart. He jumped up off the ground, then lay still.

"All done," came Dave's whisper.

This tent had ten fellows in it. After some head-scratching and a whispered conference, Gavin came up with a way of moving the big man. We took belts off five corpses. One went around his neck to hold him from buckling forward, four laced into his belt as carrying handles. So, five of us managed to carry him upright. The other corpses were easy.

Again we collected their weapons and rejoined our friends, to set off for the creek.

I sent Jim to lead, and kept myself last. Eventually, we all lay on the ground, between the northernmost tents and the line of sentries along the creek. I now waited, observing the moon through the slow passage of clouds. When a particularly dark one got in the way of the light, I moved on the corner sentry. A hand over his mouth, a knife though his heart, and I sank down with him as the fellow cowering beside me stood.

I could hear the rustling of our inexperienced recruits taking up position, but no Englishman seemed to worry. Dave went by me for the next guard on the right, and I went past him for the last one we'd take out. There was no point in making things hard, dragging bodies to the creek over a long distance. I winced at the noisy crawl of the fellow with Dave. I was alone, because I reserved this, most risky, position for myself. I wanted to be the one on hand if a guard on my right got active, or if a superior came prowling. For the same reason, Jim had the other end.

As the clouds came and went, I tracked our progress by sound. Occasionally I even glimpsed movement as a body was lowered over the edge. All the same, I could see that the plan was being followed to perfection. I and two new men stood on guard on the eastern side. Jim and three were at the other end. The five other old hands were ferrying bodies to the creek, which had fallen sufficiently to provide a muddy but passable crawl space. The seven remaining new men were towing the bodies through the water, up to the twisted oak.

A clear patch of sky approached the moon, and I watched the Englishman thirty yards to my right. He seemed uninterested in me, which was how I wanted it. A glance to my left showed the two false soldiers, and I clearly saw the lack of guards on the northern side. If a real soldier looked that way... but at last a cloud covered the moon again, and I saw the barest motion. Presumably this was the team collecting the muskets, to be ferried out.

After another eternity, the corner guard doubled for an instant. That was John, replacing the new man and giving him a chance to go. Then the same happened in the next position. I focused to the right again, willing the soldier to go to sleep, or dream of his sweetheart, or anything but look left.

I heard the last new fellow crawl to the creek, waited for a dark cloud to hide the moon, then dropped to the ground and ran on palms and toes like a lizard, rifle slung over my shoulder. Here was the creek, a figure, presumably David, ahead of me, and hopefully the team of four behind. I lay in the mud for a while, recovering after my sixty-yard crawl, but all of us gained the old oak by the time a terrified yell came from behind. I saw the flash of a gun fired up toward the sky an instant before I heard the bang. An Englishman was being smart, raising the alarm in the quickest way.

The men had already moved half the bodies along the second stage, still dragging them in the water. I hoisted a smallish corpse over my shoulder and ran uphill. I kept going till my legs and lungs were afire, then dropped the body and returned for the next one, stepping out of John and Gavin's way. They were carrying a big man by his arms and legs.

All nineteen of us were working well. I was wondering how the new fellows could keep going given their weakened state, but keep going they did. After my second body, I climbed the tree and peered toward the camp. All I could see was the movement of indistinct shapes against the lighter darkness of the square tents. So, happy to see no organized chase, I grabbed several muskets and hurried up the path. The bodies I'd dropped were gone, and I kept almost running all the way to the campsite, with others running the other way.

When the area behind the tree was free, we relieved the new men of their loads, which they were still dutifully towing upstream, though here they could do so almost upright rather than crawling. At last, we were all assembled.

Kieran and the two women had a nice little fire going. Katie gave me a mug of hot soup, saying, "Oh, we thought you were all dead! Thank the good God you're all right."

I was too busy enjoying the soup to do more than grin at her.

At last things settled down. I said loudly, "Men, we're not done yet. We now need to line up our English at the end of the overhang, and pile stones in front. Then, in the morning we'd better move out. I know another place that'll serve."

"Why do you want to move?" Kieran asked.

"We've been here too long. The English may be poor at tracking, but we've just about worn a road to here. And it's too small for this many people. And in a few days, the place will stink. I don't feel like digging graves for our latest visitors."

Kieran pressed a piece of cooked meat into my hand. As I bit into it, I tasted pork—Howard Pig no doubt. While chewing, I went to inspect Howard Sub-Pig's grave. It had been completely filled, and the ground smoothed by our home team of three. Excellent.

"Right people," I said on my return. "Get all the rest you can. We're moving at dawn."

8.

Cockroach

The first light woke me. I saw the other old hands also stir, but the new people lay as if dead. After all the deprivation and slave work, I wished I could leave them to rest a while.

Katie's face caught my eyes. After only two days of freedom and food, it had started to fill a little. In the repose of sleep, she looked beautiful. I wished for her that her husband and children, if any, also survived, and if not, that she'd find a good man for herself.

I opened my mouth to wake everyone, but the distant sound of shooting did it for me. A few popping sounds rapidly grew into an almost constant peppering. Everyone stirred, and I saw several new men checking their muskets.

"Which of you fought in the war?" I asked in the way of a "good morning."

Five raised their hands.

"Follow us at a walk. Everyone else, pack up and hide the signs that we've been here." I started running down the path, hearing the other old hands behind me.

The shooting increased. It was like when a potful of water starts to boil: a bubble here and there, then more and more till it's constant. But by the time I was halfway, a new pattern emerged, the one familiar from the war. A loud bang sounded, and came regularly over the continuous shooting of many individual guns. In the war, this had been the disciplined English loading and shooting together, three shots to the minute, while the Irish each acted alone.

I slowed to a walk. If an Irish force was attacking the camp, they'd take us to be English in our stolen uniforms.

Cautiously but still fast, we walked to the old oak. Dylan and I climbed it. What I saw made no sense. There were no Irish, only redcoats. Many were way down the hill, running west. A large number were among the stumps, in the cleared area south of their camp. They were shooting, loading and shooting while steadily walking downhill: the terribly effective advance of the English soldier. Only, they were shooting to the right, toward their own camp. The disciplined volleys came from there, and some redcoats fell. As we jumped down, the five new men arrived, puffing. They'd disobeyed orders and ran after us, despite their weakened state.

"I don't understand it," Dylan said. "It's English against English."

I quickly organized a skirmish line, with Jim on the left flank, me on the right, and old and new men paired in between. We rapidly advanced across the clear ground to the top line of tents, then split up along the corridors between them. When I checked, there was no one in the first tent, none in the second. Soon we reached dead soldiers. I passed a wounded man, bleeding to death, and I was frustrated that I couldn't question him. He looked at us without interest, preparing for a journey to a different place.

Fewer and fewer soldiers remained in the open space south of the camp, and the sound of shooting reduced. So, to speed them on their way, I shot the nearest redcoat. My friends joined in, though only having muskets, they missed at this distance.

By the time I'd reloaded, we reached the cooking area. It was empty of the living, and no fires were lit. Silence descended, almost shocking after the sound of battle. An ox lowed in his enclosure, no doubt past his feeding time.

Movement ahead: a compact group of soldiers emerged into the open, marching west. Something was odd: I saw a couple of senior officers, lieutenants, and perhaps ten soldiers, but they all seemed to be sergeants and corporals, with the morning sun reflecting off the emblems of their rank. The three traitors were among them too. Even the officers carried muskets, which was unusual. One of the traitors bent next to a fallen soldier and picked up his gun, searching the body, no doubt for ammunition. The group marched on, leaving him behind, and he ran to fall in at the back.

I figured that the lower ranks would be the better shooters, so raised my rifle and blew the head off a sergeant. My friends shot too, and three more went down.

There was a shout. They turned and fired off a volley in our direction. I didn't know if they'd hit anyone, but no bullet came anywhere near me.

I reloaded and ran ahead. Again I shot a soldier, ran, then dived for the ground to reload.

The English had reloaded too, but were holding their fire. They stood out in the open, waiting. So, I popped off a corporal and ran to a new position while their volley struck everywhere around where I no longer was. Two more fell at the same time. My crew were using the sound of the volley to hide their shots.

I briefly saw Gavin's distinctive silhouette between two tents, then he was out of sight. I shot a lieutenant, having ran out of lower ranks. Another two fell even as their volley came again, nowhere near me. It now sounded pathetic, no longer the intimidating bang but rather the scattered sound of a few guns.

I advanced to the southernmost row of tents, lay on the ground in the shelter of one and shot another lieutenant.

"Leave the traitors till last," I shouted while moving again. The English shot for my voice, but by then I was well away and rolling.

Four or five shots came in close succession. One of the senior men and the remaining lieutenants all fell.

Having reloaded, I came out into the open, since only two of the enemy had guns, and one was a civilian. Both pivoted toward me. I shot the colonel, as I could now see from his insignia. The traitor missed.

There were the rest of my team. As I advanced, reloading, a glance showed me that two of the new men were missing, but the six old hands looked fine, and ready to shoot.

"Drop your weapon!" I shouted to the traitor. Not that he could shoot an unloaded gun.

He did so.

I stopped five paces from him, bayonet pointing at the ground. "Talk, traitor," I said.

"I am no traitor but a loyal subject of his majesty King George. All my ancestors were Normans. I'm unsullied by base Irish blood."

Arrogant bastard. I jumped forward, and slashed his throat with the bayonet. His head flopped back, and he collapsed into a heap.

"Dermot!" David shouted, but I already saw the danger: the big blond fellow coming for me, hands outstretched. He grabbed the barrel of my rifle and twisted it aside, so I missed him.

A fusillade of shots came from my men, and he went down. All the same, both my arms hurt from holding against him. And, for the barest instant, I saw him wearing armor, the first light of dawn on his bared teeth, though his face was different. He held an axe, which was coming for my head. I actually flinched but then the... what? vision? was gone.

One man remained. I said to him, "Talk. I'll let you live if you tell us what we need to know."

He looked surprised to hear a redcoat talk the Gaelic to him. "Can I trust your word?"

I laughed. "What have you got to lose? Tell me, what happened this morning?"

"Mutiny. Word was coming in that maybe sixty of the guard disappeared, and five or six tents were completely empty of men!"

I managed not to laugh at the way things grew.

"And?"

"And the men panicked. A private refused to do his duty, so Lieutenant Somers shot him. So, they killed him, and it exploded from there."

"Look you, the Irish are still locked in your disgusting enclosure. Do you have a key?"

"No. All the non-commissioned officers have those."

"Thank you. Now, would you like to know how those English bastards disappeared?"

He looked at me.

"The Little People did it. We serve them, and they do the magic."

"Superstitious nonsense!"

"What they do is to turn a man into a cockroach. Highly appropriate for an Englishman. They're still there of course, but when you seek, you look for a man not an insect."

My men behind his back were trying not to howl with laughter, but he went pale.

"I told you I'd let you live, and so I shall. But I didn't say you'd stay a man. As soon as my masters arrive, they'll deal with you, and then I'll happily see you crawl away."

He took off and started sprinting downhill, tripped and fell, rolled and was up again.

We managed to wait till he was well out of hearing before laughing ourselves silly.

Once I could breathe again, I sent John, the fastest runner, back to the camp to bring our recruits. Dave searched his pockets, found the key he'd used to remove the shackles an eternity ago, or was it only a few days? He ran off to free our people.

Bride's Bay

The newly liberated Irish had ransacked the camp for food. All the animals were looked after, and at my request the oldest and wisest men were gathering.

"Dermot!" I heard, and this skeleton in rags rushed toward me, arms outstretched. At first I didn't recognize him with the white, shaggy beard, but it was Da all right, aged a century. We hugged. He smelled terrible of course, but so what.

We sat on the ground in a circle, Da on my right, Dylan on my left. I'd invited Ryan to sit in too. I said, "We need to decide what to do. This many people couldn't survive in the wild places, even if you were all fit and strong."

We talked about it for a while, but no one could offer any choice but to return to our villages. People need plants grown in the fields, and domestic animals, and fish from the sea. The English? I hoped that the traitor I'd spared would infect more English with the fear of being turned into cockroaches. All we could do was to hope that the mutiny might spread. As one man said, "They treat their private soldiers near as bad as their enemies. Maybe a taste of freedom will be too good to give away for them."

As the council ended, Katie came to me. She still wore men's clothes, with the breeches held on with a bit of rope and the cuffs of sleeves and legs rolled up. But she'd washed and brushed her dark hair, and her blue eyes shone at me. "Dermot," she said, "a favor I'd ask of you."

"Ask away."

"Everyone I've loved is dead. May I... may I come with you to your village?"

"Surely. You'll be welcome. We've suffered losses too." Of course, this brought Maeve to the eyes of my heart, and I had to try my hardest not to make a fool of myself by crying.

I sent people to yoke up horses to the few carts, and to improvise carts from the pairs of wheels-on-axles that had been used to carry logs, with oxen to pull them. We loaded all the tools, lots of tents and anything else we could find, and set off downhill. Of particular attraction was their store of powder and bullets.

Walking beside me at the front, Ryan said, "I can't wait to get out of this soldier's rig. And soon as I can, I want to go home to see if my family is still alive. They of course must think me long dead, as I would be sooner rather than later, except for you."

"Where is home?"

"Sligeach."

"I was there recently. The English lord it over us, but there is peace of a sort."

We arrived at the coast road. I stopped and climbed up on a cart. "We need to check what's happening at Bride's Bay. Get armed if you can handle a gun, and come along for the fun."

All the uniformed new men volunteered, so there were seventeen of us false soldiers. I got the men without uniforms to walk slowly. We red-coated Irish hurried ahead.

With a couple of miles to go, I noticed smoke rising into the sky. We kept walking, ready for instant action. As we rounded the final curve before the village, I saw a small group of redcoats, lying on the ground. They were alive, and stank of whiskey. We happily bayoneted them, hardly slowing. After this, we encountered other drunken soldiers, and killed them too.

Here was the village, with the bay behind it. All the houses were burnt, bitter-smelling smoke still rising from the roofs. Dead soldiers lay everywhere, but all in all, there weren't anywhere near as many, counting both alive and dead, as had been at the camp above, and the village had a substantial garrison too.

One fellow looked reasonably sober. He didn't carry a gun. Ryan asked him something. Seeing the corporal's markings, the Englishman looked both hostile and scared, but relaxed as the conversation progressed. Ryan smacked him on the shoulder as you would a friend, and we went on. Unfortunately, having him translate would have betrayed us.

The Irish slaves who'd been made to work here were still locked in a fenced enclosure similar to the uphill one, and looked like they hadn't been fed even the usual pittance yet, and it was past noon.

I took my group to the largest building. Corpses of several officers lay inside.

We had to return, and organize our contingent of Irish. When we met them, I got them all to turn around, and return to Glasagh, the next village north. Again I asked for a meeting of the respected elders to plan our actions.

"They're a rabble," I said. "Our people are locked up and starving. But we're outnumbered maybe three-to-one?" I looked around at my mates.

"About that," Gavin answered, "though it's hard to tell. Maybe more."

"They are trained. They can load and shoot maybe three times as fast as any of you, and far more accurately. A bull at a gate rush will see us defeated."

Dave said, "Let's wait till dark. I'd be surprised if any of them will stand guard. We wait till they're asleep, and kill them then."

"Any objections to killing a sleeping man?" I looked around.

A tall bald man, who must have been very powerful before being starved, spoke. "Not after what this lot have done to us!" There was a general nodding of heads.

Those of us in uniform searched the ruins and found clothes to change into. I didn't fancy being attacked by a friend in the dark.

We settled down to wait for the night.

An hour or so later, everything changed. Bang... bang... bang came the sounds of disciplined volleys, a little sporadic shooting, but it was soon over.

The English army was here, to put down the mutiny.

I looked around at my small, untrained force. To be seen with weapons was death. It'd be utter folly to oppose them.

I thought of scattering up into the hills, but the women and even less fit men were a few miles behind us. Could we desert them? Also, how well could these starved, exhausted men cope with rushing up a steep hill?

I shouted, "Hide your guns behind the houses." That would be all we'd have time for.

Men were still doing this when the ground vibrated to the thunder of massed horses at a gallop. Here they came, bursting around the curve of the road. They pulled up in a disciplined way. Even this advance guard at least matched our numbers.

A colonel led them. He looked fit and strong and very intimidating. Another surprise, he shouted in Gaelic, "Men. I take it you're forced laborers, escaped thanks to the mutiny?"

"Yes Sir," I answered.

"The mutiny is over. Those criminals are dead, or wishing they were dead. As for you, I have an announcement to make. His gracious majesty, King George the Third, has authorized his Grace Earl Camden, Lord-Lieutenant of Ireland, to annex this region for his personal use. His Grace has determined that all residents are guilty of treason. The punishment is transportation to the colony of New South Wales for the terms of your natural lives."

9. 1802-1803

Exiled

I have suffered much in my life, but that three month death march was the worst. The soldiers herding us were not Englishmen. Ryan couldn't understand their speech. They had black coats, like the patrol I'd seen when getting our uniforms. Only, our lot had blue facings not yellow. I'd thought the English cruel, but compared to these men, they were angels. We were fed, but never enough, and forced to march for hours without rest. They took delight in torturing anyone who collapsed, be it man, woman or child.

During our nightly stops, they amused themselves with little games. For example, they'd hoist a rope over a high branch, and make a noose at each end. They put this around the necks of two victims and tightened the rope, forcing them to stand on tip-toes. It was obvious that they then took bets on which would collapse first, choking them both.

I could have escaped many a time, but people looked to me for leadership. The general of the walking dead, that's what I was. That's why this time is so painful for me. I had to lead, to support, although I had no power to protect. I had to keep people alive—and they died anyway. I was a false hope, and it hurt far more than anything I could suffer personally.

The English kept bringing new groups to swell our number, handing them over to the black devils, as we called the foreigners. Until hunger weakened them too, the newcomers were stronger, and I organized them to support the weakest among us. Mostly, they were glad to do so, but not always. Then my little force dealt with them in the night. And none of these good men chose to escape either, although they had the skill to succeed and survive.

Every day, people died. The lucky did so without assistance from the black devils. I'd say less than a third of those forced off the land finally made it on board a ship.

Each ship took 300 of us. They separated the men from the women, who also had the very few surviving children. I was fortunate to be herded onto the same ship as my father, brother Dan, Gavin, Dave and Ryan. What happened to the rest of my companions I know not. This was not the first ship by any means, since we waited for months in hellish conditions.

As a boy, I'd seen full-rigged ships in the distance, but never close by, and didn't realize how large they were. Now, I'd have been happy never to have seen one. We were in a low flat area, crowded so close that breathing was difficult. Cannons on a higher level pointed down at us. A gate closed off the entrance to our area, with red-coated soldiers on the other side.

A man in a blue uniform walked forward on the higher level. Looking at him, I immediately thought of Lieutenant Howard. This fellow could have been his older brother: the same body build, the same gross obesity, the same disdainful sneer on his face.

By then, I had a smattering of the English, learned from Ryan during the death march and after. So, I understood when he shouted, "Any of you speak the King's English?"

Ryan held up his hand. The gate was unlocked, and two redcoats escorted him out. He soon appeared up by the officer, who said something to him.

Ryan shouted, "This is Captain Caruthers. He represents the King on this ship and–"

The Captain smacked him on the side of the head with an open palm. It was not a hard blow, but in his weakened state, Ryan collapsed. The soldiers hauled him to his feet.

The Captain said something, and Ryan spoke: "This is Captain Caruthers. He represents his majesty the King on this ship and his word is law."

Sentence by sentence, Ryan translated the fat bully's words. "We'll be decently treated as long as we obey the rules. Any disobedience will be severely punished. We'll be fed, allowed to wash ourselves, and will get clean clothes. When the weather permits, some of us may come up to this space. It's up to us to organize who comes up when. That's all."

I stared at the man, hate eating my guts. This promise of fair treatment was made a lie by the fact he'd hit Ryan. Besides, didn't he look like Howard Sub-Pig? I wished for my rifle.

As the Captain's eyes swept us, contempt in his bearing, his gaze fixed on me. His face grew red and he snarled something. The gate opened and four soldiers came for me.

Weakened by starvation I may have been, but I was not going without a fight. As the first fellow reached for me, I swayed aside and kicked him in the groin, spun away and hit the next one in the guts with an elbow. A hand grasped me by the throat. I grabbed a finger and snapped it. Then the back of my head exploded.

When I came to, the top half of me was naked, and I was tied to some timber contraption with my arms spread wide. I heard a whistling sound, and what felt like a dozen whip-blows split my back like fire. "One," I heard.

I was not going to cry out.

Again a forest of whips struck me. "Two," the calm voice said.

I don't know when I fainted, or how many times I was struck.

Shipboard

"I think he is waking," I heard my father's voice from far away.

"Da," I managed. I was face down on a hard surface. My back felt like it had been chewed by a shark. Everything was moving and swaying. As I opened my eyes, I saw I lay on something maybe two feet off a timber floor, although the light was very dim. Young Dan gazed up at me. He knelt on the floor and held a bottle with a hollow reed sticking out of it. He put that in my mouth and said, "Suck, Dermot."

I sucked. Weak soup came into my mouth. Awkwardly in that position, I swallowed, and kept sucking till only air came.

An Englishman spoke, then Ryan: "The doctor says he should now survive."

"Ryan, why?" I demanded, sounding to myself like a child.

"You dared to look at the bastard. Insolence. But the doctor told me, he does this every trip. During the first meeting, he has someone lashed, so we all see what can happen. You were just a convenient warning to the rest of us."

"Maybe we should invite the Little People along." I had to rest. "Do a Howard on him."

"Forget it, son," Da said. "For now, just recover. You've been unconscious for three days."

One day I could sit, and later stand, and walk, and eventually even lie on my back. The doctor gave us cream people dabbed on my healing scars, and instructed me to do stretching exercises to return movement. He was the first decent Englishman I'd ever met, and got him to teach me as much English as he had time for. This was difficult at first because his speech was quite different from Ryan's. When I'd learnt enough, he explained that Ryan's speech was "Cockney," what poor people in London speak, while his was that of wealthier people. Apparently, among the English, how you speak indicates whether you're scum or gentry.

When at last I could climb the ladder out of the dim, dark hold, I felt like I was born again, breathing real air, seeing God's sky. The sea was hidden, because our low deck was enclosed on all sides, but I heard the sound of the ship working its way through it, the sighing of the wind in the great sails above, smelt the salt.

Bored sailors stood by the cannons still pointing down at us, and equally bored redcoats beyond the gate. I heard sailors going about their duties. Now I understood some of their words, but even so made little sense of their activities.

We captives had settled into a routine of doing nothing, treating each meal time as an event of interest, though the food was bland: twice-baked bread with weevils providing the meat, soup, which was a few limp vegetables floating in hot water, maybe a potato.

We wore shirts and breeches, and had to wash once a day up on our deck. We had to strip off, and they turned a pump on us that sprayed sea water.

There was a defeated air about everybody. This was accurate of course— we were defeated. All the same, I asked my small group of friends to have a talk about it. "Look you," I started. "All we do all day and all night is nothing. We were starved and mistreated on the road, but at least walking gave us some exercise. Here, nothing. By the time we arrive at this New South Wales, wherever it might be, we'll be weaker than kittens."

Gavin replied, "I've been thinking the same, but couldn't be bothered to do anything about it. See, when we get there they'll just do to us what they did at home. Why should I be a strong slave instead of a weak slave?"

"Because a strong slave survives better. Because a strong slave might escape. Or fight back."

"Not sure I want to survive," my father said. "What for?"

"Because two sons still look to you. Dan is only sixteen. I certainly want him to survive!"

"What do you have in mind?" my little brother asked.

"We exercise to get strong. We learn their language." I had my way, and we talked with all the others. Some couldn't be bothered, but others filled empty hours by exercising, slowly gaining strength. The doctor agreed to teach us. A group of about thirty were keen to learn, and soon we talked in English, for practice.

Sometimes, great storms hit the ship, and then we were battened down, with water sloshing under our feet, and vomit too because not everyone had been fishermen at home. We called in at ports, but of course spent all the time then locked below. After these occasions, we were given strange new foods, occasionally even a scrap of meat.

One day, the doctor told us, "Won't be long now. I heard that we should arrive at Sydney Town in about a week." But the next day, I got in trouble again.

We were having our usual wash. The two men working the pump had fun suddenly spraying sea water into the faces of people. I could understand their shouted jokes as they made bets with other sailors about how many Irish animals they could knock down.

The first one down was my father. I gave him a hand up, then of course the stream of water hit me. I set myself, closed my eyes and mouth, and used a hand to shield my nose so I could breathe. The bastards would not budge me.

At last the jet of water swung away. Glancing up, I saw the lounging sailors laughing at the two pump operators, who seemed displeased.

I looked them in the eye, and said in English, "You're very brave at this distance. I wonder how brave you'd be two steps away."

They stopped pumping. I felt like smacking myself upside the head for being stupid enough to be provoked. Another lashing would kill me for sure.

The gate opened, and ten redcoats marched in, muskets pointing. They spread into a line. The corporal looked at me. "You will come. If there's a struggle like last time, we'll shoot you in the arms and legs."

They surrounded me and marched me out. Up some steep stairs we went, into a busy place though I had no opportunity to see anything. Then we went up again, into a little room-like enclosure with a man holding a large vertical wheel, and others doing I know not what.

The fat captain looked down his nose at me. "You speak English?" he demanded.

"Yes Sir, I can speak a little English. Not very good yet."

"You're still insolent. Didn't the cat-o'-nine-tails teach you?"

"I beg your pardon Sir. I don't know that cat word."

"The lashing you got." Well, the scars on my naked body were plain to see.

"Sir, those sailors were hurting my father. For no reason."

He looked at the corporal of my escort. "In chains, solitary confinement till we arrive."

"Aye aye Sir."

I soon learned what "solitary confinement" meant. Rough hands grabbed me. They marched me down, down, to some deep hole. There they shackled my left ankle, attached to a chain about three yards in length, which was fixed to the wall. In the light of a lantern carried by one man, I saw an empty bucket, no doubt for the wastes of my body, and nothing else.

They went out, leaving me in pitch dark.

Water constantly seeped through the timbers of the ship. I had no way of measuring time, except that every now and then two men came, one carrying a lantern, the other a bit of food. Four extra soldiers came the first time, and the doctor carrying clothes. They allowed me to dress before shackling me to the chain again. On every second or third occasion, they also had an Irishman along, who exchanged my bucket for an empty one. I did have company: rats scurrying around. At first, I was concerned they might bite me, but this didn't happen and after awhile I ignored them.

At first I was energized by anger. Then I spent the uncounted hours dreaming of the good times: dancing with Maeve, hunting in my hills, fishing, playing with my little sisters and brothers, riding Harry. Then I dreamt of the bad times: sharpshooting in the war, slitting the throats of English sentries in the dark, doing the magic of the Little People.

Then I stopped it all. Maeve was dead—raped, tortured and killed, never mind the baby, my baby, within her. Those hills were no longer mine, but owned by Earl Camden, and if I ever were to return, the place would be changed beyond recognition. And for all the English I'd killed, they had won all the same.

For the first time ever, I felt defeated. In the dark, in the silence made worse by the creaks of the ship, I stopped moving, just sat on the slimy floor and waited for the next visit from my captors. Then, I didn't even look up, for the dim flicker of the lantern hurt my eyes with its brightness. I even stopped eating the food. What for? The rats could have it, and welcome.

10. 1803-1811

Neville Carney

Without interest I heard a lot of feet on the stairs. A corporal came in, with a bunch of redcoats.

He stopped, his booted feet in front of my nose. "End of the journey, you stinking Irishman," he said. I thought that if he changed places with me for a week, he'd stink too, but knew enough to stay quiet.

He snapped his fingers and two men grabbed me. They hauled me upright while a third unlocked the shackle, but when they let me go, I couldn't stand.

They dragged me up the stairs, up again, up. I gradually managed to get my body to work after awhile, and was able to walk, but the steadily increasing light was a torture for my eyes. Even when I squeezed them shut, the brilliance through my eyelids stabbed right into my skull. I felt myself shoved forward, and would have fallen except that several hands grabbed me. I heard words of encouragement in Gaelic.

Gradually my eyes got used to the light enough that I could open them in short bursts, then for longer. I was at the tail end of the three hundred passengers, walking over a gangplank to a wharf. Two men whose names I didn't know supported me. "Sorry for the stink," I said.

One answered, "That stink is from associating with the bloody English. It's not your fault."

Soldiers escorted us to a large building, and we had to wait forever as each man was admitted. When at last it was my turn, I faced a corporal with gray at the temples. "Name?" he demanded in some approximation of Gaelic.

"Corporal, my name is Dermot O'Halloran," I answered in English.

He looked surprised, then wrote on the board in his hands. "Your Irish names give me a lot o' trouble," then, "You're in a sad state. What 'appened?" His speech was like Ryan's rather than like the doctor's.

"One week of solitary confinement, in chains, in complete dark."

To my surprise, he looked sympathetic. "What'ya do to earn it?"

"They were being cruel to my father."

"I 'ate all this. 'Ave to do as I'm told, but I try to 'urt no man."

All the other Irishmen were inside, and the last of other soldiers who'd been writing down their names were just entering the door. He signaled inward with his eyes, and we walked side by side like two friends.

"So why are you a soldier?"

"Because it was that, or bein' a sailor, or bein' a convict. Least bad of three choices, like."

I grinned at him. "What'ya do to earn it?"

"A little boy stole an 'andkerchief out of a nob's pocket. 'E was a starved little feller, so I tried to help 'im escape, and instead got caught meself."

I saw men milling around in a large barn-like enclosure, but he took me through a door to the left. I asked him to explain "handkerchief" and "nob."

We were outside again, by the shore of a creek with a fence on the other side. "Strip and wash," he ordered. Gladly I did so. He tossed me a shirt and breeches. As I dressed, a door opened and the great crowd of Irishmen started coming out, no doubt for their wash.

He led me inside again to another room, where a row of men waited, each next to a chair. I was made to sit, then the man shore off all my hair and beard. "We don't want no vermin in the colony," my corporal explained. "Fleas, lice and that."

The next place he led me to had a long counter near one wall, with more men standing behind, and steaming pots. I was given a metal bowl and a spoon. He turned to leave, but I asked him for his name.

"Neville Carney."

"Neville Carney, I thank you from the bottom of my heart and will say a prayer for you."

Jack Smith

I felt like a beast at the cattle market. Here we stood, dressed in our new but shabby clothes, facing an unruly crowd of cattle buyers. Some were fussy and inspected men, others just grabbed the number they wanted, and the soldiers herded them out. Steadily, the number of convicts reduced, as did the crowd on the other side. I was starting to think that I might have been lucky enough to defer my new life as a slave, when a big fellow pushed to the front. He had a shaggy head of gray hair poking out from under a wide-brimmed hat, and a long bushy beard. I heard him say, "I'll have twenty of these here," pointing in my general direction.

Next thing, I had a shackle around my ankle—the right one, not the one with the still scabbed sores from the ship—and was part of a line of men chained behind a cart with two big horses hitched to it. The old fellow climbed on the driver's seat with surprising vigor and got going, with us behind him. An hour or so later, we were well out of town. He stopped at a creek, jumped off and went to rummage in his cart. By then, I was death on legs, supported by my two neighbors. Surprising what strength a man can lose in a week.

We flopped to the ground, and after awhile I had energy enough to look around. Tall trees lined both sides of the track, but they were nothing like any tree of home. By then, our owner had a cheerful fire burning with a cauldron in the middle of it, steam just starting to rise. He walked along the line of men, giving each of us a large chunk of bread and a slab of meat nearly the same size.

"Thank you," I said as he handed me mine.

"You can speak English?" Delight and relief showed on his face.

"A little. I've been learning."

"I'll be back, mate." He finished handing out the food, then lifted the cauldron off the fire, put a double handful of tea leaves in, stirred it, then dipped metal mugs in and handed these along the line too. I was surprised to see the owner serving his slaves.

He grabbed bread, meat and tea for himself and returned to me. "Right, mate, I'm Jack Smith."

"Dermot O'Halloran, Sir."

He laughed. "Don't Sir me, Dermot. Just Jack will do. I'm delighted I can speak to one of you at least. Was worried about that. This way, I should be able to let you men off the chain. Now I want you to explain some stuff to your mates, right?"

Being let off the chain made me relieved too. "I'll do my best, Jack."

"I'm employed by the government to build roads. Our first job will be a bridge right here. Now, tell this to the others."

I did so, although his speech was different from both Ryan's and the doctor's. I continued translating as he spoke.

"I don't like using convicts as if you was slaves, but see, I've got to do as I'm told or they punish me. All the same, I want to treat you men decently— but if you run, I'm done. Anyway, no point running. You can't live off the land here. Oh, the natives do, but all the plants and animals are different from home, and we don't have the knowledge. And those natives will just as soon eat you as eat a kangaroo."

I translated, after he explained the last word, drawing an outline in the dust of the track with a stick.

"I suppose if you had a gun you could hunt till you ran out of powder and shot, but what then? You go back to any British settlement, and you can't imagine the horror of what the soldiers will do to you."

"Oh yes I can," I told him. "They had their fun with us in Ireland many a time."

"Righto, if I have a promise of good behavior from all of you, I'll unlock the chain. I'll feed you well, only work you as much as is reasonable, and protect you from the bloody soldiers. And you might teach the others to speak English too, so I can chat with them."

"Righto, Jack," I replied, liking the new word. He was my third decent Englishman, and I knew how lucky I was to be with him rather than some cruel bastard.

Having finished his tea, he returned to the cart to fetch a bottle. Walking along the line of men, he sloshed a bit of liquid into each mug, again serving himself last. I had a sip. The taste instantly took me back to the doctor's after the English had killed Harry and near-killed me.

"Rum," Jack explained.

Within two weeks, I regained my strength. We worked with a will for a man we liked. He often rode off on one of the horses, or took the cart for materials, leaving us unsupervised. We talked among ourselves, and decided that our best place in the whole colony was with Jack Smith.

We gradually learned his story. He'd been a sailor, and when old enough to be released, chose New South Wales as his home, to get as far away as he could from the cruelty of the ruling class and those who served them. As he explained, "To the nobs, we're cattle. The bastardry starts from the top, see? They care nothing for the common man, no more than for heathens in the places they conquer and plunder. To them, I'm no better than you, and that's the one thing I accept from them. Jesus said all people are the same."

"So, are things better here?" someone asked.

"Only because I can get away from the crowds. Y'see, we have a ladder. Just like at home, top of the shit-pile is the nobs. Then there's the soldiers, although a common soldier is scum to an officer. Then there's the free men, like me. And a long way below that is the ticket of leave man." He could see we didn't understand this. "When you've done eight years of slavery and behaved, you're freed. You get a piece of paper saying so. Then you can go anywhere in New South Wales, but you're not allowed to leave it. You can earn money, though always less than a free man doing the same work. And if you step out of line, you go back to being a convict. Of course, convicts are not even considered human by the bastards."

Another time, he asked us what our crime was. "Being Irish," someone answered.

"Figures. I've heard, mates, that in England rich bastards make lots of money from spinning fleece into yarn in big factories, and they can't get enough wool. That's why they wanted you lot gone. They've stolen your land, and now sheep graze there."

It was good to at least have an explanation.

Sadly, after three years, Jack had to return us to the government. We all asked him to keep us on, but it was against the rules. He had to start again with a new lot of convicts.

Stonemason

We were all fit and strong, suntanned and with some knowledge of English, and got snapped up by a small wealthy-looking man with a big moustache. We had to unload sandstone blocks from bullock carts, and carry them up scaffolding to where craftsman stone layers put them into the rising walls of a church. We also mixed mortar and carried that up too. Unlike with Jack, here we were overseen by big men carrying whips who didn't mind using them, and were watched all the time. We worked from dawn to dark with hardly a break. At least, food was adequate.

Occasionally, a man fell from the scaffolding from tiredness. This didn't worry the overseers. They just got another convict to "clean up the mess," and the next day a new man worked with us. On one occasion, after a nasty whipping, a convict from London dropped a big sandstone block on the head of the overseer who'd assaulted him. Although he swore loudly that it was an accident, he was hauled away. We had a brief holiday the next morning, and were required to watch him being lashed to death with a cat-o'-nine-tails. Standing among the crowd of convicts, I said a prayer for his soul. After all, it was a church we were building. I'd learned my lesson though. There was no point in defiance.

Over time, I became one of the experienced hands, and when the church was completed and we started another building, I was allowed to help with laying the huge stones of the foundation. This work was not too different from what I'd often done with my father as a boy, and I was promoted to stonemason. While the hours were as long, I had higher status, meaning no random hits with a whip for no reason, and the work was no longer back-breaking. I also got a lot of pleasure from the artistic arrangement of big and small blocks.

One morning, I was up on the scaffolding laying a bed of mortar, when I saw Katie walking below. She was neatly dressed, well fed, and her dark hair shone. She was big with child. I felt delighted that my wish for her, way back in ancient history, had come true. I knew she'd been sweet on me then, though of course no woman would ever fill my heart. Perhaps in consequence, that night I dreamed of Maeve, dancing the stomp with her. I woke crying in the dark, though fortunately the sound didn't wake my exhausted fellow slaves.

This builder fellow didn't seem to have the same time limitation as Jack Smith. I worked for him for five years, until I earned my freedom.

11. 1811-1820

Dunadd

Being a free man had its disadvantages. From one day to the next, I had
nowhere to sleep, no money, and needed to buy food. Being sick of the city,
I found the markets, hoping to work for a farmer. Unfortunately they all
used convicts, and had no interest in paying even a pittance to a freed man.
In the evening, I earned some food by helping several of them pack up, then
slept under looming clouds in the empty market ground. At about midnight,
I was roused by a patrol of soldiers, who inspected my brand new ticket and
walked on. The next morning, I got breakfast by helping the new lot of
vendors set up. As I stood around at a loss, an arrogant-looking man strode
up to me. "Are you looking for a job?"

"Yes Sir."

"Can you ride a horse?"

"Sir, I could ride a horse as soon as I could walk."

"Come with me."

I followed him to an enclosure, to join a dozen other men. Three
beautiful black and tan geldings had feedbags over their noses. The man
went off, soon returning with another fellow, then one more. "Right, men,"
he said, "the best two riders have jobs." We each had to ride around the
enclosure, jump the horse over the fence, guide him through the crowd and
back through the gate without dismounting.

The first fellow had a hard hand, and the horse skittered around a little.
As he lined up for the jump, the prospective employer shouted, "Stop!"
You're out." I approved.

Eventually, it was my turn. Unlike those before me, first I introduced
myself to the horse, and checked that the harness was comfortable on him
but tight. Then I vaulted up, and took the horse through the routine like
we'd been together for years.

"You're in," the man said as I dismounted.

His name was "Mr. MacTavish," and he said he was "breeding horses
for the New South Wales Corps and whoever else values fine horses." He
supplied us two recruits with decent clothing including an oilskin coat, a
wide-brimmed leather hat and good leather boots. We were equipped with a
whip, cooking and eating utensils and food for several days. He told us that
the cost of our kit would come out of our wages. That was fair enough, I
thought, but the other man asked about our rate of pay, and the cost of the
kit.

He said with a sneer, "You don't have to come. Plenty of others will
gladly take your place."

We rode off at dawn the following day and spent three days on the track. During this time, MacTavish talked more to his horses than to us. The other man was Richard, who grew up on a farm in some part of England called Kent. He went to London to find his fortune, and instead ended up as a convict in New South Wales, thanks, he said, to liking gin too much.

We passed an arched gateway with "Dunadd Stud" burned into a plank. A five-strand wire fence stretched out of sight both ways. We rode a mile along a winding road. By now I knew enough about the countryside to see that the grass around us was introduced. A few gum trees still stood, but the landscape could have been from home otherwise. Groups of horses grazed in several places. We rode over a bridge across a creek with a gate on the other side. MacTavish opened it from the saddle. Coming last, I closed it.

A loud neigh came, and a magnificent stallion trotted up to us. He was black and tan like our mounts, but larger. He put his head on MacTavish's shoulder.

"Get away, you big baby," MacTavish said, pushing at him, but with obvious love. The horse breathed a cloud around his head, then walked beside him toward the house ahead of us. I decided that however rude and arrogant he may be with people, this man must have something good about him for a horse to love him so. With a shock, thinking back, I realized he'd spoken to the horse in something very close to Gaelic rather than in English.

The big house had a red iron roof and split planks clothing the walls in a way that would shed the rain, although a wide veranda protected it. Many other less impressive buildings surrounded a large open space, with post and rail fencing holding different kinds of animals beyond the buildings. There was a thriving vegetable garden and a small field of wheat by the creek. Several men were busy at a variety of tasks. To my surprise, some of them had dark brown skin. Also, I saw what were obviously serving women near the big house, with similar appearance to these.

We were led to one of the smaller buildings. Inside, it had ten narrow beds, each with a doorless wardrobe. "This is your home, men," MacTavish said, and left us. I stacked my scant belongings away in an empty position.

This being the first time we were out of his hearing, Richard said, "Typical Scottish bastard. A smile would crack his face."

"Turn yourself into a horse," I suggested. "He'll love you then."

He laughed. "Wonder what we're to do now. A bit of rum would be good."

"Didn't you say that's what got you to New South Wales?"

He laughed with me as we walked out into the bright sunshine. MacTavish stood with his foot on the bottom rail of a post-and-rail fence, watching a dark-skinned man school a yearling on a lunge rope. We walked over. Without looking at us he said, "You two are under instruction from Jimmy here. He's the best horse breaker there is. Do as he says."

Jimmy certainly looked competent with the filly. He was perhaps forty, with gray in his curly black hair and fuzzy beard. His nose was broad and flat and he had prominent eyebrows. On one of his turns he flashed us a white-toothed grin. He said, "Climb in, but don't startle my little girl here."

Judging our time, we walked up to him. He gave the rope to Richard who continued the circling without a break. "Good girl, Susie," Jimmy said, then took me along a fenced corridor to a large stable. Neat corrals held other young horses, all with water and feed in easy reach. He opened the gate of one corral and said, "Put a halter on him and lead him out."

I made friends with the colt, who followed me like the rope wasn't between us. Soon the three of us each worked a young horse independently, although I saw Jimmy's dark eyes often flash toward Richard or me, checking.

This set the pattern for my new life. We ate well, had the joy of working with horses, not only the young ones but all ages, occasionally taking our graduates to the city to accustom them to crowds and noise. Five others slept in our shed, but not Jimmy. He went home to his wife and family, in a camp along the creek. Lucky man, I thought, since the wife I'd never had the chance to marry and family were only memories within my heart.

The occasional trips away allowed us to buy rum, and that made life bearable.

MacTavish worked with the horses all day, and a marvel he was with them, but still the same grumpy bastard with the hired hands.

Jimmy and I became good friends. On the second day, I asked him where he came from, thinking it may have been India or somewhere.

He looked at me like I was crazy. "From here. This land is me, and I am this land. You white men stole it. Long before you called it New South Wales, my ancestors lived here."

"Oh. Sorry Jimmy, but don't put all white men together. The English stole my land from me too. Only, I was not even allowed to stay there."

"If I was removed from my land, I'd die. But Dermot, tell me your story."

I started, saying as much as I could without crying, till we returned to work. We continued at other times, and somehow talking to this wise man with the dark face helped.

One day I asked him how, unlike the other natives, he could speak English so well.

"When I was a little boy, the Reverend John Hartfield found me starving and alone. White men had killed all my family, but I somehow got away. I can't remember any of it. He took me into his home, and taught me English, the love of Jesus, and how to read and write. Then he tracked down my people and handed me over to my mother's brother. For my people, my mother's brother is my father too. He didn't know that, but it was God's work."

As I continued telling my story, I reached my three years with Jack Smith, and mentioned him saying that the natives eat people.

He laughed so hard he had to hold his stomach. When he could speak again, he told me, "Oh, he was a smart fellow! Stopped you running away. Why would we eat tough convict-meat when we can have a juicy wombat or kangaroo?"

After work, he usually took me to his people, who lived in temporary shelters for a week or so before moving. I'd have thought the little bark humpies to be miserable, but they kept the place clean, and smelling good. Despite their sorrows there was an innate happiness about them that lifted my spirit. I got lessons in finding food, enjoyed playing with several children, and felt I'd found a family.

One day, as we were walking toward his home, Jimmy said, "Dermot, your skin may be white, but we're brothers."

I had to stop, my heart became so full. Finally I said through my tears, "You've been my elder brother for a long time."

"When all my family was killed, way back, I had a brother, or so I'm told. He was intended to marry a girl. She married someone else, and now has a daughter who has no husband, because all the men she could marry are dead."

"What are you saying?"

"If you become my brother, she can marry you."

I felt incredibly honored. I managed not to cry. "There's only one thing wrong, Jimmy," I said at last. "I... I am still married within my heart to Maeve."

He sighed. "I predicted you'd say that, but you know, you can love more than one woman, like me." He did have two wives—a woman older than him, and a girl barely out of her teens.

But in the end, they respected my choice.

The seasons turned, and the years, and one day, looking into some still water in a bucket, I was surprised to see gray in my hair and beard.

Cameron

Then life changed again. A nob on a magnificent stallion arrived, and MacTavish escorted him into the big house. I separated his horse from Caleb, MacTavish's current stallion.

When the nobs came out again, MacTavish called us all together. He looked around with his usual disdain. "Men, explorers have crossed the mountains, and found fine pasture with rivers watering them, wide open plains. This gentleman is Mr. Cameron, who was my mentor at home, and again on arrival into New South Wales. He has invited me to accompany him to take up a holding. Those who wish can continue your employment with me. I'll be selling this property, so others may want to stay with the new owner."

Jimmy spoke up. "Boss, I cannot go. For us blackfellas, land is not something we own but it owns us."

That decided me to stay too, Jimmy being so much part of my life, but then MacTavish looked at me. "O'Halloran, in that case I need you."

"Sir, Jimmy is the only friend I have in the world. I'd prefer to stay with him."

I could read his mind from his face: "Figures, animal Irish and animal Abo." He looked daggers at me for a moment, then said, "Come into the house for a private word."

During my years at Dunadd, I'd never been into the big house. We kicked our boots off, and he led me to an office. He turned to face me. "O'Halloran, you're a ticket of leave man. If I accuse you of some crime, I'll be believed, and you'll be back to being a convict."

Nine years ago, I'd have killed him and run, but Jimmy had changed me. I held my rage. "Sir, would a Scottish gentleman stoop to blackmail?"

His face grew almost purple, and his already thin lips became a straight line. I could see he wanted to strike me, but my eyes, my stance, told him he'd die then. He took a deep breath. "Don't twist my words. I meant no such thing. I value your skills, and need a good horse breaker. I'll pay you a sovereign a year if you come."

"And falsely have me convicted if I don't."

"You denied yourself the right to justice when you became a criminal."

"Mr. MacTavish, do you know the crime I was convicted for?"

"Treason no doubt."

"I owe no loyalty to the English king. Why should I? But had they known it, they could have convicted me of killing hundreds of Englishmen. Push me too far, and I might kill again. Now, do you still want me along?"

He actually took a step backward. We looked into each other's eyes. At last, he said, "I do. I've found you to be a decent fellow, a hard worker, and intelligent at anything you do. If you come, I'll arrange a full pardon for you."

I thought a while. "Sir, I'll talk it over with Jimmy, and go by his advice."

"But he is an Abo!"

"He is the wisest man I know, and I consider him to be my brother." I walked out, without waiting for permission.

The next morning, Jimmy said to me, very seriously, "Dermot, I've prayed to Jesus, and asked the spirits of my ancestors to give us advice. And I've been told. Your destiny is to go to this far country. There, you'll be given a choice one day, and how you choose will determine the eternal life of your spirit." Oh, if I had only remembered this advice when the choice came!

12. 1820

The Outback

Six weeks we traveled, after months of preparation. It was a great awkward caravan of ox carts, a carriage for MacTavish's family, riders, and breeding stock for horses, cattle, sheep. Cameron led us, frequently checking a hand-drawn map I was told had cost two hundred pounds. Of course figures grow in the telling, but I was sure the price was considerable. We rode into rugged mountains clothed with gum trees, and made our way along an elevated, winding path. Often, we had to make the barely visible track into a road the carts could negotiate. I also found my scouting ability used, with me going ahead to find the easiest way, or toward evening, a place with water.

Occasionally I saw dark faces peering at the procession they no doubt found incomprehensible, but I'm sure no one else detected their presence. I respected their wish to stay hidden, though I hoped to come across some while alone. This didn't happen. Perhaps they were so good at hiding that they could observe even me undetected.

Eventually we descended onto a wide plain that stretched forever. Unlike the green of home, the sparse grass appeared gray. We swung south, following the undulating base of the mountains, and kept going day after day till we came to a largish creek, though Cameron called it a river. Strange, rather beautiful gnarled trees lined its banks. We rode for another day before we set up for good.

The first year we camped while constructing the essentials: fenced enclosures that would one day become parts of the home paddock, a water pump, sheds for the poultry so they could be released from their cages, the sowing of seed for wheat, vegetables and other crops.

MacTavish ordered me to contact the natives. I found the tracks of a small group. On the way back I shot a huge flightless bird, skinned and gutted it, thinking it'd make a fine gift. MacTavish insisted that I take four other men with me for safety. I timed our approach for just after dawn at their camping place by a waterhole. The children were naked, adults wore only something around the crotch. I hated the looks of lechery on the other men as they gazed at the bare breasts of the two young women, who were clearly unaware of this effect.

I was sure these people had never met horses, so we'd tethered our mounts a fair way off and came on foot. Even then, the locals were obviously frightened. The five men formed a line between us and their women and children, spears ready.

I approached the oldest, and spoke in Jimmy's language, which I'd learned over the years.

He said something incomprehensible in response.

Two of the men carried my bird. I got them to lay it at the elder's feet on the sparse grass. I also had a bag of trinkets with me. I pulled out a necklace, showed it so the morning sun glittered off it, and flicked it to settle around the neck of the oldest woman.

She squealed, then fingered the gift in delight.

The five men relaxed their guard. Had we been hostile, now would have been the time to attack. I'd agreed to take part to protect them from just that.

We handed out other gifts: more trinkets, a spade, an axe, a knife. They were treasures to these stone-tool using people, but cheap, poor quality goods.

I sent the youngest, Tom, to lead my horse forward. I mounted, got off again, then motioned for them to try. This caused a great buzz among all the adults, male and female. Finally, a young fellow stepped forward. Within minutes he was riding around in circles, a look of ecstasy on his face. Judging from Jimmy's people, I was sure they'd have a natural affinity for all animals, and was right. In half an hour, all the men were confident with a horse, although the women declined to try.

We then left them. I was pleased with this peaceful first contact, but didn't anticipate its sequel. Four mornings later, eight brown men approached our camp. They walked in, obviously confident of a good welcome, and speared a sheep.

The two nobs rushed out of the office tent, both with two dueling pistols, and shot four men. The elder I'd gifted with the bird threw a spear with incredible force into Cameron's right shoulder, but MacTavish's second shot killed him. The hands converged on horses, using various tools as makeshift weapons. Within a minute, all our would-be visitors were dead.

Burning with fury, I stormed up to the two Scots. MacTavish was reloading a pistol while saying in their version of Gaelic, "Duncan, we'll have to get that stick out of you."

I shouted in Gaelic, "You murderous idiots! How dare you kill those poor men?"

MacTavish raised his weapon toward me. Before he was anywhere near ready, I kicked him hard in the guts and snatched the gun from his hand.

I pointed the little gun at MacTavish's head. He was on all fours, gasping for breath and not even aware of my action. But Cameron shouted, "O'Halloran, don't!"

"Why not? Do only gentlemen have the right to murder?"

I heard hooves on hard ground and whirled. The men were riding for me. In front was Richard. I snatched his hat off with a bullet through the brim. This pulled them up short and I saw the killing fury leave their faces.

"Think a moment!" I shouted. "You're hired hands like me. How much loyalty do you owe these gentlemen?" I put contempt into the title. "They pay you a pittance for hard work, so they can make a fortune by stealing those poor natives' land. This is not your fight. Piss off and leave me to deal with it."

Charles, the foreman under the two bosses, wheeled his horse and rode away. The others followed.

I turned to see MacTavish going for his second gun.

"It'll need loading," I said in Gaelic, "You want to fight me, it's man to man."

"How dare you!" His voice was still distorted by the kick to the guts.

"Your kind stole my land, killed those I love, subjected me to torture and deprivation, enslaved me. All for greed. I did no wrong to anyone, except to defend me and mine. Can you say the same?"

"I've never been to Ireland," Cameron said. Clearly, despite the spear in him, he was thinking the better.

"What you're doing here is exactly the same. This land belongs to those natives. You've taken it without their permission, and without any intention of paying them for it. And then–"

"You're wrong," he cut me off. "His Majesty has declared New South Wales to be terra nullius, because the locals are mere savages without culture."

"I don't know what terra nullius means, but what right has the king of England to authorize theft, on any grounds? These people have never heard of England, never mind its king. And while we're at it, he calls himself king of England, Scotland and Ireland. You may be happy to have him, but he stole my land from me, and there was no excuse that my people are savages without culture."

He actually grinned at me, with a spear in his shoulder, and my rage no doubt visible. "Well, well, many in England think you're savages with no culture." He actually chuckled at what he must have seen in my face. "But I disagree. I don't know how much history you know, but before the Vikings, Ireland was the center of learning in all of Europe. So I respect the Irish."

Knock me over with a feather. I couldn't help laughing out loud. He started to laugh with me, but the pain stopped him.

"Mr. Cameron, we have eight bodies that need burying. We need to do doctoring on you. Then, gentlemen, we have a wider situation to deal with. Mr. MacTavish, a truce for now?"

He nodded.

I tossed the gun to him. He fumbled the catch and dropped it.

"Mr. MacTavish, please bring some spirits, and clean cloth for a pressure bandage."

Wordlessly he left. I turned and let out a loud whistle. The men came running. They must have been hiding behind tents, watching the show.

Cameron said, "Charles, please organize the burying of those bodies. The dead sheep might as well be butchered."

Richard said to me, "Thanks for putting the bullet through my hat, not my head."

"Mate, I bear you no ill will. Why should I kill a friend?"

"Thanks anyway."

MacTavish came running, with a bottle and a white sheet. I got out my knife and quickly converted the sheet into long strips of cloth, getting him to hold them.

I cut the shirt off Cameron's shoulder and opened the bottle. Gin. I sloshed it around the exit wound and the protruding tip of the spear, relieved it had no barbs, then around the entry. Then I gave it to Cameron. He took a good swig and passed it back to me.

I exchanged the bottle with MacTavish for a strip of cloth, rolled it up and gave it to Cameron to bite on. Then, before he could think about it, I planted my foot on his chest and pulled the spear out.

MacTavish was ready with a bandage but I said, "Let it bleed a little, to wash out any muck." After a minute or so the two of us put pressure on it, holding it for maybe five minutes, then bound it up in the tightest bandage I could manage.

"I think all three of us could do with that gin," Cameron said, still sounding calmer than he had a right to be. "Then, O'Halloran, we have to decide what to do about you."

I did enjoy the first drink I'd had since leaving Dunadd, before explaining the situation to them. "Look you, I'm no longer interested in killing people. Oh, back in Ireland I killed plenty of Redcoats, and no doubt that included Scots. One was a Lieutenant Gordon, and that's Scots, hey? But, Mr. Cameron, at Dunadd I became friends with a wonderful man who is a true follower of Jesus. And that's why I'm not the same violent man I was as a youngster. But... but don't push me too hard. I still have the skills."

"I could see that."

"Anyway, think on this. Say I kill the both of you. You saw how much loyalty those men have for you, and why not? They're just scum like me. Ticket of leave men, poor peasants come out here to get away from the poverty at home. If I became boss, I'd pay them a fair wage, treat them decently. You think they'd run to Sydney Town to betray me?"

MacTavish stared at me with horror. I think until this moment, it hadn't occurred to him that a peasant, an ex-convict, could be his equal in any way. But Cameron again managed a grin. "Even more, O'Halloran. If you were in danger, you're one of the few men who could run and live off the land. I have no doubt that in a few months you'd have a black wife and be one of the natives."

"All the same," MacTavish interrupted. "You've acted with insolence and defiance. If we were anywhere near civilization, you'd swing for it."

"Lucky for you that's not so, or I'd kill you."

"Look Rory," Cameron said, "we need to be flexible. The situation has changed and we must change with it. Now, O'Halloran, since you're not immediately intending to kill us, what do you propose we do?"

"We need to make peace with the natives, and make restitution to them for the murders. Those men had loving wives and children, parents and brothers and sisters. But I was not able to talk with them. Our first need is for an interpreter."

MacTavish still looked daggers at me. "They shouldn't have killed a sheep."

"Sir, they obviously have no idea that animals can be domesticated. They're hunters, and they hunted. No doubt they expected to share a feast with us. They came in friendship, and made a mistake from ignorance."

Cameron said, "Actually, that's not what I wished to address. How do we deal with you?"

I thought for a space. "Sir, nothing has changed, unless you choose to have it changed. I can simply stay one of the hands, doing my jobs as directed. As long as you treat the natives decently, and me with dignity, I'll make no trouble."

"Sounds good in theory. All right, about an interpreter. Any ideas?"

"Only one, and it takes time. I ride back to Dunadd, and ask Jimmy's help."

"Jimmy?"

"The wonderful friend I mentioned. He is a native of the Sydney area. Imagine him as French. Then the people in the mountains are Germans, and our natives are Russians. It should be possible to find a mountain man who can speak with them, and understand Jimmy's language, which I can speak."

"I didn't see any natives in the mountains."

"I did, but they didn't allow me to contact them. Jimmy is our key."

I could see MacTavish think deeply before he said, "Actually, I've been planning to return to bring more supplies. If you promise to do no violence to me, I'll give my word to stay quiet about your... escapade today."

"Very well, Mr. MacTavish. I agree. But also, you promised me a full pardon. Maybe we can organize that on this trip."

Cameron put a hand on his wound. "Oh, please don't make me laugh. That's priceless."

I looked at him. "Is it an unreasonable request, Sir?"

"You're lucky I'm left handed. I'll write a letter of recommendation for you myself."

"I'd also like the pay I've earned to date, so I can buy a few things in Sydney Town."

13.

Self-defense

Without the encumbrance of wagons, our group of five made the return trip in a bit over a week. I had a wonderful reunion with Jimmy and his family. He told me the new owner, Mr. Holmbury, was a far more decent man than MacTavish. When I explained my need for an interpreter, he asked for a few days.

I showed him the two letters of recommendation for my full pardon. He read them out to me. Cameron's was full of praise for my reliability as an employee, my initiative and decency. MacTavish, knowing I couldn't read, had written: "Dermot O'Halloran is a self-confessed multiple murderer. He is insolent, defiant and the worst kind of Irish scum. I request that he be tried for crimes against me and my partner, and am available to testify against him."

So, I called in at the big house, and said at the door, "Mr. MacTavish, Jimmy is organizing the interpreter, and wants us here in a few days. Perhaps we can now do our business in Sydney Town."

"Gladly," he answered with something like a smirk. While he went inside, no doubt to say his good-byes, I spoke to the other three men. From memory, I recited the two letters to them.

Sammy, a bow-legged fellow from Cornwall, swore colorfully. "The bloody treacherous bastard!"

"I expected nothing less. If I deal with him, will the three of you stand by me?"

Pete, a Londoner where he'd driven coaches for the gentry till caught for theft, said, "I've never liked the cold Scottish bastard. Do what you like, and I won't notice nothin'."

The third with us was Richard, who just grinned at me.

We set off for the three-day journey. The first evening, we camped by a swiftly running creek. In the evening sunshine, I saw fat trout and said, "Sir, I could catch one of those, without a rod and line."

"How?"

"About now, and in the morning, they find a quiet spot and just hover there. You then approach them from behind, slowly put a hand under them and flip them out." While saying this, I strolled along the creekside, and without thought he came with me.

I moved fast: grabbed him by the jacket and twisted, so he landed in the water. I was on top of him before he even realized the attack, then had his right arm behind him and up, forcing his face under water. He struggled, but after awhile bubbles came around his head, and then I held him a little longer.

I hoisted him over my shoulder, climbed out and took him back to our camp. "Something terrible happened, mates," I said. Mr. MacTavish fell in the creek and drowned."

Richard said, "I can see you're all wet too from trying to save him."

"Well, a man's got to do his best by his employer."

All three cracked up laughing.

During the next two days, I briefed my mates on what we were to do, being very firm about drink. "Buy all the grog you like. On the way home, drink all you can hold. But please, not one drop while we're there. One incautious word, and all four of us will hang if we're lucky, lashed to death otherwise."

Back in civilization, we led MacTavish's horse, with his body draped over the saddle, to the Magistrates' Court, one of the buildings I'd worked on as a slave. Solemnly we told our story of the nasty accident that had cost him his life, and I made an appointment to face the Court with my appeal for a full pardon.

I found a gun shop in George Street, and bought a breech-loading rifle with ammunition for it. I also bought a bag of barley, and a few bits and pieces for constructing a copy of my father's still. I figured that making my own beat buying the stuff. Besides, whiskey is nicer than rum. Then I returned to our camp, waiting for the other three. They arrived laden with bottles, but I was relieved to see that all were sober.

I found MacTavish's list of things to buy, but none of us could read it. Richard said that before his ticket of leave, he'd worked for a fellow who hired a scribe to do the reading and writing for him, and no doubt such people were still around. So, I gave him the list and MacTavish's money, and the following day they went shopping. As for me, I presented myself at the Court, to wait around for most of the day. The magistrate eventually saw me. He duly read the letter from Cameron, then to my surprise asked questions about the bible. Thanks to Jimmy I could answer many of them, though not all. I explained that I'd never had the opportunity to learn my letters, so needed to learn through what others told me.

I got my pardon, and returned to our hideout, for a marvelous drunk with my mates. They'd bought all the stuff on the list, though also a few other things for their private use. I figured that was none of my business.

In the morning, we were variously hung over, so it was almost midday before we started our return trip to Dunadd. We got there without trouble, and I could show Jimmy my new certificate of freedom.

A young man waited at Jimmy's camp, patiently shaving at a curved piece of wood with a flint blade. Jimmy introduced me as his brother Dermot, which brought a tear to my eye. The other fellow had a long name I couldn't get my ear around, never mind my tongue. All the brown people laughed. "Call me Ged," he said, in Jimmy's language. He spoke no English.

Jimmy explained, "Ged is from the mountains, but has married into a family of my people. We had to do that when too many of us were killed by white men. He'll go with you. His intended wife is a girl there and he is happy to visit her. There you'll find someone who can speak the language of the people of the plains. None of us here can do that, because they're too far away."

"Can he ride a horse?"

"No, but he can run as fast as you'll ride. He'll prefer that."

Off we went in the morning. As soon as we were away from land tamed by the white man, Ged undressed, making his clothes into a bundle. At a certain spot he left the track for a moment, and reappeared carrying what at first seemed like a bundle of sticks. It was several spears, throwing sticks like the one he'd been making back at Jimmy's, and another piece of wood, which was a sort of a launcher for the spears. It was the length of his arm and had a spur that fitted into a little hole at the base of the spear. He could hurl a spear about sixty yards with incredible force and accuracy.

We had a two-language conference, and decided that the other three would take the packhorses and my mount and possessions along the track, while I'd walk with Ged and visit the locals. Ged was confident that we'd catch the others well before they reached the plains.

"Just one thing," I said to my mates. "Steal my stuff and I'll cut your pricks off and choke you with them."

Sammy looked offended. "I'd never steal off a friend."

"Glad to hear it, mate. All right, good journey. I'll have some exercise and see how I can keep up with this young fella."

That did prove to be a problem. My booted feet and clothed body were not up to Ged's bare ones, and even traveling light, I carried a lot more than he did. I could see that he was going slow, often waiting for me, but he had a courteous patience that said without words that this didn't matter. As we went up and down steep slopes and wound our way through narrow valleys, he gathered food for us, though initially I found it hard to accept. The first thing he offered me was a fat yellow grub he eased out from under the rough bark of a tree. He laughed at my expression, then ate it himself. He produced another and I forced myself to try. To my surprise, it tasted delicious.

It took us two days to suddenly arrive at a secluded little valley with a chattering creek, and a small, almost smokeless fire with a bunch of dark-brown people busy at various tasks. We were treated with suspicion till Ged spoke in words I couldn't understand, then there were smiles, and the offer of a hot tuber for each of us, raked out from the fire with a stick by a woman. We spent the night here. Ged explained that they were able to tell him where his bride's family was, and we'd go there next.

The locals were very interested in me, and asked many questions through Ged. They knew about white men, and were horrified by the stories they'd heard. Sadly, I had to confirm their horror. I hoped that their rugged mountains would stay free of invasion.

We moved on at dawn, arriving at a similar little valley that afternoon. Here, Ged was welcomed as a dear friend, and after his explanation, I was welcome too. To my surprise, his intended was a little girl, five or six years old, who was delighted by his presence. He treated her the way a loving father might. He explained that they'd marry in about ten years' time, when she became a young woman. Then, she'd choose her next husband-to-be. I didn't share my thought: she'd then be the same age as Maeve was when she'd given herself to me.

The next morning, the little girl's father came with us, and took us to yet a third family. Here I was introduced to another man with an unpronounce-able name, whom I could call Cory. He spoke the plains people's language, and we managed a reasonable conversation in Jimmy's. Cory was perhaps in his mid-thirties, a slim but muscled man with a calm gaze. I felt I could trust him.

I explained the reason: we needed to teach the plains people to act in ways that would keep them from conflict with the invaders. Otherwise, they'd all be killed.

I said good-bye to Ged, who returned to the previous family. Cory and I went on together, and indeed waited at the foot of the wheel tracks before my three mates and their packhorses arrived.

Cory had never seen a horse, and was amazed that they allowed people onto their backs. I easily taught him to ride MacTavish's mount.

When we arrived back, Cameron was running things, his right arm in a sling. His eyebrows rose when he saw a naked native riding his friend's horse. "Where is Mr. MacTavish?" he demanded.

"Sir, there was a terrible accident. I have a piece of paper about it from the magistrate in Sydney Town."

He read the paper, then called me into the office tent. "O'Halloran, did you kill him?"

"Sir, I would not kill anyone, except in self-defense." Then I handed over the letter of recommendation MacTavish had written for me.

We looked each other in the eye, for a long time. "How will I tell this to his wife and bairns?" he asked, more himself than me.

I took the paper back, and burned it that evening.

14. 1820-1830

The choice

When the cold winds of winter struck, they struck me hard. The scars from the cat-o'-nine-tails and the many whip-blows contracted, and my left leg and arm constantly ached from the ancient breaks. Each of those pains were reminders of the English, and I didn't even have rum to ease the agony. My future whiskey was still a small barley field.

Thanks to my work with Cory, the natives left our animals alone, and we paid them compensation in articles of luxury they could not have imagined: steel tools that made their lives much easier. Six young men were sufficiently interested in the novelty of our presence that they started working for Cameron, soon picking up enough English to get by. I spent time with them, learning their language.

Once the rains eased, a large contingent of us returned to the foothills and cut down three tall, straight trees. We dug a pit and ripped the logs into timber, which was as difficult in New South Wales as in Ireland. We then used the oxen to haul the timber "home," and started building. We knew that this gum tree wood could only be used green. If left to season, it warped, and became so hard you couldn't drive a nail into it.

We built a big house, quarters for the men, stables, and storehouses for produce, returning for more trees as needed. Within three years, Carlton Station, as Cameron named it, looked as well settled as Dunadd.

During all this time, I made sure to be just one of the men. I did as I was told, and while I was friendly to all, I preferred to keep to myself, and the others respected this. I caught the occasional measuring look from Cameron, but our truce held.

Once Richard said to me when the two of us were alone with a mob of sheep, "I heard that back when the blackies got killed, you threatened to off the nobs and take over."

"Mate, that's ancient history. And Cameron is a decent enough boss."

"Still..."

"Spit it out."

"If you'd done it, how'd you have organized things?"

I thought about this. "I reckon all of us put in the work, all should share in the profit. Bit like a family, y'know?"

Richard laughed. "We're crazy. As if His Majesty and his loyal gentry would let us get away with such a thing." We dropped the matter.

Using timber left over from the main house, I built a hut a bit out of the way, and set up my still. In the winter of the fourth year, I had my first produce of whiskey, which I kept to myself, and kept quiet about. It did help to dull the pain my scars gave me in the cold.

Then visitors arrived: an older man, a lovely young woman with flowing dark hair, and an entourage of servants. This was Cameron's father's best friend back in Scotland, and the girl his daughter. Before Cameron had left Sydney Town, they'd sent letters to each other, and now she came to marry him.

Cameron left Charles in charge and went to Sydney Town with them. He returned a month later a married man.

I couldn't help it. Envy ate my heart. Just because he was born in Scotland he could be the squatter, in the big house, with the servants, and above all with the beautiful wife. Just because I was born in Ireland, I was the freed convict, the hired hand, working for a pittance, living in the scarred, painful body, and the wife I hadn't even had the chance to marry just a painful memory. I admired the man but hated him, and would have done anything to change places with him.

Perhaps because of that, my dreams got more frequent, and worse. Often I shouted in my sleep, and once I found myself on the floor, having fallen out of bed. Understandably, the other men complained, so I moved into my shed with the still, where I could suffer my nightmares without imposing suffering on anyone else.

Even when I slept, I woke tired, so got into the habit of using a bit of whiskey to help with the sleep. And over the years, I needed more. There came the day when I couldn't function unless I had a sip first thing in the morning.

I still enjoyed my work. I came to love this land with its wide horizons. The plains were sometimes green, sometimes red when a drought struck, and on some of our more distant drives I admired purple jagged hills on the horizon. I could still bring down a kangaroo or an emu with a shot from three hundred yards, and although I was one of the older men, I still held my own with the young fellows.

All the same, while I loved the work, I hated life. I looked at Cameron in the big house, with the lovely wife, and the lovely children that came along, and the servants, and the automatic respect of every man. I thought of my child, who'd by now have given me grandchildren, and Maeve, the constant occupant of my heart, and the green hills of Ireland I'd never see again, and I hated. The hate ate me up, and nothing eased it but the whiskey. Round and round this lament went, in endless repetition, and Mrs. Faith Cameron was the focus of it all. She was alive, and a mother, while Maeve was all so long dead.

Many an evening I stood outside my door, metal mug of whiskey in my hand, and watched the big house. It could have been mine, had I not spared Cameron. There he was, getting ready for bed with her. In all my life, I'd enjoyed a woman once. He had the pleasure available on demand, night after night. And after an evening like this, I sometimes woke from vivid dreams of my mouth on Mrs. Cameron's mouth, her breasts against my chest, and deeply within her. I then had to angrily jerk myself off so I could return to sleep—and hated myself for it.

One day just at sunset, I stood outside my little shed. Rough slab walls, bark roof, compacted earth floor—home, such as it was. There in the distance stood the mansion of his lordship. Inside was his woman. *Why him and not me?*

I needed to strike out. But first, I needed a good slug of whiskey.

I walked over, for the first time in my life staggering a little.

I knew the layout of the house, having been involved in building it.

No one used the front door much; it was there for formal occasions. I barged in, leaving my boots on. Child sounds came from a room to one side, and a woman speaking to them. I went past along the dark corridor, toward the main bedroom. I opened the door.

She wore a long nightdress, brushing her hair, facing a large mirror. There she stood—the symbol of all my suffering.

In a bound I was at her, picked her up and threw her face down on her bed. Then I had my trousers down, and I was within her, pumping away.

She was screaming, but I cared not.

A roar came from behind. As I shot my seed, my head exploded.

Somehow, I was up high, looking down. Cameron stood there, panting, the smoking pistol in his hand. The poor woman lay on the bed, face up now, sobbing, looking at him. At her feet, that heap of rubbish was what I'd become.

Terrible remorse, shame, regret twisted my being. "Oh no! I am sorry!" I kept shouting, but no one heard.

A memory came to me: Jimmy saying, very seriously: "You'll be given a choice one day, and how you choose will determine the eternal life of your spirit."

Too late. I had chosen wrong.

"Come," a Voice that was not a voice said. I traveled through darkness over a forever journey that took an instant, and then I faced... Somebody. I could not describe Her, but felt small, dirty and unworthy.

"I'm sorry," I said. If I still had eyes, if I still had tears, I'd have been sobbing from shame.

"I know."

"I've become the enemy. I'm as bad as them."

"I know."

"I acted from hate, in order to hurt."

"What do you propose to do about it?"

I thought, then, "I should become her, the squatter's wife who suffers rape. And... I should have the power, the ability, to ease hurt, to lead people from despair and helplessness to strength and love."

"You can do both of those, in different lives. Go now and pay your restitution."

"And oh, loving hurts so much."

"If you need to, you can one day experience what it is like to be unable to feel that love."

Book 2: Amelia

1. 1830-1848

Waiting to flower

I have a distinct memory of being a baby, suckling at the breast. It had to have been Nanny's breast of course, not Mother's. If I close my eyes, I can feel the nipple in my mouth, the soft yielding of the breast, the comfort of being held, secure and warm.

Then I felt wetness between my legs, and somehow, even to a baby, it was surprising that it came from the center, not the front.

My next memory is when I was perhaps three. Mother held me on her lap, and Nigel came in. I struggled off and ran to him. His face lit up as he kneeled to cuddle me. "Here I am, home from school for a while, and you now have to entertain me," he said.

"What's enter... what you said?"

Father, Mother, Nanny and Nigel all laughed. My big brother said, "Make me have fun."

"I can play the piano for you!"

We hadn't had the piano yet when he'd left for school, and now it stood in the corner, having come on a ship all the way from Home, and Mr. Perkins coming twice a week to teach me and Mother. Nigel lifted me onto the seat, but I said, "I need that pillow under me." When he made the correction, I proudly played my exercises for him, and everyone clapped.

This was a rare occasion, all of us together. I spent more time with Nanny than with anyone else. I knew she was forcibly taken from Ireland although she'd done no wrong, and then the man whose house she was made to work in did something nasty to her and so she got a baby, and then the baby died just as I was born and Mother was too busy helping father to run the hotel, and so Nanny became my special friend. Mother and Father worked long hours to make our hotel the best in the land. When they were home, they were wonderful, but sometimes I woke in the morning and they were gone, and went to bed at night and they were still working.

Nanny was special. She often said that when she first saw me as a baby, she'd felt as if she'd known me for a long time already, as if she had loved me before, but how could that be? And I knew ever since I could think that I'd always loved her, and always would.

Often she hummed wonderful swirling Irish tunes. My favorite, which I worked out for myself on the piano, had an odd pattern: the melody going up and down for six beats of two-two, then three rapid beats, over and over.

Mr. Perkins also used to be a convict. He was a musician and man of letters, and had hoped to do great things with his life. Then he fell in love with a young lady, and she with him, but her father caught them being too close to each other—and I could never get him to explain what that meant—and next thing he was convicted of theft and sent off to New South Wales. I felt very sorry for him, but all the same I was glad he was here, because he taught me such wonderful things.

I had friends too: other young ladies whose family father approved of: Rosie, Ethel and Mary. We went on picnics together and visited each other's houses. Mother arranged that Mr. Perkins could teach them too, and we all went regularly to Ethel's house, where Mrs. Martin taught us sewing and embroidery. When we got older, Rosie's mother arranged dancing classes for us, so we could grow to be accomplished young ladies.

Father loved me. Whenever we were together I saw his cares fall away, and a smile light up his round face. I may have been twelve when I saw him slumped in an armchair. I plunked myself down on his lap and drew his arms around me. He kissed the top of my head and murmured, "Thank you my poppet. That's exactly what I need right now."

Then Mother came in. She smiled at us, but needed to have a business discussion with Father. I knew that Mother was the brains and drive behind the hotel, but of course the world expected the man to lead.

Playing the piano was my favorite activity. I remember the first time Mr. Perkins got me the music for a Chopin nocturne. The wonderful liquid chords stole my heart, and all I wanted was to go to Poland on the other side of the world and meet wonderful Frederic who could write such beauty.

The Governor held an annual ball, and when I was eighteen mother escorted me to my coming out. I danced with the young men, though they seemed like a different species. My interests had been shaped by Mr. Perkins into philosophy, history, geography, the study of ideas and the advances of science. These boys only talked about sports and hunting—why would people enjoy killing?—and how much money their father made.

Back home, Father reassured me. "Amelia, my dove, don't worry. You're destined for better things than those snotty-nosed larrikins. We'll find you a good match."

After this, we had regular dinner visitors in the private room of the hotel. Mother, Father and I were there of course, and sometimes Nigel with the young lady of the moment and her parents, and some single gentleman. Frankly, I found them as boring as the boys at the ball. Some were widowers seeking a replacement mother for a brood of children. Some were ambitious wealthy men from over the seas coming to Sydney to make their fortune. There was an Italian nobleman, escaping the storms of revolution in his country, whose passion was to establish a vineyard. Even though father owned a hotel, I've never enjoyed alcohol in any of its forms, so I certainly wasn't interested in someone who made it. There was a lawyer whose entire conversation was about his ambition to become a judge. None of them interested me in the slightest.

Then, one day, the dinner guest was Mr. Charles McQuade. He was older than the other contenders, nearly forty, a quiet man refreshingly free of chatter. A funny thing about him was that his face was like mahogany from being out in the sun all day, but the top of his forehead was pink from always having a hat on. He had strong dark hair that contrasted with my blonde mane, and deep brown eyes that smiled when he looked at me.

I am tall, taller than Father even, but I barely came up to his shoulder.

He was a squatter, with a large holding in the outback. That sounded romantic. Father said, "If you marry a squatter, you'll be queen of your domain."

He was told he was welcome to visit again. Next time, we received him at home, and I played Chopin for him. When I finished and stood, he gravely kissed the back of my hand.

Then he had to return to his holding, for, as he said, he was a busy man. "Miss Poole," he said as he got ready to go, "Do check the mail, for there will be a surprise."

The surprise arrived two days later: a golden necklace, with a strangely shaped pendant. Father examined it through a magnifying glass, then muttering to himself looked up a reference book. "By God, it's the McQuade family crest!" he said. "If you like this fellow, you can marry into nobility."

I didn't actually like him, but felt a strange compulsion to think about him. I saw his face when I closed my eyes, felt the strength in his hand when he'd held mine.

I wore his pendant all the time, actually uncomfortable if it wasn't nestled within my bosom.

He returned a month later. After the conventional greetings, he said, "Bruchan Station has been very lonely since I've met you, Miss Poole. So, I've made a little purchase." He took a small velvet-lined box from his pocket and flipped it open.

I heard mother gasp just behind me. Within the box was a gold ring with a huge diamond, surrounded by smaller ones like sparkles coming out of the sun. He eased the ring onto the third finger of my right hand. "Please say you'll marry me," he said, his voice deep and quiet.

He hired a fine carriage with two matched horses, and took mother and me to places of interest. To my secret amusement, this included the vineyard of the Italian nobleman. A memory that stays with me is sitting up front on the driver's seat. I wore a light-colored dress with big yellow flowers printed on the material. Mr. McQuade towered over me even sitting, with his body steel-hard as he steadied me against the jolts of the carriage over the cobblestones.

At last it was time for the wedding. At his insistence, this was at his home. It took us weeks of travel, camping out. Father was in a cheerful mood, saying this was his first holiday in twenty-five years, but at the same time wondering aloud how Mr. Carter was coping with the hotel, and at other times hoping Mr. Carter wasn't stealing him blind.

The only one complaining was Nanny, who was of course to stay as my companion. She said she liked a comfortable bed to sleep in, and a kitchen to cook in rather than an open fire, and how could a body keep clean by washing in a creek with maybe some men gawking in secret?

The last two weeks or more we traveled across wide open plains. I didn't realize there was this much space in the world. From morning to evening we moved forward with only short rests, yet we still seemed to be in the same place. At last, we came to a sign by the road—more a wheel track left by carts—with "Bruchan Station" in fancy letters upon it. Mr. McQuade had us camp there, saying the homestead was another day's travel!

The land was fresh and green, this being the start of winter after the autumn rains, and there were flowers everywhere, and birds. All he same, as we arrived at the homestead, I noticed that every building had a large water tank. I knew from my studies that things could get dry here. A line of trees I knew to be redgums, though I'd never seen them before, indicated a watercourse.

It was a large and graceful building, with a leadlight front door and a high ceiling with plaster roses and cornices, like the pictures of European mansions I'd seen in books.

It took us three days to settle in. During that time, three other families arrived: Mr. McQuade's brother and sisters with their spouses and children.

In the turmoil of preparations, I barely had a chance to more than be introduced to them. I did note however that while the other three seemed close, all treated my bridegroom with reserve.

Mr. McQuade had found Mr. Parker, a Church of England minister, to officiate, which pleased father, who'd been worried at first that a man with his name might have been a Papist.

So, on the Saturday Nanny and Mother helped me to dress in white lace that displayed my figure to best advantage, making my bosom seem larger. They braided my hair, and even applied rouge to my face, for the second time in my life.

In a simple but impressive ceremony, Amelia Margaret Poole became Mrs. McQuade.

2. 1848: The squatter's wife

Nanny said, quietly, "The wedding night can be a little painful, my lamb. But whatever he does, make it easy on him."

I had not the slightest idea what she meant, and didn't even know what to ask. She assisted me into my beautiful new silk nightgown, then left.

Not knowing what to do, I sat on the edge of the four-poster bed with its colorful quilt cover. A side door opened, and Mr. McQuade came in. Only... he was stark naked, and growing out of his crotch was this bizarre sticklike thing poking forward. It wobbled as he walked and I didn't know whether to laugh or be scared.

"My love," he said, "I've been waiting for this moment since we've met."

He pulled me upright with irresistibly strong arms, his mouth swallowed mine so I couldn't breathe, and a hand fumbled at my breast in a most uncomfortable way. He let me go for a moment and tore the expensive nightgown. He bent and swallowed my right breast, then picked me up, threw me upon my back and dived forward.

There is a great weight pressing the breath out of me, and all I can see is the hairs on his chest tickling my face, and that strange growth between his legs is banging at me, striking the inside of my thighs, a different place each time but hard enough to bruise, and then... agony. I'm being ripped apart. I know I'm bleeding. I'd scream, but can't because I don't have breath enough.

That thing is inside me, rubbing in and out, and the pain is horrific, a burning ripping sensation. Then there is something moist, which helps a little.

The huge man on top of me relaxed, forcing even more air out of me. At last he rolled off. "Amelia," he said, "thank you. I love you so much."

If this is love, give me hate any day.

Three times more that night he assaulted me with that horrible thing. After the second occasion, I fantasized finding the kitchen, coming back with a carving knife and cutting it off while he slept. But I doubted I could walk, with the join of my legs so macerated. Even in the dim light I saw my blood covering the sheet.

The strange thing was, he did this terrible act accompanied by words of caring, as if he was doing something nice for me.

After the fourth occasion, I knew I needed help. I struggled out of bed, but lacked the strength to stand. I sank to the ground, then crawled to the door on all fours. I pulled myself up using the doorknob, then went out into the corridor. I knew that Nanny's room was to the right. I barely managed to support myself upright with one hand on the wall as I hobbled along, hoping I was not still bleeding all along the carpet.

The next two rooms were empty, but I heard quiet breathing as I opened the third door. "Nanny?" I said, softly in case it was someone else.

"Hmm? Oh, Miss Amelia. Oh my lamb, something's wrong."

I heard bedclothes stir, then strong but gentle hands led me to the bed, where I could sit.

"Wait, Miss Amelia. The kitchen fire is banked up. I'll light a lamp and come back." Then she was gone.

When she returned, she inspected my private parts in the light of the lamp. I heard the hiss of her indrawn breath. "Oh, the idjit!" she muttered. Then, "Wait, I saw something in the kitchen may help." She tucked me into her bed and went off with the light.

I was asleep, must have fallen off immediately. The light woke me, and then Nanny exposed me again and gently dabbed something soothing onto the painful parts, even working it into the so-damaged hole that horrible thing had made in me.

As she just about finished her ministrations, the door behind her opened, and Mr. McQuade marched in, carrying another lantern. He was bare-chested, but wore a pair of trousers. "You, hinny," he said loudly, "What are you doing to my wife?"

Nanny whirled. "Sir, you should be ashamed of yourself! You've grievously hurt her! She may never be able to bear a child from the damage!"

He looked at her long and quiet, and in the bed, I became afraid for her. At last, he grated, "You dare too much, you Irish scum. You're not welcome here. When Mr. Poole returns, you shall go with him."

"No," I shouted. "Nanny is part of me, I cannot live without her!"

Even in the dim flickering light, the sneer on his face was utterly intimidating. "You're now my wife, for better or worse, in sickness or in health, as long as both of us shall live. You're my possession, and shall do as you're told."

In the morning, Mr. Parker conducted a Sunday service for everyone, including the Aboriginal people. I noted that two white station hands had wives and children, who all stared at me with big eyes, but when I smiled their way they looked down, abashed. Sadly, after the service, father backed Mr. McQuade up. "A husband's word is law, my dove," he said, though I could see the pain on his face. "If he doesn't want your Nanny here, then she needs to return with us."

In my ignorance of how to talk about the unspeakable events of the night, I couldn't explain the reason why I also wanted to return to the safety of our home. My parents could no doubt see my difficulty in walking, but I didn't know if they guessed the cause. If they did, perhaps this also was beyond their ability to interfere.

So, that day I saw everyone I loved disappear from my life. I was left alone, at the mercy of a man I now knew to be a monster.

That evening, after a most uncomfortable, quiet dinner with my self-declared owner, I prepared for sleep with the utmost trepidation. At least, the blood-soaked sheet had been replaced, no doubt by the two Aboriginal women who seemed to be the sole serving staff. I had with me the jar of soft fatty substance Nanny had anointed me with, and took the precaution of again liberally smearing it within my crotch, and just as well. Mr. McQuade came to bed stark naked once more, and again that horrible growth upon him stuck out ready to do more damage. Again, he covered me so I couldn't breathe, and he shoved that thing at the join of my legs. Blessedly, the unguent helped, and he entered me at the first callous thrust. He grunted and pumped, and within a few minutes again I felt some liquid inside me, and he rolled off.

Well, if that was all it took to protect myself from further damage, then I could live with it.

Yet at breakfast, he treated me with consideration and apparent liking, as if we were old friends. He said, "Amelia my lovely dear, I'll be busy all day at the workings of the Station, but am looking forward to seeing you again at dinnertime."

I looked down, so he should not see my thought, that I hoped his horse might throw him, and get him to break his neck.

After his departure, I found the kitchen in order to meet the two brown women. The younger introduced herself as Clara, the other as Sollie. Clara was a mere girl, even younger than I. Sollie was about thirty.

Clara said, "Missy Mac, I see you walk painful. We both know why."

I felt my face flush as they giggled. "What do you mean?"

Sollie answered, "Mr. Mac do ficky-ficky to all blackfella women. Maybe now you here he stop."

Clara said, "My husband's father say old Mr. Mac not stop when he married."

"Ficky-ficky. Is that what it's called?"

Clara answered, "That white man name for it. Something like that anyway."

Sollie looked angry. "You been learn nothing. That is terrible. You white people teach children bad way. Among blackfella people, little one learns how to be husband or wife good way, so everybody happy and have fun. But white girl never even told name of how men and women make a baby. Know nothing."

My surprise must have shown on my face. "Is that how babies are made? But then why is it so painful?"

"Not always painful. With my husbands is beautiful."

"You have more than one husband?"

"Sure. Old husband was wonderful big boy come often, and when I marry him, it so much joy! And then I find baby for young husband, and I am wonderful big girl to him, and now him father of my son. And when ficky-ficky with him or old husband, feel very good. But you see, Missy Mac, white boy not learn how to be good with woman. He not learn as little boy how to please woman. That's why I say white way bad."

"And Mr. McQuade has been doing this to you women?"

Both pulled a face. Clara answered, "We no like. Even if it was good, we no like. For blackfella people, only husband and wife do ficky-ficky, not like white people."

"Why do your men allow it?"

Sollie said, sadly, "My father's father old man. He tell me. When white men come here, the blackfella men try stop this. Terrible things happen. Some white men kill children, do things to give much pain. And they have guns, things we cannot fight. So, blackfella people go away, leave white men alone. But white men hunt blackfellas like animals, and now so much land is for sheep and cattle that hard to live. And if we go somewhere we not suppose to, they can kill us."

I thought I was going to faint, so sat down on a chair by the kitchen table. Tears blurred my vision and it was hard to breathe. Finally I managed, "I am sorry. I'm so sorry."

Clara's warm voice sounded next to my ear. "Missy Mac, I want cuddle you. Only, not allowed."

I turned and then we held each other, and the loving contact was heaven. We both cried, and Sollie too, holding both of us.

"Of course it's allowed. I allow it."

"Must not let anyone see. Blackfella servant woman must not touch lady."

"Well, it feels wonderful to me. I'm so glad to have you for my friends. I have no other now."

Sollie said, "We have a little jar of emu oil we always used when we think Mr. Mac maybe want fun. Now where is it?" She scratched around without success.

"Oh, I think I have it now." I explained about Nanny finding it.

"Goody. We make sure we get you more. When you make ficky-ficky with good man, it easy. You become slippery. But stupid white man just jump at you. So, emu oil help. Also, it very good for healing."

I was about to answer when I noticed that both of them seemed a little edgy. "What's wrong?" I asked.

"We must do work. When Mr. Mac come in, sometimes he check if everything free from dust, and clean, and just right. If not, look out!"

"Well, I'll help."

"Oh no! You lady!"

"And how will I spend my time? Come on, show me what needs to be done."

The week passed. During the day, I was the third maid with my two brown-skinned friends. We did cleaning and cooking. I couldn't join in with the washing because that was done outside, and someone might have taken notice. I'd never used an iron, so had them teach me how to heat one just to the right temperature on the cooktop of the iron stove, how to sprinkle water and smooth ahead of the iron, and to keep exchanging irons. I was much slower than them at first, but knew I'd learn.

My parents had brought considerable quantities of materials of various kinds, so I set up an empty room to sew in. Since the work was done faster, my two friends had time on their hands and I enjoyed teaching them. Both were very quick to learn. We started making beautiful lace curtains for all the windows, and new, graceful uniforms for the two real maids.

Naturally, we chatted during these times. They were amazed at the things I told them about the world, something that continued for years. In turn, I became fascinated by the details of their culture, which proved to be very complex and sophisticated, the opposite of savage. Sadly, the savagery had been by the British, in their treatment of the natives.

During our sewing session on the Friday, Clara started to hum a tune, probably without even realizing it. The hairs rose at the back of my neck and on my arms: this was my favorite Irish tune learned from Nanny: swirling, rising and falling, with three pairs of two-two beats followed by a rapid triple.

"Clara," I interrupted. "That tune you're singing. What is it?"

She stopped. "Oh sorry. You no like?"

"Oh no, I love it. But where did you hear that?"

She looked confused. "I never hear it. But... was not going to tell you. Missy Mac, since you come, I have a dream. Come back every night. Had it last night again. Music from there."

Fascinating. "Tell me. What can you remember from the dream?"

"Very strange." She stopped for a while, looking down. "Always same. I am in place with little houses. Roof very tall, like dry grass or something. White walls, not stone but like stone. And grass around very green. Beautiful. Not like grass here. And people. All white people. Why I dream of white people?"

"Do go on."

"There are young men and girls. Line of boys, line of girls, and they jumping around all together, look good, look fun. Old white man next to me, has something shiny to his mouth, and the music comes from there." She whistled the rollicking tune for a short while. "And me, I have something in hand. Like frying pan shape but no handle, and skin on top. I hit skin with a little stick and make very nice bang-bang sound. That part of music too. And I look down and my hands, white!"

Her look of amazement would have made me laugh if I hadn't been so fascinated.

"Also, Missy Mac, they big hands, long fingers, and hair on back of hand." She extended her little, brown, chubby-fingered hands.

"And I look at the young people. I look with love at a boy and girl. He has dark brown hair, not black but nearly, and it has waves like some of the white men here. And his eyes brown. The other people there, in dream, blue eyes like you. Girl opposite this boy very lovely. Hair like sunshine, darker than your hair, and not straight like yours but little ring-things as it fall behind her. Very long. And face like this..." She outlined a square shape by holding her two hands in front of her.

"And in this dream, you're a white man who plays the drum, and looks on this boy and girl with love."

"Yes, I no understand."

Sollie said something rapidly in their language. In response, Clara made an odd head movement, a slight raising of her chin combined with a tiny turn of the head to the left.

"Oh sorry, Missy Mac," Sollie said. "I say to her, talk to wise old people about dream. They then talk to spirits of old-old people, who tell us what this mean."

Being with Clara and Sollie was the pleasant activity of the daytime. Mornings and evenings were something else. He was there then. Most of these times were spent in silence, since I was not at all interested in the details of his life out there, and he certainly wasn't interested in mine. We shared breakfast, he went, and I breathed a sigh of relief. In the evening, we ate dinner together, then I spent the time till bed in apprehension, wishing to be anywhere else.

The nights were torture. He had an inexhaustible need to do this ficky-ficky, and I would have died except for the emu oil.

3. Sunday service

Sunday morning was a surprise. As he rose from breakfast, Mr. McQuade said, "Church service." He picked up a leather-bound bible, and took hold of my elbow to escort me out the front door.

The whole population of the Station was gathered in the space before the house, as during the service the week before. That however had been conducted by a man of God. I made sure nothing showed on my face, but I felt disgusted that someone who forcibly did this ficky-ficky with the Aboriginal women would have the temerity to take on a priestly role.

When he had everyone's attention, Mr. McQuade said in his strong voice, "Today is Sunday, the day of the Lord. It's the day for giving thanks for the good things in our lives. For myself, I'm delighted to give thanks for my lovely young wife, who has consented to share her life with me. Thank you God."

I managed to keep my face expressionless, although the healing wound between my legs was itching, and this reminded me, if anything had to, how false his statement was.

He continued, "We've been reading through the bible, and have come to King David. Here is the next part." He opened the bible at a marked spot and started reading.

> And it came to pass, at the time when kings go forth to battle, that David sent Jo'ab, and his servants with him, and all Israel; and they destroyed the children of Ammon, and besieged Rabbah. But David tarried still at Jerusalem. And during an eveningtide, David arose from his bed, and walked upon the roof of the king's house, and from the roof he saw a woman washing herself; and the woman was very beautiful to look upon.
>
> And David sent and inquired after the woman. And one said, "Is not this Bath–she'ba, the daughter of Eli'am, the wife of Uri'ah the Hittite?"
>
> And David sent messengers and she came to him, and he lay with her; and she returned unto her house. And the woman conceived, and told David, "I am with child." And David sent to Jo'ab, saying, "Send me Uri'ah the Hittite." And Jo'ab sent Uri'ah to David. And when Uri'ah was come unto him, David demanded of him how Jo'ab did, and how the people did, and how the war prospered.
>
> And David said to Uri'ah, "Tarry here today, and tomorrow I will let thee depart." So Uri'ah abode in Jerusalem that day, and the morrow.

And it came to pass in the morning that David wrote a letter to Jo'ab, and sent it by the hand of Uri'ah. And he wrote in the letter, "Set ye Uri'ah in the forefront of the hottest battle, and retire ye from him, that he may be smitten and die."

And when Jo'ab observed the city, he assigned Uri'ah unto a place where he knew that valiant men were. And the men of the city went out, and fought with Jo'ab, and there fell some of the servants of David; and Uri'ah the Hittite died also.

Then Jo'ab sent and told David all the things concerning the war; and charged the messenger, "When thou hast made an end of telling the matters of the war unto the king, and if so be that the king's wrath arise, and he says unto thee, 'Wherefore approached ye so nigh unto the city when ye did fight? Knew ye not that they would shoot from the wall? Why went ye nigh the wall?' then say thou, 'Thy servant Uri'ah the Hittite is dead also.'"

So the messenger went, and showed David all that Jo'ab had sent him for. And the messenger said unto David, "Surely the men prevailed against us, and came out unto us into the field, and we were upon them even unto the entering of the gate. And the shooters shot from the wall upon thy servants; and some of the king's servants be dead, and thy servant Uri'ah the Hittite is dead also."

Then David said unto the messenger, Thus shalt thou say unto Jo'ab, "Let not this displease thee, for the sword devoureth one as well as another. Make thy battle more strong against the city, and overthrow it, and encourage thou him."

And when the wife of Uri'ah heard that Uri'ah her husband was dead, she mourned for her husband. And when the mourning was past, David sent and fetched her to his house, and she became his wife, and bore him a son.

Mr. McQuade looked up and shut the book. "That's all. Men, we have animals to look after."

I doubt that anyone else knew the bible, but I did. I knew he'd left out some parts, the most important being the last sentence: "But the thing that David had done displeased the Lord."

A bond

Monday morning we were in the kitchen, cleaning up after breakfast, when Clara said very seriously, "Old man Gurry talk to me. Spirits give him answer. Him very special, like father's brother to everybody."

"Uncle?"

"All right, Uncle Gurry. Spirits say strange thing. I born to be with you. Spirits know you coming here. So, I born here, when you come as baby there." She waved east. "Then I wait for you. Before I born, I was this white man. You my child. Maybe the boy. Maybe the girl. Uncle Gurry not know that part."

Then we were hugging each other, both crying—crying with joy, with sadness for whatever tragedy must have separated that father and child. I had absolutely no doubt that this was right. It just felt right. Clara, a little rounded Aboriginal girl, was my father from some previous life, never mind what the bible said.

So, Clara and I spent our days in a constant loving bond. Sollie was also a friend, but she respected our special closeness, obviously delighted for both of us.

When my monthly time came, I found the courage to mention it to him. To my relief, he replied, "Very well, my dear." But the following morning, Sollie told me he'd been to the natives' camp and had done his thing with a young woman, against her will.

I could not believe that a supposedly civilized, Christian man could be such a horrid beast. I expect he imagined himself to be David, above the laws of decency governing others. I wondered if all men were like that. But surely, Father didn't have a disgusting protrusion between his legs? Perhaps he did, for didn't Sollie say that's how babies are made? So, Nigel and I were both the result of Father and Mother doing this? Unbelievable. And then it also occurred to me: when Mr. McQuade did this with the native women, did he cause them to have half-white babies?

Next time I was with the girls I asked them.

Sollie started to cry. Sniffing, she said, "I have three children. Two proper color skin. Other one white."

Clara added, "I had baby in tummy from husband. And Mr. Mac ficky-ficky me anyway, and baby come early. Husband wanted to kill Mr. Mac but old people stop him."

I looked at them, pain wringing my heart. "Maybe I should kill him." But I knew I could never bring myself to an act of violence, and obviously my two friends could see this too. Once more, in the security of our sewing room, we held each other.

Sollie explained, "Long ago we ask advice from the spirits, and they tell us white baby our baby anyway. We love them like brown baby."

So, for a week he tortured the Aboriginal women, and through them, the men. Then he was back at me.

One day I plucked up my courage. After dinner when he looked at peace, and gazed at me with something I'd have taken for fondness if I didn't know better, I asked, "Mr. McQuade, remember the first time you visited me at home?"

"Of course."

"I played the piano for you. It'd be wonderful if we had a piano here, and I could do the same."

"I'm not interested in such fripperies. Your task is to grace my home with your beauty, to give me a warm welcome when I come home tired, and to bear my children. Speaking of that, let us prepare for bed."

I hated the look of anticipation on his face.

Gardening

Gardening is a suitable occupation for a lady. The beautiful gardens around the house were maintained by a few men, so I thought it best to ask his permission before venturing into their territory. Again I was careful to choose my time.

"The garden? Certainly. My mother used to busy herself there. I'll give Jones instructions."

Jones was a wizened little man who fell over his tongue in embarrassment at having contact with The Lady. His two helpers, Taylor and Churchley, were younger, but still treated me as if an accidental touch might be a capital offence. Given what I'd learned so far about Mr. McQuade, perhaps it was. So, I spent time in watering and pruning, germinating seeds and planting them out. At first I knew nothing about such things, but enjoyed learning from Jones, who had a magic with plants.

Naturally, there was a large vegetable garden that fed everyone. After awhile, I got my three men to establish a smaller household one for my use, which we filled with herbs as well as the more practical plants.

I still missed Nanny, and Mother and Father and Nigel and Mr. Perkins and my friends, and things like the piano—oh how I missed the piano!—but life went on, with reasonable contentment except for the nightly torture by my husband.

Then I got a holiday. One evening he said, "Amelia my dear, I'll have to deprive you of my company for a couple of months. It's time for the annual roundup, and I'll be camping a long way from home."

I felt like cheering. Instead, I looked him in the eye and asked, "How can I be of assistance in preparing for it?"

"Oh, I have it down to a fine art. You can just give me an extra-good session of your wifely duties tonight."

Wifely duties. That was his name for ficky-ficky. I thought the black girls' term was more fitting. I made sure I had plenty of emu oil handy.

In the morning, I dutifully waved him off. He took most of the men, including Taylor and Churchley, but Jones was one of the few left behind. He said, "Ma'am, I'm most grateful for your interest in the garden. In the past, I was forced to use only the work of the Abo women, and they're a lazy bunch."

"Do they get paid for their work?"

"I dunno. Mr. McQuade handles all that. But I need to ensure all the vegetables are watered, or they get burnt by the sun, and then Mr. McQuade will whip the flesh off me bones."

I had the feeling that he meant this literally, but was too afraid of confirmation to ask. So, during the monster's absence, I allowed Jones to concentrate on the vegetables with his brown helpers, and the two girls and I tended the garden around the house.

My monthly time should have come around, but didn't. This got me worried, for such a thing had not happened since my fifteenth year. If Nanny had been here, I'd have asked her, but she was an awful distance away, in Sydney. Oh, if I could have been there too, instead of in this prison! So, I asked Sollie while we were embroidering, another skill the two girls picked up with rapidity. I was working on a tablecloth, and had them make matching placemats.

"Mrs. Mac, you having baby," she said, excited.

"Oh, how do you know?"

"That what happen when woman's blood no come... You not know that? White man learning crazy."

"Please, Sollie, teach me. Tell me all about what will happen now. Where is the baby?"

She gave me instruction for over an hour, and I found it unbelievable. How could a little child find its way into my abdomen? And grow there? And how could it then come out through a hole that was still too small for Mr. McQuade's horrible appendage?

She told me that many women get sick and vomit when growing a baby inside, but fortunately I was spared this. Indeed, I felt better than I had since arriving at Bruchan. Of course, the absence of the monster, and uninterrupted sleep, had something to do with it too.

I decided to get acquainted with the other white women, and went to call on them. At each house, the reception was identical: the woman seemed unable to talk with me. She looked anywhere but at my face, mumbled, seemed ready to sink through the hard-packed dirt floor from embarrassment. The children of various ages of course imitated their mother's attitude. Sadly, this was not a possibility for friendly human contact.

A dusty man arrived about noon one day. Clara talked with him then came to tell me: "Mr. Mac here tomorrow."

My insides twisted in apprehension. The two girls and I ran around the house, ensuring that everything was perfect. We planned the welcoming dinner and prepared the materials. Clara gave me a jar newly filled with emu oil.

"Surely, he cannot do that thing if I have a baby inside?" I asked. "You said your baby…"

Oh, Missy Mac, he can. Is safe for long time, until you big. I am sorry, he will."

He did.

About midmorning of the next day, a dust cloud to the west signaled his coming. It was a huge mob of wild cattle, with whip-wielding horsemen and yapping dogs around them. I watched though a window, noticing that the Aboriginal herders seemed the most skilled. The herd was squashed into a large area with timber fencing around it: posts in the ground joined with horizontal lengths of wood. When the gate was shut after the last beast, Mr. McQuade rode over to the house, sprung to the ground and marched in. He entered the lounge room, and I could smell him from thirty feet away.

That didn't stop him. "My Amelia," he shouted. "I've so missed you!" Then I was enveloped in that stench, lifted off the ground by my arms so that afterward I had bruises on my skin, and he sucked my mouth into his. I wanted to vomit, wanted to die.

At last he put me down, saying, "I cannot wait for tonight. I need your sweet body now!"

"Sir, I have news for you."

"What?"

"I'll be having a baby."

"Wonderful! That calls for a celebration." He marched across to the glass-fronted cabinet and took out a flask and two glasses. I noted his dusty bootprints all over the carpet. It had taken us considerable work to make that carpet spotless.

He poured, and came over to me, the stench increasing with every approaching step. "Here." He gave me a glass of amber-colored liquid.

"Mr. McQuade, I… I do not enjoy alcoholic drinks. I prefer not to…"

"Nonsense! Drink up now!" Instantly his face assumed that frightening hardness.

I took a tiny sip, which burned the inside of my mouth. He tossed his down with every sign of enjoyment, then looked at me, hard. I forced myself to have another sip, then had to cough. "Sir, please, it does not agree with me."

Looking annoyed, he took it from my hand and tossed the contents of this one down too. "Right, my love," he said, "Let's go to the bedroom."

"Mr. McQuade, will I organize a bath for you first?"

"A what? Oh, you're right. That might be good. Very well."

Thank the good Lord. And while men brought in heated water to fill the tub, and he soaked, I could anoint myself with emu oil.

4. Censorship

For three weeks, the men worked from dawn to dusk. Mr. McQuade ordered breakfast he could eat while walking over to the cattle, and we had dinner by candlelight. Even the Sunday church services were curtailed. Blessedly, he was too tired at night to bother me.

I didn't know, and frankly didn't care, what they were doing to the animals, but whatever it was must have been painful because it resulted in an almost constant chorus of bellowing. Some animals were herded through into a smaller enclosure. Others were let loose, to wander off and graze on the yellowed dry grass. I now realized why the wheat field, vegetable garden and house garden were fenced.

Then one day, soon after the two girls and I had eaten luncheon, Clara came running. "Missy Mac, they finished. Mr. Mac coming," she shouted.

I walked over to a window to see the big enclosure empty. Mounted men were cracking whips, chasing the loose cattle away. Mr. McQuade strode toward the house, a smile of satisfaction on his face. I went to the front door to receive him.

"Amelia! It's done." He kicked his boots off and stepped into his inside shoes. "I'll just wash up. Get the Abo women to make me a bite to eat."

I organized it, and dutifully sat with him as he ate. He did eat like a gentleman, which had fooled me, and I suspect my parents, back in Sydney. He was in high good humor, saying, "My dear, the best year for a long time."

"How do you mean, Sir?"

"The cattle for sale of course. It's my second most important source of income, after the shearing. Tomorrow I'll take them to the Murray so they can be shipped in barges."

Oh joy. He was to go again. But this gave me a thought. "Mr. McQuade, does this make it possible for me to write a letter to my parents?"

"Certainly, if it's ready by dawn tomorrow."

"Oh... if you'll excuse me."

I retired to my sewing room and was soon pouring out my heart: the joy of starting on the road to motherhood, but the isolation, loneliness and lack of mental stimulation. I paused. What could I write about my husband?

The door opened and he barged in, filling the feminine space like a pig at a tea party. "Show me what you've written," he demanded.

Shocking. I put my arm over the letter. "Sir, that's... that's unheard of."

"You're in my charge. I need to know." Imperiously, he held out a huge hand, and once more, looking at his face, I felt frightened.

I refused to move. Silence filled the room, and he kept looking at me. I remembered, that had been his reaction to Nanny ministering to my hurts upon my first night of torture.

At last he stepped forward and simply lifted my hand off the letter. His strength was irresistible. He skimmed the page, his face growing even more thunderous. Then he crumpled the letter and walked out.

And yet, that night he again spoke words of endearment even while assaulting me as usual.

He rode off in the morning, taking only five men this time.

In his absence, I had fantasies of organizing an escape in the other direction, toward Sydney—but the men would obviously not obey me, and I couldn't even ride a horse. I had fantasies of killing him upon his return, slitting his throat with a kitchen knife while he slept, or poisoning his food. But I had not even been able to kill a little mouse-like animal that had entered the house. When Sollie did so, I couldn't watch. Then I fantasized about killing myself. But there was a baby growing within my body, and also, Clara had specially chosen to be born to be with me, and how could I give her grief?

The two girls became worried about me. Sollie said, "Missy Mac, you not eat. Must eat for baby."

Clara said, "Missy Mac, why you no sewing now? And no do nice things in garden?"

It was impossible to explain to them. They had the barest concept of writing, and none of communicating through letters. How could they understand what it meant for me to have my correspondence censored? This was the ultimate proof of my status as a mere possession. Had I been a convict, I could not have been more powerless.

Obviously, he'd never allow me to visit Sydney. Heavens, I might disclose that life at Bruchan Station was not the height of delight!

So, even the activities that had given me peace were without joy. Life was bleak, and I could look forward to it staying that way till I died.

One morning I lay in bed, lacking the energy even to arise, when Clara knocked. "Missy Mac," she called. Please come. Something special."

I quickly dressed and went to investigate. My friends led me to the back door, where two Aboriginal men waited. They were dressed like all the stockmen, and carried an intricately woven large basket between them.

Sollie said, pointing to each, "My old husband, George. And that Clara's husband, Ken."

"How do you do," I said automatically.

They grinned at me. George answered, "We fine, Missy Mac. Brought you basket for baby."

Clara said, "They take much time to make beautiful home for new baby. For you."

The cradle was indeed beautiful. It was made from reeds that grew along quiet stretches of the river. The pattern captured the eye and led it along many directions, making me think of a subtle visual symphony.

"Oh, thank you."

Ken—what improbable names for these brown men—grinned with pride. "You good to my Clara. She wonderful for me. I want her happy."

Why couldn't I have a husband like that?

The men turned to go, no doubt required at their normal tasks. Sollie said, "Missy Mac, now we must sew many things for baby."

And that was how my dear friends defeated my terrible depression, but there was still a problem. We could make a mattress and soft furnishings for the cradle, but what else did a newborn baby need? For my Aboriginal friends, a baby was just carried around by mother, wrapped in a soft fur in cold weather, naked otherwise. I had no idea whatever of the requirements for an European baby. If I could have had advice from mother, or Nanny, or preferably both... So, I marshaled arguments to present to my lord and master upon his return.

Mrs. Holbrook

As before, he sent one man in advance, and arrived the following day. He'd gone away with young cattle, and returned with a small herd of sheep. To my surprise, a covered carriage accompanied them, driven by one of our men.

I was pleased to note that this time he didn't stink, although, naturally, his clothes were covered in dust. "My Amelia!" he shouted upon entering, and I was forced to endure a maul, and what he considered a loving kiss. "Come outside my love, and meet my surprise."

The driver was just assisting a woman out of the carriage. Gray hair poked out from under her bonnet, and she had a lumpy shape even the loose dress couldn't hide. She walked toward us then stood there, her eyes avoiding mine.

Mr. McQuade made the introductions: "Amelia my dear, meet Gertrude Holbrook. She is an experienced midwife, and I've hired her to help us look after all the necessary preparations for our son. Mrs. Holbrook, here's your employer, Mrs. McQuade."

"How do you do, Mrs. Holbrook. No doubt you're tired after the journey, and would like to wash up. I'll have a room be made ready for you."

"Thank ya, ma'am." She spoke in an uneducated, Cockney way. At the same time, her eyes flashed toward me for an instant, and I was shocked by the animosity there. Why?

"Please come with me to make the arrangements. Mr. McQuade, perhaps you could get one of the men to bring Mrs. Holbrook's possessions?"

"Certainly."

I showed the woman where the privy was, and the pump for a wash. When she came in again, I introduced her to Sollie and Clara. I disliked the contemptuous way she regarded them, and decided to grab the cow by the horns, to twist the saying. "Mrs. Holbrook, the four of us will be together for several months. So, I want to make this a pleasant time for all of us. Right?"

"Yes ma'am." She still sounded resentful.

"While Mr. McQuade is here, naturally we'll need to observe proper formalities. However, when it's just us women, I'm happy for you to call me Amelia, and I'd like to call you Gertrude. And these two girls are Aboriginal, but also they're my dearest friends. They're more my companions than servants."

I restrained from laughing at the expression on her face. Her eyes opened so wide that white showed all around, and her mouth formed an O. "But, but, Abos don't have no more brains than an animal!"

I saw that my friends were deeply offended, so waved to them to let me handle it. "Do you have any evidence for that? "I've found them to be intelligent, creative and decent people. I have noted that out on the farm, the Aboriginal hands are far more skilled than the white ones. And I'd like to show you a beautiful work of art Clara's and Sollie's husbands made for me."

"All Abo women is sluts."

I felt like hitting her on the head with a vase. "Mrs. Holbrook, please answer my question. What evidence do you have that Aboriginal people have no more brains than an animal?"

Her face went red and she seemed to swell like a bullfrog. "They just is."

"In this household, you will deal with Clara and Sollie with decency, as if they were people like you and me. Because they are. And tell me, Mrs. Holbrook, why are you so hostile to me?"

"Not me place to argue with ya, ma'am. I'll just go to me room please."

Sigh. What have I done to deserve such an attitude? And I was afraid the presence of this person would also get in the way of my usual pleasant work with my friends.

The next question was, would I be expected to have her dine with us, or with the girls in the kitchen? On balance, I thought it better to have her where I could keep her from being cruel to my friends, and made appropriate arrangements.

When we sat for dinner, Mr. McQuade raised his eyebrows at seeing her with us, but said nothing. Mrs. Holbrook ate in a disgusting way. I managed not to look at her, but Mr. McQuade was not so reticent. At the end of the first course, when Sollie had left, he said, "Woman, you eat like a pig. I won't have you at table in the future."

Her hands trembled, and she looked down, but hate and resentment radiated from her. Without a word she stood and flounced from the room.

This was my chance to get rid of her, and to advance my plan. "Sir, this woman is impossible. You saw her insolence right now. She's been like this all day. Can we please return her to wherever she came from?"

He looked at me kindly. "She is a pain, isn't she? But she comes with the highest recommendations for her skill with delivering babies. I'd hoped she'd be able to instruct you in all the aspects of caring for our son, and–"

Without thought, I interrupted, "Or daughter?"

He stopped, the tyrant instantly replacing the kind friend. "You shall give me a son as eldest child. It's the family tradition. And he shall be named Charles."

"Sir, if it were within my control, I'd ensure that, but God determines such things, and–"

"And you shall have a son. But to return to our problem. We need the services of this scum of a woman. There simply is no one else."

"Sir, I do have a possible alternative."

"Go on."

"There must be many competent midwives in Sydney. Can we contact my parents to organize one for us?"

"Yes, that'll work. Well done, Amelia." Once more, he smiled at me with benevolence, as if I'd demonstrated a major achievement of intelligence. Clearly, within his world women were idiots.

"In fact, Mr. McQuade, my father has a woman who'd serve admirably."

I hesitated, and he simply looked at me.

"Her name is Grace Dennehy. She raised me from infancy."

"You mean that Irish scum I sent packing?"

"Sir, she is no scum. This Holbrook woman is uncivilized. But the woman I refer to has manners, decency and kindness. Please give her a chance!"

"It's out of the question." He rose from the table and walked out.

5. 1848-1849: Taming Trudy

Well, I could still return to asking for a Sydney midwife, only I'd have to bide my time. Meanwhile, I had a female ogre to cope with. First I told Sollie that while she was with us, Mrs. Holbrook would eat in her room. I thought this better than to lumber the two of them with her presence in the kitchen. Then I knocked on her door.

"Whddaya want, ya black bitch?" came the unpleasant voice.

Feeling like murder, I pushed the door in and entered. "You will not speak to my friends that way!" I said with heat. "We need to have a serious talk."

She was sitting on the chair facing the mirror, in a shapeless nightdress, a hairbrush in her hand.

Even by the late evening light through the window, I saw her wrinkled face pale. "I didn't mean no harm, ma'am."

"Then don't do it. Look, you're not welcome here. Tomorrow morning, I shall arrange with Mr. McQuade that you be sent back to where you came from."

"Then what? There ain't no other midwife in these parts."

"I've suggested to my husband to seek one in Sydney."

She laughed, not a pleasant sound. "Others 'ave tried that. They can't, 'cause the Sydney ones is busy enough and paid well enough not to want discomfort, like. So, then they beg me to come back. One hoity toity lady got a snotnosed girl from Sydney, then she died in childbirth, and serve 'er right. I'd have got her through."

I hadn't realized one could die from childbirth, but now was not the time to reveal that. "So, Mrs. Holbrook, you act so unpleasantly because you believe that you have the upper hand and we can't do without you?"

"Yeah. That's right."

"I've got news for you. The Aboriginal women have babies. There are wise older women among them, and if necessary, I'd much rather have them assist me than to put up with your rudeness and hostility."

Once more she went pale. I could see I'd scored a hit.

"So, Mrs. Holbrook, expect to leave tomorrow or the day after."

"But... but I ain't got nowhere to go!"

I just looked at her, I guess copying my husband.

She shrunk in on herself, defeated.

I continued when she kept silent. "While you're here, you'll have your meals in this room. You will keep this room spotlessly tidy. I don't require your help with the rest of the housework. But you will treat my two friends with decency, the way you'd want to be treated."

"Yes, ma'am."

I went to grab the bedside chair, noticing an extra piece of furniture: a plain chair with a half-moon cutout in the front of the seat. I pushed past it to get the proper chair, put it to face her and sat. "Look, Mrs. Holbrook, I have no intention of being cruel. But why were you hostile before we'd even been introduced? Please speak freely. Nothing you can say will offend me more than your behavior already has."

"Why? 'Cause you's the enemy. That's why."

"I've never met you until this morning. I've done no harm to you or to anyone else."

"Nah? Here you lives in luxury, every wish granted, servants, big 'ouse, 'usband, baby comin'. Me? I got nothin' and nobody, and it's your kind what's done it to me."

"Oh... Let me explain the reality in this household. I'm not the mistress of this house, but its prisoner. I have the use of what I want, as long as it pleases my husband to allow it to me. But I cannot visit my parents, or even write a letter to them. No wish of mine is ever granted, unless my husband chooses to approve, which is rare. I haven't handled any money since my marriage, and if I had some, I'd have no opportunity for spending it. Apart from those two nice Aboriginal young women, I have nobody. No friends at all. And as for my husband, he's a monster. I wish I could pass him on to you, and welcome."

I must have spoken with sufficient passion that she accepted it. We looked at each other. Finally, I asked, "What did you mean by saying that 'my kind' is the cause of your misfortune?"

"I had an 'usband, two nice children, and worked in the trade I learned from me mother. Bein' a midwife. Good lookin' I was in them days. And I was with this lady what was 'aving 'er baby. And 'is lordship raped me, and I kicked up a fuss. Next thing, I was on a prison hulk, and me 'usband and children didn't even know if I was dead or alive. And 'ere I am, in bloody New South Wales, no 'ome, no nobody. Me children be grown by now if they be alive, but they's dead to me and me to them. So, I 'ate all gentry."

I gathered from this that Mr. McQuade's nightly assault against me was termed "rape." Aloud I said, "But you're forced to work for them, because poor people can't afford your services."

"You got it."

"Well, Gertrude–"

"Trudy be nicer, ma'am."

We smiled at each other. She got up and lit a candle.

"Trudy, I know this happens. The woman who raised me, and is dearer to me than my own heart, was a girl from Ireland. She got transported because some nobleman wanted the land of her village, and in Sydney was assigned to a man who raped her and got her with child. And right here, my lovely Aboriginal people suffer the same from my husband, and I don't know how many other white men. They hate it, but are powerless to resist. We're all sisters, fellow victims of that thing between a man's legs."

"Ma'am–"

"Amelia."

We shared another smile. When the sourness left her face, she looked like a nice grandmotherly person. "Amelia, you's right. Me father said, a man's brain's in 'is penis, like. But I never met no lady like you. Always, they's too good for the likes of me."

So, the monstrous weapon was called a penis. "Well, I was raised by that Irish girl. Also, maybe other ladies have husbands who don't rape them, and don't treat them like idiot prisoners."

"Amelia, ma'am, I apologize. I promise to do me best for ya."

"Thank you, Trudy. I have a secret to share with you. When my husband is outside, I help Sollie and Clara with the housework. It's pleasant company, and fills–"

"AMELIA! Where are you!" came my master's shout.

"Oh dear. And I haven't had time to grease myself."

Trudy sprung up and grabbed a jar from a bag at her feet. "This's what you need, lass."

She uncapped it and handed it over. I stood, put a leg upon the chair and anointed myself while still wearing my underclothes. Then I rushed out to meet my nightly fate.

Charles

After this Trudy behaved politely to me, and at least short of abusive to the native girls. She had no contact with Mr. McQuade at all. Within a few days, the four of us shared the housework, though Trudy usually chose to work alone. However, she joined us in the sewing room, and proved to be a marvel at knitting and sewing. Two days after her arrival, she produced two pairs of very thin knitting needles, and balls of fine wool. She said, "Amelia, I always buys wool like this when in a big town. Part of me fee is to pay for the materials I bring, like." She set up a pair of needles for me to knit a tiny jacket.

The next day, Clara and Sollie came with needles of their own they'd made from polished reed slivers, and soon picked up the skill. I could see that Trudy was surprised at their speed of learning. Never again would she be able to consider Aboriginals as stupid.

So, the months passed. My belly grew, I needed to relieve myself more often, and the heat of early summer took a terrible toll on me, even within the dark relative coolness of the house. I was unable to work outside for more than a few minutes during the day, so gardened before breakfast.

Trudy also got involved in the garden, where to my surprise she quickly built an easy, friendly relationship with the men. My three gardeners treated her like a beloved aunt.

As summer progressed, I was more uncomfortable than ever. The only compensation for my huge belly, painfully distended breasts and awkwardness of movement was that Mr. McQuade now left me alone at nights. Sadly, this was bad news for the Aboriginals.

Backache became an everyday experience. One morning it was so bad I couldn't get out of bed. My husband looked at me, brows raised, but then the pain passed. I managed to lumber upright, but a few minutes later, while washing myself, my back started hurting just as badly for a short while.

This continued through breakfast. Mr. McQuade looked at my wincing. "My Amelia, something is wrong? Perhaps your baby is coming?"

"Oh. That hasn't occurred to me." I rang the bell, and Clara came in. "Clara, can you please call Mrs. Holbrook to come?"

When the midwife made her appearance, I told her about my backaches. She said, "Ma'am, you's in labor, but it be a long time yet. It takes many hours, like, 'specially the first one. 'Ave your breakfast, and I'll get prepared."

"Good," Mr. McQuade said, rising. "I'll go about my work then, and look forward to meeting my son tonight."

"Mebbe, Sir," Trudy answered. "It'll prob'ly take longer."

It did.

The pain moved from my back to wander around my lower body, always like some part of me squeezed in a mighty fist. Trudy used a sandglass to measure both the length of the pains and the gap between them. She got one of the girls to support me while I was required to walk up and down, up and down the corridor. They gave me plenty of water to drink, and snippets of food whenever Trudy managed to talk a bit into me, which was not often.

When Mr. McQuade came in, I was utterly exhausted, but Trudy said it would still take many hours. "Her water's not broke yet, Sir," she said.

He clearly understood this, just nodded and went to the dining room to eat alone, but I had no idea what she meant. When I asked, she said, "The baby's in a sort of a bag that 'as to pop, and then the water in it comes out. That's the start of the second stage."

Dear God, all this time had only been the first stage? "How many stages are there?"

"Then the baby is squeezed down the birth canal, and everything inside you needs to open up, like. That takes a while. Then the birth 'appens."

Looking at my face, she offered, "Don't worry, ma'am. Women's been doin' this since Eve ate the apple, like. When ya get your baby, ya forget the pain in the love of the little mite."

"Oh, I hope so!"

My three attendants took turns, two with me, the third resting, though Trudy was very firm about being roused if there was any change. At last, past midnight, I suddenly felt a gush of warm liquid down my legs, pooling on the carpet. Clara ducked into the nearest room, grabbed a chair, sat me on it and went to fetch the midwife.

"Trudy, must I keep walking?" I asked her. "I'm ready to fall over with tiredness!"

"Come into me room, Amelia." Now that Mr. McQuade was well asleep, I was glad she'd dropped the formality.

She had a white sheet over her bedclothes, with the edges of an oilskin showing. She settled me onto it, saying, "When it's time for the delivery, I'll get ya to sit on the birthing chair. Now, just rest between the pains."

Over and over, closer and closer together, my body was wracked by that terrible inner fist. Dawn light peered through the window when Trudy sat me on the chair, which stood on another sheet with an oilskin under it. She ordered Sollie to bring some boiling water, and Clara to stand behind me for support.

She scrubbed her hands in the hot water with soap till her skin was red, and also soaked a pair of scissors, some white cotton yarn and a curved needle in a smaller bowl.

Apprehensive, I asked about the purpose of doing this.

"The gentleman doctors is a dirty lot. They lose mothers and babies 'cause they don't wash their 'ands. Me mother taught me: keep clean, and no baby fever 'appens, like."

"The scissors? Ohh..." That was a worse pain than any before.

She laughed. "Not for you, Amelia. That bag I told you about, the placenta. It's attached to the baby, like. I need to cut the cord and tie it."

"And the needle?"

"Jus' in case. Sometimes, the mother gets torn a bit and I sew it up. You won't 'ardly even feel me doin' it."

I heard the rumble of my husband's voice, speaking to Sollie outside. I really, really hoped he'd come in to see my suffering, but he walked off.

Sollie put her head in. "Missy Mac, I give breakfast to Mr. Mac. Be back soon."

Time was still punctuated by the rhythm of pain, but now I felt an immense stretching within me. Trudy lifted my nightgown to above my knees and I felt cool fingers probe. "Summat's different," she muttered. Then I remembered Nanny saying my wedding night might have damaged me so I might not be able to bear children. I reported this to her.

"Amelia, may I look?"

"Please do. I don't care about mod... Ohh!... about modesty now."

She got me to lie on the bed again and inspected my private parts. "I see what ya mean about your 'usband bein' a monster. You got very badly torn, but it's 'ealed well. Not the right shape, like, and there's scars. I think the emu oil your girls gave ya helped to heal."

Both girls were in the room, and both nodded.

"I'll fix it up for ya. No worries, ya won't even know I'm doin' it. And the baby's almost comin'." She got Sollie to bring more boiling water, and put more instruments in it.

They helped me back onto the birthing chair. Clara lovingly massaged my shoulders, Sollie offered me a sip of water, and Trudy again inserted a couple of fingers into me. I found her touch soothing.

"I can feel the 'ead," she said calmly, then, "Don't push now, but push 'ard when I say."

I was being torn apart. I saw her doing something, her hands hidden by my nightgown, but I could feel nothing above the stretching pain. Then she called, Push!"

She stood, with a tiny red form in her hands. "An 'ealthy boy, Amelia."

"Thank Heavens for that. My husband..."

"Yeah, stupid man. Sollie, bring the next lot of 'ot water."

"You won't wash him in boiling water?"

She cackled. "Of course not. Trust me, I's been doin' this for a long time."

She and Clara helped me over to the bed again. She gave me the tiny new person. "Let 'im suck on ya," she commanded. I bared a breast and held the tiny face to it. As I felt him suck I realized, yes, it was all worth it. After a few moments, Trudy passed me a drink. I raised myself on an elbow and took a sip. "Ugh, it's bitter," I said.

She laughed. "It'll get the placenta out quick, like."

I forced it down, then lay back to enjoy my little baby. I hardly noticed Trudy's ministrations below as she first pulled something from me, then got busy with needle and thread. That was a mere repeating sting.

In the evening, I was prettily arrayed in my own bed, with the tiny baby in the beautiful cradle. My husband was delighted, and if I hadn't known better, I'd have thought he loved me.

6. 1849-1851: Grace

The work of the Station took Mr. McQuade away, a blessing since I wasn't sure when he'd want to resume the nightly rape. After some weeks a man came to warn of his return, making me highly apprehensive. Trudy's surgery had only recently healed despite daily hip baths in hot salty water, and my abdomen was still distended. I squeezed into a corset and waited. Looking out at the blinding morning heat, hardly able to breathe because of the corset, wishing for him to drop dead rather than ever to come home again, I felt this to be the pattern of my life forever. Little Charles was asleep in my bedroom, but I planned to hide behind him to interfere with Mr. McQuade's usual welcoming maul.

Outside, through the graceful folds of the lace curtains the girls and I had made, ages ago last winter, the air shimmered with heat. It never got this hot in Sydney. Did I have to endure a lifetime of such summers? Sweat covered my body, and I was thirsty all the time. Of course, Charles sucked a lot of water in his milk.

A dust cloud announced whatever herd they were torturing. I fetched Charles, my shield. During the past week, I'd written a very carefully worded letter to my parents, who after all needed to be informed of their new status as grandparents, and part of my worry was, would the tyrant allow me to send it? While waiting, I marshaled my arguments all over again.

There he was. He sprung to the ground off his horse and came striding in the front door.

"Welcome home, Sir," I said. "Little Charles has been awaiting your coming."

His face lit up. He remembered to kick off his boots, and, miracle of miracles, said, "I must stink after days in the saddle. I'll wash up first." God be praised, he was capable of learning.

He soon appeared in clean clothes, and I passed Charles to him. The baby lay comfortably on his huge palm. He lifted the child to his face, and kissed the top of his head. "My Amelia," he said, "you've made me a happy man." It was actually no hardship to put my arms around his neck and kiss him.

"Come and sit down, Sir." I led the way to the dining room. "I've prepared some cool drink and a cold meal." I rang the bell, and the girls brought it. We started with a long drink of lemonade. I begun my campaign. "Mr. McQuade, Charles is a healthy little boy. Mrs. Holbrook has been very useful in guiding me in the skills of motherhood, and everything is going well."

"Excellent."

"I'm still healing after the birth, but she says I should be whole in a few more weeks."

"Oh? I thought you'd be over that. After all, sheep, cattle and horses get over it in a day."

Wretched man. Am I no more than an animal? I put civility into my voice. "Mrs. Holbrook has explained that. A human baby's head is much bigger relatively speaking than an animal's. Look at Charles. His head is about a quarter of his body at this stage."

"Hmm. That's true. You must forgive me, my love. I've never been a father before."

Stupid fellow, where did he think the Aboriginal women's white babies came from? Still, I'd gained one victory: no rape tonight. Now for the second objective. "And it's a first for me too. I'm glad that after all we decided to keep this midwife. She's been a valuable teacher. But, Mr. McQuade, my parents need to be notified they have a grandson, and such a delightful one."

"I do have some business in Sydney. Naturally, I'll call on them."

"Oh... when can we go?" This was better than I'd expected.

"We? Amelia, it's out of the question. As you said, you're still convalescing, and we cannot expose Charles to the hardships of the journey. It is after all the hottest time of the year."

He was right, God in Heaven, he was right, so I tried a different tack. "Perhaps, Sir, we could invite them to Charles' baptism. And while waiting for your return, I've written them a letter."

"I shall deliver it, provided it's suitable of course."

Immediately after our meal, he inspected the letter and took it away, no doubt so I couldn't add an invitation to it. I was equally sure that in Sydney he'd discourage their visit.

He left for Sydney in a couple of weeks, and thankfully he'd left me alone during this time. And indeed as I'd predicted, he returned two months later, in the relative cool of autumn, with only the men who had accompanied him. Two packhorses were laden with gifts from my parents, but they were not there.

Life resumed its former rhythm. When Charles was six months old, a lone rider came to talk with Mr. McQuade. I saw through the window as my husband headed for the house. He opened the front door and shouted, "Amelia!"

"Yes, Mr. McQuade?"

"That midwife is needed elsewhere."

Trudy had never become a friend, but I'd got used to her presence, and she'd been a fount of information. She packed up and left in her carriage.

My monthly bleeding failed to come the next time it should have. So, eight months later, in the autumn of 1850, she returned to deliver a daughter, a far easier labor. When I showed her to Mr. McQuade, he gave every appearance of genuine love for her.

"I'd like to name her Grace," I said, then held my breath for his answer.

"Very well," he said, passed the tiny little person back to me, then watched me give her a breast with a benevolent smile.

Charles was at first jealous of my attention to Grace, but he soon settled, although, acting on Trudy's advice, I weaned him. He made little sounds that were almost like speech, and learned to crawl, then walk with assistance. By the time Trudy left again, he was running everywhere, and was well on the way to using a chamber pot.

While Trudy was packing, she said, "Amelia, I knows you wants to write to your folks, and that man won't let you, like. Write one now and I'll take it and post it for you."

Tears of joy came to me and I felt like hugging her. But a thought came to me: "Posting a letter costs money. I can't pay you."

"Amelia, ya done somethin' for me I can't never repay. Ya took the load of hate off me back."

This time I did hug her, then retired to the sewing room and poured out my heart on paper.

Eagle

This was a year of drought, the river shrinking to a chain of pools connected by mud, and red, cracked soil showing through the dry grass. Mr. McQuade and the men needed to go far to water the herds, so I had relative peace, seeing him at the most twice a week.

One morning, Clara was pegging out the washing and I needed to ask her some question. I walked out onto the back veranda, leaving the door open. Immediately, I heard the rapid patter of tiny feet, and Charles banged against the back of my leg, hugging it. I turned and picked him up, to see an incredible sight.

A huge brown eagle was flying straight toward me. Wingtip to wingtip, he must have been seven feet. Those great wings were motionless as he soared forward with great speed, then his angle in the air changed, and he landed on the balustrade, holding on with sharply clawed feet.

In my terror, I tightly closed my eyes, and hugged my son, protecting him with my arms.

Nothing happened for what seemed forever. When I finally managed to look again, the eagle was circling high above, then, the wings working powerfully, he flew straight east, back toward the mountains, back the way he'd come.

All excited, Clara rushed up to me. "You see that, Missy Mac?"

"I did. It terrified me out of my wits. I thought he'd attack Charles."

"What is English name for bird?"

"Eagle."

"For us, Eagle is father of all animals. Wise bird. He visit you."

"I don't understand this."

"I ask Uncle Gurry tonight. But he not dangerous. Just come to look. Look at you, look at me, look at Charles. Is wonderful."

Next morning, she delivered the result of Uncle Gurry's consultation with the spirits. "Uncle Gurry say, that not eagle. Real eagle never fly to people. Scared of people. That spirit person, not bird. Spirit person come look. Friendly, not want to hurt."

"Why would a spirit person want to look at me?"

"Missy Mac, you special. You friend to blackfella women, even make that Trudy become better. Maybe spirit people like that, tell you that you do good thing."

A few weeks later, Mr. McQuade came in looking worried. Since he usually made himself seem invulnerable, this was of note. Over dinner, he said, "I'll have to sell a lot of my stock, and of course other farmers are in the same situation, so I'll lose on the sale."

"The drought, Sir?"

He sighed. "Yes. Animals are dying. I need to reduce numbers."

That night, he was more vigorous than usual in his ficky-ficky, and on the next day took most of the men as for the annual roundup. He returned three months later, after the winter rains should have fallen but hadn't. Only the Aboriginal hands and the two married men were with him. Looking at his face, for the first time I realized that he was getting old. He looked weary beyond belief. For once, I couldn't resent his presence, but made him comfortable, wondering if my news for him would be welcome.

He downed a cool drink, then sipped the refill. "My Amelia, I have good news and bad news. The good news is, I got far more for the animals than I expected, because many thousands of people have swarmed into the new colony of Victoria. The bad news is, they've come because gold has been found, and all my hands have deserted to seek their fortune."

"Victoria, Sir? Where is that? I haven't heard of it."

"This year, the southern part of New South Wales became a new colony. And God has rewarded them or cursed them, I don't know which, with the discovery of gold."

My resentment returned. Why did I never hear news? In Sydney as a girl, I'd been aware of everything that happened even in far-off lands, never mind in my own country. But I needed to tell him. "Sir, I also have news for you. You'll be a father for the third time."

He smiled at that. "Wonderful. And don't worry, this reverse is temporary. We shall survive. I have plenty of wealth to draw on in the meantime."

HE had plenty of wealth, not us. I hid my reaction. "How will you do the work, with only two white men coming back with you?"

"Oh, even they're going. I told them if they went I'd kick their families off, so they returned. But as soon as we arrived, they demanded their wages, and are going too. I've only got three old men, one of whom is a gardener, and the blacks. And I'm worried about them."

"Why?"

"They do as they're told as long as they're afraid. With me alone, they're just as likely to murder me as to work for me."

I took a deep breath, afraid of his reaction to what I wanted to say. But then I remembered the eagle. "Mr. McQuade, I have a suggestion that may help."

"You?" Contempt was in his voice, on his face. "What do you know about farm work?"

"Nothing. But I can suggest a way of converting the Aboriginals into faithful friends rather than potential enemies forced to work for you. And in this time of need, surely anything is worth considering?"

"All right. I'm listening."

I put my hand on my stomach, drawing courage from the baby in there. "We need them. And we need to feel safe with only them and three old men around. We need their trust, liking and respect, without fear. This means, we need to treat them differently from the past, differently from how other landowners treat them."

"You know nothing about those savages. Only fear rules them."

"Sir, I do know about them. Ever since my arrival, I've had daily contact with Sollie and Clara, and I know for a fact that the whole tribe likes me and respects me as a result of how I've interacted with them. I'm confident that these people will not do me or my children any harm, under any circumstances."

He just looked at me, with that closed face.

"However, Sir, I agree with you. If any of those men has the chance to do so safely, he will happily murder you." Two could play the silent game. I stopped, and looked back at him.

"So?"

"So, we need to teach them to feel about you the way they feel about me." Again I stopped.

"Spit it out, woman!"

"Sir, surely I don't need to say why they like me and hate you."

Time stopped. We glared into each other's eyes, and for once I had the power. He broke the staring match. "All right. You're correct. Advise me."

"Within your mind, within your heart, tell yourself that they're people just like you are, deserving respect and decency. Their women are just like me. Treat them the way you'd treat a lady. They're not for your use. Apologize to the men for your past deeds. Offer them payment, not in money probably, because they have no use for that, but in things and rights they value. Accept them as equals, treat them better than you've treated the white hands."

To my surprise, he heard me out. Then without a word he stood, went outside and walked into his office building.

I found Sollie and Clara in the kitchen. "Listen," I said, passing on my excitement. "I think I may have managed to convince Mr. McQuade to stop doing ficky-ficky with you women, and to treat your men decently." Within half an hour, I was ready to make my first visit to the Aboriginal camp. I was aware that they moved around, along the river. This time, they were a quarter of a mile from the house. I carried Grace. Clara carried Charles, who proudly wore a new gift from his father: a wide-brimmed hat.

I counted fifteen little shelters, each an arch made from bark. Women and children were everywhere, but I only saw one man, who was very old. Of course, the able-bodied men were working with my husband. Several little fires burned. Everyone gathered to watch as we approached. All the women wore shabby European-style dresses, while most of the children were naked.

A white-haired older woman stepped forward, saying, "Missy Mac, you's welcome."

Sollie said, "Missy Mac, this Gundu. She wife in same family I am wife in."

I smiled at the old lady. "Thank you Gundu. I'm honored by the welcome."

"Missy Mac, you different. Old Missy Mac never talk to blackfella people. If blackfella servant woman do wrong thing in house, she beat them. You never do nasty thing like that."

"And I'm doing my best to make sure nobody else will. If I'm successful, Mr. McQuade will never do anything to your young women again. And I'm trying to make him apologize for the harm he has done, and to pay your men decently for their work."

There was a buzz in their own language. Clara said, "Everyone cannot believe that true. They hope, but Mr. Mac hard man. They scared you wrong."

I spoke again. "Right now, we have a chance to change his mind. He needs your men to work for him. If they can help me, we can keep going. If not, then I and my children may have to go away. Other white people will come, and will be just as cruel as white men have been in the past. I want a good life for you. I need you to help me to make it happen."

A very pretty young woman stepped forward, holding a little girl's hand. The girl was perhaps six years old, with more the color of an Italian than of an Aboriginal. "You say we now be nice to Mr. Mac? He do bad things to us. His father do bad things to us. Other white men too. And if we no like, they hurt us. Now it all change?"

"I'm trying to change it. I need your help, then we can change it. If I have to go away from here, other white people will come, and everything will be the same as before. If I can stay here, then we can work together to make life better. And maybe if we can do it here, then we can work to have life better for Aboriginal people in other places too."

The old man came forward, and I saw that his eyes had a whitish film over them. "Missy Mac," he asked, "Please, I hold hand?" He reached for me. I noticed that although his skin was more black than brown, his palms were pink.

I put my right hand in his. His grip was firm, surprisingly strong, and felt good.

His blind eyes regarded me. Everyone was silent, looking on. At last he let go, and said something in the native tongue. Then he said in their broken English, "Your spirit good. You mean good. Maybe you can do what you say. Maybe you not can do what you say. But I know you want good. Thank you."

I guessed his identity. "And thank you, Uncle Gurry."

He gave me a broad, toothless smile.

Clara then started to speak. While I couldn't understand her, she was miming as well, and obviously she was describing the visit from the great eagle.

At last, Gundu spoke. "Missy Mac, when men come home, we talk with them. But many men angry. They no like Mr. Mac being harsh. They no like him ficky-ficky women. Maybe they want go away, now that no white men can stop us."

I was relieved that the threat was abandonment rather than murder. I answered, "I also hate that. He is my husband. He should not ficky-ficky other women. And your men should be treated decently, not harshly. I have a question. I want him to pay you. He can pay money if that's what you want, or things you can use. Please think about what he should pay for the men's work, and what he should pay to show he is sorry for the past."

Charles wriggled, so Clara put him down. He ran forward—he never walked—to the pretty young woman's girl. He looked up at her face. "Hello," he said, quite clearly.

She smiled at him. "Hello, Mr. Charles."

Charles took off his hat and reached high, trying to put it on her head.

Everyone laughed. My son had won my case for me.

7. Payment

I could hardly wait to share my news with Mr. McQuade, but his face was grim as he rode up to the stable. The old man there took the lead from him, and as he dismounted, I saw him pull a gun from a saddle holster. He strode across to the house, carrying the weapon.

"I can't talk those idiots out of taking their families on a long dangerous trek to the goldfields," he said in greeting. "And the Abos are restive. I needed eyes in the back of my head all day."

Here was my opening. "Mr. McQuade, welcome home. I've got good news about that."

"What?"

"Right now, the Aboriginal women will be talking to their men, and if we do it right, we can have a permanent change there."

He walked past me, returning in a few minutes, washed and in clean clothes. "You've been up to something. Tell me." His voice was still abrupt.

"I visited them today, and talked with all the women and a blind old man. I've won their cooperation. It's up to them now to convince their men."

"Amelia, you're naïve. Only a show of strength works in this world, especially with savages."

"Mr. McQuade, the situation has changed. I don't want to be a widow yet." Actually, I'd have loved to be widow, but then I'd be in too much practical trouble to even think about.

He sighed. "Tell me, what foolish promises did you make I won't be able to keep?"

"Sir, I only made three promises. That you and other white men will leave their women alone; that you'll pay them for their labor either with money or with materials they value, at a decent rate; and that we'll compensate them for past injuries."

"Right. I know what those blackfellas will value. They like nothing better than to get drunk." He looked cheerful at the thought.

"Oh." I felt utterly dismayed. "Sir, wouldn't it be better to help them improve their lives?"

He gave me that hard, close-faced stare. "You're rising above yourself. Organize dinner—I'm hungry after working hard all day."

I wished for some cyanide to put into it. We ate without a word between us, but, blessedly, at night he didn't touch me.

Over breakfast the next morning, I braved his anger by reopening the argument. "Sir, as you know, my parents own a hotel. I've often heard them discuss the behavior of drunken men."

"You don't need to lecture me about the behavior of drunken men."

"Of course not, Sir. So, you know that alcohol impairs self-restraint. A man who'd swallow his anger might resort to violence if intoxicated. And can a drunk do responsible work?"

He gave me that hard look and walked out.

As we started cleaning up after breakfast, Sollie said, "Missy Mac, you do good thing yesterday. Men listen to us. In blackfella way, man not boss, woman not boss, but do different things for each other."

"I have a worry," I told them. "Mr. McQuade has come up with the idea of paying the men with alcohol. You know what that is?"

As I looked out the kitchen window, I saw two horse-drawn carts setting out east. Women and children rode them, with the two men walking. I hoped they'd survive the journey.

Clara asked, "Is that rum? Burn mouth, warm inside, fuzzy head?"

"Yes."

"Very bad. People do horrible things."

We looked after Charles and Grace then did the housework, and even doled out some water for the plants around the house, but my mind wasn't on it. I saw horrid images of drunken violence, things I'd never seen personally but had heard, or read in books, or... I don't know where they came from—of fathers belting children, of women lying on the ground, reeking of alcohol, of men blindly battering each other.

That evening, Mr. McQuade came in looking self-satisfied and hardly said a word. In bed, he raped me with even more force than usual. And in the morning, Clara turned up with one of the other women, whom she introduced as Tillie. Sollie, she told me, had been beaten up by her old husband, that nice George who'd spent many hours making my cradle. In the morning, George had been very sorry, and stayed home to look after her—but the damage was done.

Three changes

With only the Aboriginals helping him, my husband needed to work far harder than usual, and this had the blessing that he was too tired for ficky-ficky. Sollie returned in a few days, with a big bruise on her face. She said her husbands now refused the rum, but the other men got drunk every night, and some of the women joined them. Children were being neglected, something that had never happened before.

Three days later, George called at the back door. He'd made a lovely little chair for Charles, because that had been Sollie's choice of a sorry gift.

I thanked him, and got Charles to do so as well. Then I said, "George, please, can you convince the other people to avoid the rum?"

"Missy Mac, I try. But blackfella life bad now that white man take our land. Rum helps forget for a little while." His dark eyes glowed with unshed tears.

"Well, maybe Mr. McQuade will run out of supplies."

"He has shed full." He turned away to return to his work.

I wondered if there was a way of setting that shed on fire.

However, Clara distracted me from this worry after breakfast the next day. She rushed out the back door and vomited. When she came in, I offered help, but she said, "No, Missy Mac, is good. I think I also have baby!"

"Wonderful!" We hugged. "When Trudy Holbrook comes back to help with my baby, she can look after you too."

"Oh no. Aunt Kalabla do that very well. She older blackfella woman."

We got on with washing dishes, sharing yet another bond.

Mr. McQuade looked worn and weary when he came in that day. "Oh, my Amelia," he said, "I need more men."

"Sir, anything I can do?"

"You're pregnant. Even if you were not, it'd take more work to train you than you could accomplish. But thanks for the thought." He smiled at me in that benevolent way that I knew could change into thunder at the slightest provocation.

All the same, next morning I walked across to the stables and said hello to the old man there. I didn't know his name, after sharing this place with him for nearly three years.

"Good morning, ma'am," he said, obviously surprised.

"Good morning. Look, now that we're terribly short-handed, I want to do something to ease the load for those who are left. Can I help with anything?"

He lifted his hat, scratched the top of his bald head and put the hat back. "Righto, ma'am, one of our jobs is to raise orphan lambs. Guess you could help with that, and then Garvey and me could do other things that've been neglected."

"Oh. Yes, that sounds most suitable."

He filled a couple of metal buckets with water from the pump, then took me to a small shed by an enclosure divided in two with a fence. About twenty cute white lambs occupied the left side, with the right side empty. The lambs all crowded against the fence, bleating. We entered the shed, which was mostly full of big jute bags. He unrolled the top of one that was half full. Inside, it had a paper lining, within which was a white powder. "This is milk," he said. He tipped some water into an empty bucket, then ladled powder in, stirring with a stick. When it became milk color he picked it up and led the way outside. My tutor, whose name I still didn't know, opened a gate, let one lamb out and pushed its nose into the bucket. He put a hand in, saying, "You gotta put a finger in her mouth. She sucks on your finger and gets the milk that way."

When the lamb had its fill he put it into the empty enclosure, let a second one out and watched for a few minutes while I had the fun of feeding it. He then went into the shed and returned with another bucket of milk. Soon we worked in a smooth rhythm, and got all the lambs fed within an hour. As I straightened my now-aching back, he said, "Thank you ma'am, much obliged. I'll now have time to oil the harness for all the horses. I've had to put that off for weeks."

As I was returning to the house, I saw some moving dots along the road, far to the east. "Excuse me," I called. "Can you see what that is?"

The man came running, and followed my pointing finger. "Oh, that be wagons, ma'am," he said, excited. Someone's coming!"

"Oh." This was a first, for me anyway. "Do you know where Mr. McQuade is working?"

"They're taking some cows to drink at a billabong, some five mile away."

"Please go and get him immediately."

He ran for the stable, and re-emerged with a saddle over his shoulder. I hurried to the house, to wash up and change my splattered dress. Who could this be?

The distant dots seemed no larger or closer by the time I was ready. I needed to feed Grace anyway, so cared for her, fed Charles, then went outside again, carrying him. Now I could see four rectangular shapes, with several ant-sized dots ahead of them.

By the time Mr. McQuade arrived, with his huge horse's face covered in lather, the visitors were individually distinguishable horsemen, in front of four wagons each pulled by four horses. And the man in the lead... surely, it was Father!

I put Charles down, hitched my dress up with one hand and ran forward. He urged his horse to run, and then we held each other, both crying with joy.

"Poole, this is a surprise," I heard my husband say.

Father let me go with clear reluctance and stepped forward to shake his hand. "McQuade, good morning. I've brought nine experienced stockmen with me!"

This cheered Mr. McQuade up. "Well done, my Amelia, sending Foster to fetch me." As if that had taken an act of genius!

A flurry of activity followed, with the men shown to the bunkhouse, things unloaded from the wagons, horses cared for and I don't know what else. I got the girls to prepare the south guest room because it was the coolest, and put together a cold luncheon, talking to Charles all the time as he sat on his little chair in the kitchen.

Within half an hour, the three of us sat at the dining table. Mr. McQuade said, "Poole, thank you. How did you know I had no men?"

Father gave him a firm look. "Don't thank me till you hear all my news." He turned to me, his face softening. "First, Amelia my dear, I have sad news. Mother has... passed away."

A knife of pain stabbed into my heart, and I could say nothing.

"It's this wretched gold rush. She decided that we could triple our wealth by setting up a pub at Ballarat, where the most gold is. As I've written to you, Nigel has–"

I had to cut him off. "Father, I've received no letter from you, ever!"

The pink part of Mr. McQuade's forehead went a deep red. The suntanned part of his face looked more like a beetroot.

We both looked at him in anger.

Typically, he met this with bluster. "As your husband, it's my duty to ensure your happiness. I was aware of some homesickness for Sydney, and considered that reminders of home and family would worsen it. I was protecting you."

"McQuade, this is outrageous. It bears out what my daughter has written to me."

Instant anger replaced embarrassment. He glared at me. "How? I ensured that you could tell no lies about life here!"

"Sir, I've told no lies. And you've underestimated my intelligence ever since I've arrived. I found a way of writing to my parents."

Father said, "That's why I am here. When I arrived back home from the goldfields, I found Amelia's letter and became extremely concerned for her wellbeing. In Ballarat, I'd met many men who had no luck at finding gold. You see, a few make a fortune, many scratch a living, and most come close to starving. So, I returned by stage coach, recruited experienced stockmen into my employ, then made the best possible time to get here. And, hear me, McQuade. I have a contract with those men. I pay them, and employ them in any way I see fit. If you're willing to pay me for their labor, they'll do your work. If I don't feel like staying here, I'll readily find employment for them at any of the other stations that have been denuded of men. And if I go, my daughter and grandchildren accompany me."

Looking at my husband's face, I became frightened for Father, but then he stood and stormed outside. Probably, this was the first time in his life he'd ever been thwarted.

Now that the monster was out of the room, I asked, "Father, how did mother... die?"

"You know that in all things, she was the leader, but the world doesn't work that way, so I've always been the one to seem to make arrangements. This has meant frequent trips to Melbourne and even Sydney, and of course she was perfectly competent to manage affairs in my absence. We were making even more money than she'd predicted, and were building a proper brick hotel. Meanwhile, we served in a huge tent. One day, I came back from Melbourne with a caravan of supplies, to find the tent destroyed by fire. About thirty people had died, lots more injured. And..." His voice came close to breaking, "Susannah was one of those gone."

We stood and hugged each other, with tears pouring from my eyes.

Clara disturbed us, shouting, "Missy Mac, the blackfella men here. Rain coming!"

Father said, "I must move my wagons under cover," and rushed out.

I looked at Clara. "That's wonderful!"

"Yes but Sollie and I go help move camp."

"Why?"

"Big water coming. Please excuse." She was gone.

I looked after my children, then, being alone, needed to prepare dinner. I settled Grace on a rug on the kitchen floor, and got Charles to help me. He liked nothing more than being useful. While I cut up vegetables, he was shelling dried beans, and we practiced counting the while. He was correct up to ten, although "seven" came out as "seben."

When I'd done all I could I picked Grace up and went out on the back veranda, Charles at my side. The eastern half of the sky was black, with sparkles of lightning visible in many places. The air was motionless, heavy and stiflingly hot. I sat Charles on the handrail, and explained what was coming. He had no concept at all of water falling from the sky.

I saw the natives on the move. Mounted men carried the children, and also Uncle Gurry. The women carried loads, but surprisingly little, given it was all their possessions.

I now heard the distant muttering of thunder, and as I looked, that blackness swallowed much of the sky. It reached the sun, and the world grew dark. Charles started to cry and I spoke softly to him, promising that the rain would be interesting.

I looked left in response to a grinding roar, to see something at first incomprehensible speed along the river's bed. It was level with the tops of the redgum trees: a great tangled mess of entire trees and rubble, smashing forward at great speed, backed by black water. Now I understood why the natives had moved out of the way.

A great jagged bolt of lightning blinded me, and the thunder was almost instantaneous, so loud it left my ears ringing. Charles put his arms around my neck in a stranglehold, Grace started crying too, and for the first time, I felt the baby move inside me. A few fat raindrops crashed to the ground, then the air became solid water. I'd never seen rain like this. I thought that out in the open, it may have been impossible to breathe, and wondered about the animals. Water smashed onto the rock-hard ground and bounced up again, and the noise of the waterfall on the iron roof was painfully deafening.

I took my children inside, and hid the three of us within my bed, with the blankets over our heads to shield us a little from the din.

Some time later, I felt a tapping on my head. I lifted the blanket to see Clara's grinning face. Her lips moved, but the noise of the rain masked her voice. Her hair was still wet, but she'd changed into a dry uniform. I sat up, and she put her mouth to my ear. "Family happy now in shed," I faintly heard her shout. "Old days, no sheds. This better. Sollie and me back."

We twisted heads so I could shout in her ear. "How long will it be so savage?"

"Soon easier. But will be flood outside. And much mud."

When I moved to get up, both children clutched for me, so I carried Charles while Grace clung to Clara. We looked out the window, and indeed the ground was covered in red liquid, the raindrops patterning it with goosebumps. More lightning flashed in all directions, but I couldn't even hear the thunder.

Even as we watched, the power of the rain reduced. Raindrops raised less of a splash, and the battering on the roof eased to mere noise.

Charles' lips moved, and I put my ear close. "Scared," he said. "No like rain."

"I know you don't like this, but it'll make plants grow. You'll see."

Outside the window, it became an ordinary downpour. I actually heard the back door bang.

Father and Mr. McQuade were shedding oilskin coats when I went to investigate. My husband was saying, "But Poole, how could I stay angry with you when you've brought me both men and rain?"

I knew better, and just hoped he wouldn't fool Father.

8. 1851-1852: Murder

It rained for nine days but when it passed, the river soon returned to its normal levels, the mud dried, and a magical cover of verdant grass and flowers beautified everything. Birds were everywhere and frogs sang among the reeds. It was like the drought had never been.

My husband took the men to check on all the animals, leaving Father and me to get reacquainted. He enjoyed Charles and Grace, and it was mutual. Grace's first word was "Gram."

During our first day together, I asked about Nanny.

"That was one of the things I'd written to you, my dove. I got her to serve behind the bar, and very popular she was too. And David Godfrey— oh, that's the man who'd, you know..."

I nodded my understanding.

"...he courted her, and after three months she agreed to marry him, and now they have a little son. She seems happy."

"But hadn't he... abused her before?"

"No, not exactly. His story is, he went to choose a servant from among the new arrival of female convicts, saw her and instantly fell in love. When they arrived at his house, he celebrated his good fortune by getting both of them drunk. In the morning, when Grace found herself in his bed she was furious, being a good, decent Christian woman, and would have none of him after. But she was with child from that one occasion. She wouldn't speak to him, merely performed her duties as a servant. But, he says now, he continued to love her all the more because he learned to respect her, and was glad to let her go to us when the child was born and died within an hour."

"I'm glad things have turned out well for her. She deserves it. I only wish..."

"Hmm?"

"That I also had a loving husband instead of a monster."

"Is he that bad?"

"Father, he is worse, and I worry for your safety. He may put a good face on it, but he won't forget that you bested him. Never, ever allow yourself to be alone with him."

"Surely, Amelia you're exaggerating. The lawless days are gone in this colony."

"Darling father, trust me. I don't want to lose you too."

Quite obviously, he changed the topic. "Amelia, I've never told you how I managed to marry your mother, and I think you should know. I fell in love with her when I first saw her. She was twelve, me fifteen. We became good friends, but as she grew, her heart was for my best friend, Bertrand. They got engaged, and Bertie asked me to be his best man. Of course I agreed, though what I wanted was to change places with him. Then, there was a tragedy. He had to go on short voyage, and his ship went down, everyone lost."

"Oh. That must have been hard for you."

"It was. I'd lost a friend. And yet I was glad that Susannah was now free. Then I felt horribly guilty for feeling that way."

I nodded. It's how I'd have felt.

"Susannah grieved terribly, and I was there for her. It took me four years of dogged determination before she agreed to marry me. You know she's always said I have more sticking power than a bathful of leeches. And I believe I made her happy, well, most of the time."

Then Charles came into the room, and took up his attention. Father had an endless fount of stories for him.

During this time when, once more, only the three old men were left behind, again I helped Foster with feeding the lambs, and father made himself useful too. Wherever he went, Charles wanted to be with him, and became his apprentice in a dozen activities. Mr. McQuade had never built this bond with his own son.

At last Ken arrived, as messenger. He said he wanted to be first back, to see Clara. All the men returned on the next day.

I welcomed Mr. McQuade with a suitable dinner, and that night, I am afraid, with all too much ficky-ficky. At the table, he said, "It's just as well I sold those animals some months ago. If I'd had more, more would have drowned."

Father nodded. "How badly are you affected?"

"The cattle mostly survived, only about fifty head drowned. But the sheep, being smaller and just before the shearing, that's something else. I'll need to buy more stock."

Wonderful. That implied a trip away, but I'd been thinking about the effect of the flash flood on the natives. "Mr. McQuade," I said.

"Hmm?"

"When the rain came, the Aboriginals sheltered in a shed, and appreciated that. Wouldn't it be better for them to live in proper housing? You may remember, we once discussed paying them, and that'd be a very suitable form."

I could see him contain his automatic anger. I was more than thankful for father's presence. "They don't like living in houses, Amelia. They're nomads, and have a need to move around. And they're too primitive to be able to use even slightly civilized facilities."

"Sir, the two maids do a superior job of it."

"They had to be painfully instructed over time, in great detail, and forced to do it right through threat of punishment."

"But–"

He could conceal his nature no more. "Enough," he snapped and gave me that intimidating look.

The months passed, and we settled into a routine. My pregnancy advanced, and thankfully my husband now desisted from his nightly assaults. I regularly asked my friends, so knew that so far he'd kept his word and left the native women alone too. No doubt he knew that with the safety of Father's presence, I was willing to confront him about it. Clara also swelled, and I arranged for Tillie to return in order to reduce the workload on her. She was also a nice young woman, and soon became fully competent under the tutelage of the other two. I was hoping my husband would notice that she learned fast, and without any threat of punishment, but he showed no sign and I was reluctant to provoke his displeasure by opening the topic.

Father continued to take an active role in the running of the station, and in the raising of his grandchildren. He didn't go on the drives that took the men away, and I was glad of that. After all, he'd been a town creature all his life.

One morning at breakfast, Mr. McQuade said, "Poole, I'd like your advice on something."

"Happy to, if I can help."

"Last time I was in Mildura, I saw a steam shovel at work. Marvelous machine. I'll get one here to dig a nice deep dam, as an insurance against the next drought. It's the location I need advice on." They went out to the office building to look at maps.

The next day, they rode out together. I thought nothing of it, but in the afternoon, Mr. McQuade rode back, leading Father's horse with his body laid across the saddle.

I had to scream as I rushed out. Hadn't I warned Father?

Mr. McQuade dismounted, and men were gathering. One fellow lifted Father down. Father's head moved like it was barely attached, and I noticed dusty scuff marks on his clothes.

Heavily, Mr. McQuade said, "A snake startled the horse, and Mr. Poole was thrown. Broke his neck I'm afraid."

I didn't believe him. The snake had just spoken. I caught his eyes, and he could see I knew.

It took hours before the two of us were alone, after a flurry of necessary activities. Then I stood face to face with him and said, "You murdered him."

"Amelia, you're being hysterical."

"He retained control over the men, and has been protecting me against your vicious treatment."

Without warning, his hand moved in a blur. I was lying at his feet, the left side of my face not there. Then the pain came.

"Vicious treatment? This is a sample of vicious treatment. Until now, I've treated you gently. I will not stand for such insolence."

I tried to stand, to collapse again. I felt the baby stir within me, so, kneeling on the carpet, I put a hand over my abdomen.

"Sir, you're a real hero, daring to hit a pregnant woman!"

He didn't respond but instead said, softly, "You know, I have great wealth. There is also a mystique to being a squatter. If I were to become a widower through some sad accident, I'd have no trouble finding a replacement."

He turned on his heel and walked out, shutting the door quietly behind himself.

When I could stand, I looked in the mirror. My left cheek was swollen and red, and I felt it throbbing in time with my heartbeat.

The door opened, and Sollie rushed in. "Mr. Mac say you fall and hurt your face... oh, poor lady!"

"I hurt my face the same way you did. I fell because he hit me." My speech sounded distorted.

She looked as shocked as I felt.

As she assisted me toward the bedroom, I saw Mr. McQuade striding up to a group of men outside. I said, "Sollie, I'll move my things into Mr. Poole's room. I shall sleep there."

She stopped and turned to face me. "That make him more angry!"

"I don't care. He can kill me, then I don't have to suffer his company any more."

"And Master Charles? And Miss Grace? And your new baby?"

"I intend to avoid his company. Maybe he won't even notice I'm not around."

By the evening, all my possessions were out of the master bedroom. I got the girls to prepare a soft meal I could eat with minimal pain, and ate it in my new bedroom. However, just before dark the door opened, and Mr. McQuade strode in.

I said, "Sir, a gentleman would knock before entering a lady's room."

"You're my wife, and owe me obedience."

"If you were my husband, you'd treat me with gentleness. You don't know the meaning of being gentle. Sir, you may kill me if you wish. I don't have the power to stop you. But before God, I renounce all vows I've made to you."

He stood there, glowering, but I was now used to this device. I kept talking as if he were listening. "Would you feel any loyalty to the murderer of your father?"

He was clearly ready to try a new tack. "Amelia, you're distraught by grief. I shall make allowance for that. Very well, out of compassion for your sad loss, I give you permission to sleep here until after the birth of our child."

The next day, Sollie told me that he'd gone to the Aboriginal camp and tried to ficky-ficky one of the young women. However, he could not get that wretched penis to stay hard. He dressed and stormed away. We both laughed, even though it still hurt my face. I hoped that the shame would keep him away from the brown women. I hoped the condition would become permanent. He'd be a much better knight without a lance!

James

Trudy said, "Amelia, you 'ave another boy."

"I'll call him James, after my father." He had lived every moment in my thoughts, even in my dreams. This way, he'd continue to live on in his new grandson.

As Clara attended to me, she stopped and rubbed her back. "Oh, having a baby inside is not comfortable," she complained. I noticed, incidentally, that her English was improving.

As she arched her body backward, Trudy looked sharply at her. "Clara," she said, "I want to examine ya."

"Huh? What's that mean?"

"I think the baby is the wrong way up, 'ead on top, like."

Sollie instantly looked worried. "That can be very painful, and kill mother maybe."

"I can usually fix it. C'mon, lemme look."

She prodded around. "Yeah, 'ead up, bum down. Mebbe in a couple o' weeks, I'll turn the bub, then we bind ya up tight so it can't turn back again. Then ya be right."

Grace was very interested in James. I was surprised that a child so young could be so gentle. I was glad that neither of my "big" children appeared to take after their father. Him, thankfully, I never saw. I avoided him, and this seemed to suit him as well. I was aware that he appointed one of the men, Horton, as foreman, and he himself spent increasing times away.

One day, Charles, all of three, asked me, "Mother, why is my name Charles?"

"Because in your father's family, every first son has been Charles. That's his name too."

"No. I mean, why my name not Neville?"

"Why should it be Neville?" I knew that he'd never encountered this name in his life.

He looked confused, so I stroked his wild black hair and pulled him close. "Do you want me to call you Neville?"

"No. But sometimes at night I go to sleep, then I'm Neville."

This was interesting. "What do you look like when you're Neville?"

"Uh, sometimes I have a red coat."

"Charles, how interesting. You know, soldiers wear red coats? So maybe in your dream you're Neville the soldier?"

"Maybe." He lost interest and ran off. The imagination of little children...

The gifts from my parents— my heart still cried at the thought of them— included books suitable for children, and although he was too young for reading, Charles was interested. I read him the Grimm fairytales, simplified stories from the bible, a book he loved with line drawings of animals. This was of course in between caring for Grace, feeding baby James and looking after the household.

Soon, I could return to working in the garden. Jones again had two young helpers, but I noticed that he was getting very frail. With the cold of winter, he was in obvious pain. So, I established a custom that he was welcome in the kitchen, near the fire. To save his pride, I found inside work for him like repairing shaky chairs and keeping locks oiled. Since Mr. McQuade was away, I talked with Horton, who readily assigned a third man to work with the plants, so Jones became more an instructor than laborer. "Ma'am, there is less work this time of the year anyway," Horton said. "Of course, I'll need to clear it with Mr. McQuade on his return, but since Jones is a very long term employee, I have no doubt he'll confirm the arrangement."

Excellent. I didn't need to interact with the monster myself.

Trudy modified my corset for Clara. She looked most uncomfortable, but thankfully it wasn't for long. When her labor started, I invited the native midwife to the house, winning Trudy's cooperation by saying that she could do a lot of good by teaching her how to handle a difficult birth. After about twelve hours of increasing suffering, Clara delivered a little brown boy, head first thanks to Trudy. While I excused her from doing any work, I did insist that she spend as much time as possible within the comfort of the house. Trudy soon moved on to another customer.

With the coming of summer, Jones returned to his usual tasks.

When Mr. McQuade came home from one of his jaunts, it was in the company of a mechanical monster: the steam shovel he'd used as the excuse to get my father alone. It was a huge, noisy thing worked by its own team. They started digging, and of course Charles was fascinated. Mr. McQuade actually took the little boy with him whenever he needed to go to the excavation, and one day Charles told me, "Father going to get me a horse!"

Good. I did wish he'd take more interest in his children, as long as it didn't extend to me.

Time passed, and I felt content. I slept alone, spent the day in pleasant company doing pleasant activities, and enjoyed raising my children. In a very real way, Clara's son, who had an unpronounceable name but was universally called Steve, was one of them.

When the seasons turned, and we had an unusually cold winter, once more I contrived to get Jones inside much of the time, into warmth and comfort.

One miserable day Sollie, Tillie and I were preparing dinner in the kitchen. James was in an ingenious chair the brown men had made, which could safely hang off the table. Grace sat on the little chair, drawing with chalk on a slate, and Charles was cutting up green beans under Jones' close supervision. Suddenly, the back door banged open and Mr. McQuade filled the opening. "Jones, what the hell are you doing in here?" he roared.

I said, "Sir, he's here at my invitation. He's been very useful with a multitude of jobs."

He ignored me. "Out!" he shouted.

I persisted. "Hasn't Horton talked to you about the gardening arrangements a year ago?"

Finally he looked at me, as at a stranger. "The disposition of men is none of your business. I will not have an ex-convict within my house."

Jones went.

The girls told me, having heard from their husbands, that he was made to work outside in all weathers. Within a week he started a terrible cough, and died soon after. I hoped my husband felt happy about having murdered another good man.

9. 1855-1857: Susannah

From his sixth birthday, Charles spent time each morning with his father, whenever that man was at home. He also enjoyed learning reading, writing, numbers, and about the wide world from me, and looking after his brother and sister. When Mr. McQuade was away, I often took my children to the Aboriginal camp, and Uncle Gurry told us stories. I noted an odd thing. Although at first James could barely make up a three-word sentence, he was as fascinated by the myths of the natives as Charles. He had a special bond with Uncle Gurry, to the point that I wondered, if he had dreams like Clara's and Charles', would they be that of being one of the brown people of this land? Why not, if an Irishman could return as my Clara?

On Charles' eighth birthday, Mr. McQuade sent Clara for me. She, now a mother of three, led me to the living room, where I found him sitting at ease, sipping whiskey. When we were alone, he said, "Amelia, it's time for Charles to go to school. I've told him this morning, and want you to prepare what he needs to take."

No consultation. Arrangements made. Typical.

Looking at my face, he said, "You look like you've lost a pound and found a penny." He grinned at his own witticism.

"Sir, in a normal family, there would have been prior discussion on such a matter."

"Yes but we're not a normal family, are we? Of course, we could resume marital relations?" His eyes gleamed.

"There was no consultation before we stopped such activities. Very well, I'll prepare for him. However, I'm sure the school will have a list of materials we'll need to buy."

"My sister Joan will handle all that in Sydney."

"Well then, if you'll excuse me." I turned to go.

"Amelia?"

"Yes?"

"Y'know, I've forgotten what a good-looking wench you are. I think we SHALL resume marital relations."

Oh my God. Oh no. I went through the door, then ran to the kitchen. "Sollie," I asked, "do we still have emu oil in the house?"

"No. Will I go to the camp and–"

"Knowing him, there mightn't be time!"

Tillie rushed out the back door to the Coolgardie safe, a new invention. She flicked the wet cloth aside, opened the wire mesh door and took out a jar of butter. "This do," she said.

I went to the privy and anointed myself, then returned to Grace, James and Steve, whom I'd been teaching in the playroom.

He stood outside its door, and his hand became a steel manacle around my wrist. His breath stank of whiskey.

Any show of resistance would result in a violent battering. Besides, I couldn't let him see an Aboriginal child with his offspring. So, softly, I said, "Sir, you're hurting me. Please act in a civilized manner."

"Amelia, my love, it's time to return to being a good little wife." He started walking toward the master bedroom, and I could do nothing but follow, almost running. He kicked the door shut behind us and let my wrist go. "Strip," he ordered, and started shedding his own clothes.

When I hesitated, he reached out a giant paw and grabbed the collar of my blouse. He tugged so hard that several buttons popped off. "I'm happy to help," he said with a leer.

During the years of separation, I'd forgotten how uncomfortable this disgusting act was. He'd grown a potbelly, making things even worse. I was squashed flat so I couldn't breathe, and his stinking, sweaty chest literally rubbed against my nose while he pumped inside me for an interminable time before finishing. I did note that his penis was now smaller, and didn't stay hard as long. Perhaps age would save me from too many repeats.

When he allowed me, I dressed sufficiently to be half-decent, and went for a thorough wash.

That evening, I was eating with my children as usual when I heard the bell ring. Soon, Tillie put a frightened face in through the door. "He wants you in dining room," she said.

I went, but stayed near the door. "Mr. McQuade?" I asked.

"Since we're husband and wife again, you should dine with me."

"Sir, I am supervising the children at dinner."

"Very well. Even James is old enough to accompany us. Tomorrow morning, I'm looking forward to husband, wife and children breaking fast together."

"Sir, we are not husband and wife. Being taken by force is not the loving, consensual act the bible condones."

He heard me out with mock respect. "My lovely, if you will give it willingly, I'll take it gently. If not, I'll take it anyway. I'm expecting you back in my bed tonight. And if you're not there, I'll fetch you myself."

So, I lost my darling eldest son and returned to slavery. Ten months later I gave birth to a beautiful girl I named Susannah.

A week after the birth, I sat on a canvas chair on the back veranda feeding Susannah, when Mr. McQuade strode up to me. He stood there, looking down. "You ready to resume your duties to me yet?" he demanded.

I wished I had a gun. "Sir, I myself will never be ready. But also my body is still healing."

He went away, and I heard the back door slam. Then, just as the baby had fallen asleep and I was ready to stand, I heard a scream, then another. I rushed inside. The sounds came from the master bedroom.

I burst in. Clara lay in a twisted heap on the floor, merely whimpering now. Her bottom half was naked, and blood pooled between her legs. Her right eye was closed by a swelling, and more blood trickled from a cut above it. The monster was naked, and his penis hung flaccid, but smeared with blood.

"You beast!" I shouted. I put Susannah on the bed and fell to my knees next to Clara.

He grabbed my arm and hurled me out through the door so I crashed against the far wall of the corridor.

I needed witnesses. I struggled to my feet and turned to run outside where I knew Trudy and two gardeners were working.

He caught me before I reached the kitchen, and dragged me by the hair back into the bedroom.

The pool of blood between Clara's legs was now enormous. Even her good eye was closed and she breathed with an odd little gurgle.

"Make a fuss and you'll join her," he said in a voice of anticipation, as if he was hoping to carry out the threat.

"This is murder and rape. You can hang for this, squatter or no."

"Then I need to protect myself, don't I? I told you many years ago, you're replaceable."

"Kill me. I'd rather join my friend than breathe the same air as you!"

His hands formed an open circle, reaching for my throat, but then he drew them back and smiled, in a way a stranger would see as friendly and charming. "Actually, no. I'll enjoy having you around more than wringing your neck. But you know, I only need one son to carry on the line. The second is unnecessary, and daughters are a mere nuisance. You'll help me to cover up this unfortunate accident, or I'll kill your whelps."

"You're a monster."

He laughed. "I like being a monster. I like the power. That's why the devil gave me a big, strong body, and a position of wealth and power, so I can do his work."

He tore the mirror from its mounting and hurled it to the ground where it shattered into pieces. Clara didn't even move as the needles of glass struck her. "The little black slut came in here, and somehow got the mirror to hit her and she bled to death."

"And that tore her dress off? And cut her private parts?"

He gently picked Susannah up with one hand, and ripped a blanket off from under the quilt with the other. He put the baby down and bent to wrap my friend's body in the blanket. "We're far from the authorities here. We can't leave a carcass for any length of time in this heat. She'll be buried tonight, and who is to know after that?"

"Sollie and Tillie will have heard the screams first, the crash much later."

"Abo sluts. Will their word be accepted against mine? Anyway, if necessary I can kill them too. I'll enjoy it, especially since they're your pets."

"Well, I know. And–"

He picked the baby up and held her with two little feet in his hand, head hanging down. "And if you don't back me up, I'll belt her head into yours." Again, he smiled sweetly.

The utterly depraved monster meant it.

10. 1867-1874 Charlotte

Charles turned eighteen in 1867, and returned to learn the running of the Station from his father. He was two inches shorter than Mr. McQuade, with my slim build, but had a whipcord strength. He and I had stayed friends through our correspondence, and I knew that he'd become very close with my brother Nigel, his wife Liz and their three children.

While the three of us were home, he spent most of his time working outside. But soon Mr. McQuade went away, leaving him in nominal charge, although I noted that he treated the foreman with respect and asked his advice on all issues. During our first dinner with just the two of us, he said, "Mother, I didn't write about some things because Aunt Joan warned me that father would certainly read my letters, but I'm now aware that you've lived in hell."

"How?"

"Aunt Joan told me. When they were young, father used to force himself both on her and on Aunt Margaret. Also, he was violent with both of them and Uncle Gerard. All three of them hate him."

"I'm shocked, but Charles, not surprised. Your father... how can I put it? Has a sort of blindness. You know, some people are unable to see colors but see everything in shades of gray? It's called Daltonism. He has a similar blindness to morality, decency, the feelings of others. To him, sadly, other people are not human like he considers himself to be, but mere objects: either tools to be used, or obstacles to be removed."

"Mother, now that I'm here, I'll do my best to protect you."

"Darling, don't risk yourself. Get in his way too much and... and you could end up dead!"

He paled. "Would he murder?"

"He has in the past." I told him of my father's death, Clara's rape and murder, and Jones the gardener.

"And you've had to live with that?"

"I had no choice. At least, nowadays he has no physical capability to molest me or any other woman. All I can do is to keep praying to God, and where possible staying out of his way."

Of course, the children returned every school holidays. The first time after Charles' homecoming, Grace, a copy of me at seventeen except for her dark hair, brought along her best friend Charlotte, a slim little blonde with laughing eyes and a wicked sense of humor, who had us laughing much of the time. Her father ran a horse stud some distance from Sydney, and maybe because of this she liked nothing better than to ride horses astride like a man. She could crack a whip, throw a lasso and delighted in beating Charles and James in riding races.

On the last day they were getting into the coach when she said to me, very prettily, "Mrs. McQuade, I wish you could visit us at Dunadd. It's the oldest and best horse stud in New South Wales, and we breed the best horses."

"And clearly the best daughters too."

Grace was already in the coach. She leaned out. "They breed good sons too, Mother. I wish I could've brought Charlotte's brother David along too."

Standing beside me, Charles looked down at the little blonde. "Hmm, maybe we can do an exchange. How about your family keep Grace, and we keep you?"

"Get away with you!" Charlotte blushed deeply, and clambered up into the coach.

After this, whenever a trip to Sydney was necessary, Charles managed to be the one to go, and I was not surprised that, upon Grace's eighteenth birthday, we had a double wedding.

When Charles brought the matter up, he did so by getting his father and me into the same room, quite an accomplishment. He presented us with a letter from David Holmbury, asking for Grace's hand, and announced that he wished for nothing better than to marry Charlotte.

"I've made enquiries about the family," Mr. McQuade said, "and they're suitable. However, the weddings shall take place here."

"Oh, I was looking forward to seeing the famous Dunadd stud," I answered.

"It's a family tradition. The McQuade marries at Bruchan. Grace may marry wherever she likes."

"Father, the world is changing. In these modern times, we should not be so fixed in our ways. And the practicalities would be far easier there."

He turned a cold face to Charles. "When I'm dead, you can make the decisions. Here, or I put not a penny into it."

Eventually he won the silly argument. Well, if I couldn't leave my twenty-year prison, at least I had visitors to look forward to, and a wonderful occasion to plan. To assist me, I wrote to my four sisters-in-law. Liz was too involved in running the hotel to spend months away from home. Gerard's wife didn't reply — more likely she did but said something Mr. McQuade took offence to, so that I never saw the letter. Margaret and Joan arrived together, with a laden four-horse cart.

Joan had an easy, loving relationship with Charles, almost a second mother. I got to like both ladies, and they taught me all I needed to learn about organizing a major social function. We set up a small tent town to house visitors and imported staff. The modern techniques of preserving food allowed us to stock up enough in most things, and two butchers were hired to process the animals Mr. McQuade provided. A band of four musicians and an expert at making photographic pictures were hired.

The playroom was the second largest room in the house. I cleared it, and we had fun furnishing and decorating it for Charles and Charlotte.

The wedding went off exactly as planned. Everyone behaved, and there was a pretence of harmony. Surprise guests came as well: Mr. and Mrs. David Godfrey, with their three children. I hugged Nanny, and we cried with joy on each other's shoulders. To my eyes, she didn't look any older, and the bond of love between her and her husband was wonderful. He often reached out a hand to touch her, I suspect without even realizing he was doing so, and kept anticipating her wishes.

My main sadness was the absence of Mother and Father.

Charlotte had a good influence on the atmosphere at Bruchan. Even my husband behaved himself decently, and since his penis now refused to rise, I felt only minimal distress at having to share his bedroom. And soon, Charlotte presented us with a little boy (lucky!) of course named Charles. Two weeks later, Grace gave birth to a daughter, whom she named Amelia.

Soon after the double wedding, James prevailed upon his father to finance studies at Oxford. He wanted to become a doctor, because his joy in life was to reduce suffering. Mr. McQuade responded: "Being a doctor is no worse for a younger son than any other profession. As you know, my brother is a judge of the High Court now. But this idiocy about reducing suffering—"

"Father, why is that an idiocy?"

"There has always been suffering and always will be. As long as it's not me suffering, who cares?"

I signaled James with my eyes to drop the matter.

As for my baby: from her regular letters, and what she said during her visits, I was aware that Susannah was doing unusually well at school. During her summer holidays when she was fourteen, she confided in me that this was a source of frustration. "Mother, I have the ability to do anything. But, as a female, my destiny is to be a wife and mother."

"Darling, my mother, whom I named you after, had the same problem. She married a man who loved and respected her for her abilities. During their life together, he was the hand, she the controlling brain, and this made them both happy."

"It shouldn't have to be so! When I reach adulthood, I won't even be allowed to vote, or to sign a contract. Why not?"

I smiled at her vehemence. "Because men have more physical power than women, and they've organized the world this way."

"Well, I want to change it."

I wished her luck with all my heart.

Six years later, she married a lawyer with similar attitudes — one of Gerard's junior associates. Again, the wedding was at Bruchan, because Mr. McQuade managed to contrive it so. I think his obsession was to prevent me from ever leaving the place. A wonderful aspect was the guest of honor Dr. James McQuade, freshly returned from England with his new bride Rosanna, a lovely girl with bright red hair and a baby already on the way.

11. 1874-1894 Freedom

The tyrant was dead.

Lying in the bed that had been the location of so much of my suffering, he seemed shrunken, insignificant, a mere thing.

Charles and I looked at each other. He held out his arms and we embraced. After an unknown time, he murmured, "Mother, from now on your life can be how you want it."

"Thank the Lord, you're more like me than like him."

"Mother, the thanks is due to you. I've never told you, but when I was still a little boy, I decided that your way was better than his. I chose to shape my life with you as my example."

"As for me, Charles, my wonderful children have made my life worthwhile."

"Pity the others are all far away. We need to notify them."

The funeral couldn't wait, in the heat of the Outback. We found a Presbyterian minister, and put the mortal remains of my nemesis in the ground.

I happily moved out of the main bedroom, making way for Charles — the new Mr. McQuade — and Charlotte. The smaller room with its window overlooking my rose garden suited me fine, and the single bed held no memories of pain and abuse.

Three months later, we conducted a more formal ceremony attended by all the children and their families. Apart from James all had done well financially, but he'd done better: he held a government position looking after the health of Aboriginals in the Sydney area. He could have earned lots more in private practice, but he glowed with contentment.

We erected a headstone for Mr. McQuade, one that gave me a great deal of quiet joy for the following twenty years. Strong as he used to be, he was not strong enough to lift this stone!

Three days before Christmas, an ox cart arrived carrying a mysterious wooden crate. Charles managed to avoid my questions about its contents. One of the men accompanying it was introduced as Mr. Poynter. Charles had a number of conferences with him, so I assumed it had something to do with an improvement in the running of the Station.

When I emerged from my room on Christmas day, a beautiful chestnut-colored miniature grand piano stood in a corner of the lounge room, positioned so that the player would look out at the herb garden. Two books of musical scores were placed next to it: piano solos by Chopin and another by my other favorite, Beethoven. Mr. Poynter was there too, dressed in decent clothes but hanging back. Charles now explained that he was a piano tuner.

Naturally, I was rusty beyond belief, both in playing and reading music. Instead of stumbling around the keyboard in front of an audience, I played that ancient Irish dance that keeps running through my head, sometimes for days. It brings me memories of two beloved women: Nanny and Clara.

Lessons

I was happy as a child: loved, secure, believing the world was a flower that would bloom for my pleasure. Mr. McQuade spoiled all that. With his passing, I became content. Charles encouraged me to travel, so I spent time with each of my children, enjoying the wonderful role of grandmother. Accompanied by Rosanna and her two darlings, I traveled in one of the marvelous, modern steam-assisted ships to Britain, where I met her family. However, for a reason I cannot explain, my main interest was Ireland, particularly its west coast.

Then, over the years, aches and pains came. The top of my back bowed forward, and eventually I shrank by half a head.

At last, I took to my bed. I said to Charles, "My dear, call the others home. I want to say good-bye to them."

"I'm happy to call them, Mother, but it's nonsense. You'll get better, you'll see."

"My darling son, there is nothing wrong with dying. Everyone does it, sooner or later. I've lived a long life, and am tired."

They came, and I kissed each, giving them my blessing. Then I told them firmly to leave me alone.

The sun, the hot sun that used to distress me so much, poured in through the window. Lying in my bed, I looked out at the roses, kept lovingly blooming by the staff just for me, despite the shortage of water.

I'd spent most of my life at a place I'd have avoided had I known about it in advance, with a man I detested and feared, and yet, looking back, I was content. And then, I realized, nothing hurt any more.

The light faded into blackness, and I faced a Light far brighter. Unspoken words sounded in my mind: "My beloved child, you've paid your restitution. Have you learned your Lessons?"

With that, I remembered. Dermot: old before his years, wracked by pain far worse than Amelia had ever experienced, wrecked by whiskey, hating, committing the unspeakable crime that had led me, willingly before birth, to endure the life of Amelia.

"I've done no violence to anyone, and have avoided causing hurt or harm," I thought. "And I've rejected alcohol, and have progressed along the path to Love."

"I shall now assist you in evaluating your life, from this moment back to your birth. You'll experience the effects you've had on others, so you can feel the impact of your actions. Also, there is unfinished business. As Dermot you couldn't wait, but had to be born immediately. His life also needs to be examined in full."

I started on this task. There is no time when there is no body. There just Is. I knew of my loved ones growing, aging, the petty world of humans changing, but my existence had no time. At last, when I reached my birth as Amelia, I no longer felt so self-righteous.

That poor man, Charles McQuade, had been selected as my teacher. He was the way he was, because I'd needed precisely such a person. He was, I learned, a very young soul, this having been only his second life as a human, while I'd lived many lives before Padraig — that's why he was capable of such undying love. I also realized, I'd been given an opportunity to be his teacher, to lead him toward being able to love, and had instead confirmed his insanity by accepting his view of himself.

Mr. McQuade missed out on so much! He could not conceive of the joy of giving, only the trivial satisfaction of taking. And I had hated, hated, hated. I knew that I still had to learn the major lesson of forgiveness.

Then I needed to review my life as Dermot. I drowned with Rory MacTavish but felt the wonderful love for Jimmy, whom I knew to be Amelia's son James, just as my daughter Susannah was actually the returning spirit of my mother. I could appreciate all the wonderful qualities that had made Dermot into a leader, yet was devastated by Clinton Ryrie's terror at the thought of being turned into a cockroach; Captain Morton's dismay at realizing that the Irish had outsmarted him, though they were so stupid that only terror and pain could influence them. I felt his despair as his lifeblood gushed out of his wound, the exit hole where his penis had been. One by one, I experienced the deaths of all the soldiers I'd killed, Private John Hall being the worst. He was thinking of his Sally, hoping she wasn't cheating on him back home. He stepped into the latrine, reaching down to undo his britches, when he sensed a presence behind him. Unbelievably, two strange soldiers were there. How dare they! The brown eyes of one stared into his, then he felt agony in his chest. Pain made him open his mouth, but he felt himself picked up, tipped upside down, and... and his head submerged in the horrible contents of the shithole. Death came too slowly after that, and my spirit cried for him. I knew I'd need to expiate for such contemptuous acts.

Then there was Lieutenant Hector Howard's agony and disbelief as an Irishman half his size bested him. I learned what had turned him into the monster the Irish perceived him to be: as a boy in London, he'd seen his mother raped and killed by a gang of immigrant Irish louts. He was having his revenge on all the Irish, as Dermot was having his revenge on all the English.

There were the others. One by one, I felt their despair, understood their motivation. Particularly frightening was the death of Captain Alfred Cunningham. As the life was being choked out of him, he knew he was looking at a black-faced devil from hell.

"Enough," I said to my Guide. "I've learned that hate only begets hate. Is there a need to go on, to keep going back?"

But I was required to continue, through the three years of solitary action in which I was responsible for death after death, through the months of the war, back to Dermot's birth. I knew his great love for Maeve — my Nanny — and the terrible anguish at her fate, the tragedy that poisoned the rest of his life.

At the end, my Guide asked me, "What is your wish now? I know you've identified many lessons you need to learn, and there is also your previous determination to develop the ability to heal hurt, to lead people from despair and helplessness to strength and Love."

"Oh, is there a life where people are not divided by race, religion, belief, nationality? Where no person hates another because of minor differences? And even more, is there a life where male and female don't exist? So much of my suffering has been tied up with male and female!"

"Very well," She said, "You shall have that as your next life. You realize, that's only possible as an entirely different life form, on another planet?"

"That's fine. I'm not that fond of humans and their cruelties."

"The being I have for you is an intelligent plant who is able to walk around."

I can't imagine that. I guess... I guess I'll find out all about it."

My Guide smiled within my consciousness.

May I ask a question?"

"Of course."

"What would have happened if Dermot... I... had made the right choice?"

"Dermot's body was worn out. Had he refused to give in to hate and envy, his heart would have stopped anyway, damaged by whiskey. And two babies were conceived at the same time. Susannah Poole had a girl fetus, while Grace Dennehy had a boy. Because you needed to be Amelia, I myself inhabited Grace's child, so he could die immediately. But had you chosen right, another soul would have become Amelia, one who'd have no interest in Charles McQuade. As you know, the father of Grace's baby married her and fathered other children later on. However, you didn't know that his spirit also has a special connection with hers. In Dermot's life, he'd been her father. Their destiny in this life was to wed and live happily together. And now, my love, it's time for you to experience a life without male and female, without hate of one person against another for minor reasons."

Book 3: Other Worlds

1. 1910-1943: Walking Plant

Hatching

I hear Mother, within my being: "My darling fruit, it's time to hatch. Now you'll face danger and suffering. I'll be helping, and so will many other people, but only the fastest and smartest can survive. I love you, but now you must go."

I know what to do, but don't know how I know. I lift the part of my body with a hard thorn poking out, and draw it along the white luminescence above, which has been there as long as I've been aware. My shell splits. My thorn falls off, and I step out.

Many-many of my sisters are running about. We all emerged together. Mother stands among us, huge, powerful and protective. The earth wall she built before she'd seeded us stands all around, and God is shining down, so much stronger and more beautiful than through the shell!

Something swoops from above. Mother lifts a leg and knocks her away, over the wall.

There is a puddle of water, and we all suck up as much as we can hold. Then Mother sucks the remaining mud dry.

"Be ready to run, my loves," I hear her, and also the voices of many others outside the wall, calling out encouragement.

Mother puts four of her eight feet on the wall and pushes. The wall falls outward, and my sisters swarm that way. I hear them scream as many-many Others swoop on them.

I'm not running like my sisters. Instead, I climb up mother's leg. I don't know how I know to suck with the end of each of my legs, and let go sucking in just the right rhythm, and I can go up, up so high, till I'm sucking with all eight legs on her underside.

Mother is outside. Upside down, I see a mad turmoil of battling shapes: people and Others fighting. Some Others fly down to snatch a baby, or to attack a bigger person. Some are on the ground, many different shapes. All want to capture us babies to suck our water. Water is life.

Mother jumps on a big Other, and I'm nearly shaken off. The Other is sucking water from three of my sisters. Mother's legs penetrate her skin and she is hurting her while sucking her water. I hang on, terrified. The Other lets my sisters go, and one of them is able to move. For the other two, it's too late, They're just empty shells.

A smaller Other snatches my live sister. Mother jumps again and her eight legs rip the small Other apart. The big Other turns and its legs strike at Mother.

I fall off, so scurry to get clear. A flyer swoops for me, but I skitter to the side, then I'm among the trees. Enemies lurk here too. I find a little cavity under a tree root and cower there, although it's terrible, being out of God's light.

The fighting goes on and on, many-many people trying to save us babies, and losing water and maybe life in doing so. Unfortunately, I'm getting weaker and weaker, being out of God's light, and must move or die anyway. I crawl out, into a patch of light no bigger than little me, and soak up power. I'm looking everywhere, ready to run.

I feel stronger after awhile, and am still full of water. I climb up the trunk of the tree, out along a branch, then onto the underside of a leaf much bigger than I am. I hope that this way flying Others won't notice me, and God's light coming through the leaf is enough to keep me alive. When I get thirsty I puncture the leaf with one leg. I don't know how I know to do that, it's just natural. I suck the juice till the leaf turns yellow and dead-looking. Then I realize that's dangerous. I crawl back onto the branch, and onto another leaf.

A flyer goes by, but doesn't seem to have noticed me. All the same, I'm too terrified to move, long after she's gone. Then I suck this leaf dry, and move to the next one.

All the fighting has stopped, and I can only hear people from far away. Maybe I've survived. I keep moving from leaf to leaf, sucking life.

Somebody says, "Baby, come down, it's safe."

"How do you know I'm here? I wasn't talking."

"I can see all the dead leaves. It could be a small Other, but this is right next to the newest hatching."

"You're smart." I am climbing down the tree.

"Only the smart survive. That's why so many must die, so we can keep improving."

She is also young, only about three times my size. She gently strokes me with two legs, saying, "I'm too small yet to fight the Others and save babies, but I want to help by looking for survivors. And here you are."

"Thank you. How many survived from your hatching?"

"Only me now." She sounds very sad.

Something moves nearby and I scurry for my hole under the root. My friend flattens herself under a dead leaf on the ground. The Other going by is long and thin, with many-many legs. We wait, motionless, long after she is gone. In the meantime, I send a question to my sisters. Only four answer. Of those many-many babies, five of us are still alive.

Growing

Each time I suck water from something alive, I grow. God always shines with Her blessed energy. But then someone says, "Rain coming." Hiding with my friend, always hiding, I ask her why this is important.

"Clouds get between God and us, and it can get so dark that if it goes on too long, little people like us can die. But water falls from the clouds, and that's good." Soon it grows darker and darker, and we slow down. A very bright light strikes from the cloud to the ground, and everything shakes. Then indeed, water falls from the sky. We scurry around sucking it up, but it's tasteless, without nourishment. My friend says, "This is how all water comes. The standing plants need it, and everyone and everything lives by sucking good water from them. All moving life needs the standing plants."

I get terribly weak before the clouds go and God shines again. But then everything else moves too, and a large flyer nearly catches us.

Later, two people find us. One is Mother. She's been badly hurt. One of her legs is half-length, and her color is too light. She says to the other adult, "Thank you sister."

The other one has many little bumps all over her. They're seeds, so she is ready to fruit too. She says, "You're growing back. When you're well again, I'll build my wall."

Mother says to me, "I knew you'd survive. You think differently, and that's good."

"Five of us are still alive."

"I know. Friends are looking after the others. We'll now protect you."

So, my friend and I grow in safety. Sometimes Others come near, but very few are as big as the two adults.

I find our body to be marvelous, so simple yet graceful and strong. Everyone else accepts it without thought, but it's as if I were comparing to something else. All life is more or less like us, only the shape is different. Even flyers and standing plants are like us in many ways. Also, every person has her own voice, so we merely need to listen within to know who the speaker is. All the same, I miss having a special thought to identify each person.

Mother's damaged leg grows back, and she becomes the right color. So, her sister goes away to fruit, and Mother needs to go with her to feed her. All the many kinds of Others will know about the fruiting, so that'll be a dangerous place. It's better for us little ones to stay here, but life is danger.

I have grown. My legs are now twice as long as the thickness of my body. I'm among the grass and other small standing plants, looking for danger, always looking, but everything is safe right now. I stand so that half of me is in God's light so I can grow, and half in shadow so anything seeing me won't notice my shape. Everything is still safe, so I lift a leg, and put it against a standing plant, make a hole and suck water.

My friend screams! I run that way, but something big has her. Three of the Other's legs penetrate her body. I can do nothing but hide. Far away, people are screaming, being angry. There is fighting, so I know nobody will be able to help me. I'm alone. Life goes on, and my task is to grow and stay alive. I'm terribly sad for a long time. Death is always with us.

Sometimes clouds block God's light and rain falls. Sometimes the ground shakes so that even big trees fall over, and sometimes everything is still and quiet... but dangerous because Others can be anywhere. Still, I keep growing.

A big Other comes so I climb a tree. I recognize her: she is the first one Mother had fought at my hatching. When she is under me I jump on her with all my feet penetrating. I'm hurting her and sucking her water, then I jump off and run up the tree again.

The Other is after me, but she is too big to climb up. She charges into the tree, trying to shake me off, but the tree is too thick. I send her a rude thought, although Others can't hear people, just like we can't hear them. At last she lumbers off.

2. Adult

I'm half grown, and now big enough to help at a hatching. I've often spent time with people, but we soon need to separate when we run out of food. I wait outside the earth walls the new mother has built. Rain has just stopped, so the babies will have water to start their lives. The mother is inside with all the seeds waiting to hatch. We know this, and so do many Others.

I use my trick of hiding on a high branch. A big flyer goes by, not noticing me. I jump, all my legs sinking into her. I work my legs in deep, and we fall down together. As the flyer hits the ground she splits. That's one Other who won't hurt babies!

Something big is coming so I run. She stops to suck water from the dead flyer and I turn, jump, hurt her and run again. As she comes after me, another person not much bigger than me attacks her, so I turn and hurt her again. She runs away.

The wall falls down! Many-many babies swarm out, with the mother stepping among them. Now everything is confusing and terribly fast. I attack and am attacked. Something comes up out of the ground and its front grasps a baby. I jump on her, three of my legs penetrating. She lets the baby go, so I pick her up in three other legs, and jump away toward the forest. There is a moment of quiet. "Climb on me," I say to the baby, then again climb a tree, searching for flying or climbing Others, but we're alone.

I tell the baby to hide on the underside of a leaf, the way I did when I was her size. I hide in a spot between two branches and watch for flyers.

A long Other is climbing up the tree. I think she has noticed the baby, but I'm waiting. When she is near, I suddenly shove her with four feet, holding on with four, and she falls, twisting and turning in the air.

I'm full of water, or I'd climb down to empty the broken body.

"Thank you," the baby says. "You're so clever!"

"You need to be clever," I pass on the lesson. "Only the smart survive. I'll look after you and teach you tricks."

Still, I know I could die, just like my protector did.

So, there are two of us. She grows, I grow.

Again, the ground shakes and there is a black cloud in the sky. Only, this cloud stays still far away, and no rain comes. I ask and an adult explains, "That's God making a new mountain. Rock is so hot it flows like water, and kills everything in its path."

After a long time, the earth stops shaking, and the black cloud shrinks. Then I hear a call for help. I say good-bye to my little friend, hoping she'll survive. I go fast, but still very careful, always careful, and join many-many people watching a hole in the ground. It's the nest of a long many-legged Other, and now it's our turn to attack their babies when they come out. They're water and so life for us, and also if we kill them when they're little, they won't grow to kill us.

Many different kinds of Others are around too, and I catch one and suck her empty.

Here comes the swarm of little ones. They aren't protected by adults of their kind in the way we protect ours, but they're very hard to catch. I try my best, but am unable to get hold of even one. All the same, people and other Others are everywhere, and I think most of these babies are caught.

At least I killed one Other, although of a different kind.

Many more times I cooperate with other people, and many more times I defend a new hatching. I'm now too big to climb trees, but am known as a very good protector of babies. Many younger people are alive because of my help and teaching. I keep growing, and at last I'm an adult. Eight people, the ceremonial number, come to me. One of them is Mother, and I'm glad she is still alive. Another is the Old One, the biggest person. She likes to welcome as many new adults as she can.

First, we fill ourselves with water, as much as we can hold and then more. Then, we go toward the High Place. This means walking up a steady, gentle slope. First we pass through forest like everywhere else, but the trees get smaller and smaller. The air gets cooler, but God's light gets stronger. As we climb, we get to where there are no trees at all, only grasses of different kinds, and that gets more and more sparse, till there is nothing but bare ground. This is too high for rain ever to fall. The High Place is a plain, but it's closer to God than even the tallest mountains elsewhere.

The others stop and give their blessing. Each blows her pollen all over me in a golden cloud. Now I must go on alone, and stand under God's light at the High Place where nothing can live. I keep going up, as fast as I can. Sometimes, people run out of water before they can return, then they die.

After a long walk, I'm at the closest point to God. There She is, right above me, huge, white and hot although the air is icy cold.

I stand there. Around me is a flat plain, curving down in all directions.

This is absolute peace, and I thank God for my survival. Very few babies live long enough to get here.

I enjoy God's fierce light upon my body, and after a long time feel itchy all over. That's the seeds germinating. It takes the light of the High Place to start new life for my kind.

Now I walk back, down to my waiting mentors. When I reach them, I'm almost empty of water.

To complete the ceremony, each of the eight allows me to suck water from her body. I take as little as I can, imposing as little pain as I can. When I've received the eight gifts, we return to our natural home.

My mentors advise me on a good spot. Many-many mothers have seeded here, so no standing plants grow. We wait for rain to soften the ground, hunting widely, and when we can't find prey, we suck from the standing plants, but never so much that we damage them. All this time, I'm itchy all over, and the bumps of seeds keep growing. Mostly they're on my top surface, but even my underside has some.

At last the rain comes, and we need to stay quiet while God's light is hidden, but when the cloud passes, I start to mix mud for my wall. I've never seen anyone do this, and have never been taught, but it's one of those things we know. I move my eight legs rhythmically, churning up mud, and raising it into a wall that will enclose me within an area the same shape as me — twice as long as wide — with a smooth curve all around. When it's finished it's taller than me, with a hollow in the middle of a flat space. When my babies hatch, they'll need that hollow filled with water.

I can't get out of course, but my eight loving mentors hunt for me. We talk all the time so I know what they're doing. They kill some Other but leave plenty of water inside, and toss the body over the wall for me.

Working with care, I scatter my seeds on the flat surface, so each gets plenty of God's light. Now my only task is to guard them, and to build up strength for the coming battle. Every mother gets hurt, sometimes killed, but it's worth it if a few babies survive.

Three times, an underground Other pops up, but before she can grab a seed I pull her from the ground, suck her dry and throw the empty body over the wall. Meantime, my mentors and I have a game with flyers. They warn me when one approaches. As she swoops I bat her outside, to be caught and killed by somebody, who then throws the body back to me to feed on.

The ground shakes from an earthquake. I'm terrified my seeds may get hurt, but no cracks appear in the ground within. The wall does crack in several places. Me on the inside and my mentors on the outside glue up the cracks, sacrificing water from our bodies.

All this time, my darling seeds keep growing. At last they're the right size, and I haven't lost even one.

Now we need rain. I hear people gather, ready for the coming battle, and other big people also pass me bodies full of water, strengthening me.

I see a very bright flash — distant lightning. Gradually, there are more of them, closer, until a thick cloud dims God's light. Then rain pours down. It goes on and on, and I'm getting weaker. As an adult, I know I'll outlast the darkness, but I'm worried for the younger people out there, waiting to fight for my babies.

At last the rain stops. A flash of God's light shines onto me and my seeds. The edge of the cloud blocks it again, and the light comes and goes for a while. I wait. I wouldn't want my babies to start with the handicap of clouds in the sky.

Then the Old One says to me, "Darling, wake your fruit."

So, I tell them to hatch. Everywhere, the many-many seedpods split open, and cute little people emerge, running around in every direction. I get them to have their first drink from the puddle, which is bigger than I expected, then I have my fill too.

We're ready. I knock down the wall, weakened by the rain.

Instantly, I'm in the middle of a terrible fight. I'm attacking four Others of different kinds at the same time, jumping around, rescuing babies, also rescuing smaller friends who have come to be here for me.

A terrible pain lances into my top surface and I can't get at the attacker, the biggest flyer I've ever seen. In desperation I roll over, with my body on the ground and legs in the air.

As I roll to stand again, two others pounce on the flyer, but as I look, I see that, sadly, I've squashed several of my own babies.

No time to cry now. The battle goes on. I'm getting weak from many injuries, but there are fewer Others. I call for my babies. Eight-plus-two answer. Other people hear them, and we all move to protect them.

Mother comes to me. "You've done enough for now. You need to heal, and get strong again. Leave your babies to us."

I've survived. Over eight of my babies survived the first battle. I've done well. Mother and her sister protect me while I recover, then life goes on. The Old One invites me to be a mentor for a new adult, and to my delight she is someone I'd protected when she was a baby. So, for the second time, I walk to the edge of the High Place. When she goes on, we eight descend again, low enough to find abundant life, and we feed as much as we can. And when at last she returns, with the tiny bumps of newly formed seeds all over her body, I have plenty of water and am overjoyed to make a gift of a little to her.

We choose a place, and after the next rain she starts to build her wall.

It's maybe half finished when the earth shakes. It's a terrible earthquake, the worst of my life, and suddenly great rocks rise into the air far away, and come crashing down. One just misses me and I move sideways, then—darkness.

Recall

I faced an incredibly beautiful Light, far brighter than even God at the High Place. She said, within my being, "My love, what have you learned from this life?"

I remembered Amelia and Dermot, every instant of their lives, as well as this last life. "I learned that the human body is a very poor thing compared to the Walking Plant I've just been."

There was a smile in the answer. "A Walking Plant couldn't live on Earth, needing a continuous, huge energy input as she does."

"Also, I've learned that love is the most important force, and transcends everything else. A Walking Plant will die for the love of others of her kind."

"Yes. Any regrets?"

"Well, it's a jungle world. Sadly, each species can only live by killing others. Dermot lived like that, but Amelia rose above violence. I feel that now, for the time being, I've returned to Dermot's way, because that's the reality for Walking Plants."

"Do you want to do something about that?"

"I think, in my next life, I need to continue to defend the weak, the victim, but then progress to doing so without hurting the aggressor."

"Excellent. You'll have that opportunity. Anything else?"

"I don't understand some of this world's features."

"I can explain if you wish."

"The God of that world is its sun, but why is it always in the same position? And what's the High Place? And how do Walking Plants communicate?"

"Mr. Perkins taught you that the Earth's Moon makes one rotation per revolution, so it always shows the same face. The same is true for that planet. Its star is far larger and hotter. The face that was your home is always oriented to all this energy. The opposite side is always frozen. Of course, most of the water is locked up in the ice of the winter side, but over millions of years, the gravitational pull of the star has distorted the planet, so it's like an egg, not a globe. The High Place is the point of the egg. The curvature there is such that the flat plain falls away on all sides. Also, because of the distortion, the planet has a slight wobble. And this process of distortion is still going on."

"Oh. That's the cause of the earthquakes and volcanoes?"

"Yes. And volcanic action on the winter side evaporates water, which makes its way to a ring of very violent climate between eternal summer and eternal winter."

"And the wobble will do the same. All right, but communication?"

"That's something humans discovered on Earth while you've been away, called 'radio waves.' Leave that for now. Instead, we have work to do."

"Yes. I have all too many lessons to learn, all too many things I need to make restitution for."

"Please list them."

"I need to learn the lesson of forgiveness. I've asked to experience what it's like to be without the pain of loving. I need to become a person who can heal hurt, and lead people from despair and helplessness to strength and Love. Finally, I need to have experiences that expiate for Dermot's cruelties: the callous killings, putting men into pits full of feces, terrifying that Clinton Ryrie with the threat of being turned into a cockroach. Dermot was a good man, but he became a bully. He... I... need to experience the other side, what it feels like to be victimized."

"Your list has been anticipated, and a child is available for you. You'll share life with many of your past teachers, because you need to learn from them, and they from you. But also, this is the last life you have available for fulfilling a far earlier destiny. I now want you to remember how you became a person on planet Earth."

Terrible sorrow and regret gripped my being. Guilt... guilt beyond belief for an inexcusable act. I went back... back... and remembered the crime that condemned me to many lives as a tiny, ephemeral creature bound to the surface of a planet. Compared to this crime, the worst act of a human is nothing.

3. ~10,000 BCE: Space Flower: Lost

It was time to leave Flettar. The space around it was getting too infested with various pests, and keeping them at bay was taking up more and more attention. So, all five of us decided to go to the nearest star, Kol. I converted my peripherals into energy, though they'd been judged second best in the recent visual-music contest, said good-bye to my friends and blasted off.

However, I woke in a strange place. The star was barely close enough to activate my systems. On one side was the galaxy, on the other merely a sparse sprinkling of stars. Somehow, inexplicably, I'd missed my aim, who knows how long ago, and I'd drifted right out into the periphery. The good thing was that at least this star woke me. Otherwise, I could have ended up in the emptiness of intergalactic space.

Or... was I still in my home? Had I spent an unbelievably long time drifting, until now I was entering a different galaxy altogether? The thought was terrifying. All the people I loved could be lost to me forever—maybe my entire species.

First, I needed to get closer to the star, to access enough energy to communicate. If there was anyone to communicate with. If anything lived in this galaxy. If this place was not inhabited by some hostile alien life form. We, the People, have long renounced all forms of killing except in self-defense, but of course many other kinds live by different values.

I studied this system. The star was an above-average yellow dwarf. Gravitational analysis identified eight hard planets, six gas ones further out, and of course heaps of junk. Three gas planets had lovely rings. Two hard planets were smaller than my current mass.

The fifth planet was unique in my experience. It twinkled everywhere with low-energy emissions over a wide band of wavelengths. That was pretty to look at, but utterly baffling. I couldn't think of any natural phenomenon that'd account for this kind of radiation, and it clearly had a water-oxygen sheath. I'd heard of small, primitive, unintelligent life forms on planetary surfaces, but of course they were not in a deadly corrosive environment like this planet's.

For now, I had to drop into orbit. I threw away mass to slow relative to the star, on a gentle spiral toward the outermost gas planet. It had a good crop of moons, one of which would serve for fuel. Then, given the low energy supply, I shut down everything except a gravity monitor and returned to sleep.

Eventually, the monitor woke me. Spectroscopic analysis showed the triple ring around the planet to be frozen methane, carbon dioxide and water—useless. The nearest moon was maybe half my size, but I couldn't tell how much of that was frozen water, and therefore dangerous. I also detected lots of liquid oxygen. Ugh.

I dismantled my currently nonessential components and extracted all the available gold. Gold is inert, and takes less energy to melt than other metals. Naturally, I had considerable lengths of steel tube, and coated more than enough with gold to penetrate oxygen and water. Then I drilled to the center of the moon, planted an explosive, withdrew my probe and threw away a little more mass to separate from the moon.

My calculations were exact: the explosion neatly split the moon in two. Indeed, about a quarter of its mass was water, but now I could stay away from it and extract the rock. Much of that was aluminum-based, so with some ingenuity and considerable care I produced an aluminum-oxygen engine. I aimed for the puzzling fifth planet, again following an economical spiral. Once more, there was nothing to do for a long time, so I slept until my gravity monitor woke me.

This close to the star, I had plenty of energy, so reconstructed my communication equipment. It was of course part of what I'd had to wreck to get at the gold.

Emissions poured off the planet in the radio bands and shorter wavelengths. So, I didn't bother with light-speed communication, because any sentient being within range would have come to investigate. I charged up my energy accumulator, warped space, and sent a query toward the bulk of the galaxy.

No answer.

I changed aim and tried again.

After the eighth failure, I was ready to give up in despair. Maybe this was a foreign galaxy, empty of life. Or its life forms didn't use kappa waves for communication. Or they did, and chose to stay silent and were now coming to attack me.

On the ninth try, I got a reply! It was a stranger whose identifier was incomprehensibly different from any I'd encountered. The communication link showed It as an intensely beautiful ballet of multicolored spirals.

I explained my predicament, including the reason that I was currently a plain sphere.

It said, "You're in the right galaxy at least. But we'd better work out how long you've been drifting. Were there public events roughly when you'd set out?"

I introduced myself, to get a response of incredulity at my identifier's age. Then I told It about the visual-music contest with my second placing. We disconnected to save my still-low energy store.

Eventually It contacted me again. "I've searched the records. Your contest was over two hundred and fifty half-lives of radium 226 ago!"[1]

A great emptiness filled me. All my loved ones, all my friends, had died eons ago. I was a relic of the distant past. And if I ever got home again, it'd be after a similar time lapse, so this Person and Its contemporaries would be long dead too.

However, It said, "Let me see... I think space warp for matter transmission was developed since your time."

Promising! "We only had it for kappa waves with their zero mass."

"I'll send you the specifications. You can build a transmitter, and rejoin the People within ten half-lives of thorium 234. You'll need that long to produce the main propulsive material."

The plans arrived, and while I studied them, my new friend contacted two others a fair distance apart, and we set up a triangulation, giving me somewhere to aim for.

The main ingredient I needed was uranium, as raw material for an artificial metal with an atomic mass of 519. Surely this planet below me had to be full of uranium to radiate energy in so many places?

I had to admit, it was a very attractive-looking planet, precisely because of its nasty oxygen-water coating. The surface was brown land set in deep blue water, with endlessly changing white swirls of water vapor in its nitrogen-oxygen atmosphere.

I studied the pattern of energy emissions. They were mostly on land, with water surfaces being almost but not quite free of them. On the side facing the star at any one time, most of the output was radio waves. On the dark side, shorter wavelengths joined these.

My distance viewer showed that my mass had a significant influence on local water levels. Directly below my orbit, the water rose, submerging some land when I was over a boundary. Interestingly, the emissions ceased in the areas that were affected by this phenomenon, and this change seemed permanent.

I focused on the very short wavelengths that indicate fissile materials, and to my delight found them in abundance. While it was going to be a shame to destroy such a pretty planet, it had just what I needed to return to my People. After all, no one else would see it in such an empty place, and

---

[1] Our way of measuring time depends on the movement of our planet, which is irrelevant to space creatures. They have to use invariable phenomena, being the decay of radioactive materials. The half-life of radium 226 is 1600 years; of thorium 234 it's 24 days.

probably no one would ever come here again. Of course I made recordings, so people could view it at leisure if they were interested.

Once more I needed to coat my mining equipment with gold, but even if I dismantled everything inessential, I wouldn't have anywhere near enough to penetrate through the thick atmosphere. Then it occurred to me: I could blow the atmosphere away with a suitable explosion. That'd also freeze all that water, making my work much easier.

While preparing, I noticed a change in the radiations from the planet. In a great many places, the shorter-wave emissions became rhythmic, and they seemed to focus on me. The radio waves came in step with the same rhythm.

It went like this:

Blip.

Blip-blip.

Blip-blip-blip.

And so on, until there were sixty pulses, then the count returned to one.

No life is possible in the presence of oxygen and water. And yet... this definitely seemed to indicate intelligence.

I still had plenty of aluminum and oxygen from the outer moon. I decided to investigate the other hard planets. I set my engine in motion, spiraled out from the planet, then set course for the hard planet closest to me, which happened to be the one furthest out. I reached it after another sleep, to find two problems: the energy flux from the star was low this far out, and I found very little uranium.

And I wanted to go home!

This planet had little gaseous atmosphere because most substances were frozen. I mined it for gold and more fuel, doing well for both, then sadly, set out for the fourth planet. This one was smaller than me, with no fissile material.

I wanted to go home! How much longer was I willing to blunder about this system?

The second planet was the largest hard planet. I decided to inspect it, but it would be absolutely the last. Now having lots of weight to throw away, I blasted off on a shortest-time trajectory, which still took me twenty half-lives of radon 222[2], every instant of which was a torture.

I detected plenty of fissile material, but it was an impossible situation. The atmosphere was mostly sulfuric acid, and too thick for me to blow it away like I could with the fifth one.

---

[2] Radon 222 has a half-life of 3.8 days.

All right, so some bizarre little life form seemed to have evolved on a ball of rock surrounded by water and oxygen—and they were on the only practically available fuel for my return home.

We do no harm. It's the first tenet of the People.

But surely that only applies to real life, not to some aberration like this? Would such things have feelings and emotions like real living beings? They could count to sixty, and so what. Did they have any appreciation of beauty? How could they, being bound on the surface of a planet? Could they even see the stars?

Anyway, how long could an individual live in such an environment? My expected life span exclusive of interstellar sleeps was about two half-lives of radium 226. Could these little things live as long as the half-life of thorium 234 even? They just had to be short lived beyond belief, and if I shortened their lives, would it make any difference?

I wanted to go home.

Once more, I used maximum mass for minimum travel time, back to the fifth planet.

A change

Back with my People, I tried to join in with life, but found it very difficult. I was an oddity everyone wanted to meet, but apart from historians, I held no one's interest. Things had moved on; not only science but art, tastes and fashions. I made many acquaintances, but no friends. The novelty of my journey soon wore off, and even the historians left me alone.

Before my drift to the periphery, life had been vital, interesting and meaningful. Now it became a bore. I used to be famous for the beauty of my forms. Now, my best was nothing compared to the ordinary by others. I used to be involved in many endeavors. Now I could only observe.

So, at last I stopped trying. Even when pests nibbled at my body, I ignored them. I didn't bother to monitor for danger, stopped seeking out the company of others, just orbited around some star, never mind which. Thinking of nothing much, I listened to conversations of which I was not a part. What else was there to do? Some alarm activated within my body, but I couldn't be bothered to investigate.

A sensor suddenly showed a movement within my brain cavity.

Then terrible pain as the worm chewed the very crystals of my being.

Then darkness.

In the distance, I beheld a light of incredible beauty. I heard, "Come."

An indescribable Presence faced me. It said without words, "It's time for you to plan your future."

"What future? I'm dead!"

I felt a smile in Its thought. "Death is an illusion. Life is an illusion. You and I as individual, ongoing entities are illusions. There is just the One, and we're all parts of It. The purpose of the illusion of life is to allow the One to grow by having the illusion of your eternal spirit learn Lessons. Now you need to examine this just-finished life, and extract the Lessons you've learned. Then, you need to set up a new life in which you can be exposed to opportunities to learn Lessons you decide you need."

Instantly, I felt the savage joy of the worm as it chewed on my brain, then the pity of people who had wanted to be my friends, wanted to support me, but were repulsed by my attitudes.

Then I experienced an utterly alien perspective. I had a fixed, soft body with various appendages coming out of It. I saw a swiftly spreading black hole in the blue surround of my planet. The atmosphere moved with great force, lifting me up, then smashing me onto hard rock. At first, I was drawing atmospheric gases into myself through a particular hole, and expelling them in a rhythmic manner. Now, when I sucked, nothing came, and this was incredibly frightening and incredibly painful.

Over and over, as suffered by being after being, I experienced variations of the same torture, till I cried, "Enough! I've got the message."

Time moved back. I was one of these beings, standing near the water's edge, looking up at a great globe above the atmosphere, reflecting the star's light on half its surface. I realized, that was me, seen from below. Then suddenly, a huge rush of water hit me. My hole for pulling in gases got filled with water and I knew I was dying, even as the force of the water smashed me onto jagged rock, causing agony in many places. Dying was a relief. Again, this tragedy kept repeating with minor variations. Then I was in an enclosure I knew to be my space for living in, when a terrible weight of water crashed into it. I became trapped in a small gas bubble, my body agonizingly damaged in several places, till the atmosphere around me became unable to support life.

Again, time moved back. I was one of these beings, an old and wise person according to those of Its kind. I lived all Its memories, thoughts and emotions from Its birth to death and realized, this little, short-lived thing was as valuable, as worthy of respect and care, as any of my People.

I had destroyed Its world, billions of intelligent lives, for what? So I could die of boredom and despair?

"Please," I said to the Presence, "allow me to cease. I don't deserve to exist. I am sorry. I'd do anything to reverse this terrible, evil thing I've done, but I can't. Just let me die, truly die."

"My love, that's not possible. You're an essential part of the Universe, and this was a Lesson you needed to face. You made the wrong choice, and so an entire nursery habitat was destroyed. Now, design your next life, to suitably expiate this deed."

I didn't know what a nursery habitat might be, but it wasn't my place to ask. What did MY puzzlement matter? But the Superior Being obviously detected my thought. It explained, "The Universe is alive. You and I are both Its parts. I'm merely further along the path to growth. My task is to guide younger spirits like you toward the point where you can evolve into a higher form, and will no longer need to return to three-dimensional life."

Surely, someone who had committed such a crime would never achieve perfection like that.

"My dear, that very thought proves the contrary. You're learning, and have grown a great step toward the ultimate Lesson. Your development is necessary for the Universe, which has stages of growth. Soon, as the Universe measures time, It'll reach a stage when many more like me will be needed. So, billions of habitats for short-lived beings arose. There they live and die over and over, and progress toward the ultimate Lesson far faster than is possible for the much older, long-lived life forms like you've just been."

My necessary fate became clear. "In my next life, I must be one of them. And not just in the next life. For life after life, round and round, I must stay there, until I can expiate my guilt by being present during the destruction of one of these nursery habitats."

"Or perhaps," the Presence gently said, "you may be instrumental in saving such a nursery habitat from destruction?"

"If that's possible. Yes. That would be wonderful."

I became a primitive little mind, within a warm, soft cocoon, filled by a rhythmic vibration: tha-thump, tha-thump, tha-thump, comfortingly forever. There I grew, until I was born into my first human life. That was many lives ago. Now, my Guide told me, I'd be facing the last such transition. This time around, I'd either witness the destruction of all humans on earth, or be instrumental in preventing this destruction. And then, hopefully, in the next life, I might be allowed to return to my natural environment of the spaces around the stars.

Book 4: Pip

1. 1966-1967: Love

The third time I saw my love, I didn't recognize her. Here is how it happened.

My friend Brian married Leanne. I lent them my car for their honeymoon while I returned to my past, back to Hungary. My mother and stepfather paid for the trip, a horrendous cost given the exchange rate. This was to celebrate my wonderful results at university. You see, stupid as I knew myself to be, I was good at fooling examiners and their ilk.

I didn't want to meet the ogre of my childhood, but to my surprise I became friends with the old boy. I got to understand his story, so pity and admiration replaced hate. After all, by transporting me to Australia for the term of my natural life, he'd prevented a murder (we both knew that eventually either I'd kill him or he'd kill me, and he was a tough ex-prisoner of war while I was merely the naughtiest boy in the world).

Meanwhile, an autoimmune disorder destroyed Leanne's brain. After she died, Brian quit his Masters and started Medicine. He and his three best friends, including me, moved together to give him support, and boy, did he need it! For weeks, I lost as much sleep as he did, allowing him to talk, or just sit with me saying nothing. Funny he turned to me more than to the other two, who, like him, were strong Christians.

Two years later, at 23, I met Rachael, who became my first girlfriend. I know, a late starter, though not for want of trying. But when I asked her to marry me, she turned me down, confirming that nobody could possibly love me. I drowned myself in running and study, my two antidepressants since 11 years of age. My research was going well, and I ran three hours a day. This left little time to yearn after girls, though they kept sneaking into my awareness. Since starting university, I'd been desperately chasing them, a lost puppy looking for a home. The result was many "sisters," but no girlfriend.

Then I became shortlisted for the Rhodes Scholarship for New South Wales. Told you I'm good at fooling people. That removed the urge: no point in a girlfriend if I needed to leave Australia.

OK, back to my living arrangements. Apart from Brian and me, we had Neil and Keith. Neil and his fiancé Sandra ran an Episcopalian youth fellowship. He kept pestering me to go, but I told him I was not a Christian, didn't want to be one, and hated crowds of strangers. Then one day he said, "Hey Pip, we've got a new ping-pong table. Come and have a hit."

I gave in and grabbed my favorite bat, the one that had won me several contests. I got into the front passenger seat, with Brian and Keith in the back. Neil said, "I've got to pick up another passenger."

It was dark when we pulled up at this mansion, and a girl scurried into the back seat. Neil mumbled an introduction I didn't catch.

When we arrived, my worst imaginings proved to be optimistic: a hall full of strangers, all apparently in couples. Idiot music blared, and people were shouting because of the poor acoustics. I wanted to walk out, but Neil had the keys and I didn't know how to hotwire a car.

There was the ping-pong table with four guys playing doubles. Their bats were those things with pimply rubber glued on. One fellow saw the bat in my hand and shouted, "Hey, can I borrow that?"

I wanted to say no. I should have said no. Unfortunately, in those days I didn't yet know how to say no. I handed it over.

He served, his opponent drove the ball back, his partner made an awkward return, and the fourth person smashed the ball. The bloke with my bat made a wild swipe, hit the edge of the table and broke the bat off the handle.

Bugger.

He was very apologetic, and promised to replace it.

I just walked off.

Everyone knew each other. I stood around a few groups, invisible. A wall clock showed I'd been there ten minutes, which felt like ten hours. Then I glimpsed a battered old upright piano against a wall. I walked over, opened the lid and sat. Für Elise came tinkling from my fingers, no doubt inaudible in the din. Beethoven is Uncle Ludwig, though Freddie Chopin is my favorite. Music is my third antidepressant. Oh, not playing it, I've never had money for lessons, but listening to it. Rachael had taught me a few favorites.

A pleasant female voice said behind me, "Lovely, another Beethoven fan."

I turned. She had a gorgeous Junoesque figure Renoir would have loved to paint, long, heavy brown hair worn over one shoulder, and she smelt of garlic.

"Hi, I'm Pip."

"I know. We were introduced in the car." She spoke with an accent, nice on the ear.

Oops. Put my foot in it as usual. My motto then was: "If there's a wrong way to do it, or even if there isn't, I'll do it that way first." "Sorry," I said. "It was dark and I only saw a silhouette." I still didn't know her name.

Suddenly she looked distressed. "Oh no," she murmured as a bloke joined us.

He was shorter than her, with thick round glasses. "Hi Jacinta," he said, "I've been looking for you. I'd like to ask you to come to the ball with me. You know my mother is on the organizing committee, and–"

"David, I'm sorry. Pip has just asked me and I've accepted." She gave me a beseeching look.

I hate balls. I'd much rather kick the inflated kind than attend the social kind. I hate dressing up formally (isn't a tie the limpest phallic symbol?), and I hate dancing. I was in no position to chase girls, and... and I didn't know how to say no. Besides, she clearly needed rescuing from poor David. So, I didn't reveal the lie.

David chatted awhile, mostly about his mother's achievements, then wandered off.

"Tell me about this ball," I asked, annoyed with myself for getting trapped. Bugger of a night so far.

"I can't hear myself think," Jacinta said. "I hate all this noise and crowd, and hardly know anyone yet. You won't think badly of me if I ask if we can talk outside?"

I could have taken this as an invitation, though of course girls didn't invite me to anything much. I certainly shared the sentiments!

She led me out a side door, past the restrooms, into a paved area. The view was lousy: a fence and what the city lights allowed of the night sky, but it was peaceful and quiet.

"Oh that's better, Jacinta. But if you don't like it, why do you come?"

"I've only been here a month, almost six months in Australia, and don't know anyone. How else do you make friends?"

"Fair enough. And you've got David already."

"Poor David. But anyway, I don't want a boyfriend. I was engaged back in Scotland, and he turned out to be a sleaze. So, the male species can stay away."

"Um... if you'd observe me, I'm male."

"But there's something about you, Pip. I know I can trust you."

"How?"

She shrugged. "Don't know. When I got in Neil's car and saw you from behind, you seemed familiar, like an old friend. And when you played Für Elise, I had this feeling that I've seen you playing the piano before. Maybe I'm crazy."

"There are more things in heaven and earth, Horatio, than are dreamt of in your philosophy."

"That's Shakespeare, isn't it?"

"Yes. Little Ham. Oh, sorry, Hamlet to most people."

She laughed. Not everyone laughs at my jokes.

"Anyway, I'm not looking for a girlfriend either."

"You've got one of course?"

Of course? "No. But I'm shortlisted for a scholarship, and have one chance in four of going overseas." I was always careful to leave "Rhodes" out of it, not wanting to seem conceited. "Besides, I'm working on my Master's thesis, and train three hours a day for distance running, and race most Saturdays, and every Thursday night help to run a Scout troop."

"So what do you do in your spare time?" We both laughed.

Somehow, Oxford didn't feel quite so enticing. "Jacinta, what's your passion in life?"

"Heavens. Only one? I love children, making beautiful things with my hands, cooking. Will that do for now?"

"Sounds like an excellent reference. And you like Beethoven."

"My favorite is Chopin actually, but yes. Anyway, why haven't I seen you here before?"

"I don't come to Christian events much because I'm Jewish." Then I told her about the ping-pong bat, managing to make it sound funny rather than disastrous.

She laughed. "Oh, my apology for railroading you into that ball. I was desperate, and knew you'd be kind enough to cover for me. Look, you don't have to do it."

By now I'd have been happy to go anywhere with her. "What's it about?"

"A bunch of rich ladies organize it for charity, and to keep us kids off the street."

"They won't raise much money from me. I'm a starving student on a scholarship."

"And I'm an *au pair* girl working for one of those rich ladies."

"Thank heavens. I thought you were some spoiled rich kid when I saw you emerging from that palace."

"Oh, I was lucky to get the job. I've got my little room with its own entrance, and I actually like housework."

"Hmm. You'll be welcome to visit us, particularly by Keith. He is super-tidy, and works us hard to keep the place up to his standards."

"I might just do that on a day off."

"When is that?"

"Friday and Saturday, unless Mrs. Leahy is entertaining."

"Really? How entertaining is she? Would I laugh if I watched?"

Again she laughed. Most people would have groaned. "Actually, I wouldn't mind coming to see you racing."

"That's not all that entertaining: a lot of blokes going round and round the track. The 5000 meters is due next Saturday. That's twelve and a half laps. A yawn to watch."

I heard Neil behind us, "There you are! Ready to go home?"

She did visit us, when it was my week to be mother. I cooked rakott krumpli, which means "stacked spuds," one of the monthly meals demanded of me. She didn't find anything to tidy—I'd made damn sure of that—but in my room her eyes lit on my long row of trophies, all tarnished. She found silver polish and cloth, and put a shine on them.

We went to the ball. I managed not to step on her toes, and actually enjoyed myself. I found it easy to chat with her. "How did you end up in Australia?" I asked.

"My sister lives here, and had a one-year-old son while giving birth to a daughter. I came to look after the boy, run the household and help for the first few months. Anyway, tomorrow is six months since my arrival."

"Hey, that means you arrived on my birthday!"

"There, Pip, a birthday present and you didn't even know it. How long have you been here?"

"Arrived on the 10th of January, 1957."

"You won't believe this. That's my birthday! What was that quote from Hamlet?"

"Oh well, coincidences happen."

The music started again, and we stood to dance.

When it was over I drove her home, parked, and ran around to open the car door.

"Nice to see there are still gentlemen around," she said. "Let me show you Mrs. Leahy's garden." In the dim light, her white dress shone. She took my hand, hers feeling warm, soft and friendly, and led me through an arch. The garden was dominated by an in-ground swimming pool, with space for plenty else. She stepped up on the edging of the pool, saying, "From here you can see the coastline."

I joined her. Beyond the back fence, the ground sharply dropped away, the neighboring roof actually below us. The Heads to the harbor were to the left, the glittering coastline stretching away in a wavy line. It was beautiful, and we just gazed at it.

Jacinta said, "You know, I've got this strange feeling that we've stood in such a place before." She stepped closer, and I felt her arm rub against mine through my jacket.

I turned to face her. I don't know why, but I needed to stroke her face from temples to chin.

She came even closer so I felt her breath on my face. No garlic this time.

Our lips met. Hers were warm, soft, moist and sweet. As my arms rested on her bare shoulders, she wriggled, like a cat relishing a stroke does.

As always, my wretched mind got in the way of feeling. *This girl is different,* I thought. *She actually likes me touching her.* Pity I had one chance in four of having to leave the country.

She took me to her little room—a bed-sitter with attached bathroom, full of frills, dolls, cushions and family photos. It was lovely, comfortable and inviting, and made me feel I'd break something if I moved too suddenly. "I thought you said you've only been here a month."

"Yes, but I brought the important things in a cabin trunk on the ship, even the cradle my father bought when I was born. Of course, my sister has that now."

She accompanied me back to the car, my arm around her shoulder, hers around my waist, and we shared another kiss. Driving home, I knew that this was the girl for me, and yet, as always, it was all in the head. I knew from observation that love, joy, happiness were gut-things, heart things for others. I knew what to do. I'd watched guys who loved, like Brian before his tragedy, like Neil with Sandra. I just had to make a good job of copying them. I knew the source of the problem: War Infant Syndrome. It was punishment for the bad judgment of choosing to be born into a Jewish family in a Nazi-dominated country, while the bombs were falling. The baby can survive the felt terror of the carers only by shutting down emotion, including all positive emotion. The textbooks say it's for life.

She watched me running the next Saturday. Though it couldn't have been very exciting, she kept returning when she could. Somehow, I did my best times when she was there.

She came to Keith's birthday party, and in the middle of chatter and noise and people drinking, she beat me at a game of chess. Few people have done that.

Everything shut down for the silly season. I hate Christmas. Jacinta said, "I'm spending a few days with my sister. She's renting an abandoned rose farm. Would you like to come too?"

We drove across the Harbour Bridge, eventually along a gravel road, and turned onto a path with a tangle of vegetation on each side. The house was old and ramshackle, but smelt of good cooking. A tall blonde lady welcomed us with a broad smile. "Sis, this is Pip Lipkin," Jacinta said, and, "My sister Liana."

"Welcome Pip," Liana said with a laugh. "Time I checked you out, my little sister's been talking a lot about you." She had the same soft Scottish accent.

Her husband lay on a sofa, watching TV, and didn't bother to rise. "G'day mate," he said, the Australianism odd in a much broader brogue. "I'm Lachlan. If that's too hard, Sir will do."

"Or Madam as the case may be?" Two could play at being quirky.

He grinned. "OK, you pass." He returned to his show like I wasn't there.

Liana took us to the kitchen, where a little red-haired boy sat in a highchair, covered in mush he was supposedly eating from a bowl. Seeing Jacinta, he lit up like a sunrise and held out his arms.

She laughed, wetted a cloth at the sink, wiped off the muck and picked him up. "Hello Farquhar," she said, hugging him, then introduced me as Uncle Pip. He gravely regarded me, then a grin showed little teeth, and to my surprise he reached out to me. I grabbed him under the arms, raised him high and down again. Since becoming my brother's second mother when I was nine, I've had a special bond with kids.

I heard a whimper. Liana went off to return with a much smaller red-haired person, introduced as Gabrielle. Liana sat and proceeded to breastfeed her. Embarrassed, I looked away, but she demanded, "Pip, tell me about your family."

"I don't really have any. My mother lives in Hungary with her husband and my little brother. That's about it. I do have an uncle, but he's my favorite person to avoid."

"Why?"

"Only two things matter for him: to make as much money as possible, never mind who he tramples on, and to screw as many women as possible." I sat down and played a knee-riding game with Farquhar. He giggled every time I mock-dropped him.

"So, how did you end up in Australia?"

"In 1956, there was a revolution in Hungary, and it was pretty revolting. For a couple of months, the Iron Curtain had a rust hole, and people escaped. One of my uncle's many girlfriends was the dispatcher for a company bringing milk to Budapest. She organized two trucks on succeeding mornings to pick us up. Of course, her payment was that Uncle Paul pretended to form an exclusive relationship with her. I don't know how, but my stepfather arranged that I went on the first truck with Uncle Paul and Erzsi, and the rest of them would come the next day. Then, he paid off the second driver and sent him away without them."

Both girls looked shocked.

"How could he do that? And what about your mother?"

"I visited them two years ago. My brother told me, Mother cried my name every day for years. Don't know why. If I'd been my parent, I'd have felt like killing me."

Liana looked at me consideringly. "Why?"

"Because I was the naughtiest kid in the world. I fought a guerrilla war against my stepfather, things like... Imagine. You back out your pride and joy, drive down the street, and a tire goes flat. There is a four-inch nail in it. Can happen to anyone, right? But until the night before, that nail had lived in the wall next to our front door. Or, when he gets to work, he finds his nice shirt decorated with a huge blue patch focused on his fountain pen—remember those? Or, he steps on a perfectly safe floor mat, one people have walked on hundreds of times, and it slips out from under him so he lands on his bum. On and on, day after day, and always so I couldn't possibly have done it."

"You still do things like that?"

"I've never done anything nasty to anyone else, not even Uncle Paul. And as I said, although I'd won every battle, he won the war by exporting me. Then I met several angels—people I admired—and decided to copy them instead."

The baby had fallen asleep. Liana lifted her away and covered up. She held her upright and burped her, saying, "Lachlan had a rotten childhood too. His father disowned him. He left home young, became a seaman, then trained as an engineer in Australia."

I voiced a frequent thought. "Humans are crazy. In a sane society, all children would be cherished, whoever their parents are."

We stood, and Jacinta showed me around the blackberry-and-rose farm.

That evening, Liana apologetically explained that the only spare bed was in the baby's room. "As a Boy Scout, I've slept on hard ground, next to boys who snored," I answered. Given the long hours of running, I could sleep anywhere.

At 1:30, I heard Gabrielle squeak. I got up, turned on the light and found her sopping wet. I changed her, but she wouldn't settle. "Well, love, I haven't got what it takes to feed you," I said, carrying her to the kitchen, to find a baby's bottle of milk in the fridge. Beauty. I heated water, stood the bottle in it till the milk was just right when dripped onto my wrist, fed her, burped her and changed the wet-again nappy—but when I tried to return her to the cradle, she clung to me. So, I switched the light off and cuddled her in bed. I woke at 4:30 as usual, but hadn't brought my running gear. Besides, the baby might have woken if I'd stirred.

Next thing was two female laughs. Liana said, "I was wondering why I hadn't heard a peep from her all night!" Jacinta's comment was more momentous. "I think I'll keep this fellow!"

I sat up. "And if I get my scholarship?"

"Then I'll come with you."

If I'd been anyone else, I might have cried from joy. I merely had the thought, *I've found a home! But poor girl, committing herself to a stuffup like me.*

I introduced her to my friends. All thoroughly approved. My "sisters" were all glad to get me off their hands. On her part, Jacinta wanted to marry in her Presbyterian Church. Since I was determinedly non-Christian, this meant an interview with the minister, Mr. MacAndrew. We arranged a meeting, which filled all afternoon. I explained that during my childhood, words like "Jesus" were terms of abuse, as in "You Jews killed Jesus!"

He quizzed me on my beliefs, told me I was a Buddhist, and he'd be happy to have me marry in his church. He modified the service to remove all words I had negative reactions to, including "Jesus." I also wanted "obey" out. No way did I want Jacinta to promise to obey me.

That evening, I camped at the Uni. Library and read up on Buddhism. Mr. MacAndrew was right. Here was my philosophy in beautiful words.

The wedding was inspiring, spoiled only by my uncle's wife Elena, who told us off for being late. Farquhar was responsible for that. He'd climbed up on furniture to get at the shoe polish, kept on top of a wardrobe, and nicely warpainted himself.

The reception cost us $70. Liana and Jacinta had done most of the preparation (as well as making her wedding dress), and about thirty of my "sisters" brought something to share.

And all that was forty-four years, three kids and four grandkids ago. I tell people I'm no good at getting married, having only done it once.

Oh, we've had our ups and downs, misunderstandings and fights, but we share maybe twenty good experiences for each bad one. Jacinta still laughs at my jokes.

2. 1943-1950: *Country holiday*

I was seven when Grandmother and Aunt Janka took me to a farm for a summer holiday. I'm sure it was meant well, but in fact it was strange, threatening and lonely. The local children were strange, foreign and hostile. They even spoke differently from people in Budapest. Animals were strange, puzzling and scary—on the second day, a flock of geese cornered me. Their hard beaks were level with my face. Their little beady eyes glared at me as they moved their heads back and forth, hissing.

There were also dogs, every one of which growled and barked at me. But the terrible thing was done by two-legged animals wearing clothes.

I could tell no one about this, not even Aunt Janka, because the two old ladies kept smiling and looking happy, saying how lucky we were to get out of the city for awhile. All I wanted was to go home to our safe apartment.

A fascinating thing at this house was the well in the backyard. It was unused, because the house had water from taps, like normal. A round hole in the ground had a circular stone wall around it, its top level with my eyes. I wanted to look inside, to see the water below. As I stood there, wondering how to climb up the smooth surface, suddenly three boys crowded me. One was only a little bigger than me, the other two a head taller. I smelt their dirty bodies. Their hands and faces were filthy. They wore ragged shirts and shorts, their feet bare.

The tallest boy said, in a sing-song voice, "Dirty stinking Jew!"

"Yeah," the second largest took it up, "Dirty stinking Jew killed Jesus!"

"Why'd you kill Jesus?"

"Dirty shit-faced Jew killed Jesus!"

"Stinking shit-faced Jew!"

I could say nothing. I could not move. I had trouble even breathing.

They enjoyed themselves, chanting, dancing around me, their fun fed by my terror.

The biggest one stopped. "Shit-faced? YEAH!" He grabbed my arm, and instantly the other two grasped me too. The big one started dragging me toward the back fence. When I struggled, he held a fist in front of my nose. Nobody had threatened me with violence before. I could do nothing.

Tall weeds hid a big gap in the fence. Led by the big boy, they dragged me through, into an area with trees. This was utterly foreign territory.

Under a tree was a pile of human shit.

"Hold the stinking Jew," the big boy commanded. He let me go, found a stick and shoved an end into the shit. A big grin on his face, he thrust it at my mouth.

I couldn't move my body, but managed to turn my head. The shit smeared on my cheek.

The second biggest boy grabbed my hair as the big one returned for another load. "Shit-faced Jew!" he chanted.

Again I barely managed to avoid having the horrid thing hit my mouth. Time and again they tried, until the stick hit my closed lips, bruising them against clenched teeth.

Then the big boy threw his stick away and whooping, they ran off.

Somehow, my trembling legs took me back to the house. I found a tap against a back wall. I felt like crying, but that'd have meant opening my mouth. After a lot of effort I opened the tap, and water gushed out. I put my face under it and scrubbed, scrubbed, scrubbed. Then I went inside and scrubbed my face with hot water and soap until I felt the skin might come off.

But I still wanted to die.

There was a festival toward the end of that holiday, and my old ladies insisted on taking me. It was all meaningless and frightening: crowds and noise and animals in enclosures and people behind tables yelling about their wares.

In one area, soldiers of the Hungarian Army had a small square area roped off, and were encouraging boys to put on puffy-looking gloves and hit each other with them. I stood there, holding Aunt Janka's hand, when a boy ducked through the ropes and looked around. He was the smallest of my three attackers. "I want to box with him!" he said, pointing at me.

A soldier came over but I shrank back.

The boy grinned with pride.

This was when I decided that one day I'd learn to fight.

The beginning

Life for Pip Lipkin started with terror, death and misery: the fate of a Jewish family in a Nazi-dominated country. Trouble is, I had zero memories of those years until September 2007. Well, there was one hazy memory. I'm a tiny boy, reaching way up with my right hand to hold a man's finger. I've always thought of this as my only link to Grandfather, killed in the Holocaust.

I was born because Endre Lipschitz had, in Mother's words, more sticking power than a bathful of leeches. He courted Hannah Holstein for four years, from 1939 to 1942, when she finally consented to marry him. Both expected to die soon anyway. I was born in 1943, when the Brits were in Greece, so she wanted to give me a name that'd sound all right in English. I became Filip Lipschitz, which sounds fine in any language but English.

Hungary conscripted all men, but Gypsies and Jews were armed with spades rather than guns, and sent to die as work conscripts on the Eastern Front. Father's boss became a colonel and protected him, and he survived in some hidey hole. Meanwhile the rest of us endured the twice-daily bombing, the murders of Jews, the terror, the ghetto.

So, when the war ended and Father returned, Mother divorced him, allowing him access to me every second weekend.

My family was Grandmother, her oldest sister Aunt Janka, Mother and Uncle Pali. Let me describe these stars in my firmament.

Uncle Pali was a kind of god. His slightest wish had to be satisfied and his word was law. On the rare occasions when he was home, everything revolved around him. The three women spoke of his many girlfriends with prideful disapproval. I didn't understand what he did with those girlfriends, but whatever it was, the ladies couldn't resist him. I followed the family tradition and admired Uncle Pali, but I didn't like him. Mother, Aunt Janka, Grandmother did things because they enjoyed making others feel good. Even as a small child, I noticed that Uncle Pali only cared for himself.

In contrast, I cared all too much. I realized how different I was from other people on my sixth birthday, when Mother took me to the circus. Two clowns carried on. One fell, screaming, "My leg! I've broken my leg!"

I started to cry, feeling his pain, but the audience laughed, even Mother. She explained, "He's only pretending!"

I couldn't see anything funny even in someone pretending to be hurt.

Grandmother ran everything, decided everything, told me what I could and couldn't do. She was the fount of all wisdom, and trained some important beliefs into me: Only put as much on your plate as you need, but then eat every last scrap. Men are there to respect, support and protect women. If God approves of what you do, who cares what people think? The strong must protect the weak. The more you give, the more you get. Everything needs to be paid for. Every fight starts with you hitting back.

Mother was very busy, because she owned a printing business. She only employed women whose husbands were lost in the War. I wondered what would happen if one was found. Would Mother replace the lady with one still looking for her husband? The workshop was in a long, narrow cellar: a place of music from the radio, singing women, clacking machines, the smell of ink and paper, of jokes and smiles from busy workers with their long hair safely bound up.

Mother had wanted to go to university like Uncle Pali, but girls couldn't do that then. They couldn't learn a trade either, but the Principal of the Printing School was Grandfather's friend, so she got in, but then many boys treated her dreadfully because she was a girl, and because she was Jewish.

All the same, she got the top marks for her year, every year. Grandmother often told me that until a bomb hit the School building, her work had been displayed in the foyer.

When Mother was at home, she said I was her sunshine. We had fun with her reading picture books to me, although she didn't believe that I could read the words for myself. We played games with numbers, memory games, puzzles and riddles. I often invented a riddle, waited for days till she had time to play with me, then sprung it on her.

Mother was wonderful, but the best person in the world was Aunt Janka. Everybody else had other things to do. For Aunt Janka, I was the most important thing. She was smaller than other adults, with a sweet wrinkled face and a hump on her back. That's why she was an old maid. She told me I was the child of her life and the child of her heart, and I liked that. Grandmother had rules, but Aunt Janka often helped me to get around them, then we shared a secret grin.

There always was one other person: a sixteen-year old country girl Grandmother "trained" for a year. Then she'd get a higher-paid job with another family, and a new girl arrived. She lived in a little room off the corridor, and did the housework with Grandmother.

One of these girls had a trick that gave her a lot of amusement. I got very involved in whatever I was doing—assembling a jigsaw puzzle, reading a picture book, making up a story in my head—so I tended to delay going to the toilet. When I finally went, I had to rush. And, with this maid, every time I burst the door open, there she sat, giggling loudly. I felt my face go tomato-red, and had to hold my little penis so I wouldn't wet myself. By the end of that year, I was terrified of girls.

There was school too, but that was boring. The teacher taught us the alphabet, and the names of numbers. That was old stuff, so I always did two things. Outside, I did what the teacher wanted. Inside, I made up stories, poems and puzzles, thought about the magic of numbers, like finding that 24x12 was the same as 12x24. I watched the faces of the other boys and worked out what they thought from their expressions. Sometimes the inside stuff was so interesting that I forgot to do the outside stuff, then I got in trouble for being stupid.

The adults were very excited for months, because mother's business had to become part of a cooperative or the government would take it away. She was the only woman owner, but managed to be elected as president. I didn't think this to be all that wonderful, because it meant she had to spend even more time away from me. All the same, when she was home, I was still her sunshine.

There were regular gatherings, at our place or elsewhere. Éva and Kati were always there. They enjoyed a game: pretending they wanted to kiss me. The thought of somebody's mouth on mine was disgusting, so I ran and they chased me with merry screams. I hated attending these parties, but had no say. The adults, even Aunt Janka, thought I was having fun with the girls, but for me they were scary monsters best avoided.

Uncle Antal

Everything changed when Uncle Antal invaded our family. He walked in with Mother one evening, and had a boring adult conversation with Grandmother and Aunt Janka. I'd invented a new puzzle to share with mother, but when I tried to get her attention, she said, "Later, my darling." She only had attention for this man with the curly dark hair. Whenever she looked at him, her eyes glowed in the way they'd only glowed for me before. So, I instantly disliked him.

After this, I was second best in Mother's life, and it was the fault of this cigarette-stinking loudmouth. I couldn't understand how Mother could bear to stay near him, but often she kept reaching out a hand, just to touch him.

I noticed with amusement that Uncle Antal managed to make Uncle Pali like him. His voice deepened when the two of them were talking, and he kept asking Uncle Pali's opinion about things, and kept saying things like "Of course. You're right!"

Uncle Pali was tall anyway, but he seemed to grow while Uncle Antal talked to him. I was sure Uncle Antal knew exactly what he was doing: winning Uncle Pali's support for winning Mother. Not that he needed that. She loved him more than anything else anyway. That used to be my place in her life.

Usually, he didn't even notice me. When he did, his expression said I was a nuisance he'd like to have got rid of. The feeling was mutual, and the stories I now told myself focused on terrible things happening to him, like monsters from outer space eating him, and an earthquake opening the ground under him with me standing on the edge of the crack. Once, I became a great spider and sucked the blood out of him until he was just a skin bag.

The school year ended, and Mother was very annoyed with me. The teacher had written, "Filip has the capacity to do better. He pays no attention in class, just dreams the day away."

3. 1951-1956: Spanish gold

Every second weekend, I had to go to Father. He had a new wife, Aunt Irén, who made him change his name before she'd agreed to marry him, so now he was Endre Liponyi. That sounded Hungarian rather than Jewish. Aunt Irén thought she had a great sense of humor, but the laughter always made someone feel small and damaged. She held a dinner party once, and somebody farted. It wasn't me, but she looked at me with false worry on her face, saying maybe I had liver disease, because that makes people unable to control gas, and so she hoped everyone would forgive me. I could see her laughing inside, but she fooled the others.

Another time, a family with a girl came visiting. She was a couple of years older than me. Aunt Irén said, "There you are, Filip, an older woman to teach you tricks," then shrieked with laughter at my expression. She was punished for this though, because she suffered a great coughing fit. I secretly felt pleased, and at the same time found it strange that people's breathing and eating pipes should cross over. What a silly way to make a body!

Aunt Irén also got me to hate Christmas. Mother requested that Father should celebrate Hanukkah when I was with him, so Aunt Irén lit candles on the Christmas tree, then said, "Now we'll light the Jewish Christmas candles too." I knew what saccharin was: her smile. She showed me without words that she despised the wonderful story of Hanukkah, the story of courage against overwhelming odds. She knew the story all right, but made it an inferior custom of an inferior people.

At home, we went to Synagogue on Saturdays. Sometimes, I had to sit up in the gallery between Mother and Grandmother, watching the ceremony below. Usually, I was with the other children in a smaller room, where Mrs. Feldman told us stories. Some stories were from the Torah, others about what the terrible Nazis did during the War, and some about how the great and glorious Soviet Union protected the rights of everyone. Listening to the tones of her voice, watching her face, the way she used her hands and held her shoulders, I saw that she found the stories from the Torah interesting, she cried inside when talking about the war, and didn't believe a word of what she said about the Soviet Union.

At Father's, though, we didn't go to Synagogue. I once asked Father why not. He said, "Aunt Irén is a good Communist, and she doesn't like people following outmoded customs. In the world we live in, it's very important to be a good Communist, especially when Aunt Irén is around." He looked nervous and said this in a soft voice, although we were alone.

Once I heard her say to some visitors, "It's lucky Endre earns good money, isn't it? Otherwise, who'd have married him?" Then she laughed like it was a joke, but I saw Father shrink in on himself, as if something inside him had gone gray.

One time at home, I overheard Grandmother saying that "that woman" had reported some people, who were taken away by the ÁVÓ. Nobody ever explained things like that, but I knew the ÁVÓ took you away if you were anticommunist.

So, between Uncle Antal and Aunt Irén, I didn't like being anywhere, except with Aunt Janka. Then she left me too.

I came home from school one summer day in 1951, and to my surprise Mother and Uncle Pali were there, but no Aunt Janka. Uncle Pali looked cranky and impatient. Mother and Grandmother had red eyes like they'd been crying. When mother saw me she gave a little sob and hugged me. She said, "Oh, Filip my sweet, Aunt Janka has gone away. She's no longer with us, but went to God."

Now I understood why they were crying. How could I live without that little old lady? And how could she do this to me? If I was the child of her life and the child of her heart, how could she leave? If even she left me, then nobody really loved me, so I must be unlovable. If not even she loved me, then this would always be true. I was just unlovable. I was unlovable and nobody would ever love me. Mother didn't, and now Aunt Janka didn't.

This was bad enough, but worse came. One Saturday, after we came home from Synagogue, Mother gave me a hug. "Oh, my darling," she said, "I'm so happy. I want you to congratulate me: Uncle Antal and I got married today!"

I hid my face and just stood there, shocked: she knew me so little that she thought I'd be happy about her marrying that cigarette-stinking interloper! I wasn't sure what being married meant, except that husband and wife lived in the same house, slept in the same bed. So now, either I'd lose Mother altogether, or be forced to live with HIM.

Sure enough, Mother said, "Uncle Antal and I will go away for a week, and when we return, we'll live with him in his lovely house. Grandmother is selling this apartment, and we've found a nice little place for her that's close to us, so you'll still see lots of her."

Soon, my home for all my life disappeared. Everything familiar was snatched away. HIS house was not at all lovely. The outside wall was pockmarked by bullets from the War. HE said HE didn't want the house to look too good from the outside, because if a privately owned house did, it could get nationalized.

I now went to a different school, three tram stops away. I had to catch the tram right outside the big girls' school. I stood there, watching these dangerous creatures, hoping they wouldn't notice me. If they did, they'd laugh, and that'd be like being mauled by a tiger.

I was the only Jewish boy at this school. Many boys looked at me like I carried a disease. Nobody played with me. Luckily, the school had a library, and I read there during playtimes. While reading interesting stuff, I forgot about life. After school, some boys shouted nasty things at me, hit me, spat on me or grabbed my bag and threw it into the roadway so I had to duck out among the cars and trucks to get it. That was very funny, though it didn't make me laugh. I coped by planning ahead, using teachers as shields, and when I had to, running faster than even bigger boys. Soon I managed to outsmart them every time. All the same, I still wanted to learn to fight, only I didn't know how to go about it.

I was always the first to arrive at HIS apartment, which never became home. One day, I washed the breakfast dishes and put them away, and vacuumed the lounge room. Otherwise, Mother would have had to do these things, because HE never did any housework. Then I sneaked into the little room off the corridor that the maid had slept in before the War. Having a maid was anticommunist, so now the room was for junk, including shelves full of books. I picked a book and took it to my room. It happened to be about African animals, with pictures, so it was interesting, but even a boring book was better than nothing.

The door slammed. HE was home. I stayed quiet, and as usual HE acted as if I didn't exist. Unfortunately, after awhile I had to relieve myself, and this meant going past HIM. As I tried to creep by without attracting HIS attention, HE looked up. "Oh you're stupid! Why the hell are you tiptoeing like you had shit in your pants? Walk like you were a human being!"

What could I say? But while washing my hands, I noticed HIS slippers, neatly parked in the bathroom. I took one of HIS razor blades, and carried the slippers into the junk room. Enough light came through the glass door although the room had no window. I cut some of the stitching between the sole and upper of each slipper, just enough to have it wear through in a few days. With luck, HE'd trip and break his neck. Then I blunted the razor blade and put it back in its packet, in fourth position. Sure enough, later that week HIS face was covered in little bloody cuts. After this, once a month I blunted a razor blade, mincing HIS face by remote control on some random day HE could never predict.

When Mother came, she was all over HIM and, disgustingly, they mashed their mouths together. Imagine, kissing that stinkhole! Ugh! Then, after that, she wanted to hug and kiss me. I didn't let her. I certainly didn't want HIS slime rubbing off on me!

Then she was terribly busy preparing dinner, and talking on the telephone, and doing a thousand things. Why couldn't HE help too?

The book I found another day was about English sailors who attacked Spanish ships and took their gold. Queen Elizabeth had told them to do it. I decided that if this was good enough for a queen, it was good enough for me. So, I explored the cellar and found pencils, erasers, rulers, watercolor paints, notebooks, stuff like that, leftovers of HIS father's business. I took these to school and used them in two ways. I sold some to get Spanish gold, and made gifts to those boys who hadn't been actively unkind. This way, I managed to be accepted by some, and after awhile used them as shields from the bullies.

Grandmother gave me a Meccano set for my ninth birthday. I didn't understand the instructions, and couldn't make anything. Mother was too busy, Grandmother wasn't there, Aunt Janka had left me, and no way was I going to ask HIM! But HE walked in on me, with nuts and screws and little metal plates spread over the carpet. "Spare us from the idiots of the world," HE said. "If there's a wrong way of doing something, or even if there isn't, he'll do it that way first." So, the next day, when I was taking the washing out of the washing machine, I started a few little holes in HIS socks and almost cut through the elastics of two pairs of HIS underpants.

"That boy is a born stuffup," HE said to a visitor while Mother was out of the room. I had my weapon already in my pocket: a rough little stone I'd picked up on the way home. At night, I put it into his shoe, hoping it'd wear a hole through to his brain.

I hated life. I hated me. I dreamed about how good it would be to die, to not-be. I knew the reason: HIM. So, it'd be wrong to kill myself. That'd just remove a nuisance from HIS life. It'd be better to get rid of HIM! I continued doing secret things to get HIM so angry that HE and Mother would fight, then we could go away from HIS house and I could have Mother back.

I put butter on the chair HE sat on in the kitchen during breakfast, and it made a lovely wet-looking spot on HIS trousers, and HE went off to work like that. I carefully cut almost through HIS shoelace so the weakness wasn't visible—till HE tried to tighten it. I took money from his wallet, and spent it on ice creams, chocolates and stuff—more untraceable Spanish gold. Day after day, I found new tortures, and always so I couldn't be blamed for it. This was fun, and I did notice that HE and Mother now had arguments. Maybe I was winning.

One day, Mother said, "My sweet, you'll have a little sibling!"

That was wonderful. Other children had siblings, and I thought if I had a brother, I could teach him to like me before he found out what a stupid, terrible boy I was. I didn't want a sister, because she'd grow into a girl who'd laugh at me. That's what girls did.

Mother's tummy grew. She always looked tired, but still worked long hours and did all the housework. A book in the junk room was about nursing, and I found childbirth in it. Horrific! Poor mother! And, I thought, what a silly way for people to be born. Why couldn't we be an egg outside like birds do it, or maybe a seed like a plant? Because I felt sorry for her, I spent more time in helping when nobody noticed. All the washing was put away, and the kitchen clean, and the house vacuumed. I never told anyone I was doing those things. Anyway, this still left me plenty of time for reading books, and designing the next act of war against HIM.

My brother Áron was born in June 1952, and I was not alone any more. Mother took him to work where he was cared for in the child-minding center she'd started up, the first in Hungary. When she came home, I took Áron from her and loved looking after him. Every day, Mother used a pump thing to fill some bottles with mother's milk, and so I could feed him. I was very good at changing his diaper without pricking him with the pin, and all his milestones were with me: the first smile, the first time he held up his head unsupported, when he rolled over, and sat up, and started to crawl. I read him stories although I knew he couldn't understand them yet. Even when he was teething, I could always make him smile.

HE took less interest in Áron than I did, so Áron was more my baby than HIS. If I could get rid of HIM, Mother, Áron and I could be very happy together. So, I became even more ingenious in my guerrilla war. The best trick was the Battle of the Toilet. Mother kept rolls of new toilet paper on a high ledge where I couldn't possibly reach. HE was always the first to use the little room in the morning. So, one night I managed to stay awake long enough to sneak out of my room, and use the stepladder from the pantry to get a roll down. I stuffed it into the toilet bowl with the brush, then tidied everything away. In the morning, there came this great roar, and swearwords as bad as those of the boys at school. I raced out.

HE stood with HIS nicely polished shoes submerged in water and shit! HE was shouting at Mother that she was stupid, putting the toilet rolls where one could fall in and block it.

I managed to return to my room before laughing my head off.

But even then, HE and mother forgave each other. I just had to try harder. Every day, I found new secret tortures for HIM. I studied HIM with great care so I could anticipate his actions, and succeeded every time. HE often interrogated me like a policeman in a detective novel, but HE knew I was stupid, so it was easy to act stupid.

All the same, I knew HE suspected where HIS torture came from. I once overheard HIM saying to somebody, when Mother was away, "One day, that boy will murder me unless I murder him first!" The friend laughed, but HE and I knew it was true.

Changes

Two big changes in my life came when I was 11. There was a 50 meter running race, and I won it by two meters. After all, I'd had plenty of practice, escaping from the bullies. In response, Mother took me to the local athletics club. The coach told me to run around the 400 meter track. I did, as fast as I could. When I finished, he looked down at me. "Do you smoke?" he demanded.

"I, um..."

"You'll never be a champion if you smoke." That was the only thing he ever said to me, but that gave me the idea that I could become a champion, because of course I had no intention of making myself stink like HIM.

After this, I ran whenever I could. Instead of waiting for the tram I ran from stop to stop, usually getting all the way, saving the fare too. I read books about running, and learned that you need to make your upper body strong too. I started doing pushups, bicep curls, chin-ups and sit-ups. I spent Spanish gold on buying a spring thing you squeeze with your hands as exercise. One day, a bully managed to grab my bag. I grasped his wrist and squeezed. He let go and started crying, and my finger-marks showed on his skin for several days as black bruises.

Running was wonderful. Once I warmed up, I entered a space without time. The world was beautiful and my mind worked twice as fast and twice as well. Then my body hurt for a while, and when I pushed through that, I entered an even better space without thought, without sadness, without anger, without self-hate.

The second change was that I fell in love, and decided that girls were not monsters after all. This was another holiday with Grandmother, though sadly without Aunt Janka. Áron was too young. We stayed in a big house with ten children. Unexpectedly, all of them were friendly. For the first time in my life, I was just another child. I learned to play ping-pong, and surprised myself by beating all the other children, and even some adults. Of course, I could be good at something useless. That didn't stop me from being a stupid stuffup in important things.

The lady who ran the place had a ten-year-old daughter, Ildikó. When I saw her, I wished I could paint. She had blue eyes and golden hair, rare in Hungary. When she looked at me she always smiled, and only Aunt Janka had done that. I could talk with her in a way I'd never been able to with anyone, and I knew lots of things from my wide reading she found interesting. I made her laugh with poems and jokes. So, my every thought was to make her happy.

All too soon, the holiday was over. We promised to write to each other. I wrote three letters to her, but she never replied. Back in the reality of home, I realized the truth: she didn't love me either. Nobody could. But after this, I became interested in girls, fascinated by breasts, and wondered what it'd feel like to kiss a girl.

Time passed, then came 1956, and the revolution, and I found myself in Vienna, Austria.

4. 1957-1961: High school

Uncle Paul

In thinking about the influences that brought me to contentment, I need to write a very complex story, so complex that a chronological account confuses even me. So, I thought to present my high school years by themes.

Uncle Pali spoke fluent German, English and French, so the various Legations employed him as interpreter. He tried to send me to Switzerland or England or wherever, but nobody wanted an unattached thirteen-year-old. A friend in Australia sponsored him and Erzsi, and he had to take me along. We rode a train to Hamburg, Germany, then a Qantas Super Constellation turbojet. It had three tails and four great jet-turned propellers, and, incredibly, held a hundred people. We covered the immense distance to Australia in only three days. Everything was interesting. I'd read about Muslims, and saw men wearing turbans in Abu Dhabi. I saw brown-skinned people in Karachi, and palm trees in Darwin.

Sydney was so hot that the air above the tarmac shimmered as we got off the plane. A line of ladies handed out packets of Minties to all the refugees. "Welcome, love," one said to me. I remembered the sound of the words, though I didn't know the meaning yet. I was very interested in the low cut of her dress, with suntanned mounds peeking out.

We ended up in a migrant hostel at Matraville, in south Sydney. Uncle Pali and Erzsi had a married room, and I shared a tiny room with a young man within the single men's quarters. Uncle Pali told me, now I had to call them Uncle Paul and Liz. He got a job, and also went to night school.

Within two years, he bought an old block of apartments. In addition to working and studying, he started renovating it himself. I did wonder where he'd got the money for the deposit, but it didn't concern me too much.

The next year, he imported another of his girlfriends, Elena, and married her. He bought a second block of rundown apartments and settled her there.

I was outraged. Poor Erzsi... oh, Liz. She was a gentle, decent woman. How could he betray her like this? I plucked up my courage and confronted him.

He looked down his nose at me. "Filip, mind your own business. Liz is Catholic. She's always known that we could never marry and have children. Elena is a good Jew."

"You're giving Jews a bad name!"

He smacked my face, hard, and we didn't speak until Elena gave birth to a daughter. Then I couldn't resist being there, to love the child. Still, I calculated my debt to him. I cost him one pound, seventeen shillings and sixpence a week while at the migrant hostel. The government paid the rest. I worked out the total he'd paid for me, and thereafter kept a tally. I was going to repay every penny.

Soon, Uncle Paul bought a third block of apartments and settled an Australian lady named Jan there, nictitating among his possessions. Since later he bought more houses, I suspect he had more ladies as well.

What's more, right through all this, he had affairs and one-night stands.

All of his women I'd met were decent and pleasant, merely unwise in the choice of the man in their lives. I became close to Elena's three children, who are all troubled, traumatized people thanks to their father.

My mother was dying in 2000, so I returned to be with her. She told me many stories, one of which cleared up a mystery. When Antal and Pali were planning the escape from Hungary, Antal gave his brother-in-law a fortune in gold and jewels, saying, "Take the boy on the first truck. If anything happens, this is for his upkeep. If we turn up, we'll share it for our common benefit." Of course, he knew that something would happen, and Pali must have deduced it too. That was why he'd tried to offload me in Vienna, and parked me in the migrant hostel for five years, till I became independent.

Guess where the deposit for the apartment blocks came from?

Paul was worth twenty million dollars when he died. Had he left me any of it, I'd have refused such tainted money.

I'm grateful to have had Paul in my life. He taught me to be a faithful husband, that people deserve respect and decent treatment, and that money costs more than it's worth. I feel sorry for him.

School

I had to go to the local boys' high school, although I couldn't even read street signs yet.

The first day, a big boy said something to me. Everyone laughed, so I smiled. He said something else, then put a hand on my chest and pushed. I went back with the push but grabbed his fingers and twisted.

He yelled in surprise and fell to the ground. A ring of boys gathered as if by magic, and they were laughing—at him.

A teacher appeared and listened to a number of boys. He gave a stern-sounding lecture, then turned to me. "Good," he said. I already knew that word. "Tank you," I answered, not being able to cope with the "th" sound yet.

When boys learned my name, they laughed, but they didn't say it right. Instead of Lipschitz, they said Shitlips. Soon I knew what that meant, and got in trouble twice for bashing some boy. Whenever I heard "Shitlips," I was back to being seven, having shit forced onto my face. I felt the horror, anger, helplessness, and wanted to die.

I could now do thirty chin-ups, and five one-handed. Everyone knew I was strong, so they only called me Shitlips when in a group, or muttered it while a teacher was around. All the same, I could read their faces while they thought it, and that was as bad.

After I put the bully on the ground, I had friends for the first time in my life. They worked hard to teach me English, and soon I could tell them stories about Hungary, the revolution (though I embellished it a lot to keep their interest), and like with Ildikó, about things I'd learned from reading. I even knew stuff about Australia that was new to them.

The headmaster, Mr. Dutton, took a special interest in me. He presented me with a school uniform, which, unknown to me at the time, he'd bought with his own money. He gave me private coaching in English, and earned my respect by being the only person in the school who sometimes beat me at chess. He even took me home, where his wife cooked beautiful meals.

I decided that I could do worse than become like Mr. Dutton.

At the end of the first year, I passed all subjects, and got top marks in Geography, Science and Mathematics. Of course, this wasn't because I was smart, but because it was a rough suburb. Also, although I managed to fool people into accepting me, this was only because I put on a good act. Inside, I still knew myself to be stupid and ugly, an unlovable stuffup.

As my English improved, I realized why I had friends. They were the ones the bullies picked on, and I was protection. That boy I'd conquered on my first day was the worst bully, and I'd bested him. As long as they were with me, they were left in peace. This was good. All the same, I knew it was not me they liked—how could they?—but the safety I provided.

I became what I thought of as a lame duck collector. Any kid with problems seemed to seek me out. Ross said one lunchtime, "My mom and dad fight all the time. I don't even want to go home any more!"

I didn't say to him that he was lucky to have parents at all, just put an arm over his shoulder and sat with him for a while. When the bell went he said, "Thanks, Filip."

I didn't think I'd done anything, but the trouble was, the next couple of nights I lost sleep thinking about his problem. I came up with the idea that he should write a letter to his parents, letting them know how their fighting affected him. He told me three days later that they went off to the Marriage Guidance Council!

Sometimes, kids cried on my shoulder because of girlfriend troubles. If only I'd had a girlfriend to be troubled by!

In my second year, and every year after that, I topped every subject, showing what a poor school this was. The other kids were not interested in study, that was all.

I trained hard for running, and also played basketball and soccer. I wanted to be an Olympic distance runner. Every morning, I woke at 4:30 and went for a run. After a shower I ate all I could in the communal dining room, then sleepwalked to school, alert again by the time I arrived.

Life went on, but it was terribly lonely. When studying, when running or playing sports, I was fine. The rest of the time, I was an empty dead space. I was inside a black steel box with no light, no way out.

Letters from Mother and Grandmother helped, and soon even Áron wrote childish notes. That was great. Of course, they didn't know me any more, only what I wrote to them, and that was always cheerful, reporting achievements rather than feelings.

After the first year, I only had two fights. George Papadopoulos came to our school at the start of second year. He was born in Australia to Greek parents, and from his first day, copped "Greasy wog!" and the like. I kept an eye out for him, helped him to settle in and let it be known he was to be left alone.

One day, he turned up with a black eye. Three fourth-years had cornered him after school. At lunchtime, I got him to point them out to me. I knew them by sight. All three were known as good Rugby players.

I strolled up to them. As I passed, I thumped the blond one on the sternum with the ball of my palm. I knew from my reading about Tai Chi that this stops a person's heart for long enough to cause fainting, and had been keen to try it out.

Sure enough, down he went.

"What the fuck!" the pimply-faced one shouted.

"Sorry, my hand slipped," I said, smiling sweetly at him. He towered over me and raised a fist.

I turned away as if afraid, and kicked him hard in the guts. This was a Karate trick I'd read.

He fell bent double, joining his mate.

The biggest boy was coming for me. "I'll kill you, bloody Shitlips!"

We were surrounded by a crowd of boys by now. I skipped sideways, so his bull-rush carried him past. I kicked him just above the split of his buttocks, shoe against bone. "You and whose army, creampuff?"

Two teachers were converging.

He charged for me again.

I made a ball of my body, rolled forward. My feet shot out, into his groin. Kung Fu.

I was standing, the three bullies still down, when the teachers arrived.

We were hauled off to Mr. Dutton. "Filip, I'm not used to such behavior from you," he said, then to the others, "Are you three in the habit of attacking younger boys?"

Pimples answered first, "Sir, that's not fair! Shi... Lip... Whatever-his-name attacked us!"

"Mr. Dutton," I said, "it's true. I attacked them."

The headmaster looked at me.

"Yesterday, these three heroes were brave enough to beat up George Papadopoulos, whose only crime is that his parents are Greek."

"Filip, violence doesn't justify violence. Two wrongs add up rather than cancel out. You know I'll need to discipline you?"

"Yes Sir. I'm happy to pay the price, provided they get theirs too. And if anyone bullies any kid, I'll do it again."

Mr. Dutton shook his head. "You're not a policeman. If anyone bullies someone, the proper thing is to report it to a teacher."

"Yes Sir." But I knew the message would spread.

I had to admire Mr. Dutton's ingenuity in punishment. The three heroes were banned from playing Rugby for three games, while I was banned from the school Library for three weeks.

The second occasion was on the last day of my final year. We'd sat for our Leaving Certificate exams, and were spending time till the end of the school year. A bunch of us were walking down the corridor when Mr. Cartiff came the other way. He was a fattish, tired man of sixty-odd, waiting to retire. Just in front of me was John Webster. As the teacher neared him, John suddenly punched his jaw, sending him to the floor. "I've always wanted to punch a teacher!" he shouted.

I don't know what happened next, but an unknown time later, three guys held me, and John lay at my feet, his face a bloody mess, both his arms broken.

I was interviewed by the police. After a grilling, the officer said, "This kind of behavior cannot be condoned. If you ever do anything like this again, you'll end up in jail, do you hear?"

"Yes Sir."

"But privately, congratulations. Would you consider joining the police force?" He patted me on the back and let me go.

Boys' Club

I was on a twenty-mile run one evening when another runner caught up with me, a big bloke with wide shoulders. Speaking in rhythm with our breathing, we introduced ourselves. He was Dale. I did say "Filip," but he misheard it as "Pip," which I liked. It was a palindrome like Mother's name, Hannah. After this I insisted on being called Pip, removing a source of confusion for people who couldn't cope with the F.

Dale told me that he ran to train for boxing. He did this at the Police and Citizens' Boys' Club in Maroubra Junction. I went there the next evening, and it was a beaut place. They had ping pong tables, weights, and different activities every night. During the next three years, I won three cups for table tennis, my first trophies. I learned the Olympic lifts, and could clean and press my own bodyweight by my seventeenth birthday.

I joined classes on judo and boxing. I liked the training and discipline of boxing, and even more the friendship with Dale who was a champion, but I never liked the idea that to win I needed to scramble someone's brain. Mind you, what a stupid place to put a brain! In a sensible body, it'd be in the chest cavity.

Judo was wonderful. I had a natural bent for the way of thinking, that you use the power of a situation to achieve your ends. Wasn't that what I'd done with Uncle Antal and the Hungarian school bullies? I was well on the way to my black belt by the end of school.

Wednesday evening's activity was dancing. I had to go, because I wanted contact with girls. Learning the steps was easy, but I failed Girls 101. I simply clammed up. I didn't know what interested them. I didn't want to reveal my true nature, and didn't know what else to do.

One day, a girl came over to me. "I've heard that you're a Brain."

"Not really. I do well in school subjects, yeah."

We danced, and looked at each other, and I couldn't think of a single thing to say to her.

There were also school dances, and sport carnivals involving both sexes, and looking back, I know that each time, some girls were interested in me. For me, it was a torture. By fifth year, the very thought of a dance or party had me go cold and wanting to hide in a dark hole. All the same, I kept going in the vain hope that, this time, I'd find a girl to love.

Angels

Mr. Dutton was my first angel. He taught me a great deal of academic learning, probably twice as much as to any of my classmates. More than that, he taught me decency. When I decided to reject violence, I copied his way of firm discipline with absolute fairness.

We kept in touch through my university years, and he and Mrs. Dutton came to my wedding. I treasure the photo showing him in the background of a portrait of Jacinta and me.

Miss Stapleton was my second angel. She ran the milk bar in Maroubra Junction, next to the movie theater. Denis, one of the kids I protected at school, worked for her, and when she needed a second employee, lined up the job for me. We had to wear a red jacket, and held a tray on a neck strap and sold candies, drinks or ice creams before and after shows and during interval. This gave me many opportunities to moon at girls, dreaming about but not daring to approach them.

At the end of second year, I received several prizes for academic performance and as the captain of the junior basketball team that had won the district competition. Uncle Paul was not in the audience, but Miss Stapleton was. She turned up every year to witness my triumphs, including graduating with my B.Sc. Sadly, she died soon after.

Miss Stapleton never married because when she was a child, a tram had run over her hand and cut several fingers off. The hand looked ugly, so she knew no one would want her, and she built a life of contentment while avoiding romantic entanglements. Inside, she was beautiful. From her I learned the joy of caring and giving, and the idea I applied many years later, that you can feel good with what you have, regardless of what you lack.

Mr. and Mrs. Roberts and Mrs. Bourke were the next angels to move into my life. It happened because Princess Alexandra visited Australia. A big show was organized, at which boys and girls were to put on an Aboriginal pageant. The Boys' Club was sending a contingent. Dale said, "Hey, Pip, there'll be lots of sheilas there." So, we went.

Dale was BIG. On the first day of rehearsal, a girl approached him. "Hi, I'm Cynthia."

Dale gave me a wink, and introduced me too.

She was with a Girl Guide group, and had an ulterior motive. Her father was the scoutmaster of a Sea Scout troop who'd just been given a racing skiff and were looking for boys big enough to crew it. Dale qualified, while light-boned Pip didn't. It was both or neither, so next Saturday I found myself out on Sydney Harbour, swooping along the waves. Even with Dale on the monkey wire, the boat wanted to lie right over, so I soaked my jumper in sea water and put a waterproof jacket over it. The two of us then managed the job.

Dale was too serious about boxing to be able to devote time to another activity, but I stuck. We won some regattas. I attended scouts Thursday nights, finding another boy to take my place with Miss Stapleton. I learned bushcraft at camps, and became the Assistant Scoutmaster after I graduated as Queen's Scout.

Why? Because Mr. Roberts, "Skip," acted more like a father to me than my own father ever had. He'd been a Navy officer during the War, and was a small, neat, softly spoken man for whom public service was natural. He talked to me as if I was his equal, and after the first few weeks took me home on some weekends.

Mrs. Roberts was the Universal Mother, and spent most of her time in various volunteer good works. She was the first person I introduced Jacinta to. Her blessing reassured me about my choice of a life partner.

Mrs. Bourke was Mrs. Roberts' opposite: skinny and tall rather than short and rounded, a working class woman rather than an educated lady, a constant buzz of energy rather than a haven of peace. Her son Greg was one of "my" scouts, and when she heard that I lived in a migrant hostel with no family, she had me sleep at her place at least once a week. We shared a twisted sense of humor, and like Mr. and Mrs. Roberts, she taught me that I was worth liking and even loving, that perhaps I wasn't as ugly and unlovable as I felt.

Back to school for my last angel: Mr. Woods. He started as English teacher in my fourth year. His classes were FUN. We did play readings, and wrote stories in which each person had to contribute a paragraph in series. He inspired me with anecdotes about his student days, being particularly eloquent about psychology.

I wanted to be a physicist, to contribute to human welfare. When I got to first year University, the Science requirements were Physics, Chemistry, Mathematics and one other subject. Thanks to Mr. Woods' stories, I chose Psychology. Halfway through first year I became disenchanted with physics. We had all too much technology, which was destroying our world, so I switched to psychology. Mr. Woods' nudge took my life in the direction necessary to become a healer.

His second gift to me was debating. He organized a debating team in my final year. I said, "Sir, I've got an accent. I can't do it."

"Lipschitz, you've got an accent and you can do it."

I became the whip. That meant thinking on my feet. As the opposition talked, I had to listen hard, and think of ways of demolishing their argument. I turned out to be very good at this. I was careful always to treat them with respect, avoiding personal ridicule, but managed to twist their arguments so that the audience roared with laughter.

We, the roughest school in the contest, reached the State finals. There, the opposing team was from an elite private girls' school. One of the three was this gorgeous blonde with huge blue eyes, and lips I couldn't take my eyes off. We were introduced before the contest and she made a beeline for me. "Hi, I'm Leah."

"Pip."

"I know. I sat in on your semi-final, and you were brilliant." She quoted some of the things I'd said.

"Yeah, well, bulldust doeth flow from his lips."

"Where do you come from?"

"I was born in Hungary, but at a very young age, and–"

"Oh really? Most people are born at a very young age."

"Well done! You'd be surprised how many people get taken in. Anyway, then I was transported to Australia for the term of my natural life."

"Fascinating. Look..." She wrote a phone number on a piece of paper and passed it to me. "Phone me after this is over."

Wow.

We went up on stage and got going. Naturally, I was simply unable to concentrate on my task, my head being full of cotton wool—pink and starlit—and I did a very pedestrian job as whip. We came second. And when I rang that phone number the next day, the person answering had never heard of a Leah.

This led to eons of depression. All the same, Mr. Woods' legacy enabled me to fool many an audience with my brilliance and entertainment value.

5. 1962-1965: Young man

Worker

I found a summer job while waiting to see if I got into University. I knew I would, because my results were within the top 200 in the State, but I also knew I was a stuffup, so if things could go wrong, they would.

My work was with an asphalting contractor, good hard physical labor. The bad part was Dino and Glenn. They were in their mid-twenties, each a head taller and 60 pounds heavier than me. On my first day, they told me that both had a third-Dan black belt in Karate. They were immensely strong from years of manual labor. When Dino found out I planned to go to University, he instantly became hostile, as if I'd accused him of being stupid.

Several times a day, they played little pranks on me. I'd be wheeling a heavy barrow-load when two large shovelfuls descended next to the handles, nearly jerking my arms out of their sockets. Or a shovelful of hot mix fell all over my boots, and into them. Or it was merely verbal abuse: "Gee, we'd better ask the genius before we decide anything." "Accidental" knocks, half an hour of my work spoiled by a carefully misplaced footprint, dirt spilled onto my sandwiches... the harassment was not particularly smart, but certainly annoying.

I stuck it out, because it gave me a sort of a flashback. Involuntarily, I recalled the endless guerrilla warfare I'd fought against Antal, and, for the first time, I identified with him, realized how he'd felt. What he'd done to me as a little boy was inexcusable, but now I agreed with Mr. Dutton: two wrongs add up rather than cancel out.

On my second payday, Glenn glimpsed the name Lipschitz on my pay envelope. "Shitlips!" he shouted, a brilliant new invention to him.

This time, my flashback was not to those boys when I was seven, but to the Battle of the Toilet. I felt myself to be Antal, standing in shit. So, I didn't get angry, just shrugged it off. I think this was the start of my healing. I need to add Dino and Glenn to my list of teachers.

Queen Elizabeth the First had inspired my childhood, so when I turned 18, I swore allegiance to Elizabeth II. Uncle Paul was absent. Mr. and Mrs. Dutton, Miss Stapleton, Mr. and Mrs. Roberts, Mrs. Bourke, and several boys from the scout troop attended.

This was a legal opportunity for a name change, so I shucked Shitlips forever by becoming Pip Lipkin.

Undergraduate

I won a Commonwealth Scholarship. With living-away-from-home allowance, I could survive, sort of. Home became an old house in the slum of Chippendale, near Uni. It was owned by a French couple who ran a restaurant in a nearby busy street. Their main trade was on weekends. During the week, the working men renting rooms had breakfast and dinner in the restaurant. Lunch and weekend meals were not included. On my nonexistent income, I often survived on a loaf of bread and a tin of baked beans.

Four of the guys worked for the railways. Thursday, payday, was for best scotch whisky. Saturday was cheap red wine from Coles. By Monday they smelt of methylated spirits, and Wednesday was the DTs. This horrified me, and I'm afraid I must have shown my disapproval. One day, poor old Sid said, "All right for a young bloke like you to pull up your nose. But wait till some woman gets her clutches in you and sucks you dry!"

I could say nothing in reply. I didn't even know how to apologize. All the same, I was determined that, whatever misfortune may strike me, I'd never turn to alcohol for relief.

I made up a one-mile running track on campus. There was a 600 meter hill. I arose at 4:30 as usual, jogged to the campus, shed my tracksuit and sprinted up this hill. Then I ran downhill over a course I'd stepped out as 1000 meters, making a mile in total. Ten laps was a good morning's workout.

Uni. was a shock. On the first day, map in hand, I sought my 9 a.m. lecture room. Thousands of strangers milled around, all seeming purposeful. No one looked at anyone else. I felt like an insignificant mote in the ocean. The thought came, *What the hell am I doing on this planet?* This feeling of isolation got worse and worse, and when I spoke to people, often they treated me as inferior. I worked out why: I spoke like the people I'd known for five years—working class. So, I adjusted my language to that of Mr. and Mrs. Roberts, and that helped.

There were exceptions to disdain. Only five people took my four subjects: Cathy, Roger, Brian, Eric and I. We got into the habit of meeting daily, discussing lectures and brainstorming on assignments. We divided our reading lists into five. Each read one part, and supplied the others with detailed notes. Cathy and I were also in the same psychology tutorial. She had ash-blonde hair, was big where it counted and tiny elsewhere, and was acknowledged as a genius. As well as doing a full time science degree, she also studied full time at the Conservatorium of Music. Unfortunately, she was also engaged to some bloke.

During first semester, our tutor was Mr. Landauer. He gave Cathy an A for our first assignment, and me a C. Since the content was nearly identical, although we'd written it up separately, I complained. He said, "You copied off her, didn't you?"

I was outraged. "No!" But he wouldn't change my mark. He said he expected me to fail first year. This was validation that I had "Kick Me!" written on my forehead, and was just what I could expect. Fortunately, we got a different tutor for second semester. Thanks to Landauer's marks, my final grade was only a Distinction.

Brian turned into a good mate. He regularly took me home to his parents, who ran a corner grocery store. He was the first person in their family to have gone to Uni. While there, I was just another son. His younger sister Diana was particularly friendly, not that she could possibly have been interested in me as a male.

Because I had no social life and no home life, I had plenty of time despite the hours of running. So, as well as my four formal subjects, I examined the syllabuses of other courses, and sat in on selected lectures in History, Geography and English. I attended a three month course on Chaucer, just for interest.

I joined the Athletics Club, but not the Debating Club. There I might have encountered Leah, and the thought was terrifying.

Girls in general were terrifying. They were everywhere, and female was beautiful, desirable and unattainable. The reason was clear. I had no past learning. No sisters; all-boys' school both in Hungary and Australia; single-men's quarters at the hostel... how could I know anything about girls? I set up a program of learning. Once a week, I sidled up to some stranger and stammered my way through a conversation, aiming to make it last five minutes. Then at home, I minutely analyzed it. What worked, what didn't? What did I do right, where did I stuff up? How could I do it better next time?

In the Quad one lunchtime, I was laughing at the way humans walk. A girl spoke next to me: "What's so funny?"

I looked at her. Chubby, with glasses, so less threatening than most. I said, "Imagine a slow motion movie of people walking. You lift a leg, deliberately fall forward, then put the leg down just in time. That's why it takes us two years to learn it. A horse is born able to walk."

"I've never thought of it that way. How would you organize it?"

"Somehow, eight legs seems perfect."

"Ugh, a spider!" She walked off.

When analyzing this exchange, I realized two things. She'd made the approach, and my mistake was telling stuff instead of asking questions.

I worked out in the gym, participated in daily training sessions with the Athletics Club and raced with them on Saturdays. As everywhere, though, I managed to provide amusement for a certain kind of person. Here, they were young men from private schools, living in exclusive suburbs, expected to follow the shining careers of their parents. Picking on Pip became a fun activity. The best joke was when two of them whispered to all the girls that Pip had an unusually small penis. I couldn't do anything about it without becoming a flasher. I had dreams of beating Pat Greene's face into a pulp, but was finished with violence, after the damage I'd done to John Webster.

I went along to the regular Athletics parties, but hated them. Everyone got drunk, which disgusted me. Anyway, all the girls had boyfriends.

Why did I go? I wanted to belong. That was also why I nominated and was elected to the Club committee, was active in student politics, and wrote letters to the Editor in the student newspaper.

During winter, there was cross-country racing in Centennial Park, where I fitted in much better than at Uni. I'd made sprinting uphill my specialty, while another youngster, Chris, was really good at speeding downhill. The races were handicapped, with Olympic champions starting last. Chris and I were in the middle, usually together.

Side by side we ran along the grass and roads, around curves, then the hill came. I took off, passing several runners. On the downhill, I then needed to maintain my gain. Sometimes he caught me by the time we reached the flat. Sometimes it took him another few hundred meters, but he always did. Then we had a see-saw all the way to the finish line. This was so entertaining that several top runners hung back for a while, just to see which of us would best the other today.

The main change during my second year was that I progressed in my course on Girls 101. I could now hold the attention of a stranger and make her laugh.

This brunette was nearly my height, her walk almost like a soldier's march. As we came out of the Philosophy lecture, I asked, "Did you think he was fudging it a bit when talking about Gilbert Ryle?"

"You mean you understood enough to think that?"

We laughed. "Well, I read Ryle's book last week, and that made more sense than this hour's gobbedlygook. What course are you doing?" Ask questions, Pip.

"Education."

"What, you going to be a high school teacher?"

"Yes. That's what I've always wanted to do. What about you?"

Strike 1 for Pip. She is interested enough to return a question. "Got time for a coffee?"

She smiled. "Yeah, I've got two free hours now."

As we walked toward the Union building, I answered, "I'm going to major in Psychology. Save the world and all that, you know."

"How will psychology save the world?"

"We're busy destroying it. I've read a lot about what humanity is doing to this planet. We've got too much technology, not enough understanding. That's why I switched from Physics to Psych." Time to return to her. "But I'd think that being a high school teacher is a scary job. You're brave."

She squared her shoulders even more. "I can cope with the little monsters! By the way, my name is Sarah."

"I'm Pip."

"Were you Pipette when you were little?"

I liked her laugh. "No, I was Filip then, with an F." We'd arrived at the Caf, and lined up.

"I notice a bit of an accent. Where you from?"

I gave her the born at a very young age bit.

"Oh, how old were you?"

"Zero of course."

We collected our coffees, she insisting on paying for her own. "You're a bit of a rascal, aren't you?"

"Got to keep trying. Very trying, I know."

We sat at a just-vacated table. "You'd do well as a stage comic. It's nice to talk with someone different."

Here was the opening. "Sarah, um... There's a great new movie by Peter Sellers. Would you like to, um..."

"I'd love to."

Graduated to Girls 201!

After the movie, I drove her home—North Shore of course–and we talked all the way. She allowed me to kiss her outside her door.

In my head, I was in love. In my heart... nothing. I was still the dead space, inside the black steel box.

We became good friends. She said, "Look, Pip, I have this feeling that if I let you get too close, I'll have you for life. I'm not ready for that, with anyone." So, she became my first sister.

Again and again, I managed to get a date, and became friends, and was clearly liked. Again and again, I wanted a lover and got a sister.

At last, I finished my Honors year, with my research actually published in the *Journal of Cognitive Science*. Mother sent an invitation: she and Uncle Antal wanted to pay for me to visit them.

The cheapest way was a six-week cruise on a Greek liner.

6. *1965-1966: Starting to heal*

Cruise

"You going on a cruise ship? Mate, you've got it made." Chris nudged me in the ribs. "When the sheilas smell the salt air, they drop their panties." He was not alone—every bloke who heard of my coming trip assured me of this good fortune.

Unfortunately, the female passengers must have heard the same rumor. They looked at every male as a potential seducer, and kept their legs crossed. It was funny, watching randy guys chasing unwilling prey.

At least, it would have been funny if I hadn't been one of those randy guys. Not that I was confident enough to chase anyone. Admiring from afar was more my style.

Three-quarters of the passengers had migrated to Australia, changed their minds and were now returning to Greece. Dark-haired kids were everywhere. Before we'd even departed, I had fun playing and joking with a few.

It was exciting when the great ship left the wharf, and slowly moved out into the harbor. Then we went through the Heads, and the first swell hit us. A universal wail sounded, the smell of vomit thickening the air.

I was unaffected after years of sailing on the harbor, but the stink was awful. I found a possie in the bow. That became my favorite spot, even when people's stomachs settled down.

There was a fellow whose job was to entertain the passengers, and a four-piece band. I took part in the daily activities, but always as an outsider, an observer. For the first time in ten years without my antidepressants of study and running, I crashed. I did spend a total of two hours a day power walking around the main deck when most others were asleep, made good use of the tiny gym, and swam in the 12.5 meter pool. Within a few days I read my way through the very inadequate library, then waited for the wretched trip to end.

The nightly dances were a particular torture, as such events always were. Every night, the band played the same repertoire, and their signature tune stayed with me for many years as a trigger to depression. At first, I asked girls to dance, tried to chat with them, but the Greek ones wanted a husband, in Greece of course, and the Aussies were only interested in trivia that bored me to tears. I'd have loved to experience the joys of sex, but as I said, the girls were not playing, with me or any other passenger as far as I know. The ship's officers may have scored.

At long interminable last, we reached Piraeus. I took train for Belgrade.

Hungary

Belgrade, Yugoslavia. I stood in the carriage doorway, scanning the crowd, when I saw a little fur starfish racing for me. It was Mother, her arms outstretched. We hugged. She was so tiny! I could have picked her up with one hand, fur coat and all. She was sobbing, "My darling! My sweet heart!" over and over.

Maybe somebody loved me, after all.

Beyond her, smiling, stood a pleasant little man in a dark coat and hat. His eyes lit up as I looked at him over Mother's head. Being the eternal observer, I was good at sizing people up. I decided that Antal, the monster of my childhood, was actually a decent bloke.

When we shook hands, I had to be careful not to crush his.

Speaking Hungarian was difficult at first, but by the end of the drive from Belgrade to Budapest along the icy highway, I was back into it. A problem was that Hungarian has different language usage for children and adults, and I'd never learned to speak as an adult.

Eventually, there was the sandy-colored wall, with the ancient bullet marks now gone. The big gate swung open, pushed by this teenage boy with broad shoulders. I'd seen photos of course, but wasn't prepared for the reality: the tiny boy I'd left was now on the way to manhood!

Inside, Grandmother had hot food waiting. She'd aged a lot, with a dowager's hump and deep wrinkles on her face.

I towered over them all, feeling awkward. We talked about super-ficialities, me of course pretending that the trip had been fun, then Áron showed me to the bedroom. It was my old room, now set up as his, with a spare mattress under the window. Posters of bikini-clad girls and space monsters on the wall, a radio and record player with lots of tapes and records, weights in one corner, a few textbooks on a bookshelf: a typical teenager's hangout.

"Oh, Filip," he said, sprawling on his bed, "I've been looking forward to this all my life!"

"I've missed you too. When you were born, I was glad because I thought at last I'll have a friend."

He grinned. "I still remember you reading to me. I can hear your voice—not your voice now but the boy's voice, although I can't remember what you said."

"So, how is life?"

"Would be all right, except for him." He looked toward the door.

"What do you mean?"

"If you listen to him, I'm stupid, an idiot, a stuffup who can't do anything right and will never amount to anything, a waste of oxygen."

"You mean, he treats you the way he treated me?"

"If you got the same, then yes."

"Right, Áron, listen. We can fix both of us, once and for all. I used to think he was treating me like that because I was his stepson, a nuisance that got between him and Mother. I used to think that something was wrong with me, that I was a stupid stuffup. But if he does it to you too, can you see what that says?"

We looked at each other. At last, I continued, "The problem is not something wrong with me. The problem is not something wrong with you."

My little brother finished it: "The problem is something wrong with him!"

"So, if it's his problem, we can throw it away. Anything he has said to us is noise. Garbage."

We left it at that. Later I found out that Áron was doing poorly at school. My reaction to being stupid was to study. His had been to opt out, to avoid trying. And to foreshadow, from the resumption of school after my departure, he started to improve, and ended up doing quite well.

Antal was the head of a government department. Mother was still the president of the cooperative, elected annually every year since 1950. Both of them took holidays from these important jobs to be with me. We went to concerts, museums and famous buildings, as a vehicle for having contact. During all this, I became more and more impressed by my stepfather, and liked him a great deal.

We got onto a crowded bus one afternoon. The conductress seemed near the end of her endurance. The bag full of coins around her waist pulled her down like diver's weights. Clearly, her feet hurt, and her voice was hoarse. Antal looked her in the eye, smiled and said, "I bet you'll be glad to go home!"

She lit up like a lamp. While pushing through the unfeeling crowd, she kept returning to us, as if to drink some more refreshment from a fountain. When we got off, she leaned out the door to wave him good-bye.

I now understood what my mother loved about him. This was the real Antal.

All the same, he abused the children in his care.

Over the days, I learned his story. Like most Jewish men, he was sent to the Eastern Front as a work conscript. Their jobs included anything dirty, distasteful or unduly dangerous. The casualty rate was horrendous, and often they were killed by their own side rather than by the Russians. Then, the remnants of the unit were captured at Stalingrad. They were marched through bitter winter, fed almost nothing, beaten if they lagged behind. When they reached Siberia, Antal was the only one left of his unit of 100. By then he could speak, read and write fluently in Russian, the only prisoner to be able to do so. As a result, he was appointed Camp Commandant. It gave him a lot of pleasure to issue orders even to SS officers.

The Russians set them to work, and again he learnt fast. When the war ended, he was in charge of the renovation of a stretch of the Siberian Railway, being so useful they refused to release him until 1948.

Then he met Hannah. He said to me, "Your mother... you know, I've known her all my life, only I didn't know. When I saw her on a bus for the first time, it was meeting an old friend, an old love. I kid you not. I just didn't know her name."

Sitting beside him, Mother laughed. "I thought I recognized him too, and thought he must have been one of Pali's friends, so I smiled at him. He's stuck to me since, and I haven't been able to scrape him off."

I thought I'd take a risk. "Uncle Antal, I used to hate you when I was a boy. Now, I hope to stay your friend."

"Mutual, my boy, mutual."

"I've been watching you since my return and... the way you deal with even complete strangers, is wonderful."

He looked surprised. "Thank you."

"With one exception." I didn't know the Hungarian word for "abusive," so continued, "The way you talk to Áron is the way you used to talk to me and about me. And it's the opposite. It's as if you wanted to hurt us, and it is hurtful."

He looked hurt in turn, but put a good face on it. He looked down for a while, then said, "I'll have to think about that."

After two weeks, Mother needed to return to work, but she did something incredible: introduced me to a woman in her early thirties, Emili, and told me that while she was at work, this lady would show me around.

I said, "Oh, I don't need any special attention, I–"

"Filip, just go with Emili and enjoy yourself."

She was blonde—how did Mother know I favored blondes?—a divorcee who had once had a child who'd died. It was still painful for her to tell me this, and of course I instantly wanted to protect her from the hurt.

I took her to a restaurant, and thanks to the exchange rate, fed the two of us for two Aussie shillings. Then she gave me her address, and said she'd take me caving the next day.

Carefully following the directions on a piece of paper, I successfully used tram, underground train and bus, arriving at her apartment on time. I was hoping my city shoes would be up to walking around in a cave.

I was surprised at her clothing as she let me in: a multicolored, almost transparent garment that'd have looked appropriate in a harem.

"Is that your caving clothes?" I asked.

"It'll be just right for the kind of caving I have in mind." She took my hand to lead me in. Her hand was half the size of mine, and she continuously moved her fingers against my palm in a more than pleasant way. She led me to a room with a beautiful view of the Danube in the distance, and an endless vista of snow-covered roofs. The room was small yet felt spacious, with only a couch, two easy chairs and a coffee table, nature prints on the walls. She sank to the couch, pulling me with her, then snuggled very close. "You don't have to go anywhere to explore this cave," she said.

At last I understood.

I soon noted that she was a natural blonde, and enjoyed being her student in how to please a lady. I got more pleasure than I could have imagined from giving pleasure, and the physical side of it was great for me too. Predictably, in my head, I was in love, and if I hadn't been committed to returning to Australia, I might have stayed with her, devoting my life to making her happy. This was despite knowing that Mother must have paid her for the service.

Antal also engaged in an act of generosity. He lent me his car, and Emili and I drove off into the countryside. She showed me forested mountains and quaint villages, and even taught me the rudiments of skiing. We shared each other's bodies over and over, in more ways than I'd thought possible.

When it was time to return, she said, "Filip, one day you'll make a wonderful husband for some lucky girl."

Home

The return trip on the ocean liner was even more dreary. This time, the majority of passengers were Greeks who had emigrated to Australia, returned to Greece, and now were going back. I decided that dissatisfaction is an inside not an outside thing. As long as you take it with you, you can enjoy being miserable anywhere.

I settled back to University till my friend Brian's life fell apart. When Leanne died, as I've said, I was there for him. For the following two years, I did interesting research, taught small classes (and I was a far better tutor than Mr. Landauer), engaged in student politics and the budding environmental movement, and spent time running, running, running.

Emili's lessons made me bolder on dates, and indeed I was able to give pleasure. All the same, I still kept accumulating sisters, and could find nobody to fill the hole I had for a life partner.

Sadly, while the surface of my life was great, inside I was still an empty place within a black steel box. I now recognized and intellectually discounted the damaging beliefs that Antal had put there, but they still kept influencing me.

As a graduate student, my scholarship was slightly higher, and I earned a little for tutoring, so I invested in a record player. I went to buy my first record. Browsing around, I saw an LP (for those too young, that's a vinyl record). On one side was Pathetique, on the other Appassionata. I'd never come across either term, and although I knew about the composer, Beethoven, I was ignorant about his music. However, the titles spoke to me. Pathetic was how I felt, because of the lack of passion in my life. I bought the disk.

When I crashed, I listened over and over, and soon bought other records. Chopin particularly spoke to me. Listening led to reading about music. I discovered a new world, and a new way of putting peace into my life.

One day, I'd missed lunch and stopped to buy some potato chips. Walking out of the shop was Glenn, my torturer of six years ago. He grinned in a friendly way. "G'day! It's Shitlips!"

I grinned right back at him as if unoffended, although inside I was instantly back to the shit-boys when I was seven. "And it's Glenn. Still breaking your back for a pittance?"

I walked past him, leaving him open-mouthed.

In Psychology, I'd learned about exposure therapy. When a traumatic memory is triggered so you feel as if you were back there, the way to get rid of it is to allow the experience. So, that's what I did now. I sat at a table, and put myself right back: the bodily sensations, smells, sights and sounds, the emotions. It felt overwhelming for a few minutes, then faded. I deliberately rekindled it by thinking *Shitlips!* then watched it fade again. By the third time it was the merest shadow.

Rachael

A friend was getting married. I dislike social gatherings, but couldn't decline. I got into a hated suit and tie, sat through the service at the synagogue, then a posh reception. At least the food was plentiful. A live band struck up, and people started dancing. I stood. *Right, I'm out of here*, I thought, having done my duty, when a little dark-haired girl stepped in front of me. "You were just going to ask me to dance, weren't you?"

Who was I to decline? Off we went, and the ancient dancing lessons from the Boys' Club were still there somewhere.

"OK, boy," she said, "name, rank and serial number?"

"Pip Lipkin, ma'am, so private you wouldn't believe, 1612. And you?"

"Rachael Mauritz, trainee music teacher and future world famous violist."

"Wow. You play music?"

"It's my life. Actually, my three sisters and I are a string quartet. Two violins, a cello and me on viola." She had dark eyes, a Jewish nose and a feel of mischievous kindness.

It was lucky I'd spent months studying music. "I'd love to be able to play, but never had the chance to learn. If I could, I'd go for the piano."

"Why?"

"It's so portable, isn't it?"

She laughed. "OK, what do you do if you don't play the piano yet?"

"I run. It's a form of meditation, a way of getting in tune with the Universe and a delightful torture."

"You're a poet as well. Do people pay you for running?"

"Nobody pays me very much for anything. I'm on a graduate scholarship, doing a Masters in Psychology."

"You're going to be a shrink?"

"I object to the term. If I ever feel able to do psychotherapy, I'll help people to grow, not shrink. But no. It's pure research. I've found if I get involved in people's problems, I worry more than they do. Maybe when I toughen up a bit."

Rachael and I spent a lot of time together. She was at the Teachers' College attached to the University but lived on the North Shore. So, my distance runs were now over the Harbour Bridge, to her place and back again. She taught me to play several favorites including Für Elise, and the elements of reading music.

She and her sisters were in a symphony orchestra, and during practice sessions I sat among the players, getting the closest to joy I'd ever experienced. I considered learning percussion, that being the easiest.

She was also the nicest, kindest, warmest person I'd ever met. I was looking forward to loving our children.

We enjoyed what was then called heavy petting. I managed to get her to expose the upstairs parts, but never downstairs. Only my fingers were allowed to explore, and it drove me crazy.

One afternoon, sitting on the lawn at the Uni. among the unseeing crowds, I asked her to marry me.

"Pip, you're a darling. But I can't marry you."

Boom. Straight between the eyes.

"Well, you can. It's legal."

"I could never marry someone who is not a musician. And... well... um..."

"OK, tell me the worst."

"I was going with a fellow for five years. He is a top trumpeter. We decided to take a year's holiday from each other, the day before that wedding, and–"

"And you found someone to keep the place warm, and have some casual fun with."

"Oh Pip it's not like that! I didn't know you'd get so intense! I never wanted to hurt you."

Yeah, right. Of course she didn't want to hurt me. Like everyone, like me sometimes, she dealt with cognitive dissonance by doing what she wanted while believing what felt comfortable. Cognitive dissonance is "I'm 100% honest, would never steal from anyone. Now, this is a cash job so we don't have to pay tax, OK?" Or, "Your Honor, I abhor violence. But she shouldn't have nagged me!" Once you know about cognitive dissonance, you'll see it everywhere.

I kissed her good-bye. There was some party that evening, one I hadn't intended to attend. Free beer was on offer, and I went along to get drunk.

I had a beer. It tasted awful. I had a second. It tasted no better. I had a third. Then within me I saw old Sid, heard his whining voice. This was crazy.

I went home and changed into my running gear. I did a really hard 30 miles. By the time I burst through the pain barrier, I knew I'd survive, somehow.

7. 1967-1970: Thriving

Children

Six months later, I was married to Jacinta. We were two pieces of a jigsaw puzzle: different but fitting. Naturally, she left Mrs. Leahy, and we found the last cheap apartment in Paddington, which was on the way to becoming a yuppie address. She got a waitressing job, and raked in the tips.

My joy was to give her pleasure. The physical sensations of lovemaking were fine, but less important than her ecstasy. Still, even during our most passionate moments, I was an observer, an intellectual analyzer rather than the experiencer of emotion. I hated this about myself, and wished I could do something. Sadly, my studies told me that War Infant Syndrome is for life.

Her body defied the best that medical science could do, and we got pregnant. I needed a job, and found one at Monash University, in Melbourne, Victoria. I restarted my Ph.D. with a new topic and dived into research. I lectured, coordinated a first year course, trained and supervised tutors, and supervised a few Honors students. I ran half an hour each lunchtime, and an hour in the evening, but didn't go in for competition. Life was too full.

In our little rented house, Jacinta created a place of peace, comfort and beauty, and soon made friends with several neighbors. I obeyed speed limits in the morning, but always found myself speeding on the way home. I loved the thought of becoming a father, but worried about the risks to Jacinta. Also, she was mostly alone at home, steadily growing.

At last, in August 1968, we rushed to the hospital. I took time off, and spent every possible moment with her, massaging her shoulders, anticipating every wish, timing the contractions.

Some woman in a neighboring ward was doing a prima donna, and the staff revolved around her, but occasionally I kidnapped a nurse: "Excuse me, you're needed in Ward 5. The bell has been on for half an hour."

"I'll be with you when I can."

Smile. Lean forward, look her in the eyes: lessons from Antal. "C'mon, take a moment!"

She carried out an examination while I was banished outside a curtain. "Hmm. It hasn't progressed. I'll inform the doctor." Then we were left alone again.

Three days of torture passed before our little daughter deigned to be born. I was chased out at the last moment, but when I saw my child, I instantly fell in love. Narelle had a fuzz of dark hair, a mind of her own as her birth showed, and always wisdom ahead of her years.

I soon had to return to work, but begrudged the moments away from home. Each day's miracle developments were greeted with awe, and recorded in my first-ever diary.

As a new father, I became even more interested in environmental and political issues. What kind of a world did I bring my little person into? This was the time of protests about the Vietnam War, and I joined in. War is crazy: a game in which sentient beings deliberately kill each other. I was even more concerned by the damage humanity was doing to its life support system, so this became my extracurricular project. I read *The Ecologist* magazine, and contributed several articles. I read widely, and by the time my son Anthony was born (yes, named for my old nemesis), I was able to construct models of where current trends were taking us.

Then the reports of the Club of Rome were published, one after another, and I was pleased to see close agreement with my conclusions. In summary, humanity was clearly heading toward extinction. I didn't want to witness the destruction of life on this planet. I didn't want my children to endure catastrophe. I wanted a decent life for my grandchildren, and their grandchildren in perpetuity, and this has been my passion since.

Spontaneous therapy

Five minutes after I'd returned to my office following a 9 o'clock lecture, a blonde girl hesitantly knocked on the open door. Her eyes were bloodshot, shoulders drooping.

"Come in Sally."

"You know my name, Mr. Lipkin?"

"Sally Riley. You're in Greg's tutorial, and sit in the fifth row next to Bevan Stevens."

A hesitant smile fought with crying. "How can you remember that?"

"Oh well, there are only 907 students in the course. Come in and sit down."

She shut the door, slumped into the chair and looked at me. I gave her time. Finally she said, "Mr. Lipkin, yesterday I accidentally left a book at home. When I... when I went in, I found mmmy bbboyfriend in bed with my housemate." Sobs shook her slight body.

"The bastard!" I was wondering how to handle this.

"I... I'm being punished for not letting him fuck me!"

I didn't show shock at the unexpected obscenity. "Hmm."

"I'm a Christian girl. Sex is for marriage. He knew that. You know what he said when I walked in?" Anger was better than despair.

"Go on."

"He said, 'Shit, I've waited too long to get my bit in. I've only got so much patience you know!' He sounded like I was unreasonable!"

"And it hurts like hell."

"I want to die!"

"Would you give him the power to kill you?"

"Huh? I... hadn't thought of it like that."

"You know, I feel sorry for the stupid idiot." We looked at each other. "He missed out on a beautiful, intelligent, decent girl who'd have made him a wonderful wife. He'll go from slut to slut, rubbing bodies together without emotion or commitment." I saw a glimmer of a smile in the reddened eyes. "After his third or fourth divorce, he may actually grow up. But by then, you'll have built a great life for yourself, won't you?"

She squared her shoulders. "I'll make sure of that, just to spite him."

"Something else. You're a Christian girl. That gives you a wonderful resource: pray to Jesus to put peace into your heart."

"Mr. Lipkin, what you said before made me think of something else. Lucky I caught him at it now, not after marriage and a couple of kids!"

We shared a smile. "OK Sally, now listen. This isn't my job, and I have no training in therapy. Will I phone the Student Counseling service for you?"

"Mr. Lipkin, maybe you should switch jobs. You've helped me heaps."

As we stood, she gave me a big hug, and walked out with a firm step.

A warm glow filled my heart, not just the head. Trouble was, I couldn't sleep at night. Sally had more than boyfriend trouble. She'd need to split with the housemate as well, which implied lots of practical problems. Uselessly, my mind kept running around the squirrel cage of someone else's problem. However, during the next lecture, Bevan sat alone. Sally was in the front row, and clearly able to concentrate. She and I exchanged a smile before I started on the next wonderful revelation about experimental design.

Suburban peasant

How do you change a crazy culture? OK, I was on the Students' Representative Council as a Postgrad. Rep, wrote letters to the papers, joined Friends of the Earth and all that: just another young stirrer knowing better than his elders, easy to dismiss. "You can't stop progress!" was a cliché. I decided the ethical way to social change was to live what I wanted to create. We talked things over, and my lovely wife was more leader than follower toward a self-sufficient lifestyle.

Right back to that Meccano set, I'd never done anything practical in my life. We bought a run-down little house, and I blundered about renovating it, learning from my mistakes. I bought a book on organic gardening, and within six months grew 100% of our vegetable needs. Jacinta baked bread, preserved my produce, made all our clothes.

The best part was our two willing helpers. Tony hardly walked yet, but loved helping Dad. I dug a hole, he put the seed in. I climbed up a ladder to scrape off peeling paint. He insisted on climbing in front of me, and stood there, wielding his own scraper.

One day as I was digging, Narelle bent to pick up an earthworm. Gravely she studied it. "Cute. Dad, can I kiss it?"

She was way too young for school, but read books aimed at six-year-olds, and already had a way with numbers. She badgered us till we sent her to a private school, because no state school would take a four-year-old. I still treasure the first school photo: all the littlies lined up by size, with her on the end, a head shorter than the girl next to her.

One evening, Jacinta said, "Pip, I love our new lifestyle, but, you know, to the neighbors we're just oddballs. I wish we had contact with likeminded people."

"Yeah, you're right. This Egyptian architect said, 'One man cannot build a house. Twenty men can build twenty houses.'"

"We'd better form a community then."

Easier said than done. Many people shared our ideals. None of us had money to put in. All of us were involved in too many activities to make the necessary changes. And as my Ph.D. neared completion, I needed to find another job.

Debate

The Student Union held a debate between the Young Liberals and FOE, on "Economic growth is the way to social justice." I was lead speaker for the opposition. The hall was near-full—an audience of maybe 2000? Great. Jenny Standish started for the Libs. Prosperity for all, trickle-down effect, encouraging personal initiative, great Aussie tradition of freedom and self-determination without government interference, the wonders of coming technology...

I'd anticipated much of it, and could stick to my script.

> Growth is good, right? Well, friends, cancer is a growth. The question is growth toward what, for what purpose. A thirteen-year-old's growth in leg length is good. A fifty-year-old's growth in circumference is bad.
>
> Edward Goldsmith has put it beautifully. You can't cut an ever-growing number of slices from a cake, each slice of increasing size. The planet Earth is a finite cake. You can eat your piece only once.

And this is not a matter of capitalism versus communism. Those two ideologies only disagree on who wields the cake knife.

Yeah, I can hear you thinking: Malthus is dead, technology can solve it all. The Green Revolution can feed the masses. By the time oil is short, we'll get it from the sea bed.

I've got news for you. This is a dangerous illusion. When we stop here today, you owe it to yourself to go to the Library and read the *Second Report of the Club of Rome: Mankind at the Turning Point*. The Club of Rome is some of the planet's top scientists, who have spent thousands of hours of pro bono work to examine where current trends are taking us. And if Latin is Greek to you, "Pro bono" means "for the public good."

Briefly, their rigorous computer modeling shows that you can fix any problem with technology, but only by making one or more other problems worse.

The Green Revolution is a perfect example.

If you're interested, I can give you the references to the evidence. The Green Revolution is a means of increasing the necessity for pesticides and artificial fertilizers. Such chemicals are very profitable, but not for the starving masses. And pesticides in food is, well, distasteful to me.

Who can afford the chemicals and the special seed? People with money. Who needs the help? Subsistence farmers who are being displaced by agribusiness. Sure, the plantations grow more food, but where do the evicted peasants go? To swell the slum settlements around cities, with all the resulting problems. So, the Green Revolution is a means of passing wealth from the poor to the rich. Solving one problem worsens several others.

OK, offshore drilling for oil. Guess what, it costs more than putting a pipe in the ground in Texas. Recently, I filled up the tank of my car for $2. My estimate, and I'm happy to share the calculations, is that by 2000 it'll be more like $40.

Right, who cares about the year 2000? My friends, if you don't, you're idiots.

We'll only be middle-aged then, loving parents, and some of us doting grandparents. Every time we stuff up today, we're stealing from those kids, that future.

We live on a lovely planet, with only one thing wrong with it: an infestation of a noxious species. *Us.* Money is the measure of the harm we do. Every time you spend a dollar, you steal from your kids. And every kid you have above two per two adults means that the cake will be cut into more pieces.

You've seen car stickers: "Live simply, so others can simply live." That's the answer to today's topic, but it's inaccurate. It should be: "Live simply, so YOU can simply live." Be selfish. Fight for your future, and the future of your kids.

Jim has pointed to the clock, so I'll wrap up by telling you where the problems come from. In 1962, John Calhoun did an experiment on the effects of population density on rats. No crowding: normal rats. Up the density one click, and some rats developed stress-related physical problems: eczema, asthma, cancer, digestive ulcers, strokes, heart attacks and stuff. Two clicks up, and many females were unable to properly socialize their young into the rat way of doing things. With the highest population density, many male rats became so territorial they attacked their own females and young, and males formed gangs that fought to the death.

Look around at our world and think.

I received a great deal of applause, and the Melbourne *Age* reproduced my speech.

8. 1970-1996: New life

Moving out

I found a job where I could do public service while preparing for my coming life change, as Research Scientist in the government-funded Building Research Institute. My task was survey design and execution, on a wide range of issues: privacy needs, town planning to maximize community interaction, child safety in the home, the needs of the homeless, energy conservation in public housing—lots of good stuff. We also paid weekend visits to people who were building their own houses. Adobe building was the go because of its cheapness, and our kids loved to cover themselves in the raw material. I learned many practical skills from my hosts. Jacinta was already highly practical, but she learned things like hand-spinning wool. I used the Institute library to supplement my learning with theoretical knowledge. Since no one else knew about building with earth, I ended up fielding enquiries about it, not in my position specs but enjoyable.

Some of the letters mentioned issues other than building, like the young woman from the Rainbow Valley in New South Wales who had two little children, a half-built house, and a husband killed in a car smash. I exchanged many letters with her, and my words made a difference. She finished the house with the help of the local community, and our correspondence petered out when this nice bloke moved in to share her life.

Being a Research Scientist was the perfect job: creative, interesting, and oriented to improving lives in practical ways. A salary of $45,000 was huge in the 1970s, so for the first time we could afford anything we wanted.

There is always a *but*. But the job was 24/24, so I could spend little time with my lovely family. Wherever I was, the half-dozen current projects occupied my mind. What's more, I still knew: every dollar I earned, every dollar I saved or spent, was stealing from the future. I had an increasing need to do as I said. Jacinta felt the same.

We found a group who had recently bought land in beautiful countryside, and set up an intentional community they called Hope. We decided to hope on their bandwagon. (Sorry for the pun.) I retired for the first time, and started building my house. Let me advise you: build your second house first. I made many mistakes, and could have done a lot better when it was finished, but the result has stood the test of time. Once, a big tree landed on the roof. A suburban brick veneerial would have been demolished. I fixed the damage in one day.

While building, I kept learning by working as a laborer in various building trades. I worked a week or two with a concreter, wrote up the skills in an article for a marvelous magazine on self-sufficiency titled *Earth*

Garden, then poured concrete for my house. As the house grew, so did my skills. Soon I was teaching owner-building in adult education.

All the same, when the house was as finished as any owner-built house ever is, I retired for the second time, as a builder's laborer. Modern building is get in, get out, never mind the quality. Speed is everything, and this results in waste. At home, I pulled old nails from recycled timber, straightened them so they could be reused. At work, I was not allowed to pick up a dropped nail—my time supposedly cost more.

For years, Jacinta wanted a third child. I kept saying, "Zero Population Growth: two adults, two kids." One day a friend told us, "Listen, I've only got one child. Have my quota." I couldn't argue with that. Within ten months, we were blessed with Anna. Nine-year-old Narelle came up with the name: "Dad, it's your mother's name with the Hs removed, and it's a palindrome." Anna had four loving parents, the way the older two acted toward her.

Living in an intentional community was an education. There was always conflict, and not always handled well. Being a psychologist didn't protect me from it, and I got as embroiled as anyone else. All the same, we became an extended family who cared for each other.

The years passed, and even Anna got to university. One day, I received a distressed phone call. "Dad, oh dad, it's terrible."

"Tell me, love."

"I handed in this assignment, and thought I'd done a great job. Dad, it really is good. And I just got it back, and the bastard gave me a C minus!"

Flashback to Mr. Landauer. "And you feel furious, and doubting your own judgment, and maybe even thinking about changing courses?"

"How did you know? That's exactly right!"

"Darling, I know your work. I'm sure it was worth more than that."

"But what am I going to do?" Crying again.

I did my best to send love through the phone while saying nothing. At last, "What are your options?"

"Let the air out of his car tires." We both laughed. "Decide I'm not as good as I thought and aim for a career as a checkout chick in a supermarket." Again we laughed.

"Any more options, love?"

"Complain to Professor Irvine?"

"Hmm. That sounds more promising. What's stopping you?"

"Sending you all my love before hanging up. You know what, Dad? You're great!"

She took the assignment to the Head of Department, and said something like, "Excuse me, Professor Irvine, I believe a mistake has been made. Can this please be reassessed?"

The assignment came back with an A. If I say so myself, I'm a terrific father.

Healer

Once I stopped building work, I encountered another angel, who nudged me toward where I needed to go. She was one of the community members, Carol, who worked as a nurse educator. With her encouragement, I became a nurse.

On my first shift as a student nurse, I was looking after three different people sitting on three different toilets (it's more polite that way) when a girl grabbed my arm. "Your turn for a break," she said.

"But–"

"But nothing. Hand over to me, then look after yourself."

This was my first nursing lesson: "before you can care for others, care for the carer first."

The second lesson we got in lectures, by example and from sheer necessity: "It's not your pain. You're not here to share it but to relieve it." I first managed it on night duty. An old gentleman fell and got a nasty scalp tear. I had to assist in minor surgery. The doctor was Tamsin, and I thought it a nice turnaround: female doctor, male nurse. Somehow, I managed to calm our patient with a few words, and he insisted on holding my hand while she cleaned up the wound, shaved his hair and injected local anesthetic. Then he allowed me to do my job as assistant. All this time, I stayed calm, focusing on the task, minimizing distress without sharing it. I knew that now I was ready to train as a psychotherapist.

I worked as a nurse for ten more years, while doing a Masters in Counseling Psychology, accumulating supervised practice, and slowly building up a viable business. Getting joy from helping people is great, but three kids also cost money.

My first client was a lady with a food obsession. She'd be washing her dishes while vividly imagining eating ten chocolate bars in a row, or spooning down a liter of ice cream. Then she felt guilty and evil. Having an iron will, she resisted temptation, but the struggle filled her day and her mind. Two sessions of loving acceptance disguised as cognitive therapy had her go through the Christmas period of gluttony with no distress at all. Magic.

My second client was a lady with four kids. The eldest was eight, and often hit her hard enough to bruise. She was terrified of him, and took him to a psychiatrist. He diagnosed him with Antisocial Personality Disorder and put him on some nasty drug. However, the violence continued. I asked her, how long did the interview with the psychiatrist last?

"Fifteen minutes."

I was outraged. With the help of a friend experienced in family therapy, we held two family sessions. I talked on the phone with the boy's teacher, and played with each kid. The boy was only ever violent with his mother, at home. In the family sessions, and through getting the kids to talk about drawings they did for me, we found the culprit. A family rule was that you must never hurt those smaller than yourself. The five-year-old could therefore wage a secret campaign of torture against big brother, knowing he could never retaliate. Shades of me with Uncle Antal! The poor boy felt helpless, angry, frustrated. When he tried to tell his mother, she misheard him and didn't respond to his distress. She was bigger than him—so hitting her was not against the family rule.

Mother and I knew she no longer needed me when she enrolled in a university course.

Over the years, my skills have increased, and now I am the person doctors send their most difficult cases to, and other psychologists the ones they can't cope with. My success rate is not 100%, but I do pretty well. And almost always, my work is a joy.

9. 2007: *Caroline*

It's hard for a senior therapist to find someone to work with. I knew my therapist would need to be a woman, older than me. When I was ready, she turned up.

During September 2007, I was teaching weekly sessions in a course on hypnosis. In the second session, I demonstrated a guided imagery script of having your client get all the bodily, visual and auditory sensations of becoming some wonderful animal. I chose a wedge-tailed eagle, one of my favorites. Thirteen of the fifteen students had a delightful experience. We then discussed why the other two hadn't managed it.

The course coordinator sat in the background, quietly smiling. She was a breast cancer survivor who'd had a double mastectomy years ago. She then trained as a therapist, and became the internet mother of hundreds of women with cancer, pro bono. She also ran these courses for the Australian Society of Hypnosis, not bad at 70.

When the students left, she said, "Pip, that was fun. You're very talented, you know that?"

"And nowadays I can accept a compliment without that inner little voice saying "yes but.""

"The mark of someone who has defeated the monster Never Good Enough."

"Yup. I've pulled his teeth years ago. My motto nowadays is, 'If someone else can do it, I can learn it.' Pity I can't get rid of my remaining monster."

"Will I tell you what that is?"

"I thought you'd want me to tell you."

Caroline grinned at me. "It's all in the head, Pip, nothing in the guts. Your third eye and crown chakras are bright like an angel's, but your heart and Manipura chakras—that's at the solar plexus—are constricted."

"Wow, you can see auras?"

"Yes, since my clinical death experience 18 years ago. Like you, I'm here to do a job."

I've always been skeptical of these claims. People are very good at fooling themselves. Still, her diagnosis was spot on. I told her about my War Infant Syndrome, and that it's for life.

"It certainly is if you believe so. But, you know, there's a lot of new research on the plasticity of the brain. When you were an undergraduate, the brain was fixed. Now we know it can grow back to replace supposedly lost functions."

"I'm aware of that research, Caroline, and use it in my work. But damage done when you were a few days old–"

"Can be reversed. You use age regression hypnosis."

I looked at her: serene, strong, a five-foot-tall giant. I said, "Lady, you've got a customer."

Rather than weekly sessions, I stayed at her house for four days: 96 hours of continuous therapy. I was required to do self-hypnosis before going to sleep, so that while my body slept my mind worked. Eating, in the shower, whatever I did, I also grappled with my past.

When I arrived, Caroline settled me in a recliner chair, closed curtains to dim the room, then asked me to relax my body, easy for a long term meditator. She talked me through an induction then said, "Pip, that eagle. Just replay for yourself the script you showed the students, and tell me when you're up there, soaring on the thermals."

Long habit enabled me to do that in a few seconds. "I'm there."

"Pip, there you are, a magnificent bird. Perfect for your world and your world perfect for you; king of the skies. And you're a magic eagle. If you choose to flap those powerful wings, you can fly any place, any time. You've told me that your first firm memory is when you were five. Fly back to witness that scene."

My mighty muscles worked the huge wings, and I sped through the blue. Back... back... and I'm cowering in my bed while they're shouting in the other room: Mother telling Father that he isn't welcome back, that they have nothing in common any more. I haven't heard Hungarian in many years, but I hear it now: Mother's voice as a young woman, Father's deeper tones, pleading, then angry. At last, I hear the front door crash, then Mother holds me, crying.

Somewhere in the distance, Caroline said, "Once more, you're the eagle," and I was, flying high. "Back. Back to the earliest thing you can remember in this life."

Even in trance, I found the wording odd. But then I'm a tiny boy. I wear warm clothes, a bonnet on my head. My right arm is stretched way up, holding a man's finger. I see his trousered leg next to me. Oddly, at the same time I'm looking down at a tiny boy, who is grasping the middle finger of my left hand. I am me, Pip, 2007 vintage, and my heart is filled with love and pity for this poor little tyke, knowing all the suffering ahead of him. I pick him up, and little-me Filip puts my arms around grandfather Pip's neck and both my selves cry.

"Good," I heard. "Love him. He needs it. You'll be there for him for the rest of his life. Now, I'll count backward from five, and when I'm finished,

I'd like you to have full recall, and be fully alert, and rested, and feeling good. 5... 4... 3... 2... and open your eyes when you're ready."

When I complied, she got me to describe the experience. I ended with "I've always thought that was my grandfather."

"Maybe it was. But you know, time is an illusion. Reality is an illusion. It could well have been you all those years."

"I can't get my head around that."

"Don't even try. Pip, who were your primary carers in your first days?" I told her.

"Now, close your eyes and fly back... back... feel the blue sky, the power of your wings, and find what you need."

I'm in a baby carriage, but uncomfortable, with many lumpy parcels around me. I know Mother is behind, pushing. I see a great cartwheel, not quite horizontal, and slowly spinning. The air smells terrible: the stink of recent explosions and burning and blood.

"Tell me," I heard Caroline's voice somewhere. At first I couldn't move my lips, but eventually managed a mumble. "Baby. In pram. Big wheel. Spinning. After bombing. Mother."

"Good. Choose another event."

I'm looking up, lying horizontally, but swinging from side to side. Terror. Mother's terror. Grandmother's terror. A terrible wailing sound. Aunt Janka's voice. The words are just sound, but I understand the panic. Darkness, and then many people and the swinging stops. Terrible, loud banging sounds.

Caroline's voice, from somewhere, in English but that's all right: "Filip darling, you survived. Your mother survived, your grandmother, your aunty. Stay with the pain. Feel it. It's all right to feel it. Can you tell me how strong your fear is?"

"Ten."

"Ten out of ten. Good. Filip, stay with it. Watch it fade. That was then and now is now, and that was awful but you survived. How strong is the fear?"

"Seven."

Down and down we went. When I reported 3/10, she had me return to the descent of the stairs in the swinging basket, over and over until it was all right. Standard exposure therapy.

When she counted me out of the trance, I was covered in sweat, and felt I'd run a marathon.

We had a cup of tea, me telling her more of what I knew of my early history. Then we were back with the eagle. This time, she asked me to visit my mother's workshop.

I face a door, leading down to the cellar. I have to duck my head to go in. Dark inside. I find a light switch. The long cellar is empty, silent. The machines are there, covered in dust. No music, no cheerful ladies. No Mother. No Mother. No Mother. Sitting in Caroline's recliner, I cried. When Mother had died seven years ago, I'd felt an intellectual sadness. Now, I was consumed by grief, with a pain exactly in my heart, and tears running down my cheeks, and my throat feeling as if I couldn't swallow.

"Good," Caroline said. "Feel it, Pip. She's gone from this life. But you know, death is an illusion because life is an illusion. Ask her to come to you, now."

Still crying, still in trance, still in Mother's empty workshop, I thought, *Nonsense. Dead is dead.* But I said within my mind: *Anyuka?* a Hungarian diminutive for Mother. The workshop stayed cold and dead, but the pain in my heart stopped. I felt a warm glow of love. No presence came to my consciousness, just a feeling of peace and acceptance.

Caroline got me to fly back to 2007 and we discussed the morning's work over lunch. She asked an odd question: "Pip, why do you think you chose to be born to that family, in those circumstances?"

I grinned at her. "You're speaking to someone who knows all the debating tricks. That's called 'begging the question.' 'Mr. Jones, when did you stop beating your wife?' Who says I chose anything?"

"Let's have a working hypothesis that you did. If you did, why?"

"Maybe I've been very bad in a previous life and needed to be punished?"

"Spoken like a true skeptic. You don't believe in past lives, but you've said you're a Buddhist?"

"My identity separate from The All is an illusion, so there is nothing to reincarnate. All life is suffering. All suffering is from wanting, from attachment. To stop suffering, stop wanting. Choose the middle path between gluttony and self-denial. That's the four noble truths. I believe in them. Beyond that, I believe in anything that can be scientifically demonstrated."

"I'll give you a reading list for later. You're right, there is only the One, but all truth is paradox. The One needs the illusion of separation. But anyway, karma is not punishment. It's choosing to expose ourselves to lessons we need. So, what lesson could there be in deliberately acquiring War Infant Syndrome?"

"Excuse the French, but buggered if I know. It doesn't feel nice." We'd finished eating. I took the dirty plates and stuff to her sink. We returned to work.

"If you like, Pip, you can stay with the eagle. Up high, little clouds, pale blue sky, you're soaring on the thermals. Got it?"

"Yes."

"Please fly back to where you need to go."

I see the graceful folds of lace curtains, tied back on each side of a square window. Outside, the air shimmers with heat. My body is covered in a sheen of sweat—but it's not my body. I have rather small but distended, firm breasts, and find breathing difficult because of the corset under my long dress. I feel cotton stockings on my legs, and know they're white. My back feels different. I know I have long blonde hair, tied back, and if I were an artist, I could draw my face. Shapely lips, thicker than Pip's. A somewhat bony, straight, prominent nose. A long face, pale blue eyes. I cannot see this face but know it, like I know I have a baby son in another room. The main feeling is severe apprehension. Something I dread is coming.

Shaken, I opened my eyes without waiting for Caroline to tell me. When I gave the description, she asked, "Anything else you know about her?"

"How could I? I know nothing about Amelia at all... Hold it. That name..."

Caroline calmly smiled at me. "All right, Mr. Skeptic. Is this scientific enough for you?"

"I do have a very good imagination."

"You do. But if I'd asked you to make up something, would you have invented this scene?"

This was the breakthrough; the start. For the next three and a half days, the revelations came like machine-gun bullets.

The second one I called the Dancing Irishman. I had no doubt whatever about him being Irish, although I have no connection with Ireland. I, Filip-Pip, have always hated dancing, understandably so: dances have been places of suffering for me since boyhood. But the Dancing Irishman... Dermot... loves it. I hear this swirling melody with an odd beat: the main pattern is dum-dum dum-dum dum-dum tatatam, with wonderful frills and trills within, and I hold my body very straight while my feet do a shuffle. Opposite me is a lovely blonde girl. As with Amelia, I could draw her if I had the skill. I know she is Maeve, but she is Jacinta. And for the first time in my life, Pip's life, my heart is full of love for her, so sweet it hurts, in a good way. Dermot-I is happy, a young man in love, on the cusp of adult-hood. I wonder what the relationship to Amelia is.

Next I am Amelia again, Mrs. Amelia Margaret McQuade, and that's a horrid thought. I'm in a very old-fashioned kitchen, cutting up something with a knife, skilled at it from long practice. Next to me is someone also cutting. I can't see her but know she is an Aboriginal woman. The person diagonally opposite me is certainly an Aboriginal woman, short, somewhat chubby and I love her, genuinely love her. She grins at me.

Caroline counted me out and heard my report. "She hates being Mrs. McQuade? There is a reason, Pip. Amelia had some major trauma. Are you willing to invite that?"

I fly back, to a bedroom. Four-poster bed with a colorful quilt cover. I'm sitting on the edge of the bed, wearing nothing but a nightgown. A door opens, and a very tall man comes in. He is naked, with a huge erection I, Pip, recognize, but Amelia-me is puzzled. His face and lower arms are dark brown, but the rest of him, including the top of his head, are pinky-white. Somehow, he is familiar, but Amelia's emotion gets in the way. She is bewildered and a little scared. He picks her up, and I can't breathe, awful, his hand on my breast, and why does he have to tear the silk nightgown, and oh God! I know she is in agony. Fortunately Pip-I cannot feel the pain but it's horrendous.

Caroline counted me out again. My body was made of wood, and I was sore all over from muscle tension.

We returned after some progressive muscle relaxation and a break. The next scene is different: the plain of the Outback, with purple ranges on the horizon. I sit a horse, see the brown ears and mane. I'm comfortable, as if born in the saddle. Pip-I have never ridden a horse. I wear a broad-brimmed hat. I know there are cattle, dogs and other men behind me. I have no idea who the Man on the Horse is. Is it Dermot later? Or another life?

The next one was very odd. Somehow, the feeling of being an eagle is more realistic than usual. The land under me is red and parched. I'm soaring along at great speed over the red plain, with buildings ahead. I see the chubby Aboriginal woman from behind. She is pegging diapers to a washing line. Her apron is a white line around her neck, another at her waist. With my eagle eyes I can see the pegs. Each is a stick with a bit of wire tightened around it. I see the little circle where a nail had been inserted to do the tightening. Then the stick was split up to the wire. I also see Amelia from behind as I rapidly approach the location. She is on the veranda, looking at the woman.

Then I am Amelia. I hear rapid little footsteps and a child bangs against my leg. I pick him up and hug him, but all sight stops. I'm worried: did she go blind? I can feel Amelia-me holding the toddler, but I see nothing. I reported this to Caroline, who said, "Fly back to the present, back to now."

I'd got a bit tired of the eagle, so next time I walked through a door, into something bizarre. I'm at peace, quietly triumphant. I merely stand on a reddish plain, with no features except that I'm like an ant on a basketball: the plain visibly falls away all around. Above me, the sun, but it's a huge white ball. I am not human, not anything vaguely terrestrial. It's an ellipsoid body, perhaps a meter and a half long and a meter in diameter, with eight legs. Nothing like a spider's; more like thin elephant's trunks made from a tree-root-like material.

In response to my mumble, Caroline counted me out so I could give a full report. "This time, it could be your imagination, Pip."

"Why? If I can ride a horse when I've never done so before, or pick up and cuddle myself, what's so outré about me being a person on a different planet?"

"We'll have to think about it. If it's genuine, you'll get more recalls."

"If it isn't genuine, I'll get more recalls anyway, knowing my crazy imagination."

Back to work. I walk through the door, and am Amelia, younger. I sit at a piano, playing a Chopin Nocturne, one of those Rachael had taught Pip-me. Amelia-me plays it much better, her fingers bringing out the beautiful sounds as she plays from memory, swaying gently to the music. I feel her long hair moving on her back. She finishes and stands. Her audience is three people I instantly recognize. They look different, but I know them. Her father is somehow Endre, her mother Hannah, but here they're clearly in a long, contented marriage. And the husband-to-be—tall, dark, mahogany face with pink above the hat line—is without doubt Uncle Pali; in Pip's life slightly shorter, brown-haired and blue-eyed. From the wedding night I know that this man had no idea of pleasing a woman, while Uncle Pali knew how to do that all too well. Pity the lack of empathy stayed.

The next scene, I'm a boy of about twelve, fishing in a creek. Willow stick, thick coarse string, feeling of complete peace. Then I am in a flowered dress, on the driver seat of a carriage with two brown horses in front. The movement is very uneven, and a steel-hard body steadies me. In the distance, I see sun glint on water.

Changes, flitting from life to life. As we stopped for the day, I asked, "Any idea why it's mostly Dermot and Amelia? Surely if I've lived as them, there must be others?"

"Pip, you're being shown what you need to know, right now, in order to do your work in this life."

"Back to mumbo-jumbo? Am I just a puppet on a string? Who is doing the deciding?"

"Pip, you are. There is a part of you that's larger than you, and that part knows what you need and why. Look, one of my reasons for being on this planet, right now, is to be your teacher, just as you've been put in the right place at the right time for many of your clients. Do you know the feeling?"

"You mean, the instant connection, when I can put into words what the client can't or won't? When we're one without separation?"

"Yes. Doesn't happen with all your clients, does it?"

"No. When it does, it's wonderful. But designed in advance?"

"There is free will. We need to make choices. There is also a symphony of complex interactions, designed in advance. So, in bed tonight, meditate on some question about the meaning of it all."

When I was still subject to depression, a frequent inner question was *What the hell am I doing on this planet?* So, this was what I asked myself as I drifted off to sleep.

I woke at 2 a.m. and turned on the light. My pulse rate must have been 200, and I was covered in sweat, the nightmare vividly clear. I'm in orbit around a planet. It's like Earth, but the continents are different. I see twinkles of light from many places down there, but my perception is for the full range from long-wave radio to X-rays. I'm not in a spaceship, the whole thing orbiting is me. I activate something, and a vortex starts below me, and I watch the planet's atmosphere being ripped away. But there are sentient beings down there!

No! I am a criminal! Combine Hitler, Stalin, all the worst mass murderers of this planet, and they can't even touch my crime. My being is twisted with regret, self-hate. I want to stop being. I need to die. I...

The door opened and Caroline walked in. The dressing-gown showed her flat, boy-like chest. "Pip, your anguish woke me. What is it?"

"I destroyed an entire planet. Billions of people. I am evil. I..." No words will suffice.

"Describe it. Tell me."

As I started to talk, I calmed down. "This being was lost, away from the center of Its galaxy. Wanted to go home. It's all coming to me but I don't know how. It needed... what I'm perceiving is not a word but a picture of something like a model of a large atom. And It... I... killed all the life of a planet to get at it."

"Why were you shown this?"

"As I went to sleep, I asked, 'What the hell am I doing on this planet?' This must be the answer."

She sat on the edge of my bed, and we stayed quiet. At last she said, "That was then. Now is now. You made a mistake then, and have been paying for it, growing from it. Now you're here, and came to me, because you needed to know. Ask, 'Why do I need to know this now?' Return to sleep, my dear. It's all right."

I slept soon after she left, and no other dreams stayed with me.

I was in a constant trance for the next three days. While sitting in the bathroom once, I also stood next to a stinking hole, with canvas around me. I am Dermot, but wearing a red coat, dressed like an English soldier of the early 19th Century. I am waiting.

Jumping around from life to life, I'm building a confused, confusing story. My left ankle is shackled to a chain, in a deep dark place, with the boots of a red-coated soldier in front of me. I feel defeated, no more fight in me.

I stand next to the double bed, with my dead husband in there, and my son, Charles, opening his arms to hug me.

I'm a little eight-legged person, the length of my legs about twice the thickness of my body. I feel like a soldier on guard: danger could be anywhere, any time, but nothing threatens for now. I lift one leg, put it against a plant stem in front of me, puncture it and suck fluid.

I orbit a star with four others of my kind, only none of us are globes. Each has an incredibly beautiful, multicolored shape that constantly keeps changing. The colors are over the whole spectrum of radiant energy. We're Space Flowers and live for beauty.

I stand among a rhapsody of wildflowers on the top edge of a steep drop to the sea below. Maeve faces me, sixteen and lovely. I lift my hands and stroke her face from temples to chin, and we kiss, and I'm also Pip in 1966 and it's Jacinta I am kissing in exactly the same way and my love-now is the same as Dermot's for Maeve, joyful, almost religious worship, from the heart, from the guts.

There is a switch. I am still me, still kissing her in the same way, and as my hands rest on her shoulders she wriggles like a cat relishing a stroke does, but Jacinta-Maeve now has dark hair and is shorter and slighter and younger. And I cry inside, and feel tears track down my cheeks. As we stand, her arm around my waist, mine around her shoulder, we see two longboats below. There is the confusion of violence, then an axe is coming for my face.

Joy, sorrow, scenes of just living, pain, triumph, failure all mingled into a kaleidoscope.

Driving home from Caroline's place, I heard Beethoven's Fifth on the radio. I turned it way up, and shouted, "Go Ludwig!" as the magnificent chords burst into my heart. Lucky the road was nearly empty, because I cried tears of joy while driving.

10. 2007-2010

Forgiveness

In the weeks, months and years following, I carried on the work of recall. I'm Amelia, boyish figure still. Father is sitting, tired. I plop myself on his lap, drawing his arms around me. Pip-me is crying: she is still happy, doesn't know of the hell ahead. I'm on a horizontal branch, watching a lumbering shape below and jump, digging all eight legs in, joyfully hurting. I suck water then jump off, escaping up the tree again. I am barefoot, in a sort of smock, herding sheep, two dogs following the commands of my waving arms. I'm in a red coat, rifle with bloodied bayonet in my hands, watching a man sprint down the hill. I am laughing at his terror till my stomach hurts.

Caroline and I kept in frequent email and occasional phone contact, and also met while I ran sessions for her courses. So, she has continued as my guide.

At her insistence, I asked to experience the deaths of the various lives I've seen.

I lie in bed, thin to the point of gauntness. My breasts are mere skin bags, and I know my hair is sparse and white. A thought comes: *Nothing hurts any more.* In the distance, I see a Light of incredible beauty, and a command without words is within my, Pip's, mind: "You are not going there." I'm forced to open my eyes.

I am on the planet of the Walking Plants. In front of me is a brownish-red mud wall, with one of my kind on top. I know she is building it as part of fruiting, but great stones fall out of the sky. I skip away from one—then darkness.

Dermot's is terrible. I feel the heat of the Outback. In my hand, a metal cup of whiskey. I can smell it. Next to me is an old, grayed slab hut. Bark roof. I know it has a dirt floor. The door is held on with leather hinges. Home, such as it is. There in the distance is a substantial timber building with red iron roofs, graceful proportions. Then I, Pip-I, feel gut-twisting remorse and shame. "Oh no!" I keep saying within my mind without knowing what's coming. I, Dermot-I, have a woman face down on some surface, long dark hair hiding her head. I'm within her from behind, and she is screaming. Then violence, then nothing. How could he... I?

Now I know why I chose Amelia's life. I've paid restitution, and Pip-I is the person I am because I've learnt that lesson, and yet, if I could, I'd undo it. If I could, I'd find the being who was that poor woman, and do something—surely there is something—to make amends.

I phoned Caroline, shaken and feeling terrible. She said, "Pip, I've got something to tell you. I recognized you the first time we met. I was that woman, Faith Cameron. You've paid your debt, my dear, and we're sister and brother of the soul."

Over the phone, we cried together.

Purpose

I am a busy man, with more interests than the average bear. All the same, I kept exploring the treasure chest Caroline opened for me, and have recorded it all. This book is the result.

It'd be great if I had independent confirmation, in the way Peter Ramster has found for four of his clients. He got them to make testable claims—and found the evidence.

I have made testable claims, but the evidence has eluded me. That's not to say my experiences are imaginary, but I'd love to validate them with written records.

Because, if you believe my claims, you have to believe that humanity is threatened with extinction within my lifetime.

You see, I also experienced the death of the Space Flower, the original self I had been, eons ago. Willingly, I took on the doom of being a tiny, short-lived planet-dweller, living and dying and living and dying over and over, until my assigned home was ready for destruction. That home is Earth. And I've been told: this is the life, Pip's life, when the end will come.

There are only two kinds of people on this planet: Greenies and Suicides.

I've been a conservationist since before 1968, the birth of my first child. Join me, or die.

We live on a beautiful planet, an incredibly complex symbiosis of a myriad species, all acting together in a symphony of life. One species has gone rampant, and is killing everything. Did you know, two recent large-scale studies have shown that one fifth of all plant species are at risk of extinction, and one fifth of all vertebrate species are at risk of extinction? This hasn't happened since the passing of the dinosaurs.

It's not either them or us. When they die, when the other life forms that make up our ecosphere die, we will go with them. Our life is intricately bound to that of everything else.

If you believe my account, you'll know that I am here either to witness the destruction of humanity, or to help to stop this tragedy. Join my team. Work for hope and survival.

Even if you don't believe my account—it's only fiction, right?—you should still join my team. Don't believe me; believe the evidence.

In 1962, Rachel Carson published *Silent Spring*. The world took note—sort of. We stopped using DDT, but replaced it with a devil's brew of an endlessly growing list of never-before-encountered chemicals. Do an internet search, and you'll find that human breast milk often contains dangerous levels of carcinogens.

We're replacing nature with cities.

We use fresh water for human purposes at a rate higher than global rainfall over land, mining the underground aquifers.

Forests are the lungs of the planet; we are destroying them at an ever-increasing rate.

Marine fish have fed humans since the beginning of time. We've harvested them way above replacement rate so that what were once commercial species are now rarities, or completely gone. And so on, ad infinitum.

It's like ripping the door off your house to use as fuel for cooking your food. You can only do things like that for so long, then there is no house.

Why are we doing this?

Because the global civilization that is destroying us is a toddler.

Think of a lovely two year old child. She is characterized by an incredible level of energy, and an incredible rate of growth. Her two key words are: "No!" and "Mine!"

That's us, isn't it? Only, a toddler is prevented from destroying herself by (hopefully) loving older people who know better. There are no adults to pull us out of our childish acts. We need to do it for ourselves.

A toddler cannot see beyond the wants of the moment. On that basis, most humans are toddlers. Ask the average person what's life about, and you'll get, "Trying to be happy, I suppose." This endless, self-indulgent scramble for happiness is in fact the greatest cause of unhappiness. People fill their lives with things that cost the earth, and still need more because the things don't make the meaninglessness go away.

Why did those Vikings raid Sheilagh's village? They were harvesting trading stock: young women and children. Why did the British Empire destroy Dermot's land? To provide fleece for the English textile industry. Why did George Bush attack Iraq in a search for nonexistent weapons of mass destruction? Because Iraq has oil under the ground. It's all greed: the childish "Mine! I want it and I want more of it without limit and if you stop me you're bad and so I have the right to hit you."

The Roman Empire transformed the Sahara from its breadbasket into what it is now. An earlier civilization, that of Harappa and Mohenjo-Daro, created the Indus Valley desert. And remember the dustbowl of the

Midwest? Now our civilization is global, and having learnt nothing from history, we're on the way to creating a global desert.

Suppose a Space Flower, one of my kind, appeared in our solar system. This globe the size of Mars starts to orbit Earth, causing 100-meter tides, and is preparing to blast our atmosphere out of the way so It can mine our uranium.

Wouldn't all humanity unite to seek survival? Peaceful or hostile, one way or another we'd have to pull together, or die together.

We now face an equal danger. Do nothing, continue business as usual, and we'll all die together.

There is hope, or I wouldn't have been told to be an instrument of hope. It's not too late.

But what can we do?

Live simply, so you may simply live.

Replace a toddler culture with an adult culture: "No!" with "How can we cooperate?" "Mine" with "Ours. " Instead of caring for things, we need to care for each other.

The Economy is the enemy. Economic growth is a cancer. We need to cure our addiction to it. Now. If all humanity pulls together against this common enemy, we can do it.

Of course, we can't leave this to the people in power. They get the most benefit, at the most cost to others. Sure, when we die they'll be included, but they blind themselves to the fact. That's how cognitive dissonance works, by discounting uncomfortable evidence.

But leaders are powerless to lead if they go in a different direction from their followers. They become isolated loners. So, if you, I, millions of people, change course, we can transform the world.

My task is to inspire you to want a future for your kids, your grandkids, and their grandkids in perpetuity. Change "I want happiness now" to "I want a decent life for me, you and everyone else in harmony," and we're on the way.

Remember John Calhoun's experiment with the response of rats to crowding? Mammals, perhaps all animals, have automatic responses that reduce population when it has become too large. Our culture is crazy because the same forces are acting on us. If we don't reduce population in a kind, cooperative, sensible way, it'll be reduced through war and disease and mutual viciousness. Look around: it's been happening for years. Having a baby is no longer a private matter. It affects everyone.

The other consideration is making your slice of the pie smaller. Live simply so that you may simply live. I cannot say that often enough. Let's reform society so that it is no longer a cancer on the planet. Greed, the toddler's greed, is deadly. I've found a great deal of joy and satisfaction through living by the rule: THE MORE YOU GIVE, THE MORE YOU GET. Try it. Or you can copy my Uncle Paul and die with millions of dollars your heirs can fight over. What would you rather leave behind: people who bless you every time they remember you, or wrecked lives for the sake of a bank account? Only two things matter in life: what you take with you when you die, and what you leave behind in the hearts of others. Everything else is Monopoly money.

We can save humanity, and create a decent future, although it's now almost too late. People have already been killed by the epidemic of cancer and other pollution-induced diseases, by crazy wars, by increasingly worse extreme weather events like floods and wildfires and droughts. This will increase, whatever we do, but we can work to minimize the tragedy. We can compassionately look after those who are already affected.

And, actually, as my story shows, the outcome doesn't matter. What matters is that we do our best.

I dislocated a shoulder in 2009. About two months later, my rehabilitation homework was to play basketball with myself. This is brilliant: increasing strength, flexibility and self-confidence in a pleasurable way.

OK, I shoot for the basket and get it in. Beauty. I shoot again and miss. So what—I'm still exercising my shoulder.

We are on this planet for a purpose. This is not to make money or to be better than the neighbor. It is to learn Lessons, to progress toward the ultimate lesson of Love, the message of Jesus (and this is from a Buddhist Jew).

So, if you join my team and we create a sustainable society, beauty. But if we miss and humanity goes the way of the Dodo, so what. If the students destroy this school, let me reassure you: there are billions of other schools in the universe.

If I am prevented from returning to being a Space Flower, you and I might meet as tentacled people swimming in some sea, or as stable energy patterns in the magma of a planet, or as complex clouds floating in the atmosphere of some gas planet resembling Jupiter. Or of course we could be oxygen breathing carbon-based life forms like humans, or the walking plants of my immediately previous existence.

But it would be nice to score that goal, and to maintain life—decent life—for humans on Earth.

Join my team.

CPSIA information can be obtained at www.ICGtesting.com
Printed in the USA
LVOW07s2224160813

348285LV00007B/550/P